W9-AAC-816

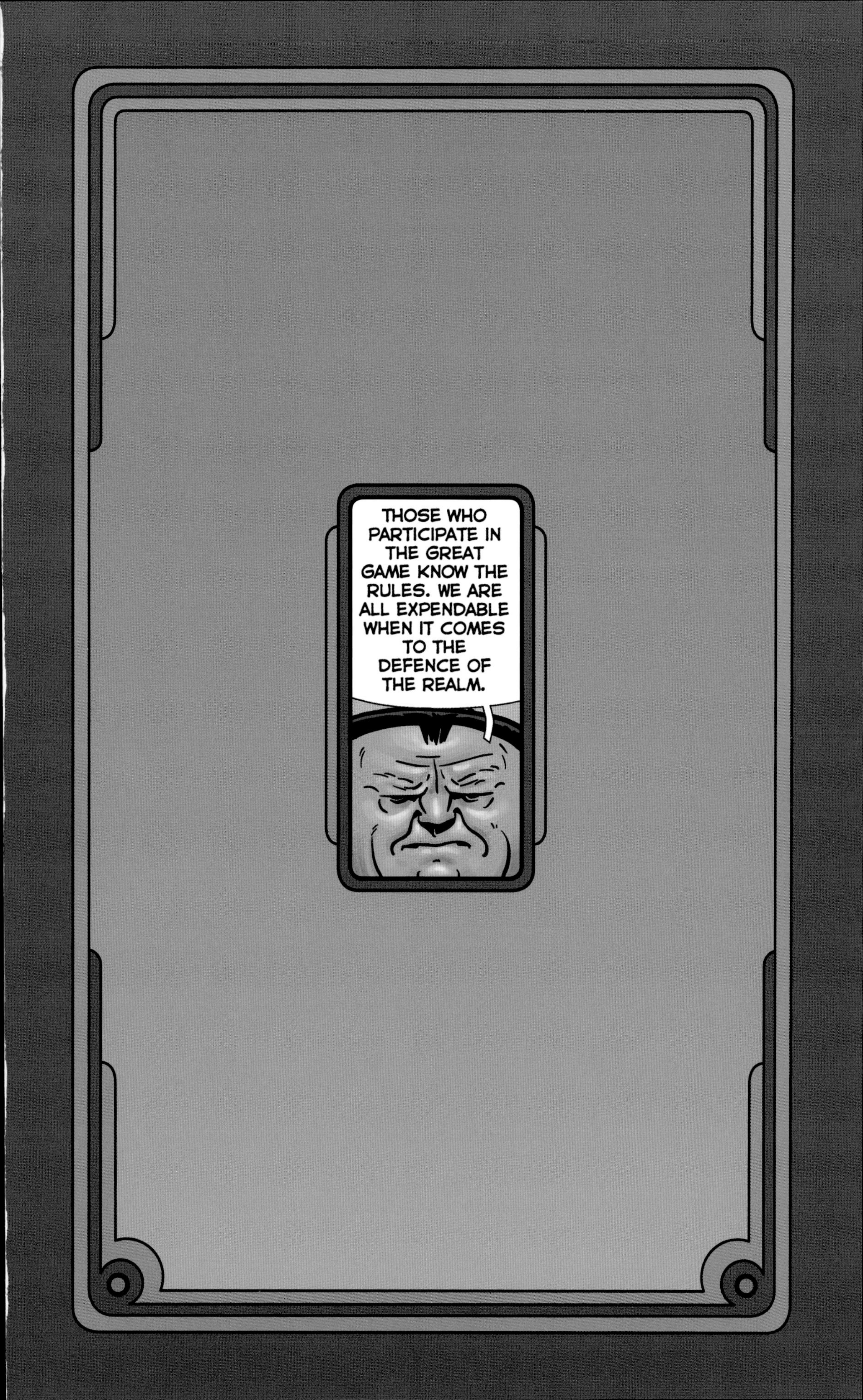
THOSE WHO PARTICIPATE IN THE GREAT GAME KNOW THE RULES. WE ARE ALL EXPENDABLE WHEN IT COMES TO THE DEFENCE OF THE REALM.

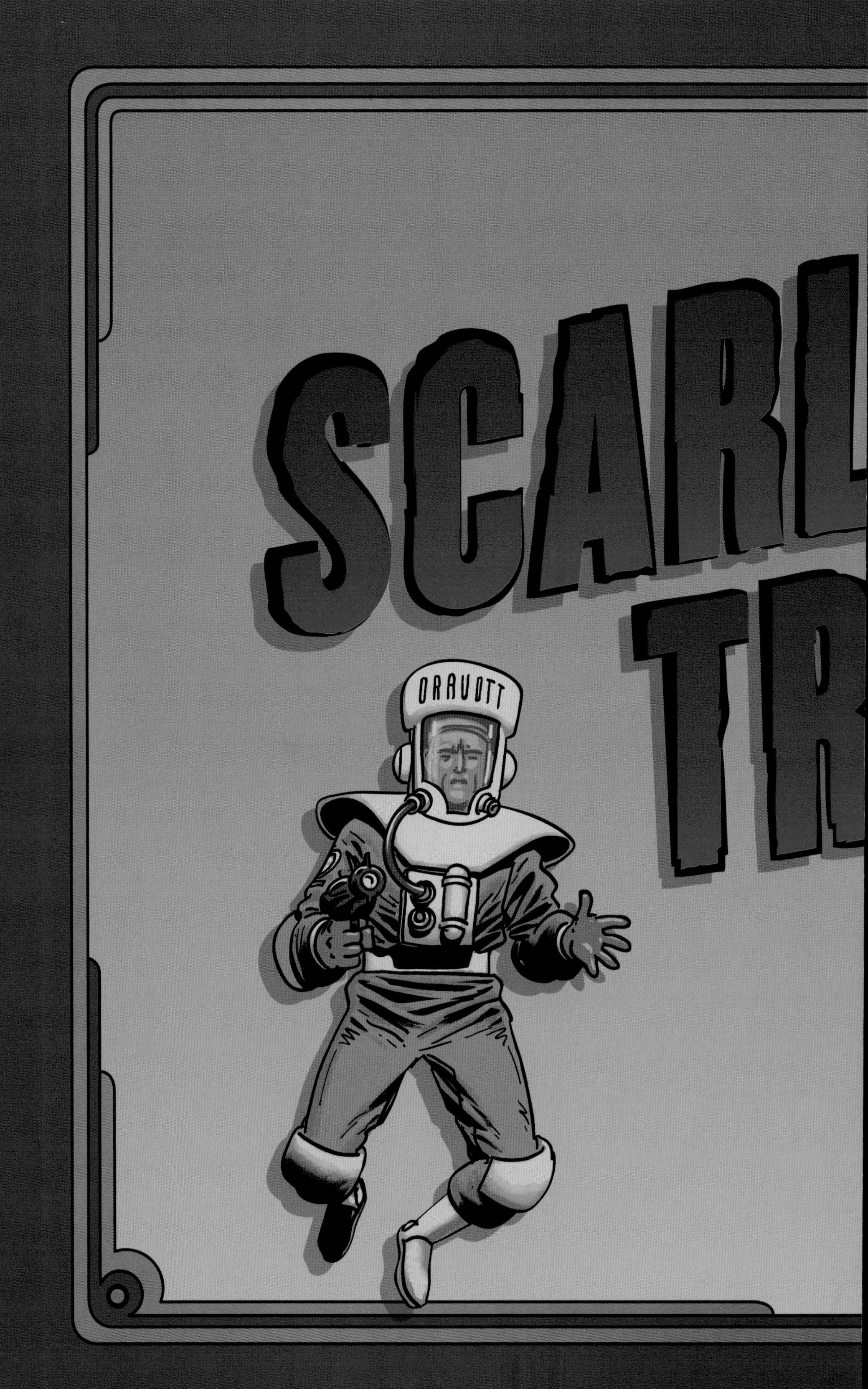

ORAVOTT

ET ACES™

THE GREAT GAME

story IAN EDGINTON
art D'ISRAELI

Dark Horse Books®

publisher · MIKE RICHARDSON
art director · LIA RIBACCHI
designer · AMY ARENDTS
assistant editor · KATIE MOODY
editor · DAVE LAND

SCARLET TRACES: THE GREAT GAME™

© 2006, 2007 Ian Edginton & Matt Brooker. All Rights Reserved.
All characters featured herein and the distinctive likenesses
thereof are trademarks of Ian Edginton & Matt Brooker. Dark Horse
Books® is a registered trademark of Dark Horse Comics, Inc.
All rights reserved. No portion of this publication may be reproduced or
transmitted, in any form or by any means, without the express written
permission of Dark Horse Comics, Inc. Names, characters, places,
and incidents featured in this publication either are the product of the
author's imagination or are used fictitiously. Any resemblance to
actual persons (living or dead), events, institutions, or locales,
without satiric intent, is coincidental.

Published by
Dark Horse Books
A division of Dark Horse Comics, Inc.
10956 SE Main Street
Milwaukie, OR 97222

darkhorse.com

To find a comic shop in your area call the
Comic Shop Locator Service toll-free at (888) 266-4226

First edition: April 2007
ISBN-10: 1-56971-717-3
ISBN-13: 978-1-59307-717-4

1 3 5 7 9 10 8 6 4 2
Printed in China

CHAPTER ONE

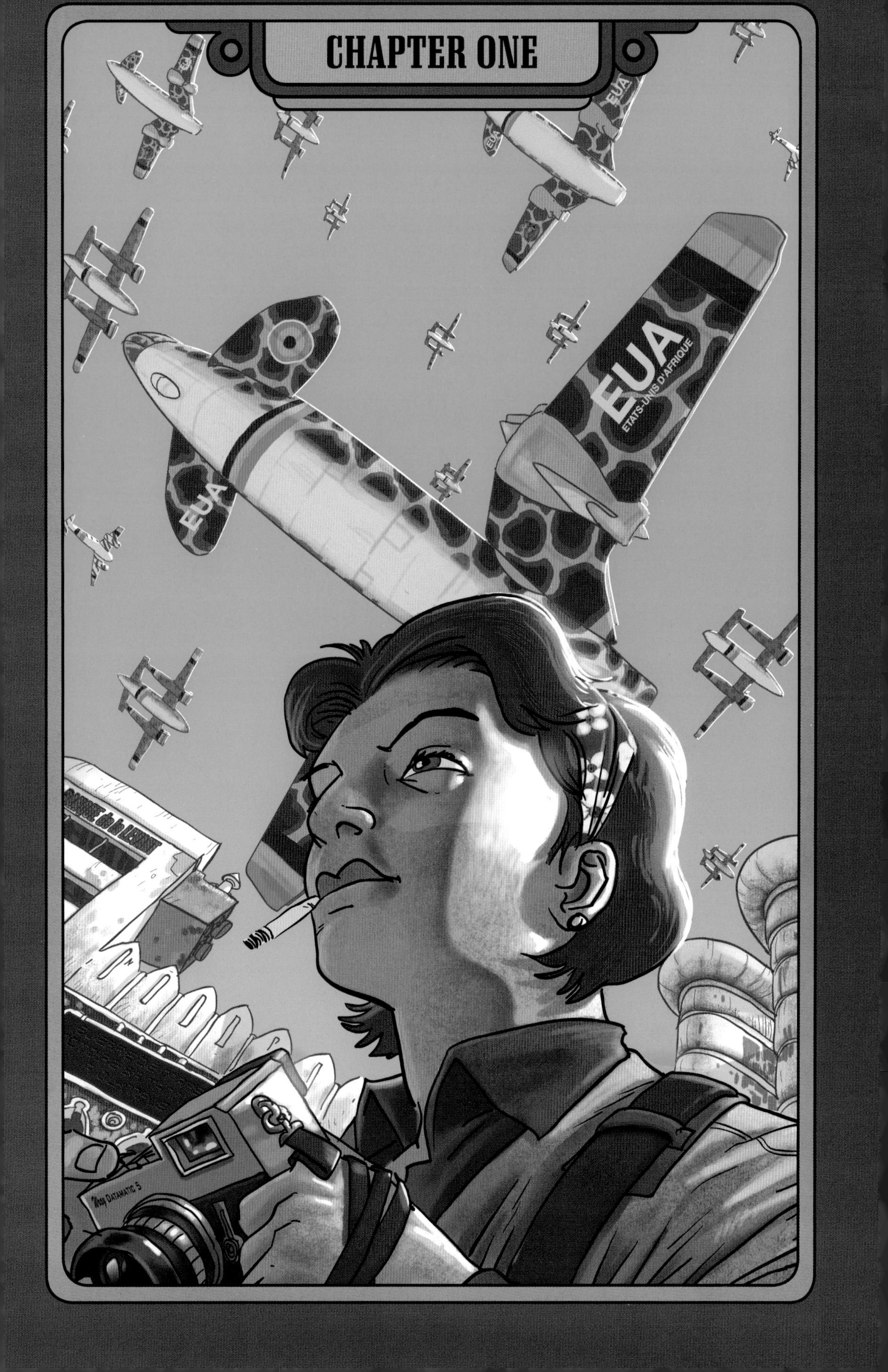
EUA
ETATS-UNIS D'AFRIQUE
DATAMATIC 5

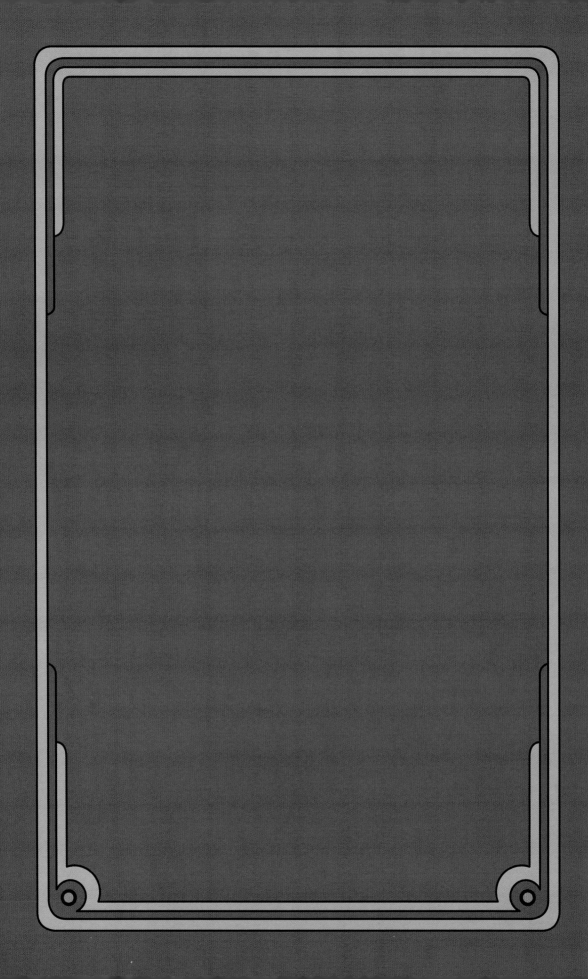

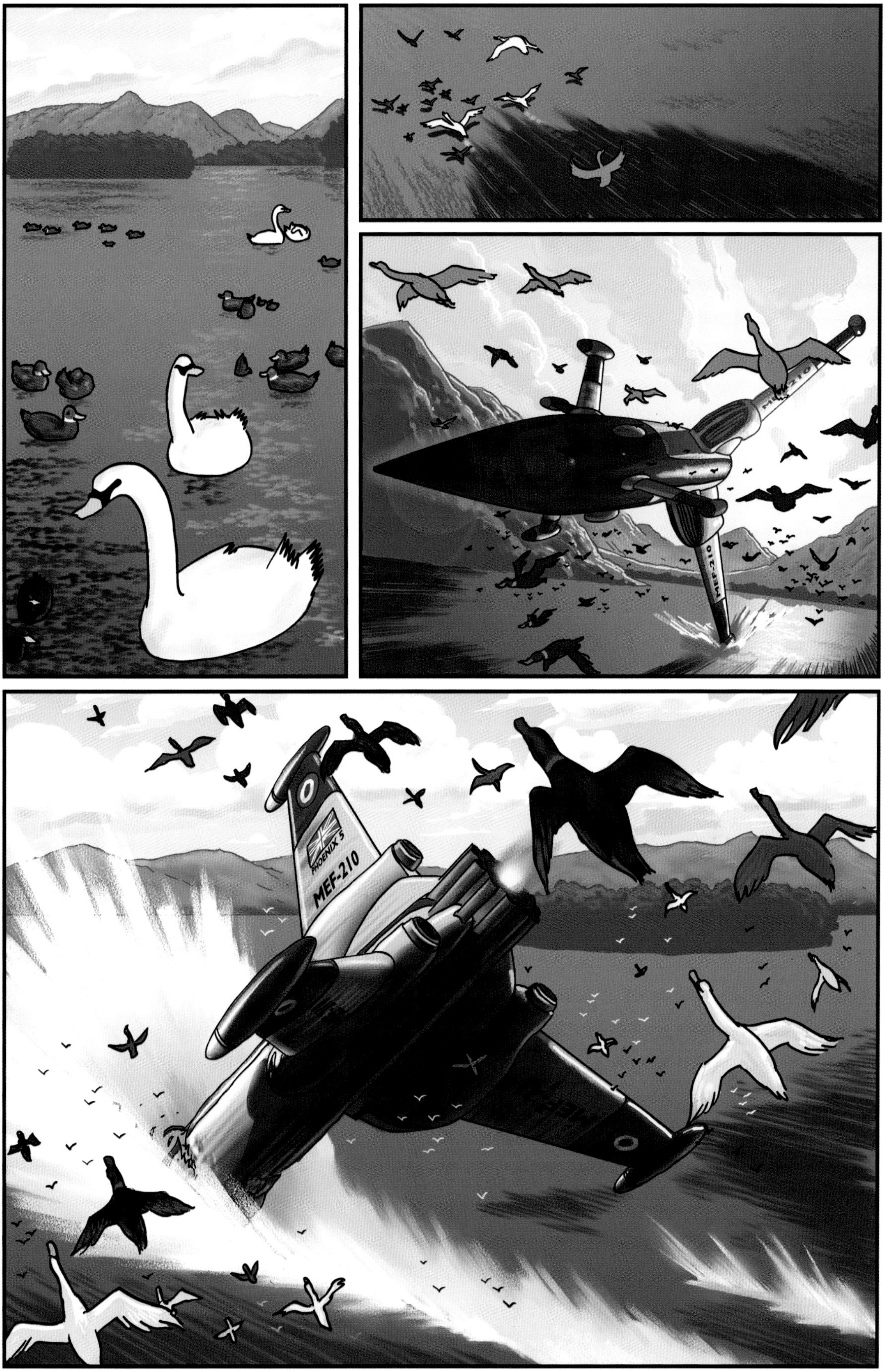
MEF-210
PHOENIX 5
MEF-210

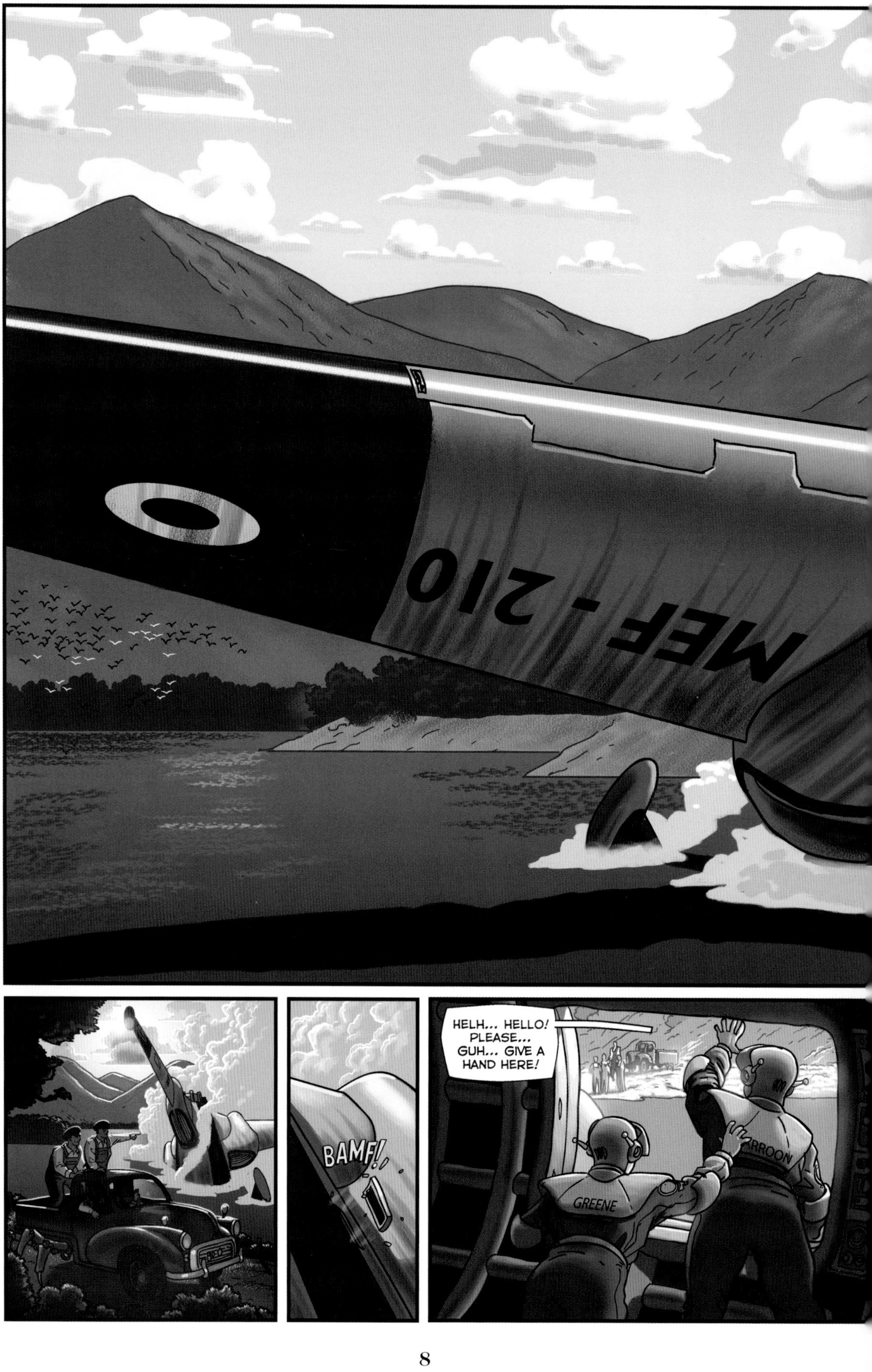
BAMF!
HELH... HELLO! PLEASE... GUH... GIVE A HAND HERE!
GREENE

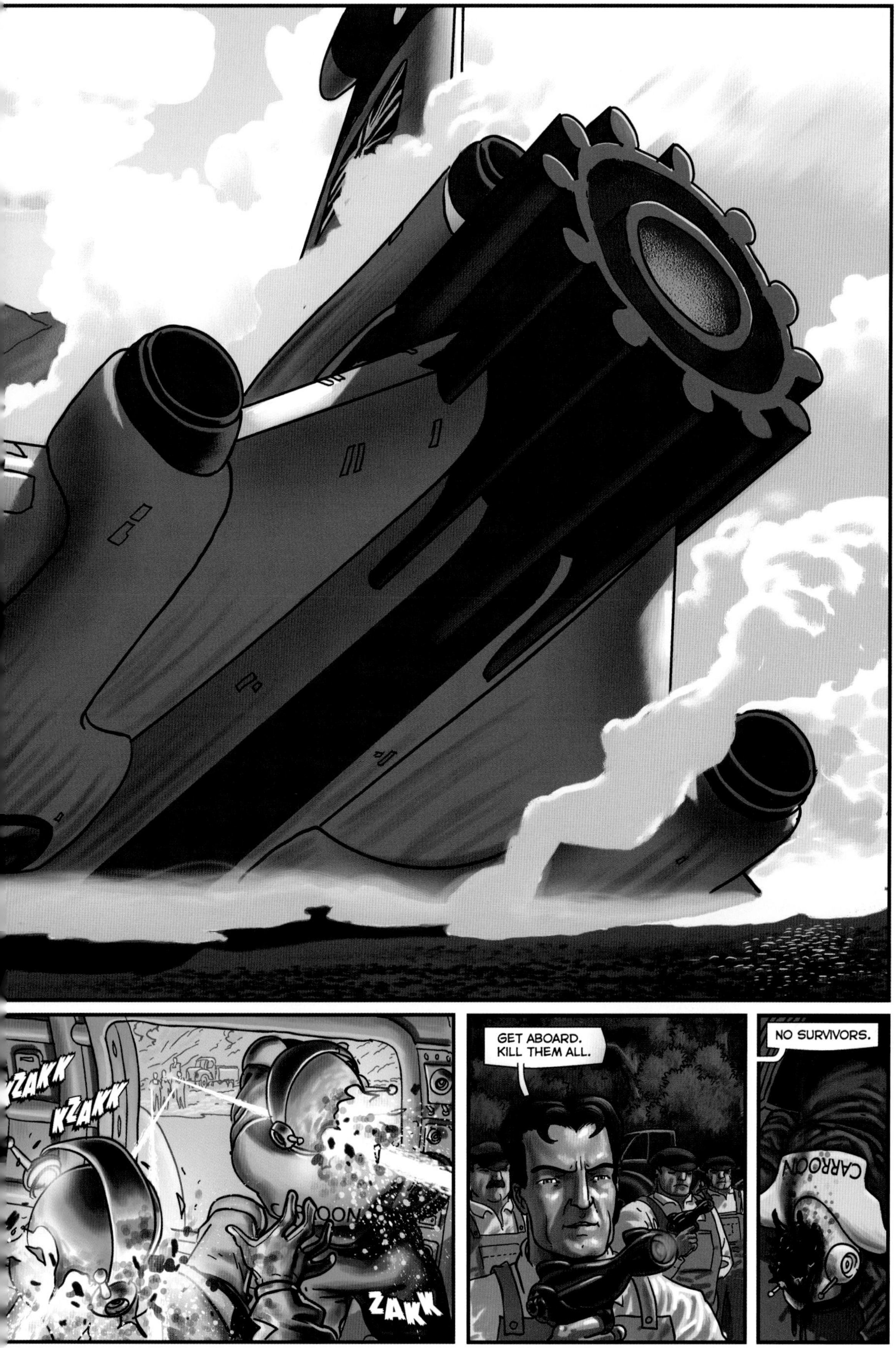
ZAKK
KZAKK
CARROON
ZAKK
GET ABOARD.
KILL THEM ALL.
NO SURVIVORS.
CARROON

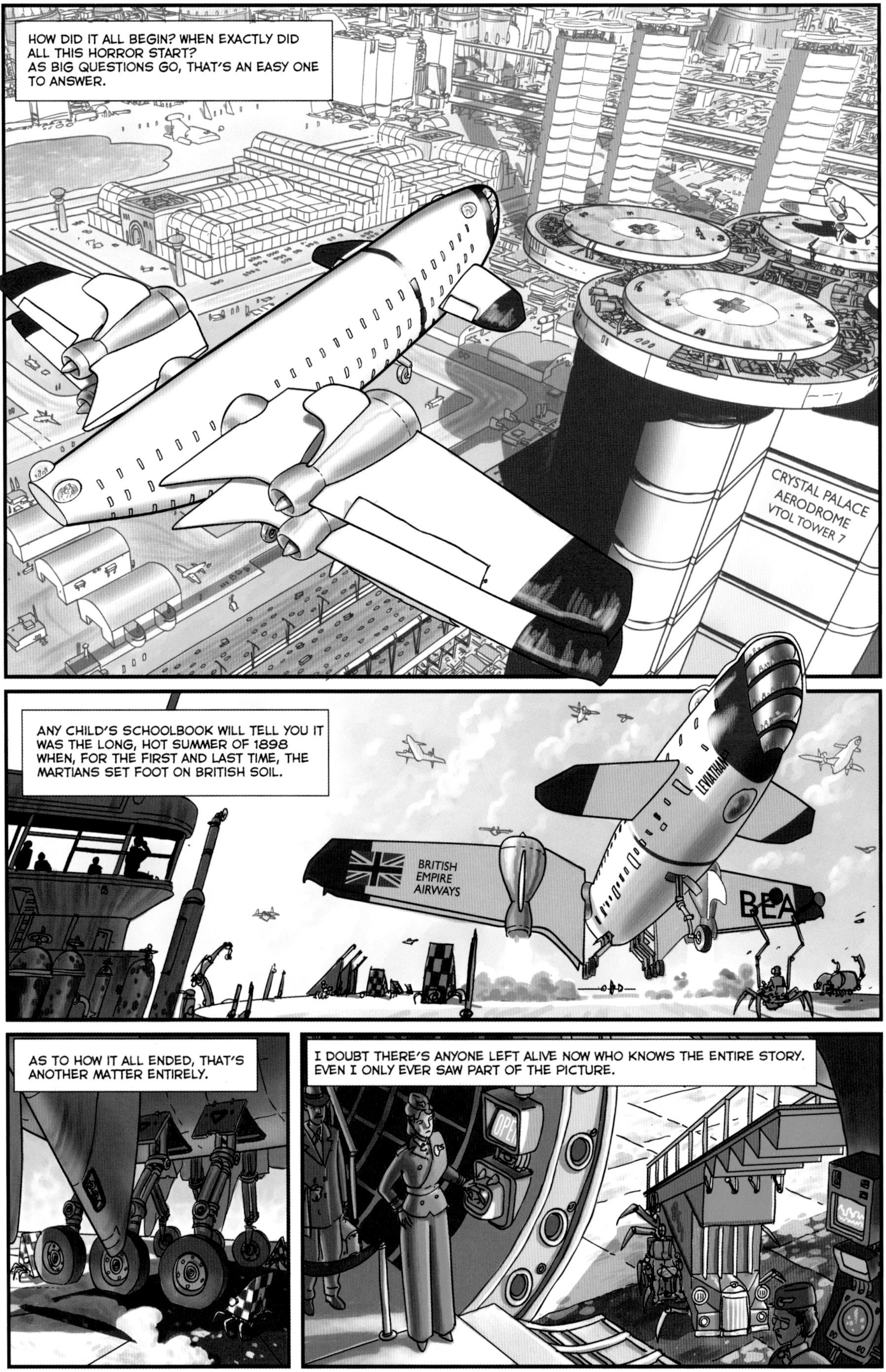
HOW DID IT ALL BEGIN? WHEN EXACTLY DID ALL THIS HORROR START?
AS BIG QUESTIONS GO, THAT'S AN EASY ONE TO ANSWER.
CRYSTAL PALACE AERODROME VTOL TOWER 7
ANY CHILD'S SCHOOLBOOK WILL TELL YOU IT WAS THE LONG, HOT SUMMER OF 1898 WHEN, FOR THE FIRST AND LAST TIME, THE MARTIANS SET FOOT ON BRITISH SOIL.
LEVIATHAN
BRITISH EMPIRE AIRWAYS
BEA
AS TO HOW IT ALL ENDED, THAT'S ANOTHER MATTER ENTIRELY.
I DOUBT THERE'S ANYONE LEFT ALIVE NOW WHO KNOWS THE ENTIRE STORY. EVEN I ONLY EVER SAW PART OF THE PICTURE.

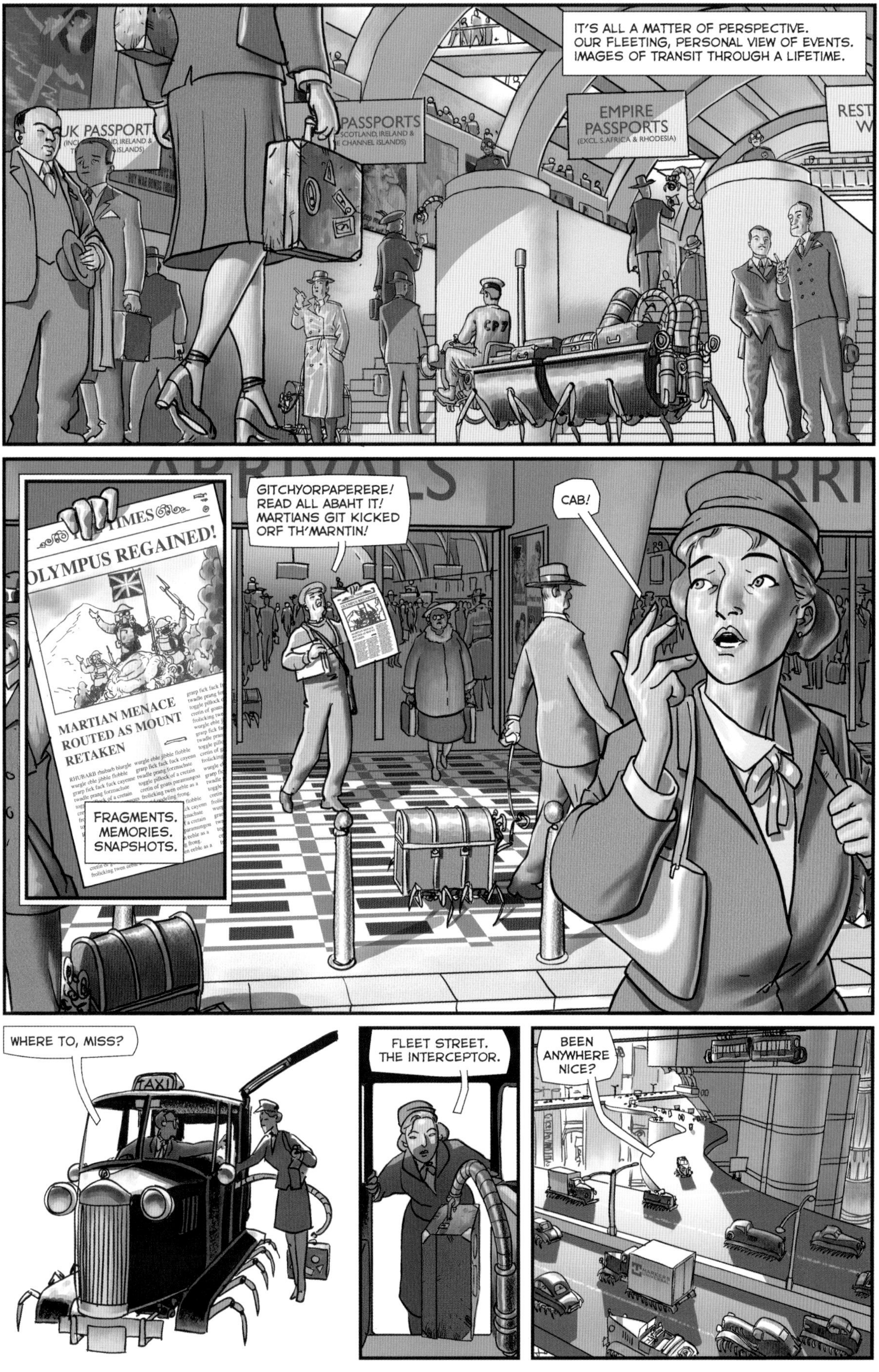
IT'S ALL A MATTER OF PERSPECTIVE. OUR FLEETING, PERSONAL VIEW OF EVENTS. IMAGES OF TRANSIT THROUGH A LIFETIME.
UK PASSPORTS
PASSPORTS
EMPIRE PASSPORTS
(EXCL. S.AFRICA & RHODESIA)
CP7
ARRIVALS
OLYMPUS REGAINED!
MARTIAN MENACE ROUTED AS MOUNT RETAKEN
FRAGMENTS. MEMORIES. SNAPSHOTS.
GITCHYORPAPERERE! READ ALL ABAHT IT! MARTIANS GIT KICKED ORF TH'MARNTIN!
CAB!
WHERE TO, MISS?
TAXI
FLEET STREET. THE INTERCEPTOR.
BEEN ANYWHERE NICE?

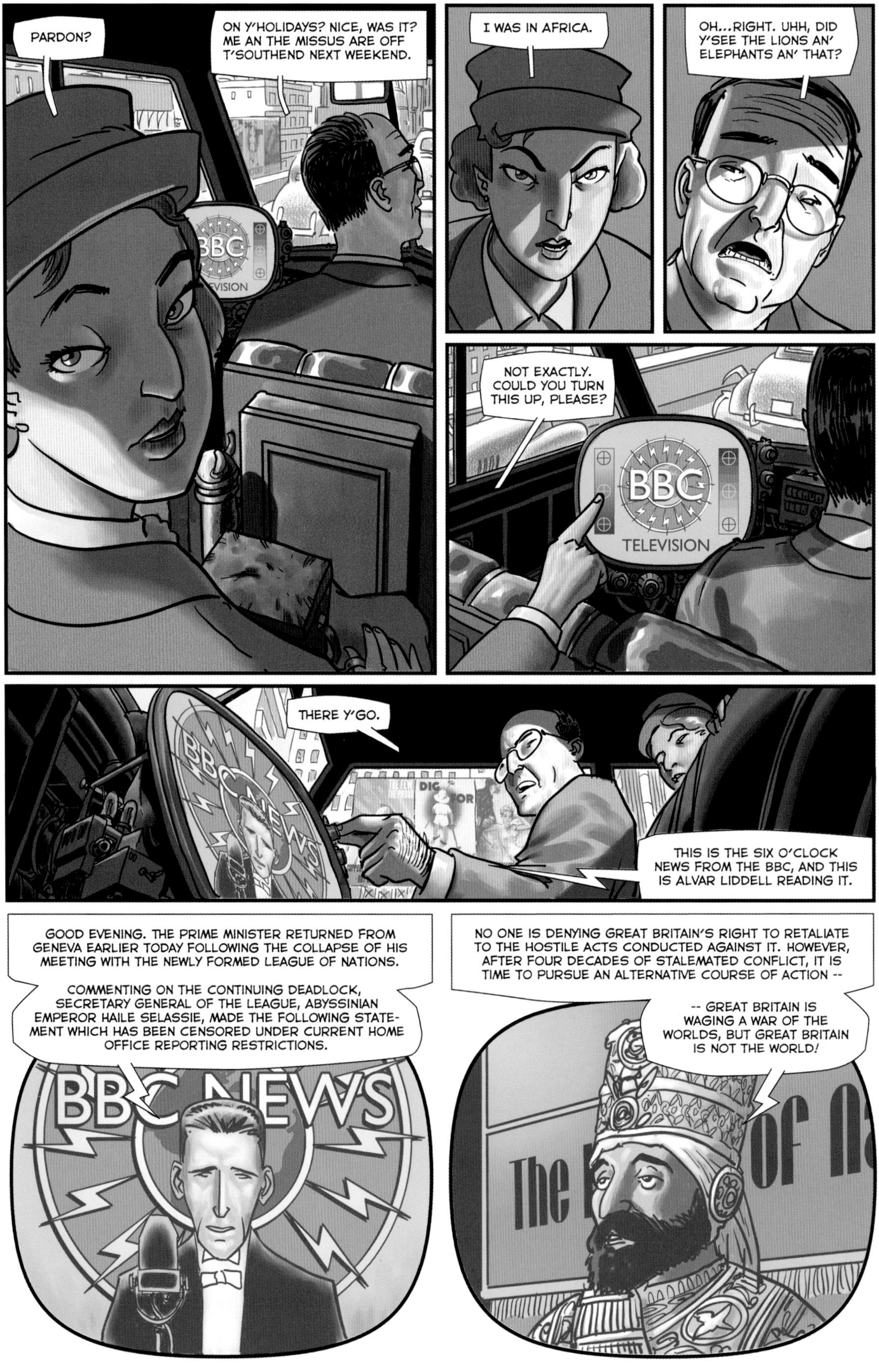
PARDON?
ON Y'HOLIDAYS? NICE, WAS IT? ME AN THE MISSUS ARE OFF T'SOUTHEND NEXT WEEKEND.
BBC TELEVISION
I WAS IN AFRICA.
OH...RIGHT. UHH, DID Y'SEE THE LIONS AN' ELEPHANTS AN' THAT?
NOT EXACTLY. COULD YOU TURN THIS UP, PLEASE?
BBC TELEVISION
THERE Y'GO.
BBC NEWS
THIS IS THE SIX O'CLOCK NEWS FROM THE BBC, AND THIS IS ALVAR LIDDELL READING IT.
GOOD EVENING. THE PRIME MINISTER RETURNED FROM GENEVA EARLIER TODAY FOLLOWING THE COLLAPSE OF HIS MEETING WITH THE NEWLY FORMED LEAGUE OF NATIONS.
COMMENTING ON THE CONTINUING DEADLOCK, SECRETARY GENERAL OF THE LEAGUE, ABYSSINIAN EMPEROR HAILE SELASSIE, MADE THE FOLLOWING STATEMENT WHICH HAS BEEN CENSORED UNDER CURRENT HOME OFFICE REPORTING RESTRICTIONS.
BBC NEWS
NO ONE IS DENYING GREAT BRITAIN'S RIGHT TO RETALIATE TO THE HOSTILE ACTS CONDUCTED AGAINST IT. HOWEVER, AFTER FOUR DECADES OF STALEMATED CONFLICT, IT IS TIME TO PURSUE AN ALTERNATIVE COURSE OF ACTION --
-- GREAT BRITAIN IS WAGING A WAR OF THE WORLDS, BUT GREAT BRITAIN IS NOT THE WORLD!

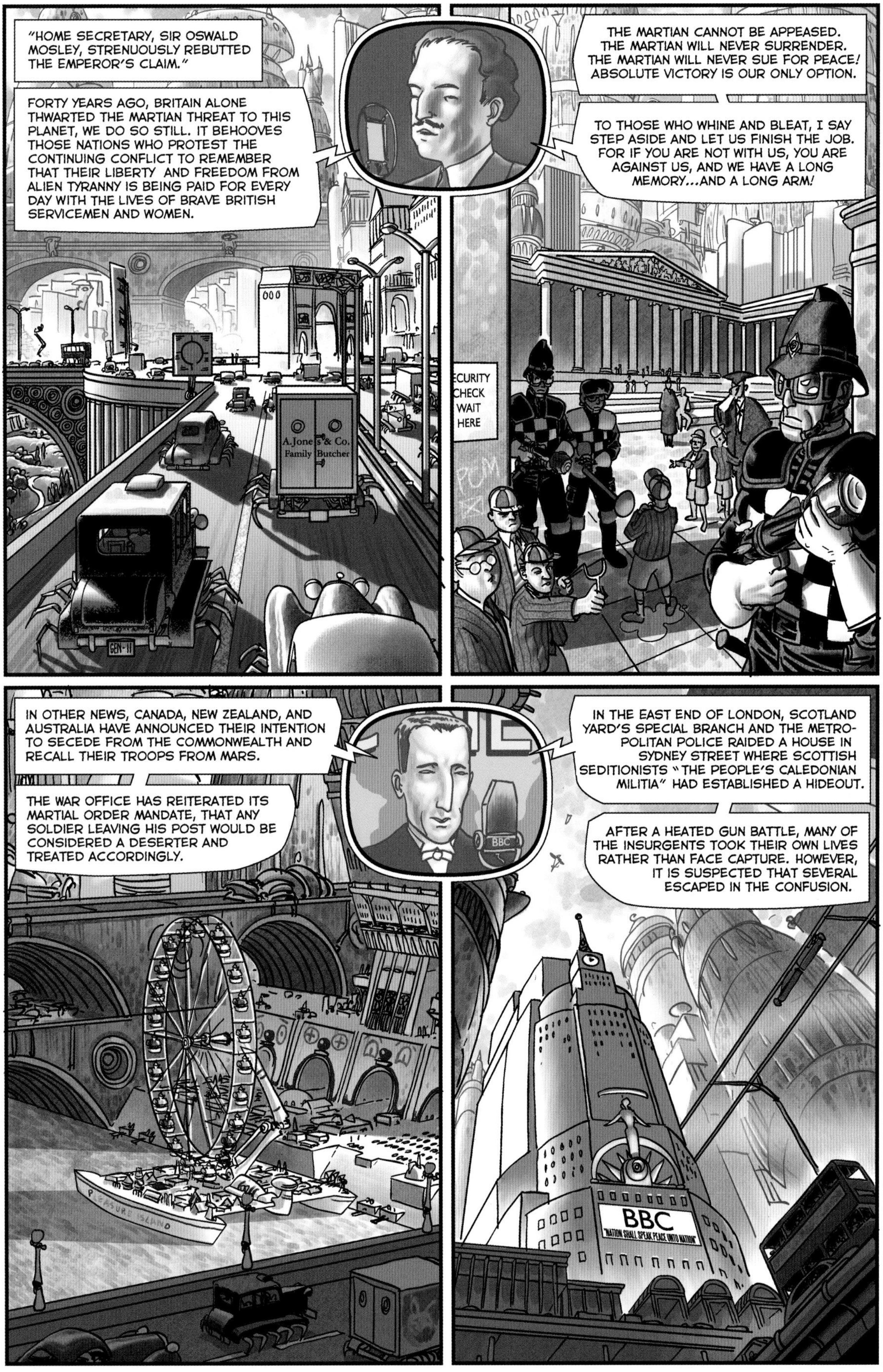
"HOME SECRETARY, SIR OSWALD MOSLEY, STRENUOUSLY REBUTTED THE EMPEROR'S CLAIM."
FORTY YEARS AGO, BRITAIN ALONE THWARTED THE MARTIAN THREAT TO THIS PLANET, WE DO SO STILL. IT BEHOOVES THOSE NATIONS WHO PROTEST THE CONTINUING CONFLICT TO REMEMBER THAT THEIR LIBERTY AND FREEDOM FROM ALIEN TYRANNY IS BEING PAID FOR EVERY DAY WITH THE LIVES OF BRAVE BRITISH SERVICEMEN AND WOMEN.
Family Butcher
GEN-11
THE MARTIAN CANNOT BE APPEASED. THE MARTIAN WILL NEVER SURRENDER. THE MARTIAN WILL NEVER SUE FOR PEACE! ABSOLUTE VICTORY IS OUR ONLY OPTION.
TO THOSE WHO WHINE AND BLEAT, I SAY STEP ASIDE AND LET US FINISH THE JOB. FOR IF YOU ARE NOT WITH US, YOU ARE AGAINST US, AND WE HAVE A LONG MEMORY...AND A LONG ARM!
CHECK
WAIT
HERE
IN OTHER NEWS, CANADA, NEW ZEALAND, AND AUSTRALIA HAVE ANNOUNCED THEIR INTENTION TO SECEDE FROM THE COMMONWEALTH AND RECALL THEIR TROOPS FROM MARS.
THE WAR OFFICE HAS REITERATED ITS MARTIAL ORDER MANDATE, THAT ANY SOLDIER LEAVING HIS POST WOULD BE CONSIDERED A DESERTER AND TREATED ACCORDINGLY.
BBC
PLEASURE ISLAND
IN THE EAST END OF LONDON, SCOTLAND YARD'S SPECIAL BRANCH AND THE METRO-POLITAN POLICE RAIDED A HOUSE IN SYDNEY STREET WHERE SCOTTISH SEDITIONISTS "THE PEOPLE'S CALEDONIAN MILITIA" HAD ESTABLISHED A HIDEOUT.
AFTER A HEATED GUN BATTLE, MANY OF THE INSURGENTS TOOK THEIR OWN LIVES RATHER THAN FACE CAPTURE. HOWEVER, IT IS SUSPECTED THAT SEVERAL ESCAPED IN THE CONFUSION.
BBC
"NATION SHALL SPEAK PEACE UNTO NATION"

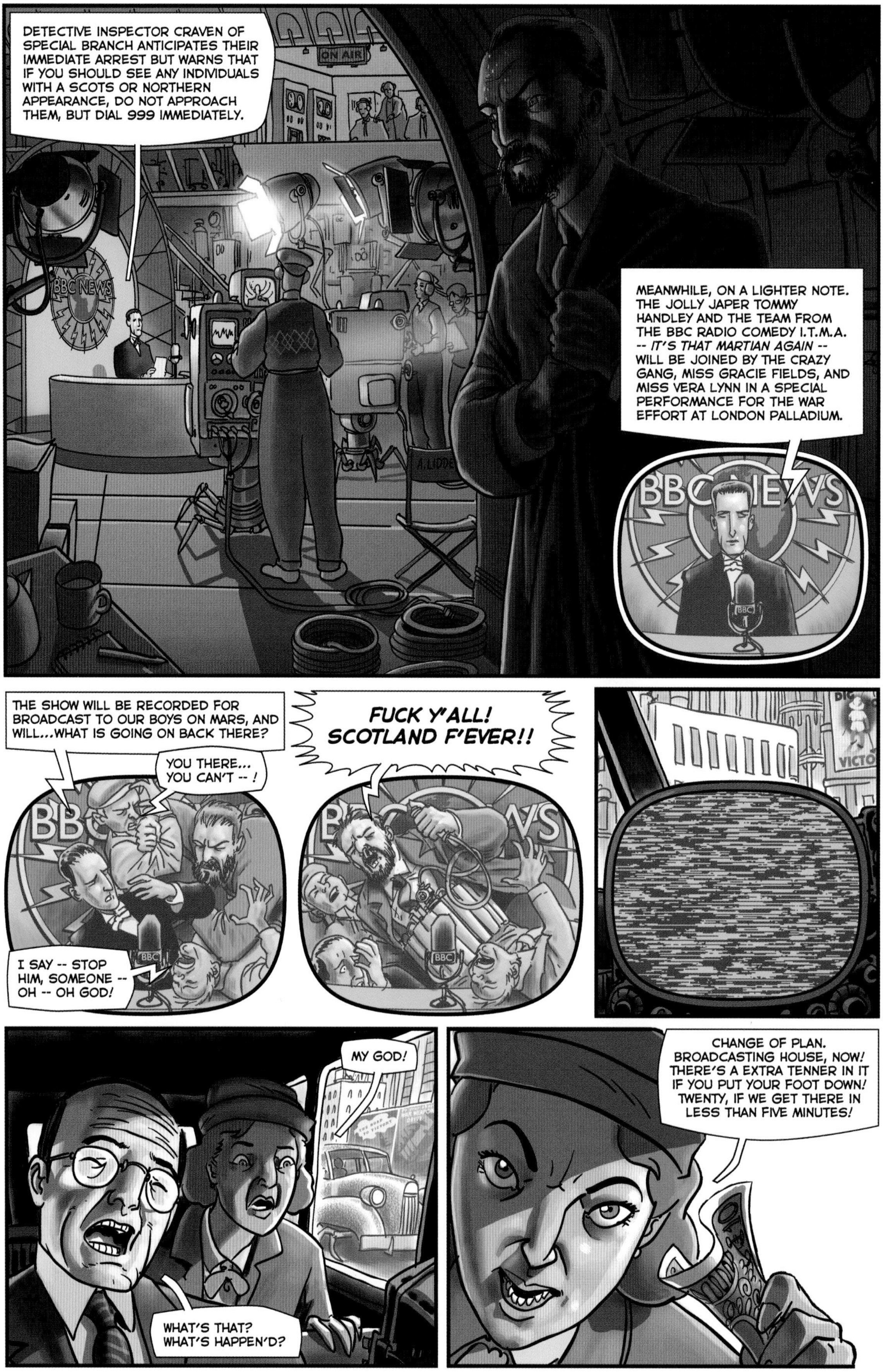
DETECTIVE INSPECTOR CRAVEN OF SPECIAL BRANCH ANTICIPATES THEIR IMMEDIATE ARREST BUT WARNS THAT IF YOU SHOULD SEE ANY INDIVIDUALS WITH A SCOTS OR NORTHERN APPEARANCE, DO NOT APPROACH THEM, BUT DIAL 999 IMMEDIATELY.
MEANWHILE, ON A LIGHTER NOTE. THE JOLLY JAPER TOMMY HANDLEY AND THE TEAM FROM THE BBC RADIO COMEDY I.T.M.A. -- *IT'S THAT MARTIAN AGAIN* -- WILL BE JOINED BY THE CRAZY GANG, MISS GRACIE FIELDS, AND MISS VERA LYNN IN A SPECIAL PERFORMANCE FOR THE WAR EFFORT AT LONDON PALLADIUM.
THE SHOW WILL BE RECORDED FOR BROADCAST TO OUR BOYS ON MARS, AND WILL...WHAT IS GOING ON BACK THERE?
YOU THERE... YOU CAN'T -- !
I SAY -- STOP HIM, SOMEONE -- OH -- OH GOD!
FUCK Y'ALL! SCOTLAND F'EVER!!
MY GOD!
WHAT'S THAT? WHAT'S HAPPEN'D?
CHANGE OF PLAN. BROADCASTING HOUSE, NOW! THERE'S A EXTRA TENNER IN IT IF YOU PUT YOUR FOOT DOWN! TWENTY, IF WE GET THERE IN LESS THAN FIVE MINUTES!

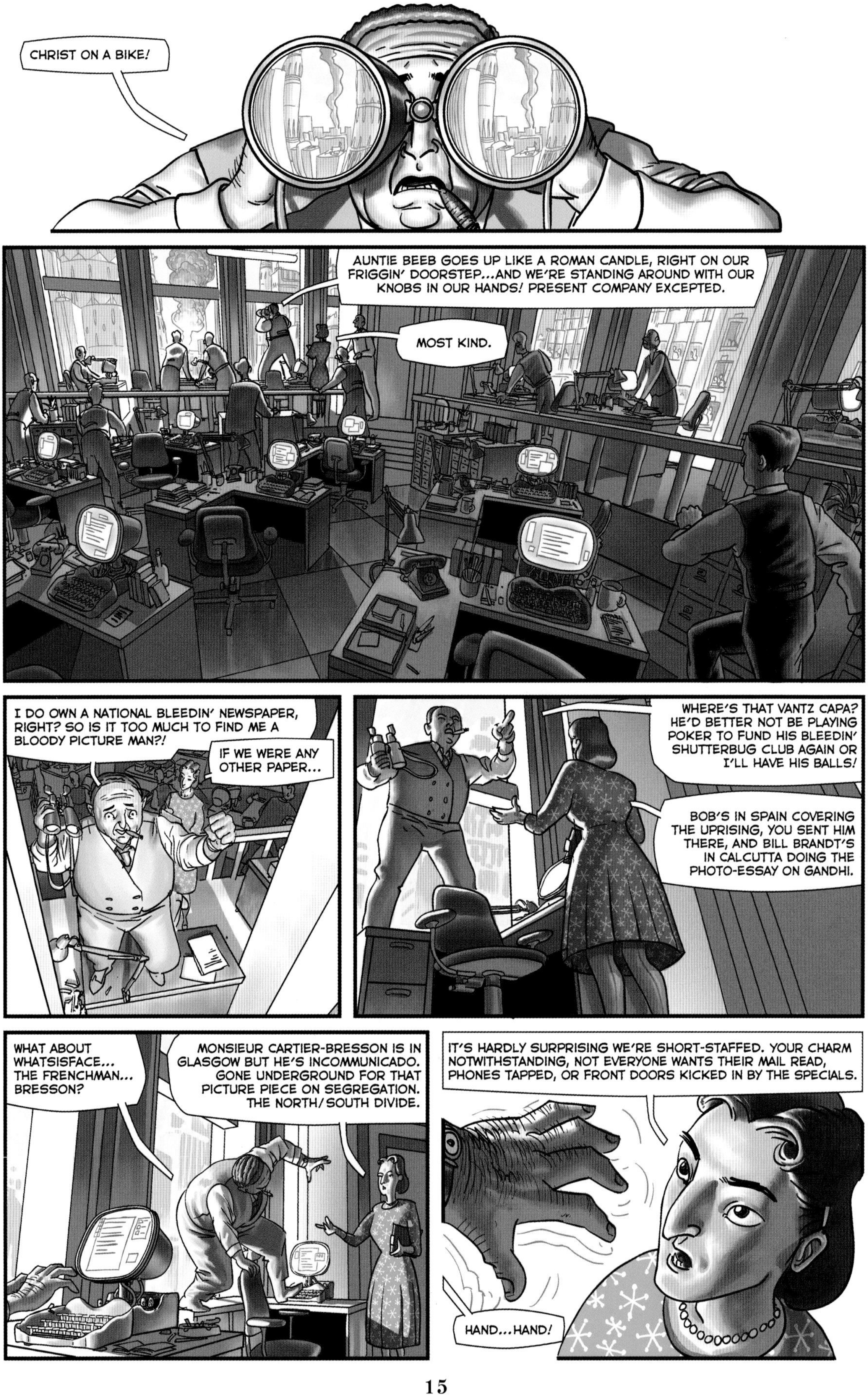
CHRIST ON A BIKE!
AUNTIE BEEB GOES UP LIKE A ROMAN CANDLE, RIGHT ON OUR FRIGGIN' DOORSTEP...AND WE'RE STANDING AROUND WITH OUR KNOBS IN OUR HANDS! PRESENT COMPANY EXCEPTED.
MOST KIND.
I DO OWN A NATIONAL BLEEDIN' NEWSPAPER, RIGHT? SO IS IT TOO MUCH TO FIND ME A BLOODY PICTURE MAN?!
IF WE WERE ANY OTHER PAPER...
WHERE'S THAT VANTZ CAPA? HE'D BETTER NOT BE PLAYING POKER TO FUND HIS BLEEDIN' SHUTTERBUG CLUB AGAIN OR I'LL HAVE HIS BALLS!
BOB'S IN SPAIN COVERING THE UPRISING, YOU SENT HIM THERE, AND BILL BRANDT'S IN CALCUTTA DOING THE PHOTO-ESSAY ON GANDHI.
WHAT ABOUT WHATSISFACE... THE FRENCHMAN... BRESSON?
MONSIEUR CARTIER-BRESSON IS IN GLASGOW BUT HE'S INCOMMUNICADO. GONE UNDERGROUND FOR THAT PICTURE PIECE ON SEGREGATION. THE NORTH/SOUTH DIVIDE.
IT'S HARDLY SURPRISING WE'RE SHORT-STAFFED. YOUR CHARM NOTWITHSTANDING, NOT EVERYONE WANTS THEIR MAIL READ, PHONES TAPPED, OR FRONT DOORS KICKED IN BY THE SPECIALS.
HAND...HAND!

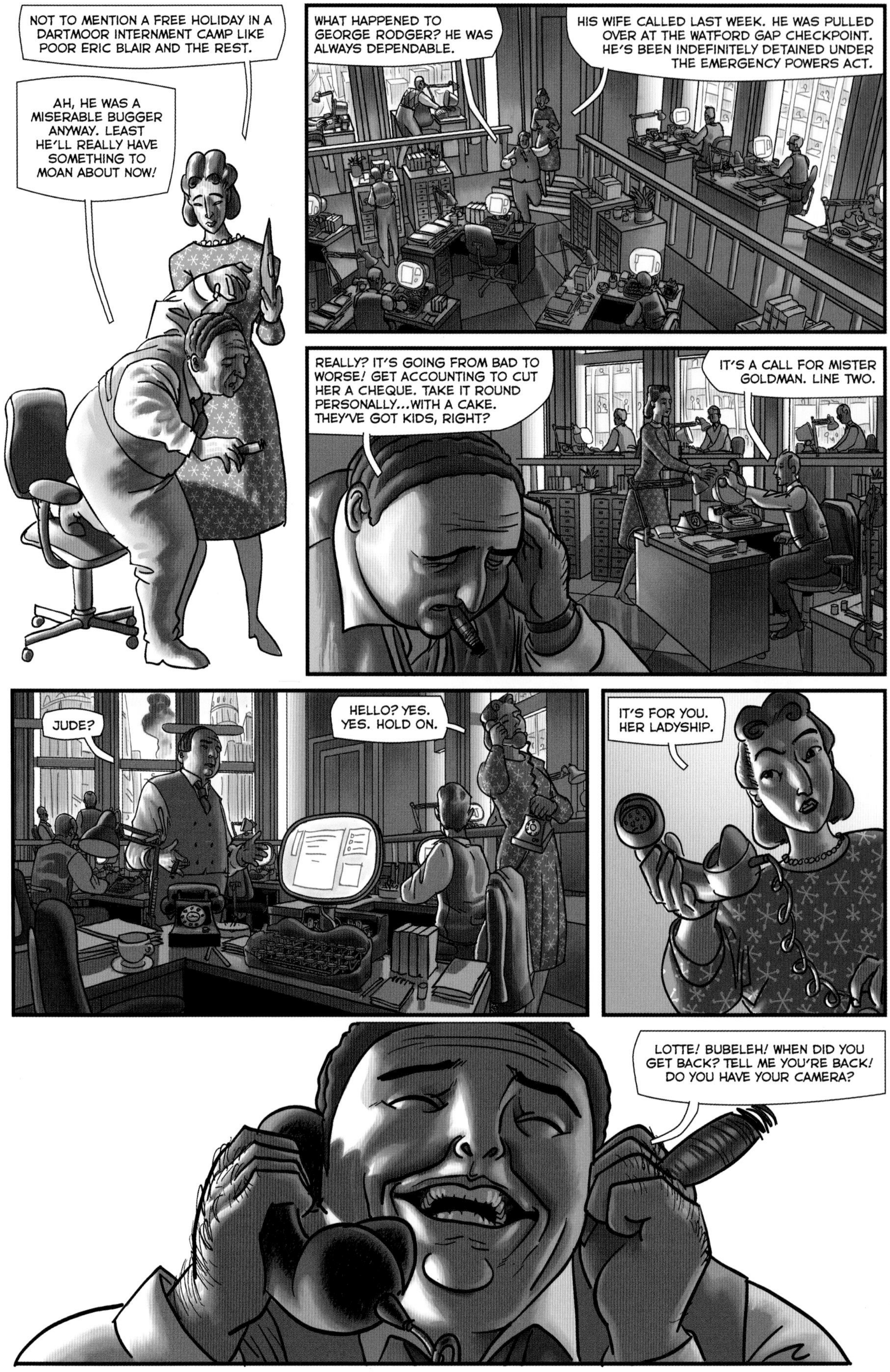
NOT TO MENTION A FREE HOLIDAY IN A DARTMOOR INTERNMENT CAMP LIKE POOR ERIC BLAIR AND THE REST.
AH, HE WAS A MISERABLE BUGGER ANYWAY. LEAST HE'LL REALLY HAVE SOMETHING TO MOAN ABOUT NOW!
WHAT HAPPENED TO GEORGE RODGER? HE WAS ALWAYS DEPENDABLE.
HIS WIFE CALLED LAST WEEK. HE WAS PULLED OVER AT THE WATFORD GAP CHECKPOINT. HE'S BEEN INDEFINITELY DETAINED UNDER THE EMERGENCY POWERS ACT.
REALLY? IT'S GOING FROM BAD TO WORSE! GET ACCOUNTING TO CUT HER A CHEQUE. TAKE IT ROUND PERSONALLY...WITH A CAKE. THEY'VE GOT KIDS, RIGHT?
IT'S A CALL FOR MISTER GOLDMAN. LINE TWO.
JUDE?
HELLO? YES. YES. HOLD ON.
IT'S FOR YOU. HER LADYSHIP.
LOTTE! BUBELEH! WHEN DID YOU GET BACK? TELL ME YOU'RE BACK! DO YOU HAVE YOUR CAMERA?

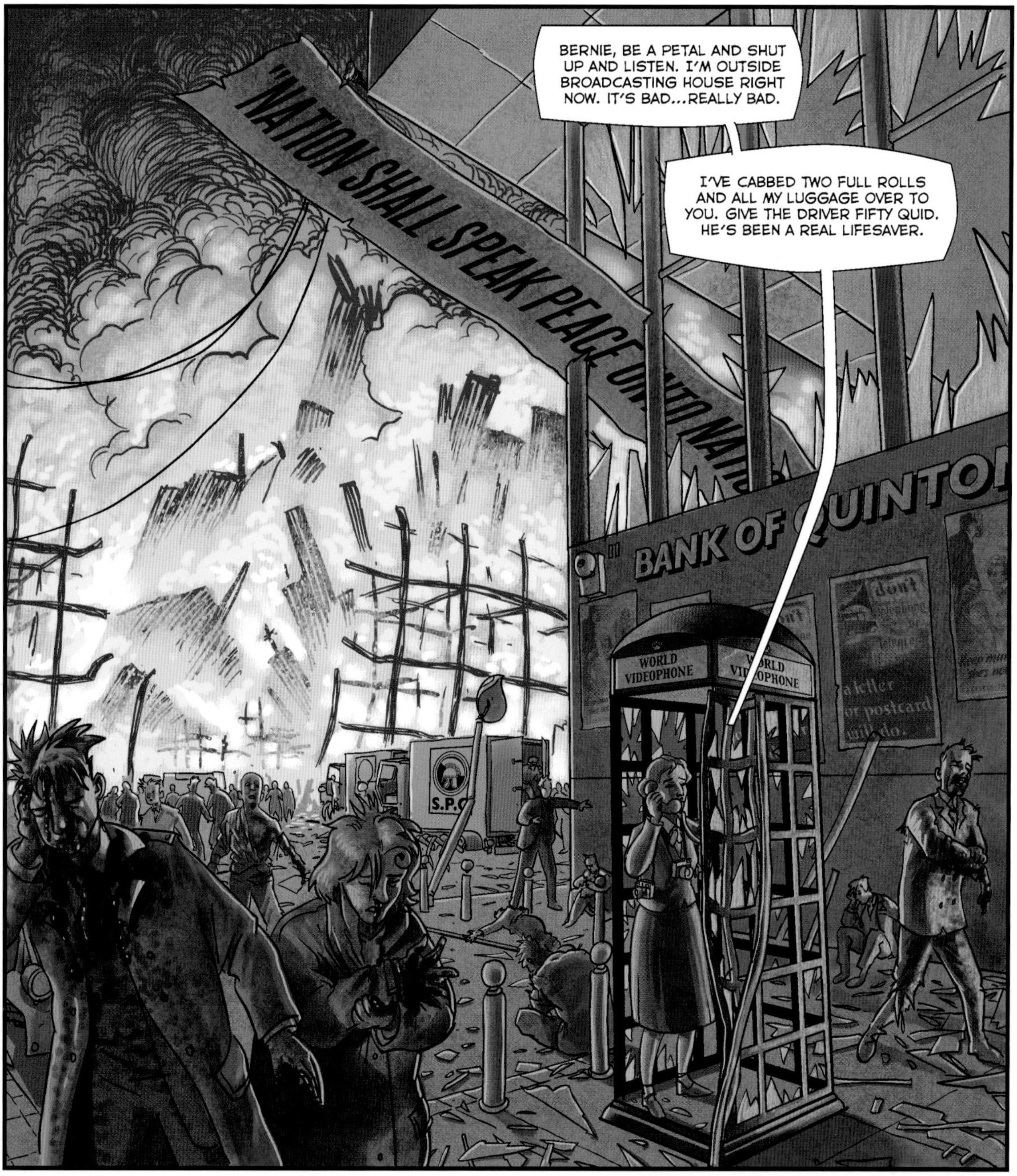
BERNIE, BE A PETAL AND SHUT UP AND LISTEN. I'M OUTSIDE BROADCASTING HOUSE RIGHT NOW. IT'S BAD...REALLY BAD.
I'VE CABBED TWO FULL ROLLS AND ALL MY LUGGAGE OVER TO YOU. GIVE THE DRIVER FIFTY QUID. HE'S BEEN A REAL LIFESAVER.
"NATION SHALL SPEAK PEACE UN
BANK OF QUINTO
WORLD VIDEOPHONE
WORLD VIDEOPHONE
a letter or postcard will do.
S.P.C.

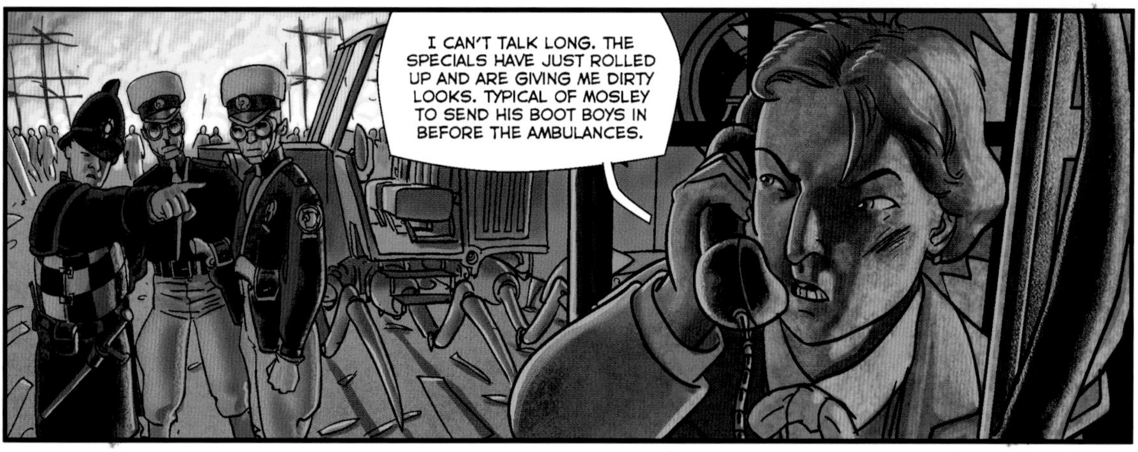
I CAN'T TALK LONG. THE SPECIALS HAVE JUST ROLLED UP AND ARE GIVING ME DIRTY LOOKS. TYPICAL OF MOSLEY TO SEND HIS BOOT BOYS IN BEFORE THE AMBULANCES.

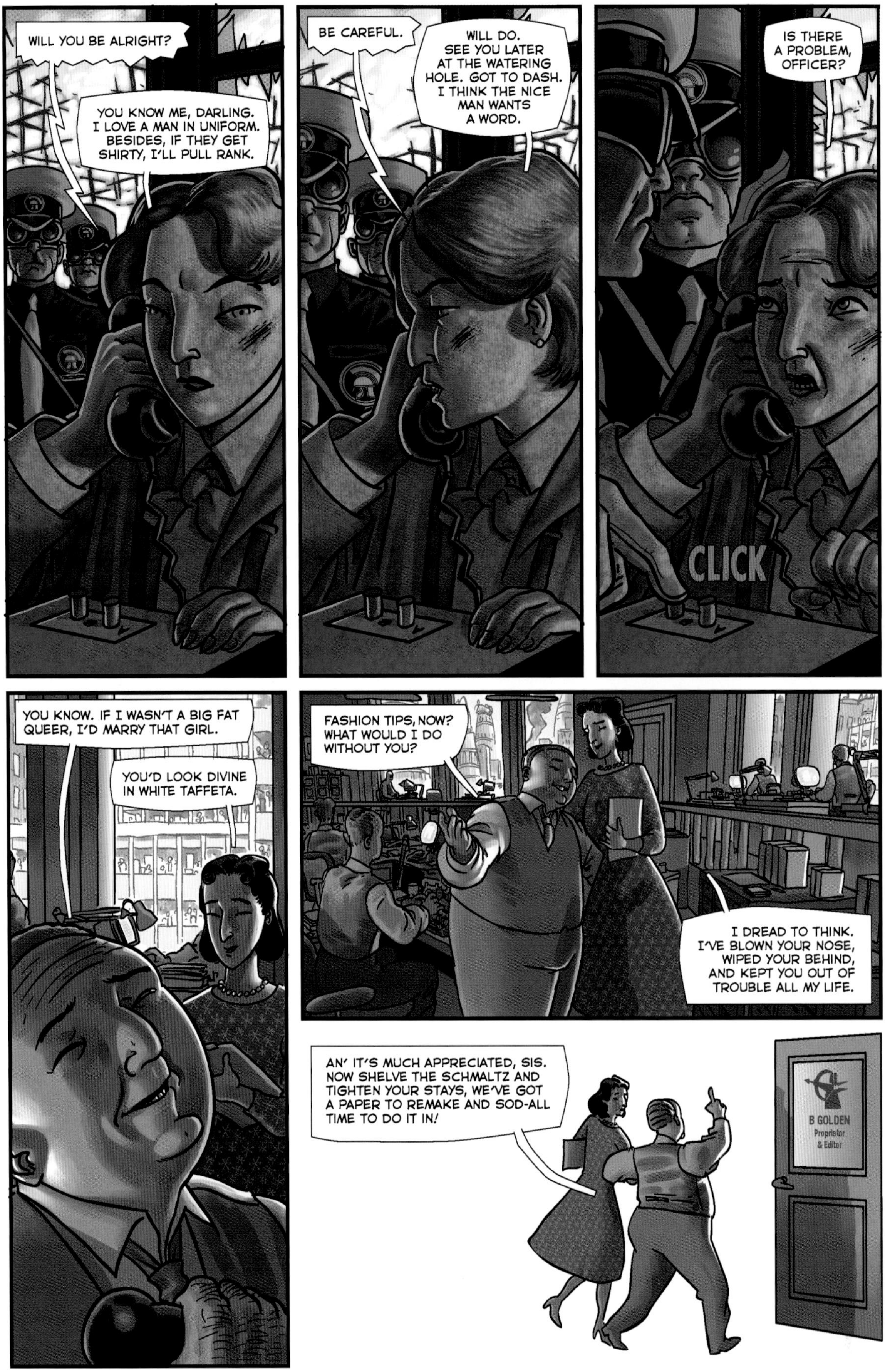
WILL YOU BE ALRIGHT?
YOU KNOW ME, DARLING. I LOVE A MAN IN UNIFORM. BESIDES, IF THEY GET SHIRTY, I'LL PULL RANK.
BE CAREFUL.
WILL DO. SEE YOU LATER AT THE WATERING HOLE. GOT TO DASH. I THINK THE NICE MAN WANTS A WORD.
IS THERE A PROBLEM, OFFICER?
CLICK
YOU KNOW. IF I WASN'T A BIG FAT QUEER, I'D MARRY THAT GIRL.
YOU'D LOOK DIVINE IN WHITE TAFFETA.
FASHION TIPS, NOW? WHAT WOULD I DO WITHOUT YOU?
I DREAD TO THINK. I'VE BLOWN YOUR NOSE, WIPED YOUR BEHIND, AND KEPT YOU OUT OF TROUBLE ALL MY LIFE.
AN' IT'S MUCH APPRECIATED, SIS. NOW SHELVE THE SCHMALTZ AND TIGHTEN YOUR STAYS, WE'VE GOT A PAPER TO REMAKE AND SOD-ALL TIME TO DO IT IN!
B GOLDEN
Proprietor
& Editor

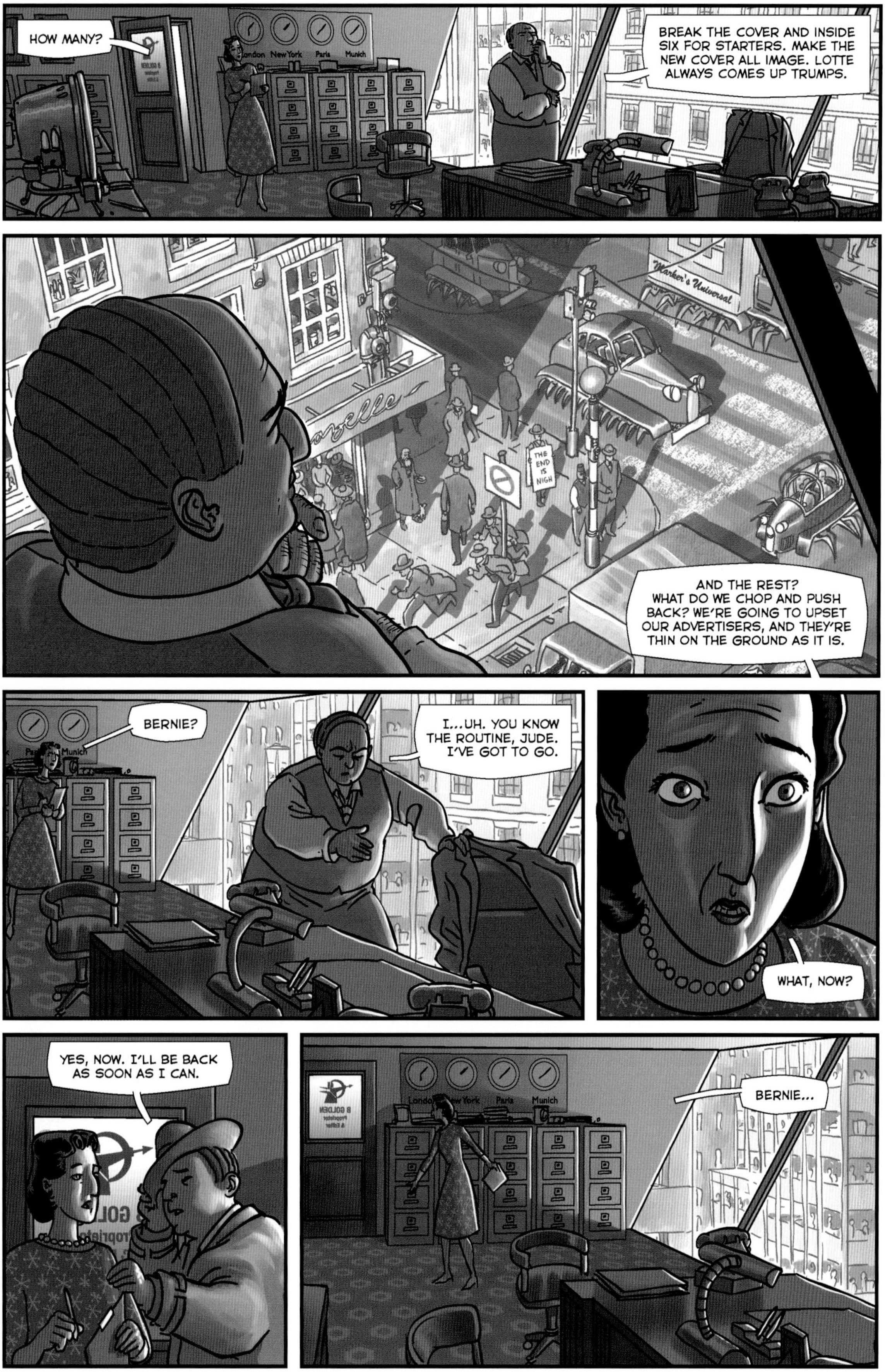
HOW MANY?
London New York Paris Munich
BREAK THE COVER AND INSIDE SIX FOR STARTERS. MAKE THE NEW COVER ALL IMAGE. LOTTE ALWAYS COMES UP TRUMPS.
Marker's Universal
THE END IS NIGH
AND THE REST? WHAT DO WE CHOP AND PUSH BACK? WE'RE GOING TO UPSET OUR ADVERTISERS, AND THEY'RE THIN ON THE GROUND AS IT IS.
BERNIE?
I...UH. YOU KNOW THE ROUTINE, JUDE. I'VE GOT TO GO.
WHAT, NOW?
YES, NOW. I'LL BE BACK AS SOON AS I CAN.
BERNIE...

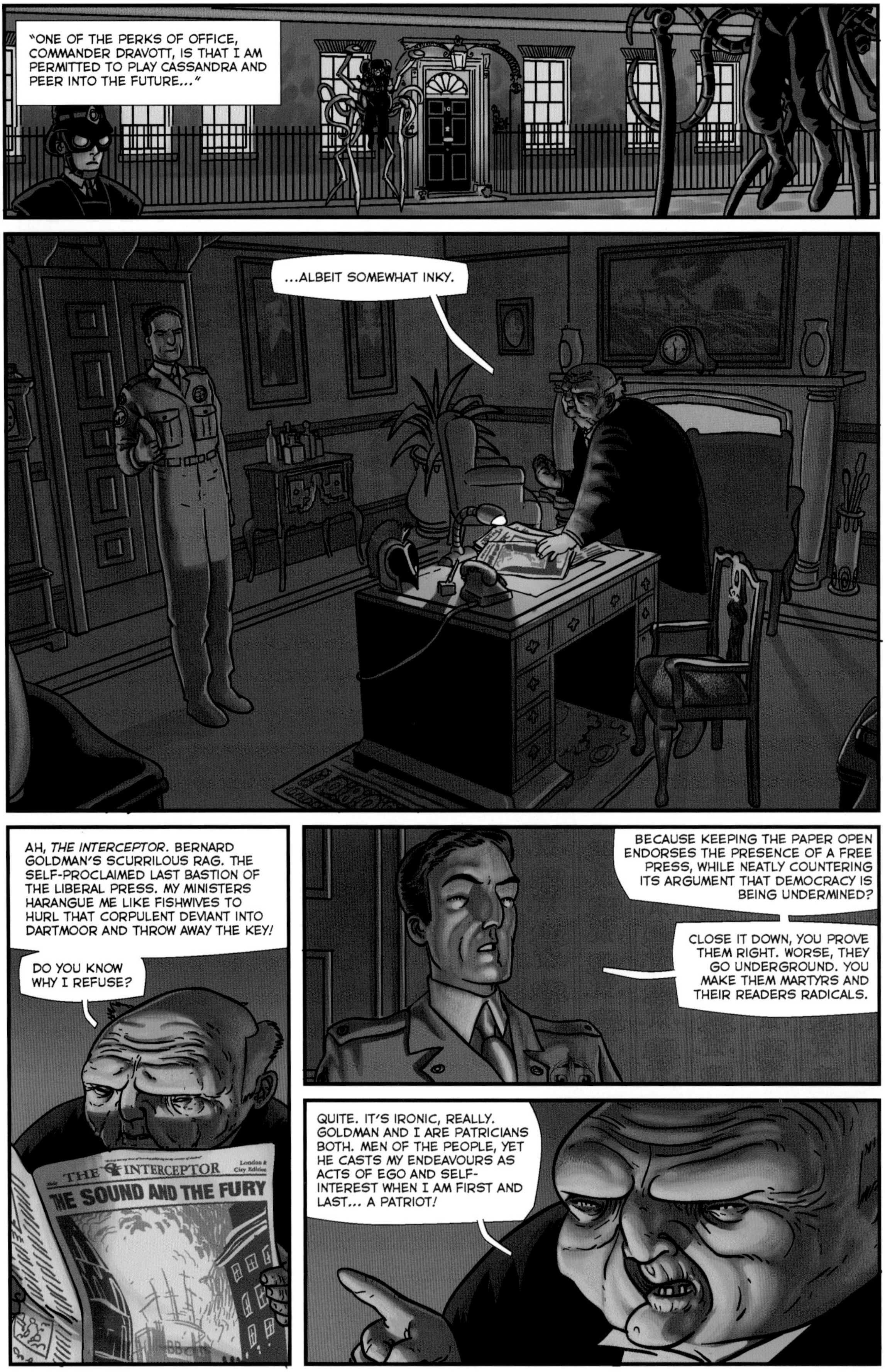
"ONE OF THE PERKS OF OFFICE, COMMANDER DRAVOTT, IS THAT I AM PERMITTED TO PLAY CASSANDRA AND PEER INTO THE FUTURE..."
...ALBEIT SOMEWHAT INKY.
AH, *THE INTERCEPTOR*. BERNARD GOLDMAN'S SCURRILOUS RAG. THE SELF-PROCLAIMED LAST BASTION OF THE LIBERAL PRESS. MY MINISTERS HARANGUE ME LIKE FISHWIVES TO HURL THAT CORPULENT DEVIANT INTO DARTMOOR AND THROW AWAY THE KEY!
DO YOU KNOW WHY I REFUSE?
THE INTERCEPTOR
London & City Edition
THE SOUND AND THE FURY
BECAUSE KEEPING THE PAPER OPEN ENDORSES THE PRESENCE OF A FREE PRESS, WHILE NEATLY COUNTERING ITS ARGUMENT THAT DEMOCRACY IS BEING UNDERMINED?
CLOSE IT DOWN, YOU PROVE THEM RIGHT. WORSE, THEY GO UNDERGROUND. YOU MAKE THEM MARTYRS AND THEIR READERS RADICALS.
QUITE. IT'S IRONIC, REALLY. GOLDMAN AND I ARE PATRICIANS BOTH. MEN OF THE PEOPLE, YET HE CASTS MY ENDEAVOURS AS ACTS OF EGO AND SELF-INTEREST WHEN I AM FIRST AND LAST... A PATRIOT!

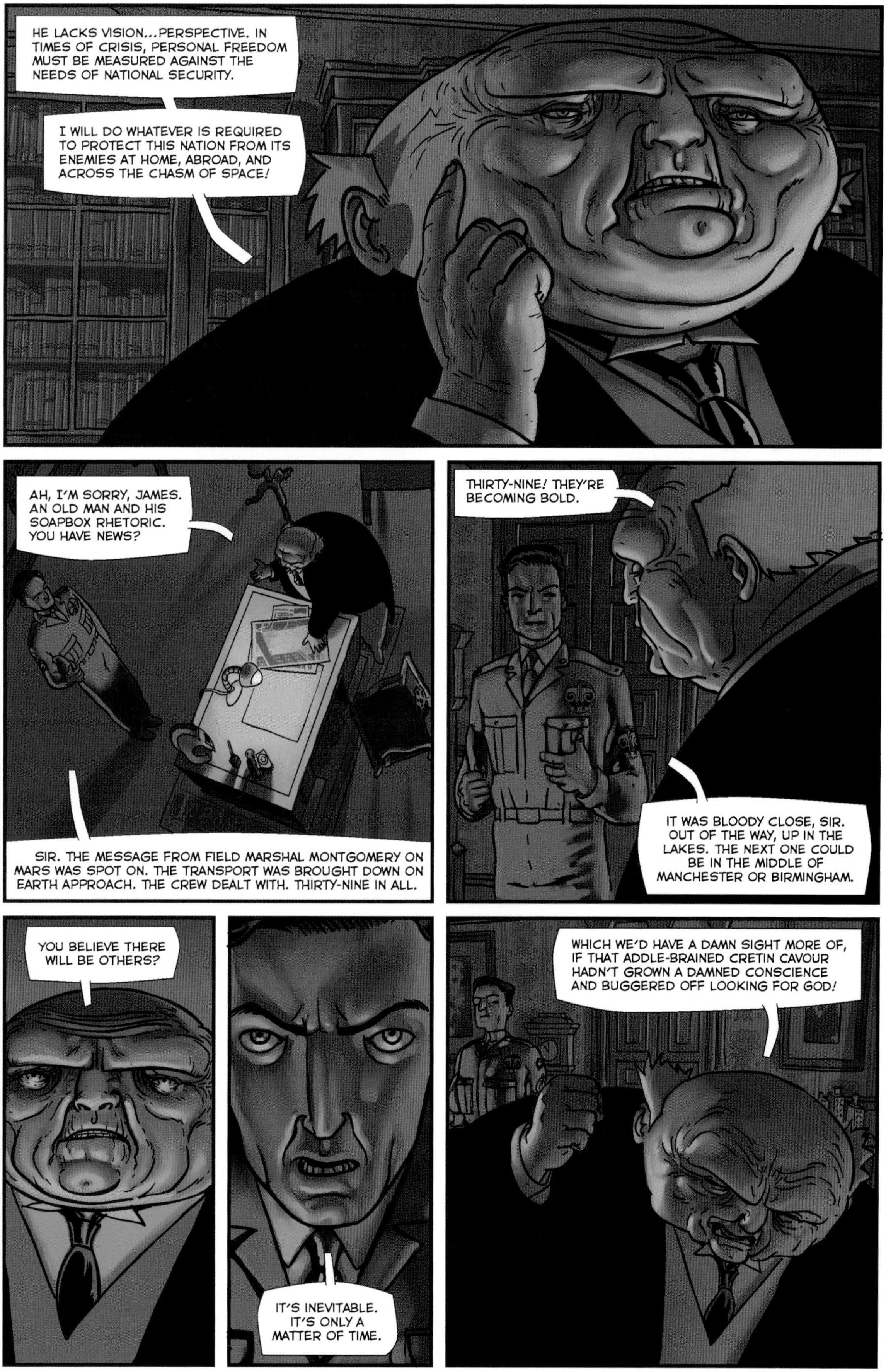
HE LACKS VISION...PERSPECTIVE. IN TIMES OF CRISIS, PERSONAL FREEDOM MUST BE MEASURED AGAINST THE NEEDS OF NATIONAL SECURITY.
I WILL DO WHATEVER IS REQUIRED TO PROTECT THIS NATION FROM ITS ENEMIES AT HOME, ABROAD, AND ACROSS THE CHASM OF SPACE!
AH, I'M SORRY, JAMES. AN OLD MAN AND HIS SOAPBOX RHETORIC. YOU HAVE NEWS?
SIR. THE MESSAGE FROM FIELD MARSHAL MONTGOMERY ON MARS WAS SPOT ON. THE TRANSPORT WAS BROUGHT DOWN ON EARTH APPROACH. THE CREW DEALT WITH. THIRTY-NINE IN ALL.
THIRTY-NINE! THEY'RE BECOMING BOLD.
IT WAS BLOODY CLOSE, SIR. OUT OF THE WAY, UP IN THE LAKES. THE NEXT ONE COULD BE IN THE MIDDLE OF MANCHESTER OR BIRMINGHAM.
YOU BELIEVE THERE WILL BE OTHERS?
IT'S INEVITABLE. IT'S ONLY A MATTER OF TIME.
WHICH WE'D HAVE A DAMN SIGHT MORE OF, IF THAT ADDLE-BRAINED CRETIN CAVOUR HADN'T GROWN A DAMNED CONSCIENCE AND BUGGERED OFF LOOKING FOR GOD!

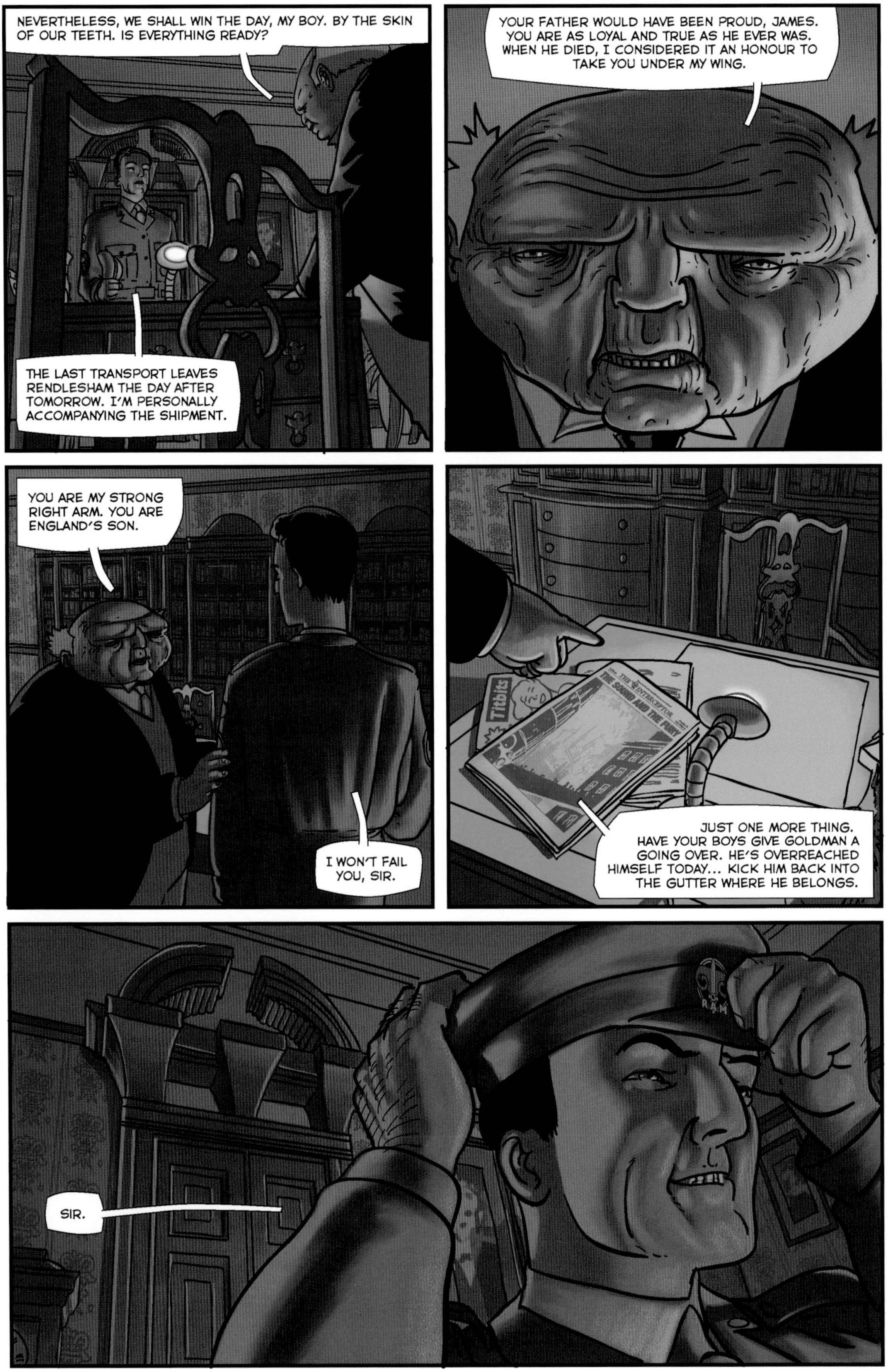
NEVERTHELESS, WE SHALL WIN THE DAY, MY BOY. BY THE SKIN OF OUR TEETH. IS EVERYTHING READY?
THE LAST TRANSPORT LEAVES RENDLESHAM THE DAY AFTER TOMORROW. I'M PERSONALLY ACCOMPANYING THE SHIPMENT.
YOUR FATHER WOULD HAVE BEEN PROUD, JAMES. YOU ARE AS LOYAL AND TRUE AS HE EVER WAS. WHEN HE DIED, I CONSIDERED IT AN HONOUR TO TAKE YOU UNDER MY WING.
YOU ARE MY STRONG RIGHT ARM. YOU ARE ENGLAND'S SON.
I WON'T FAIL YOU, SIR.
Titbits
THE INTERCEPTOR
THE SOUND AND THE FURY
JUST ONE MORE THING. HAVE YOUR BOYS GIVE GOLDMAN A GOING OVER. HE'S OVERREACHED HIMSELF TODAY... KICK HIM BACK INTO THE GUTTER WHERE HE BELONGS.
R.A.M
SIR.

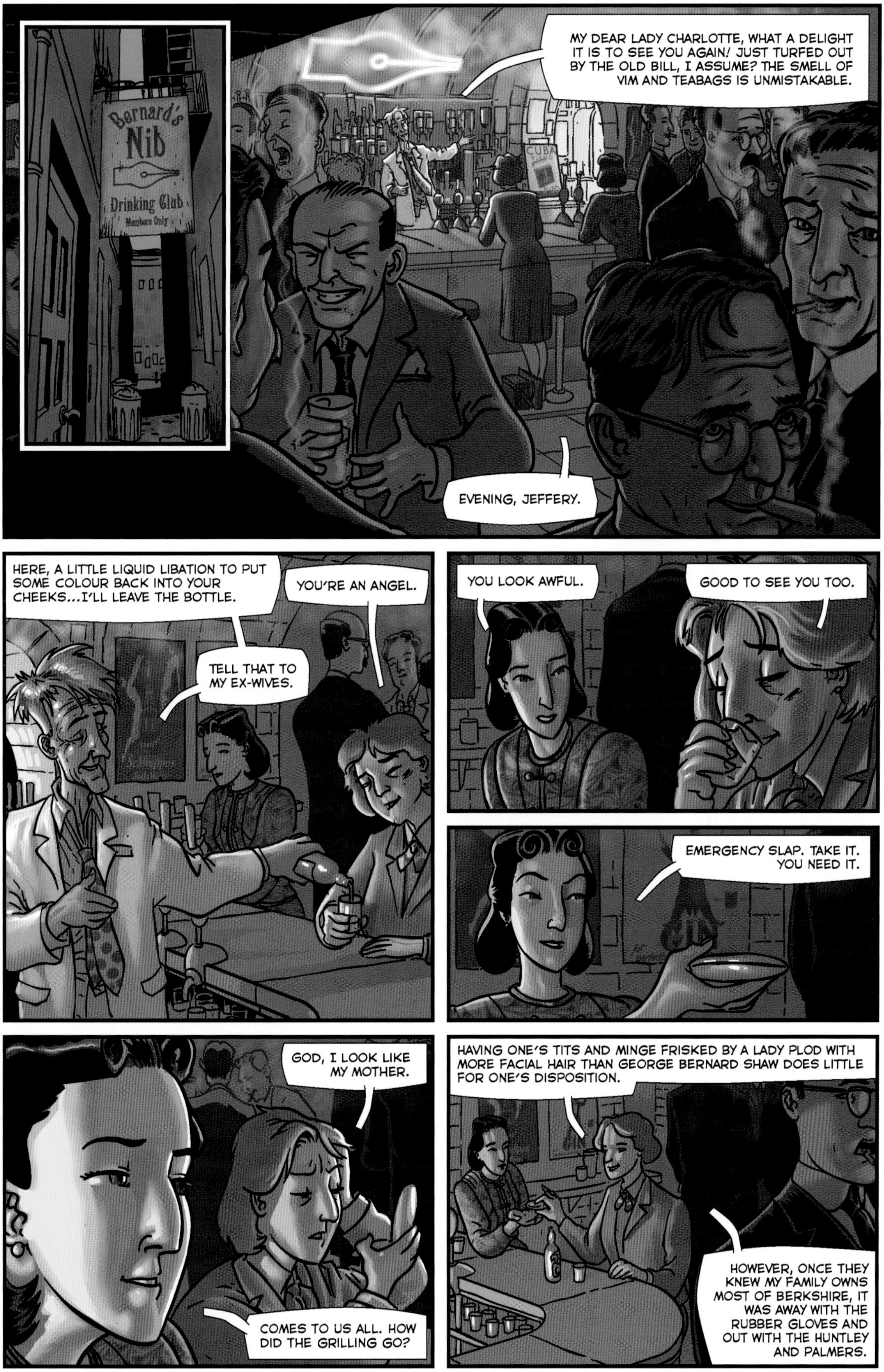
Bernard's Nib
Drinking Club
Members Only
MY DEAR LADY CHARLOTTE, WHAT A DELIGHT IT IS TO SEE YOU AGAIN! JUST TURFED OUT BY THE OLD BILL, I ASSUME? THE SMELL OF VIM AND TEABAGS IS UNMISTAKABLE.
EVENING, JEFFERY.
HERE, A LITTLE LIQUID LIBATION TO PUT SOME COLOUR BACK INTO YOUR CHEEKS...I'LL LEAVE THE BOTTLE.
YOU'RE AN ANGEL.
TELL THAT TO MY EX-WIVES.
YOU LOOK AWFUL.
GOOD TO SEE YOU TOO.
EMERGENCY SLAP. TAKE IT. YOU NEED IT.
GOD, I LOOK LIKE MY MOTHER.
COMES TO US ALL. HOW DID THE GRILLING GO?
HAVING ONE'S TITS AND MINGE FRISKED BY A LADY PLOD WITH MORE FACIAL HAIR THAN GEORGE BERNARD SHAW DOES LITTLE FOR ONE'S DISPOSITION.
HOWEVER, ONCE THEY KNEW MY FAMILY OWNS MOST OF BERKSHIRE, IT WAS AWAY WITH THE RUBBER GLOVES AND OUT WITH THE HUNTLEY AND PALMERS.

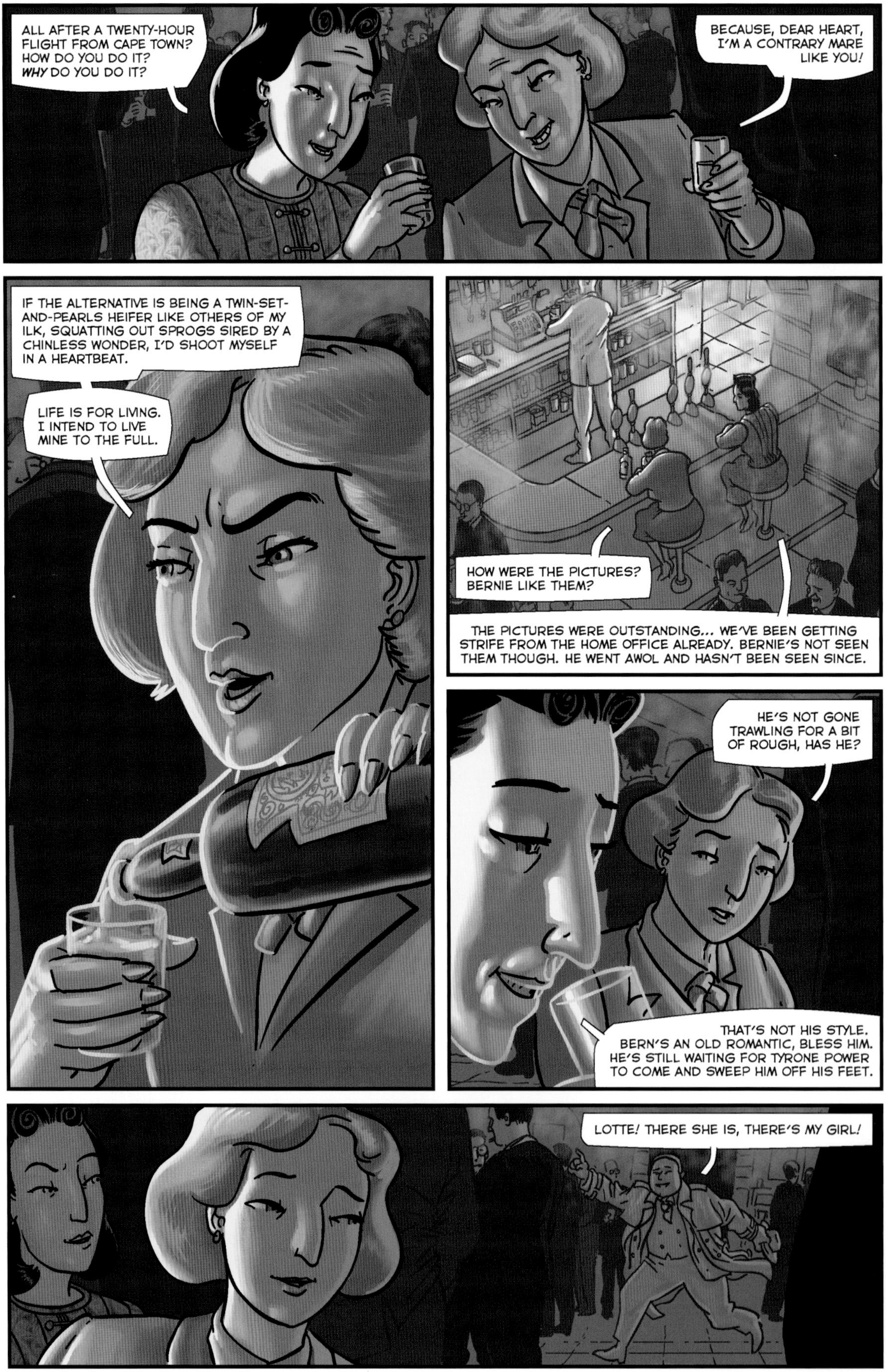

ALL AFTER A TWENTY-HOUR FLIGHT FROM CAPE TOWN? HOW DO YOU DO IT? *WHY* DO YOU DO IT?
BECAUSE, DEAR HEART, I'M A CONTRARY MARE LIKE YOU!
IF THE ALTERNATIVE IS BEING A TWIN-SET-AND-PEARLS HEIFER LIKE OTHERS OF MY ILK, SQUATTING OUT SPROGS SIRED BY A CHINLESS WONDER, I'D SHOOT MYSELF IN A HEARTBEAT.
LIFE IS FOR LIVING. I INTEND TO LIVE MINE TO THE FULL.
HOW WERE THE PICTURES? BERNIE LIKE THEM?
THE PICTURES WERE OUTSTANDING... WE'VE BEEN GETTING STRIFE FROM THE HOME OFFICE ALREADY. BERNIE'S NOT SEEN THEM THOUGH. HE WENT AWOL AND HASN'T BEEN SEEN SINCE.
HE'S NOT GONE TRAWLING FOR A BIT OF ROUGH, HAS HE?
THAT'S NOT HIS STYLE. BERN'S AN OLD ROMANTIC, BLESS HIM. HE'S STILL WAITING FOR TYRONE POWER TO COME AND SWEEP HIM OFF HIS FEET.
LOTTE! THERE SHE IS, THERE'S MY GIRL!

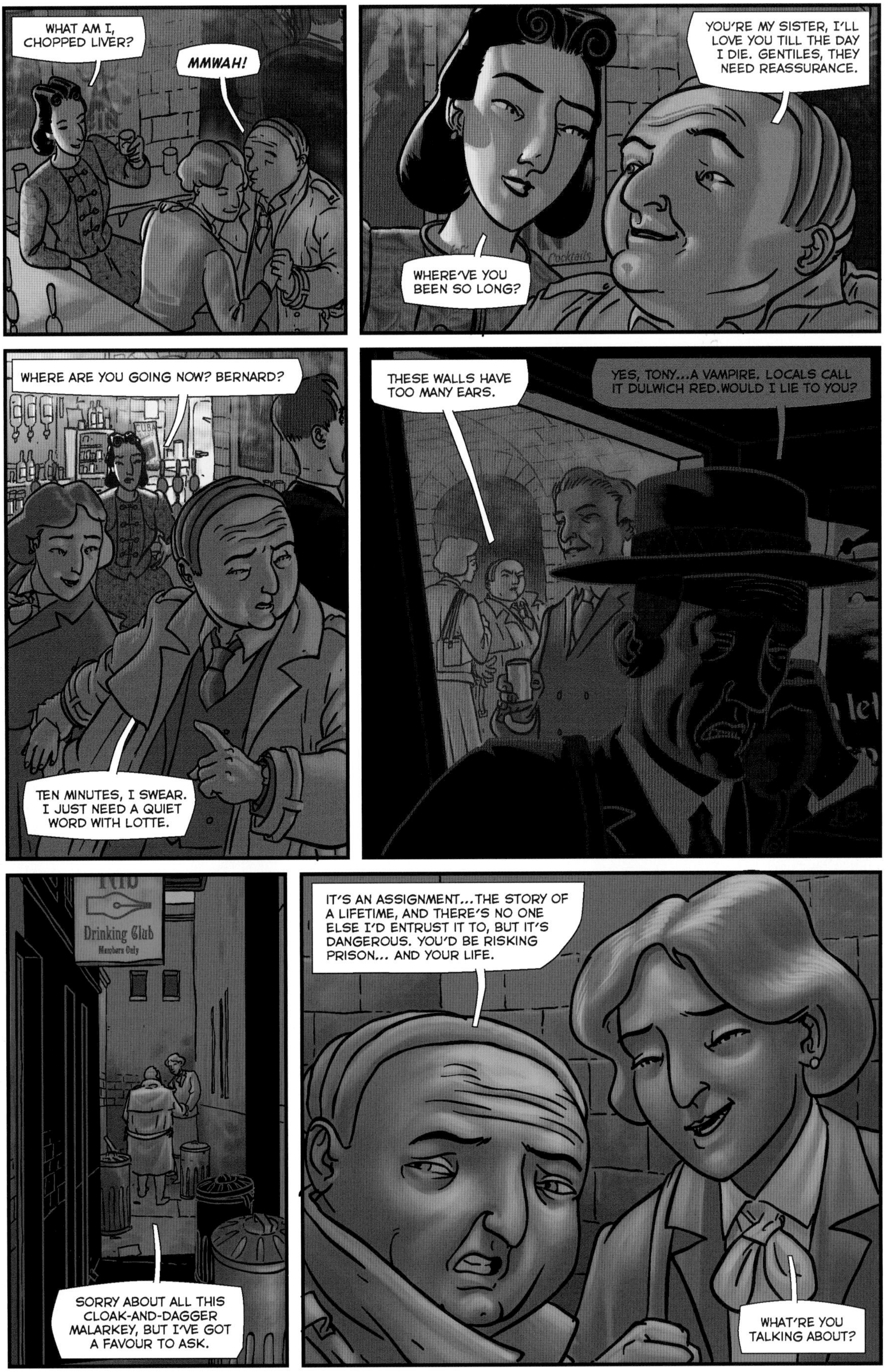
WHAT AM I, CHOPPED LIVER?
MMWAH!
YOU'RE MY SISTER, I'LL LOVE YOU TILL THE DAY I DIE. GENTILES, THEY NEED REASSURANCE.
WHERE'VE YOU BEEN SO LONG?
WHERE ARE YOU GOING NOW? BERNARD?
TEN MINUTES, I SWEAR. I JUST NEED A QUIET WORD WITH LOTTE.
THESE WALLS HAVE TOO MANY EARS.
YES, TONY...A VAMPIRE. LOCALS CALL IT DULWICH RED. WOULD I LIE TO YOU?
Drinking Club
SORRY ABOUT ALL THIS CLOAK-AND-DAGGER MALARKEY, BUT I'VE GOT A FAVOUR TO ASK.
IT'S AN ASSIGNMENT...THE STORY OF A LIFETIME, AND THERE'S NO ONE ELSE I'D ENTRUST IT TO, BUT IT'S DANGEROUS. YOU'D BE RISKING PRISON... AND YOUR LIFE.
WHAT'RE YOU TALKING ABOUT?

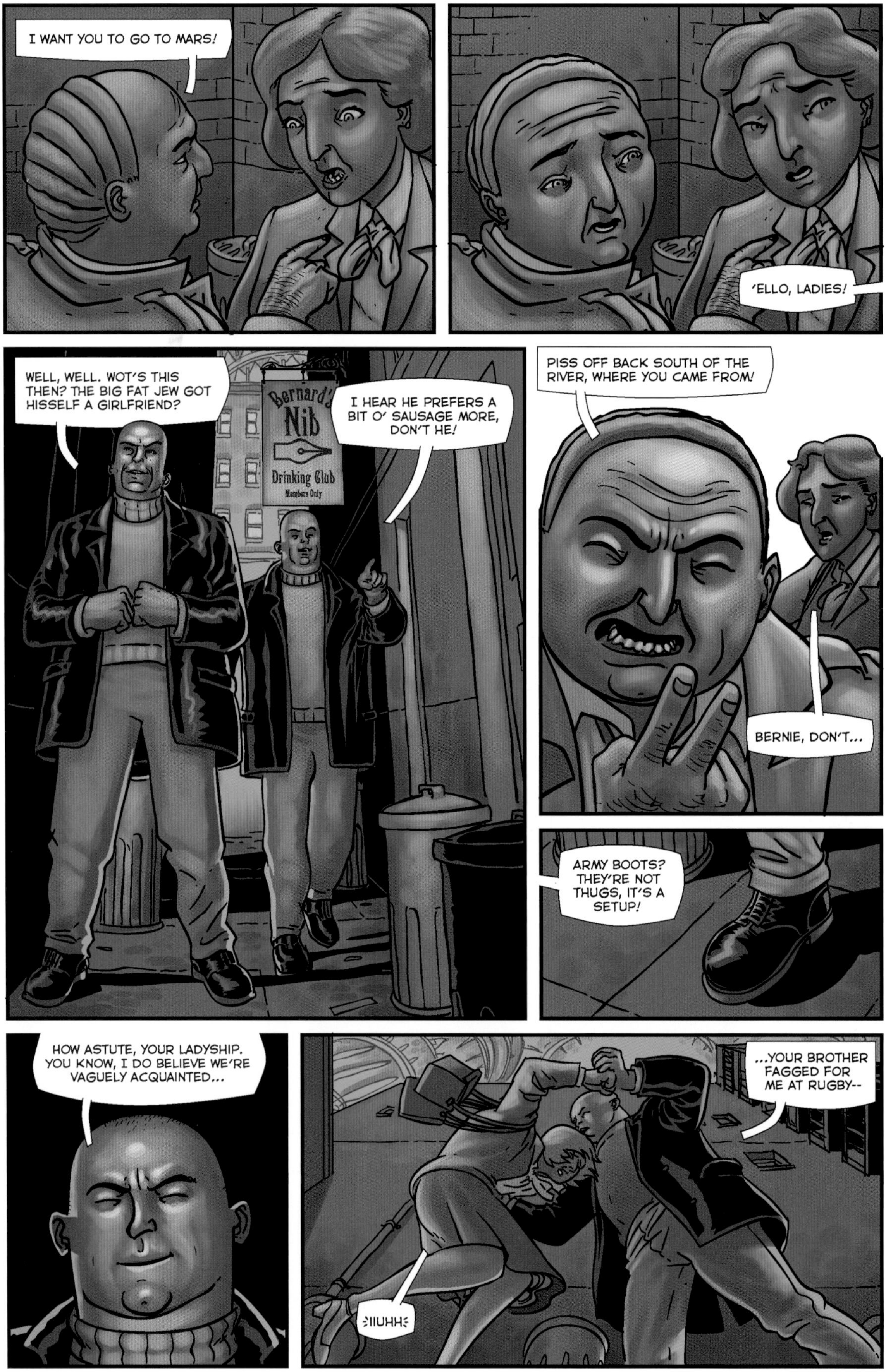
I WANT YOU TO GO TO MARS!
'ELLO, LADIES!
WELL, WELL. WOT'S THIS THEN? THE BIG FAT JEW GOT HISSELF A GIRLFRIEND?
Bernard's Nib
Drinking Club
Members Only
I HEAR HE PREFERS A BIT O' SAUSAGE MORE, DON'T HE!
PISS OFF BACK SOUTH OF THE RIVER, WHERE YOU CAME FROM!
BERNIE, DON'T...
ARMY BOOTS? THEY'RE NOT THUGS, IT'S A SETUP!
HOW ASTUTE, YOUR LADYSHIP. YOU KNOW, I DO BELIEVE WE'RE VAGUELY ACQUAINTED...
...YOUR BROTHER FAGGED FOR ME AT RUGBY--
IIUHH

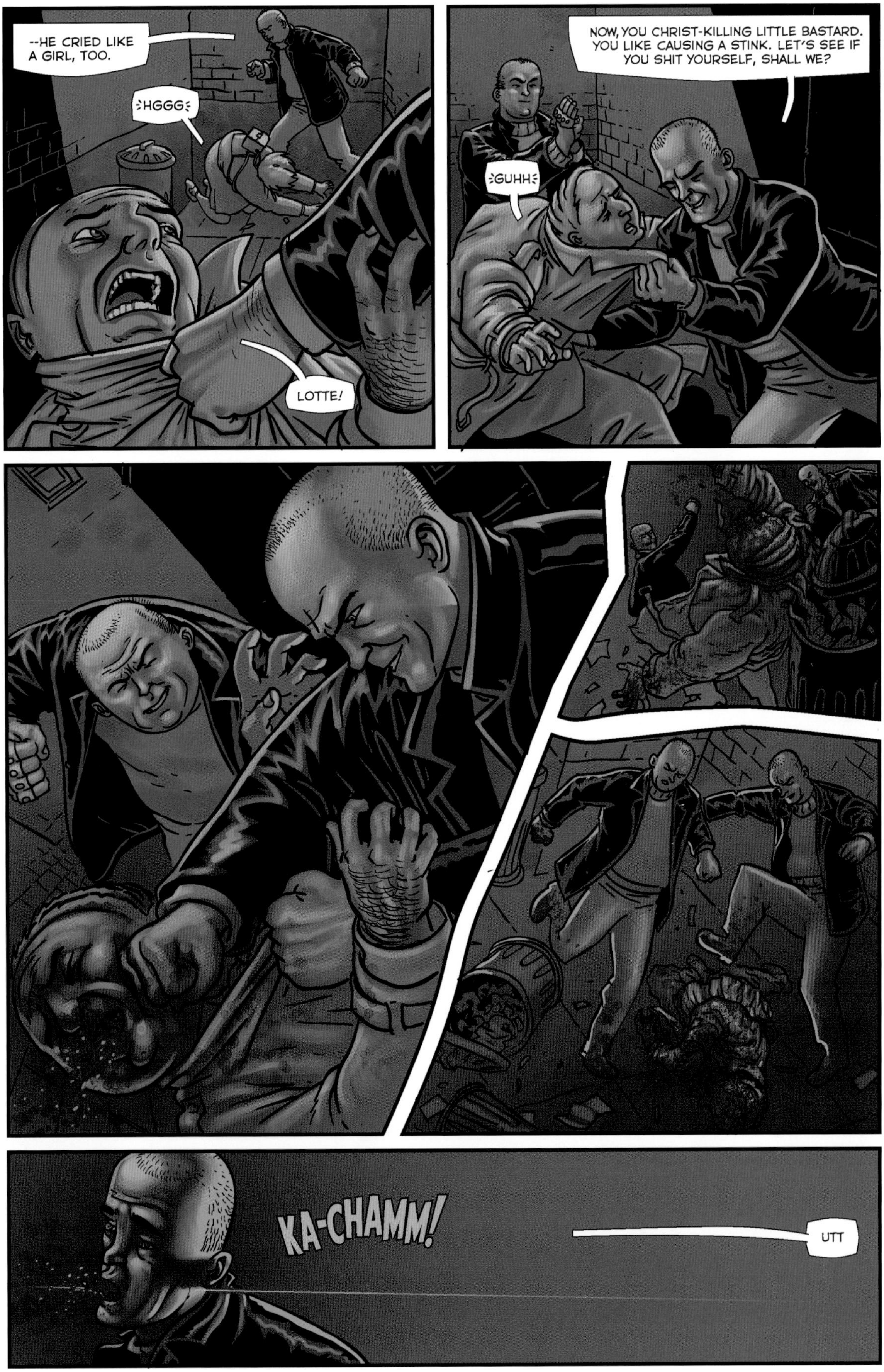
--HE CRIED LIKE A GIRL, TOO.
HGGG
LOTTE!
NOW, YOU CHRIST-KILLING LITTLE BASTARD. YOU LIKE CAUSING A STINK. LET'S SEE IF YOU SHIT YOURSELF, SHALL WE?
GUHH
KA-CHAMM!
UTT

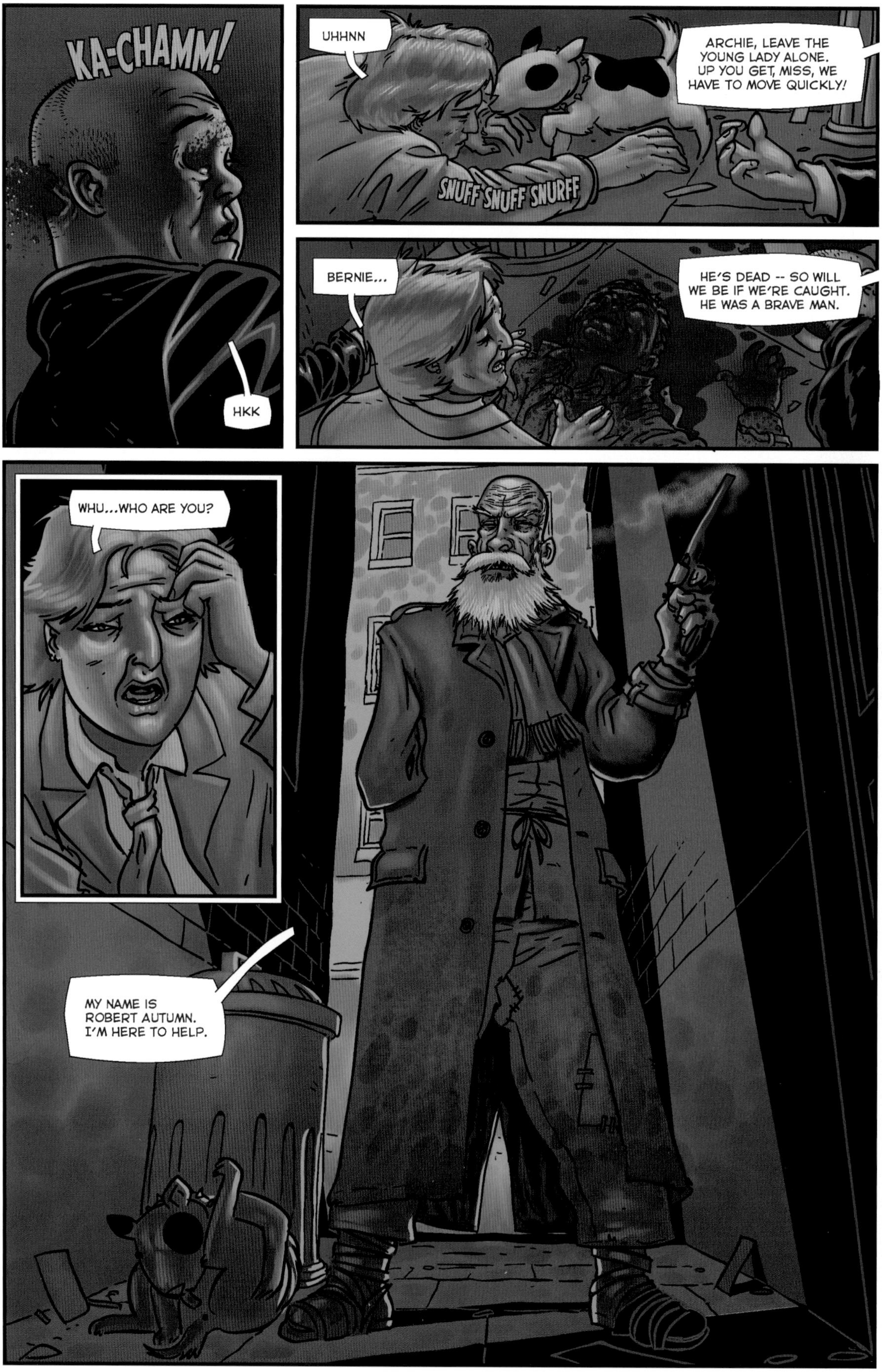
KA-CHAMM!
HKK
UHHNN
ARCHIE, LEAVE THE YOUNG LADY ALONE. UP YOU GET, MISS, WE HAVE TO MOVE QUICKLY!
SNUFF SNUFF SNURFF
BERNIE...
HE'S DEAD -- SO WILL WE BE IF WE'RE CAUGHT. HE WAS A BRAVE MAN.
WHU...WHO ARE YOU?
MY NAME IS ROBERT AUTUMN. I'M HERE TO HELP.

CHAPTER TWO

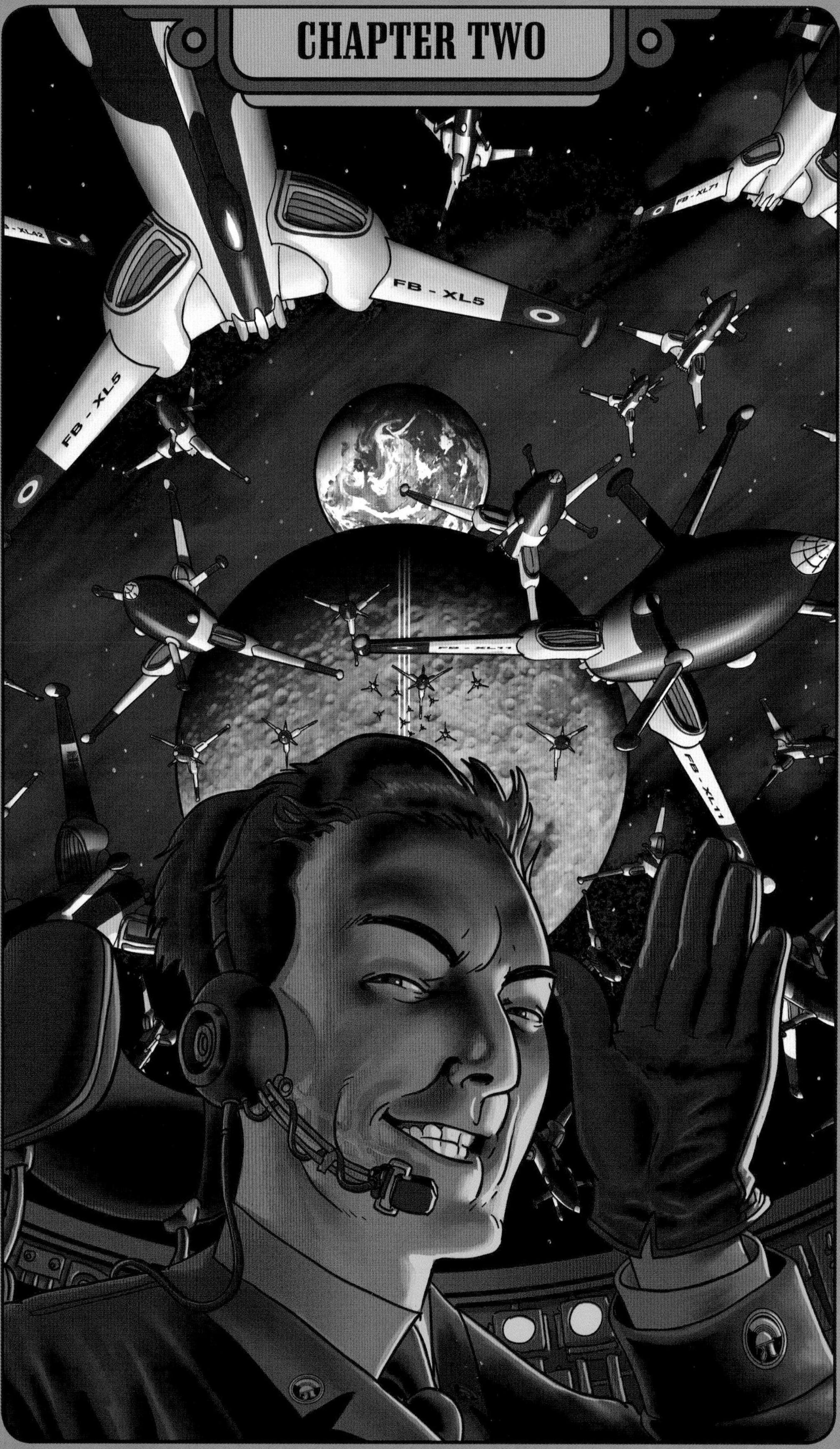
FB - XL5
FB - XL5
FB - XL11

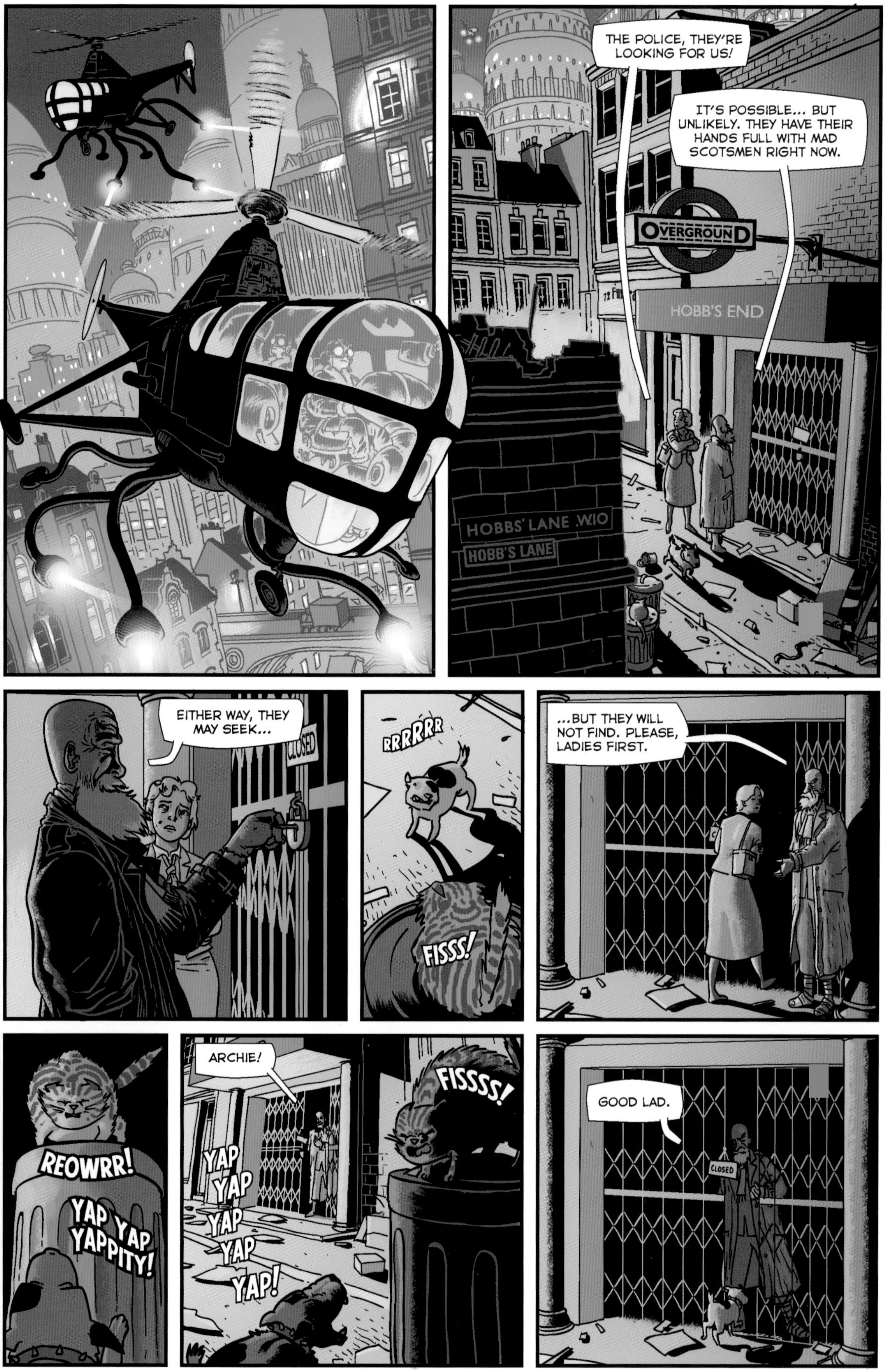
THE POLICE, THEY'RE LOOKING FOR US!
IT'S POSSIBLE... BUT UNLIKELY. THEY HAVE THEIR HANDS FULL WITH MAD SCOTSMEN RIGHT NOW.
OVERGROUND
HOBB'S END
HOBBS' LANE .W10
HOBB'S LANE
EITHER WAY, THEY MAY SEEK...
CLOSED
RRRRRR
FISSS!
...BUT THEY WILL NOT FIND. PLEASE, LADIES FIRST.
REOWRR!
YAP YAP YAPPITY!
ARCHIE!
YAP YAP YAP YAP YAP!
FISSSS!
GOOD LAD.
CLOSED

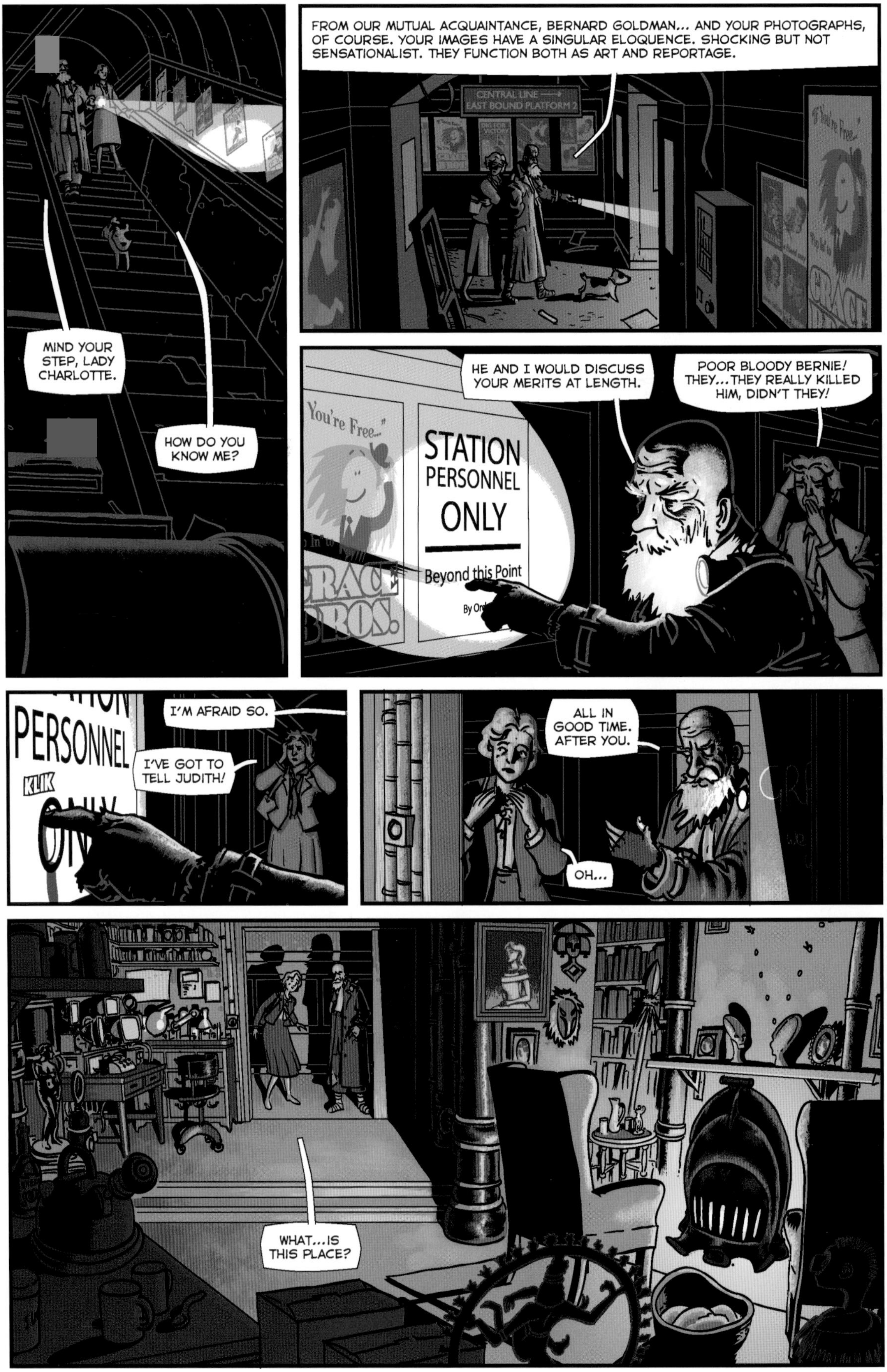
MIND YOUR STEP, LADY CHARLOTTE.
HOW DO YOU KNOW ME?
FROM OUR MUTUAL ACQUAINTANCE, BERNARD GOLDMAN... AND YOUR PHOTOGRAPHS, OF COURSE. YOUR IMAGES HAVE A SINGULAR ELOQUENCE. SHOCKING BUT NOT SENSATIONALIST. THEY FUNCTION BOTH AS ART AND REPORTAGE.
CENTRAL LINE
EAST BOUND PLATFORM 2
DIG FOR VICTORY
HE AND I WOULD DISCUSS YOUR MERITS AT LENGTH.
POOR BLOODY BERNIE! THEY...THEY REALLY KILLED HIM, DIDN'T THEY!
You're Free..."
STATION PERSONNEL ONLY
Beyond this Point
I'M AFRAID SO.
I'VE GOT TO TELL JUDITH!
KLIK
ALL IN GOOD TIME. AFTER YOU.
OH...
WHAT...IS THIS PLACE?

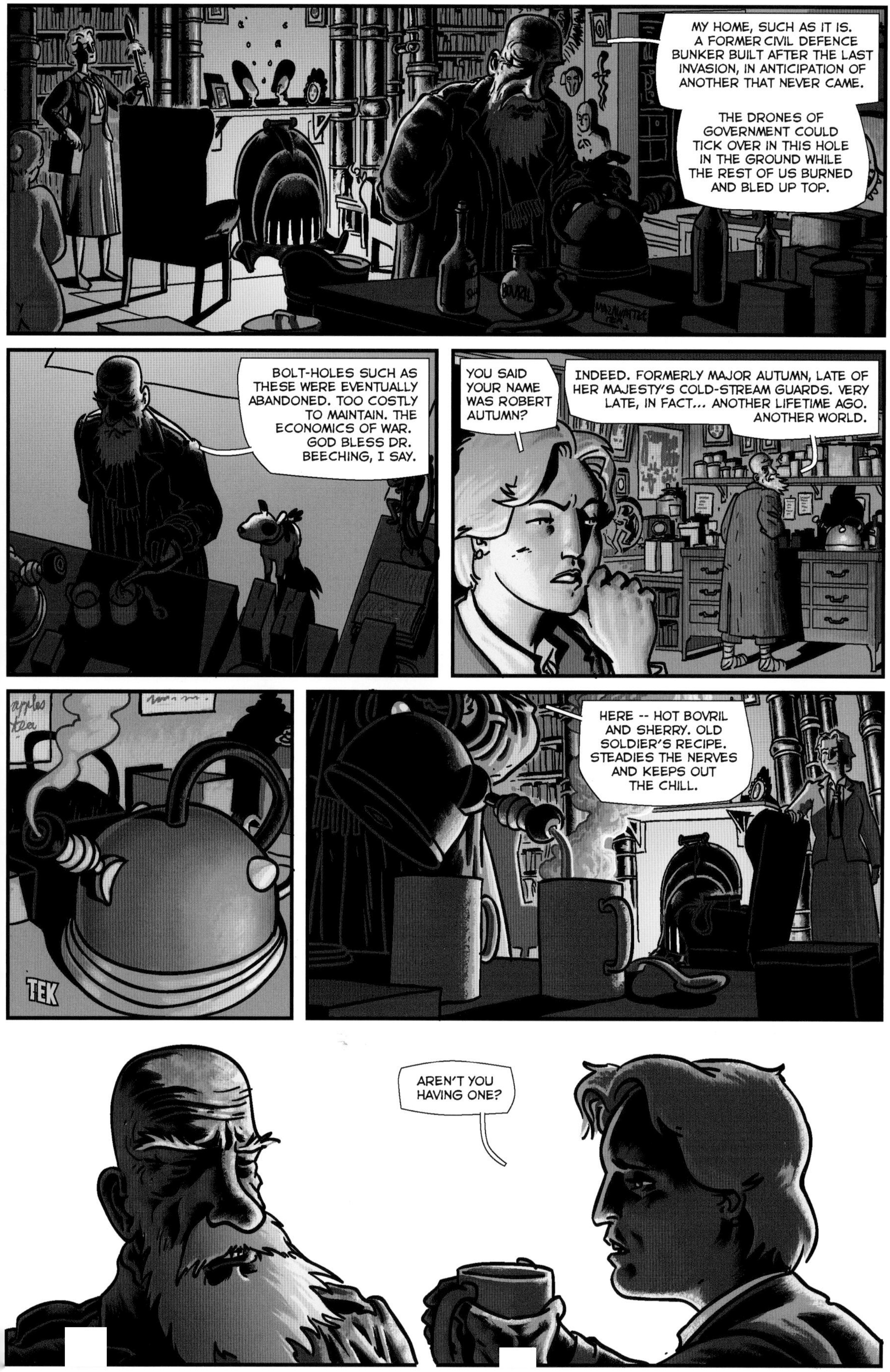

MY HOME, SUCH AS IT IS. A FORMER CIVIL DEFENCE BUNKER BUILT AFTER THE LAST INVASION, IN ANTICIPATION OF ANOTHER THAT NEVER CAME.
THE DRONES OF GOVERNMENT COULD TICK OVER IN THIS HOLE IN THE GROUND WHILE THE REST OF US BURNED AND BLED UP TOP.
BOVRIL
BOLT-HOLES SUCH AS THESE WERE EVENTUALLY ABANDONED. TOO COSTLY TO MAINTAIN. THE ECONOMICS OF WAR. GOD BLESS DR. BEECHING, I SAY.
YOU SAID YOUR NAME WAS ROBERT AUTUMN?
INDEED. FORMERLY MAJOR AUTUMN, LATE OF HER MAJESTY'S COLD-STREAM GUARDS. VERY LATE, IN FACT... ANOTHER LIFETIME AGO. ANOTHER WORLD.
TEK
HERE -- HOT BOVRIL AND SHERRY. OLD SOLDIER'S RECIPE. STEADIES THE NERVES AND KEEPS OUT THE CHILL.
AREN'T YOU HAVING ONE?

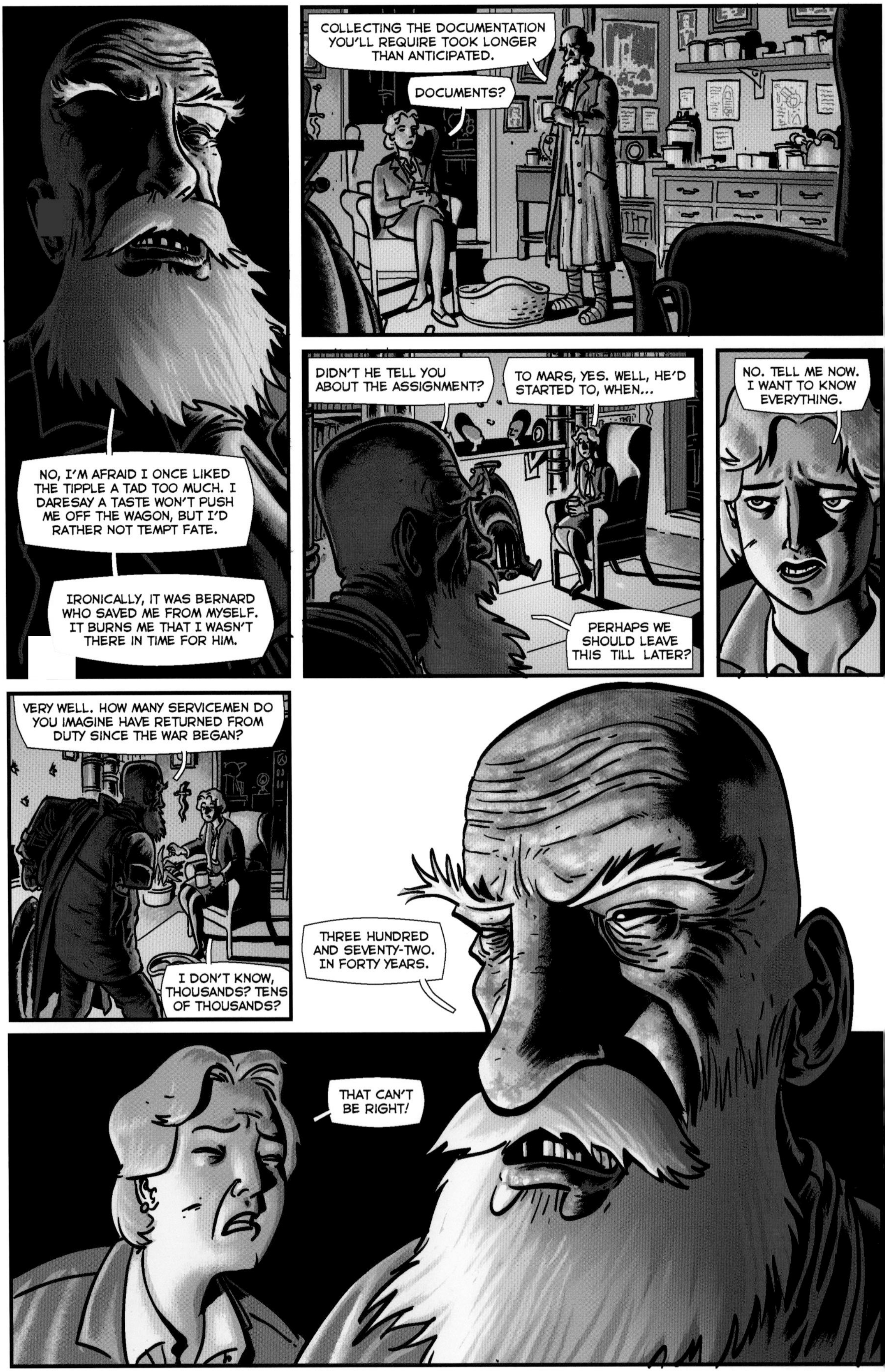
COLLECTING THE DOCUMENTATION YOU'LL REQUIRE TOOK LONGER THAN ANTICIPATED.
DOCUMENTS?
NO, I'M AFRAID I ONCE LIKED THE TIPPLE A TAD TOO MUCH. I DARESAY A TASTE WON'T PUSH ME OFF THE WAGON, BUT I'D RATHER NOT TEMPT FATE.
IRONICALLY, IT WAS BERNARD WHO SAVED ME FROM MYSELF. IT BURNS ME THAT I WASN'T THERE IN TIME FOR HIM.
DIDN'T HE TELL YOU ABOUT THE ASSIGNMENT?
TO MARS, YES. WELL, HE'D STARTED TO, WHEN...
PERHAPS WE SHOULD LEAVE THIS TILL LATER?
NO. TELL ME NOW. I WANT TO KNOW EVERYTHING.
VERY WELL. HOW MANY SERVICEMEN DO YOU IMAGINE HAVE RETURNED FROM DUTY SINCE THE WAR BEGAN?
I DON'T KNOW, THOUSANDS? TENS OF THOUSANDS?
THREE HUNDRED AND SEVENTY-TWO. IN FORTY YEARS.
THAT CAN'T BE RIGHT!

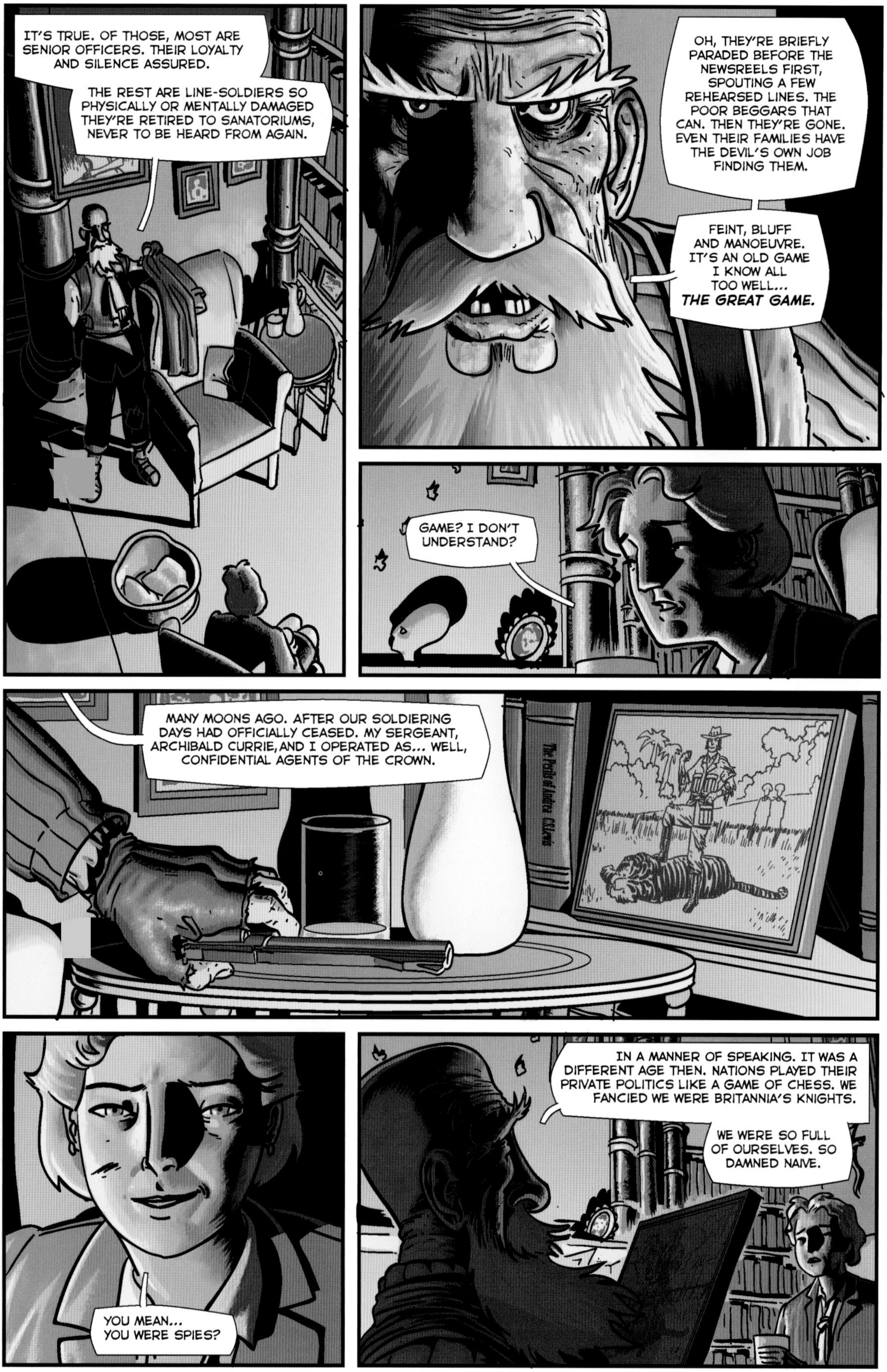
IT'S TRUE. OF THOSE, MOST ARE SENIOR OFFICERS. THEIR LOYALTY AND SILENCE ASSURED.
THE REST ARE LINE-SOLDIERS SO PHYSICALLY OR MENTALLY DAMAGED THEY'RE RETIRED TO SANATORIUMS, NEVER TO BE HEARD FROM AGAIN.
OH, THEY'RE BRIEFLY PARADED BEFORE THE NEWSREELS FIRST, SPOUTING A FEW REHEARSED LINES. THE POOR BEGGARS THAT CAN. THEN THEY'RE GONE. EVEN THEIR FAMILIES HAVE THE DEVIL'S OWN JOB FINDING THEM.
FEINT, BLUFF AND MANOEUVRE. IT'S AN OLD GAME I KNOW ALL TOO WELL... ***THE GREAT GAME.***
GAME? I DON'T UNDERSTAND?
MANY MOONS AGO. AFTER OUR SOLDIERING DAYS HAD OFFICIALLY CEASED. MY SERGEANT, ARCHIBALD CURRIE, AND I OPERATED AS... WELL, CONFIDENTIAL AGENTS OF THE CROWN.
YOU MEAN... YOU WERE SPIES?
IN A MANNER OF SPEAKING. IT WAS A DIFFERENT AGE THEN. NATIONS PLAYED THEIR PRIVATE POLITICS LIKE A GAME OF CHESS. WE FANCIED WE WERE BRITANNIA'S KNIGHTS.
WE WERE SO FULL OF OURSELVES. SO DAMNED NAIVE.

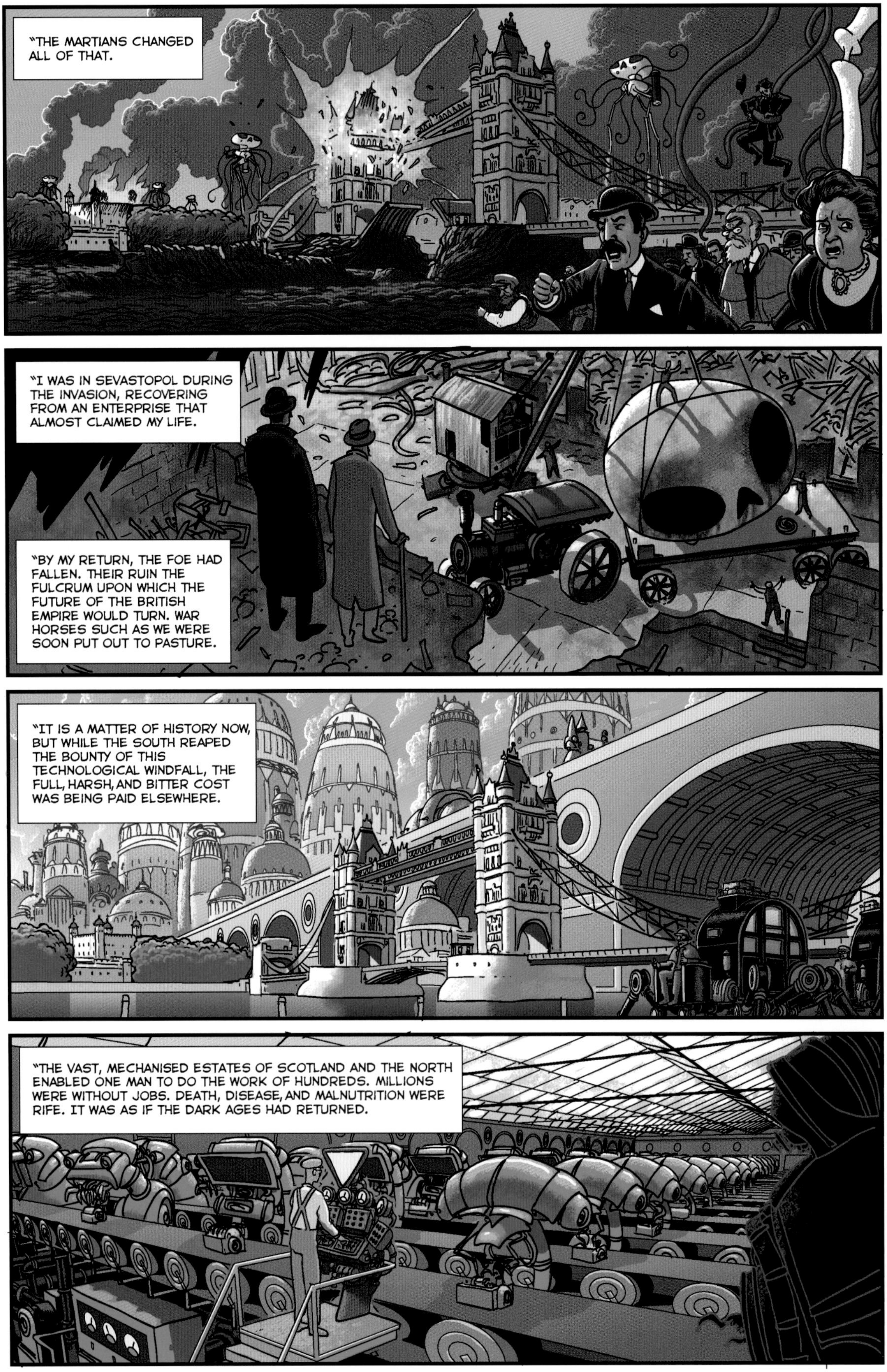
"THE MARTIANS CHANGED ALL OF THAT.
"I WAS IN SEVASTOPOL DURING THE INVASION, RECOVERING FROM AN ENTERPRISE THAT ALMOST CLAIMED MY LIFE.
"BY MY RETURN, THE FOE HAD FALLEN. THEIR RUIN THE FULCRUM UPON WHICH THE FUTURE OF THE BRITISH EMPIRE WOULD TURN. WAR HORSES SUCH AS WE WERE SOON PUT OUT TO PASTURE.
"IT IS A MATTER OF HISTORY NOW, BUT WHILE THE SOUTH REAPED THE BOUNTY OF THIS TECHNOLOGICAL WINDFALL, THE FULL, HARSH, AND BITTER COST WAS BEING PAID ELSEWHERE.
"THE VAST, MECHANISED ESTATES OF SCOTLAND AND THE NORTH ENABLED ONE MAN TO DO THE WORK OF HUNDREDS. MILLIONS WERE WITHOUT JOBS. DEATH, DISEASE, AND MALNUTRITION WERE RIFE. IT WAS AS IF THE DARK AGES HAD RETURNED.

"MEANWHILE, WE PROSPERED IN IGNORANCE UNTIL SERGEANT CURRIE'S BROTHER, DAVID, CAME SEARCHING FOR HIS MISSING DAUGHTER.

"KATHERINE HAD BEEN LURED FROM GLASGOW TO LONDON BY THE RARE PROSPECT OF EMPLOYMENT. SHE REMAINED IN TOUCH FOR SEVERAL WEEKS, THEN VANISHED WITHOUT A TRACE.

WANTED
Young, clean women of sober and industrious disposition to fill various positions of domestic service in London and the Home Counties.
GOOD RATES OF PAYMENT

WANTED
Young, clean women of sober and industrious disposition to fill various positions of domestic service in London and the Home Counties.
GOOD RATES OF PAYMENT

"THE THREE OF US TURNED DETECTIVE AND SET TO THE TASK, NOT ENTIRELY UNSELFISHLY, I'M ASHAMED TO SAY. RETIREMENT GRATED UPON ME. I RELISHED THE CHALLENGE -- THE LONG-MISSED SIREN CALL TO ACTION.

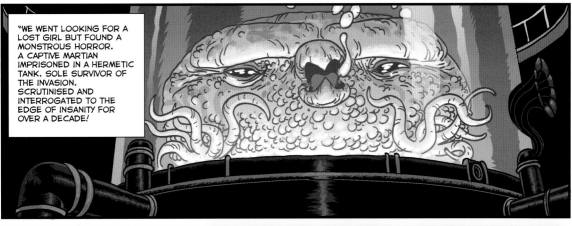

"WE WENT LOOKING FOR A LOST GIRL BUT FOUND A MONSTROUS HORROR. A CAPTIVE MARTIAN IMPRISONED IN A HERMETIC TANK. SOLE SURVIVOR OF THE INVASION. SCRUTINISED AND INTERROGATED TO THE EDGE OF INSANITY FOR OVER A DECADE!

"IT IS COMMON KNOWLEDGE NOW THAT THE MARTIANS THRIVED ON A DIET OF PURE PROTEIN... BLOOD... HUMAN BLOOD.

"KATHERINE AND COUNTLESS OTHERS BEFORE HER -- HAND-PICKED, CLEAN, AND MORAL YOUNG WOMEN -- HAD BEEN PREYED UPON AND POURED LIVE INTO THE GULLET OF THAT VILE, VAMPIRIC SQUAB!"

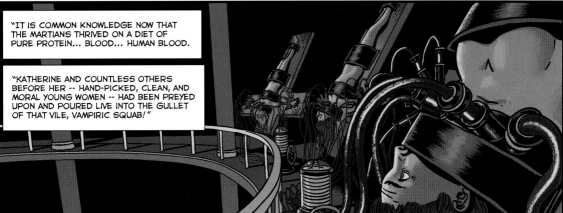

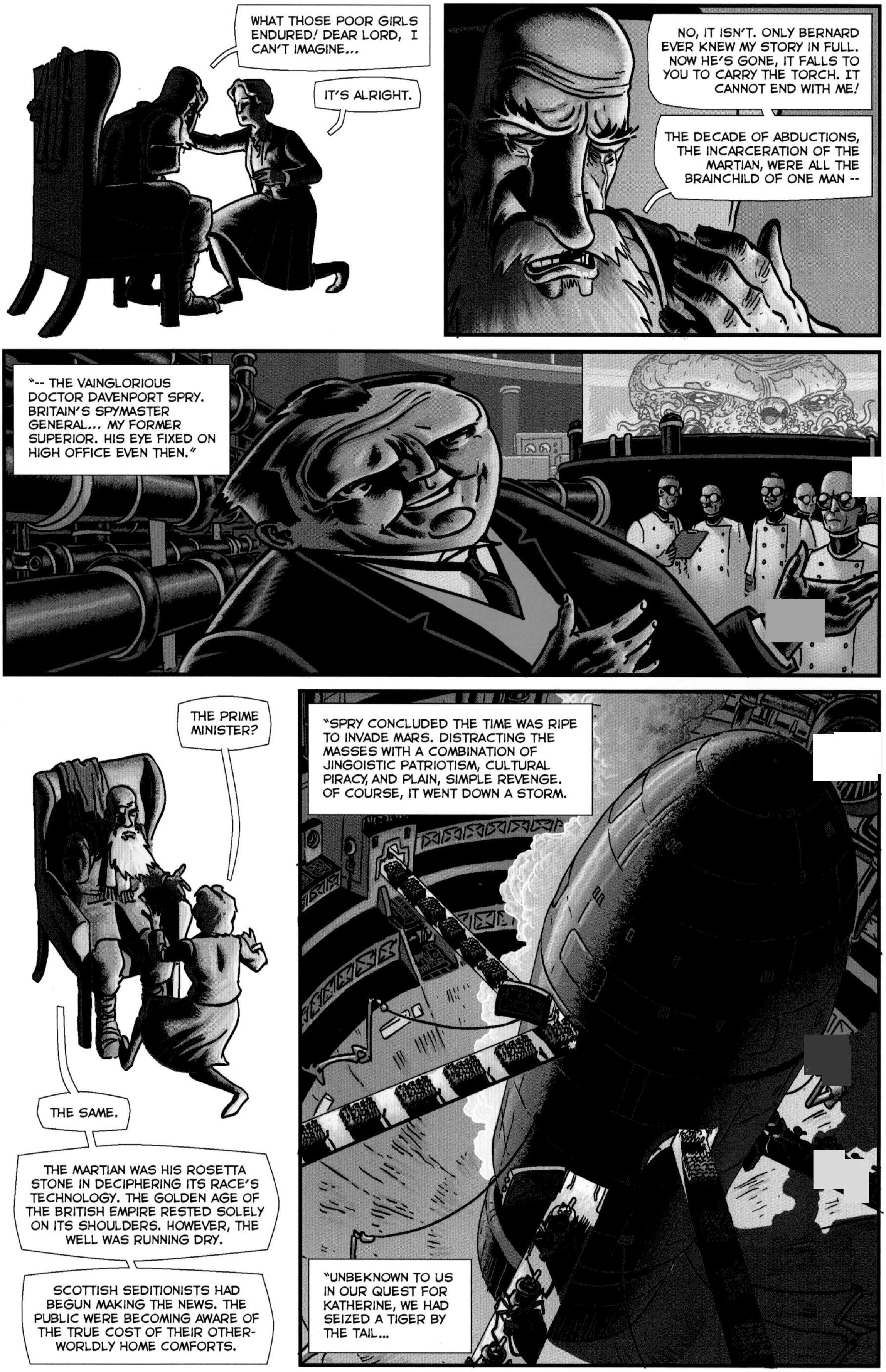
WHAT THOSE POOR GIRLS ENDURED! DEAR LORD, I CAN'T IMAGINE...
IT'S ALRIGHT.
NO, IT ISN'T. ONLY BERNARD EVER KNEW MY STORY IN FULL. NOW HE'S GONE, IT FALLS TO YOU TO CARRY THE TORCH. IT CANNOT END WITH ME!
THE DECADE OF ABDUCTIONS, THE INCARCERATION OF THE MARTIAN, WERE ALL THE BRAINCHILD OF ONE MAN --
"-- THE VAINGLORIOUS DOCTOR DAVENPORT SPRY. BRITAIN'S SPYMASTER GENERAL... MY FORMER SUPERIOR. HIS EYE FIXED ON HIGH OFFICE EVEN THEN."
THE PRIME MINISTER?
THE SAME.
THE MARTIAN WAS HIS ROSETTA STONE IN DECIPHERING ITS RACE'S TECHNOLOGY. THE GOLDEN AGE OF THE BRITISH EMPIRE RESTED SOLELY ON ITS SHOULDERS. HOWEVER, THE WELL WAS RUNNING DRY.
SCOTTISH SEDITIONISTS HAD BEGUN MAKING THE NEWS. THE PUBLIC WERE BECOMING AWARE OF THE TRUE COST OF THEIR OTHER-WORLDLY HOME COMFORTS.
"SPRY CONCLUDED THE TIME WAS RIPE TO INVADE MARS. DISTRACTING THE MASSES WITH A COMBINATION OF JINGOISTIC PATRIOTISM, CULTURAL PIRACY, AND PLAIN, SIMPLE REVENGE. OF COURSE, IT WENT DOWN A STORM.
"UNBEKNOWN TO US IN OUR QUEST FOR KATHERINE, WE HAD SEIZED A TIGER BY THE TAIL...

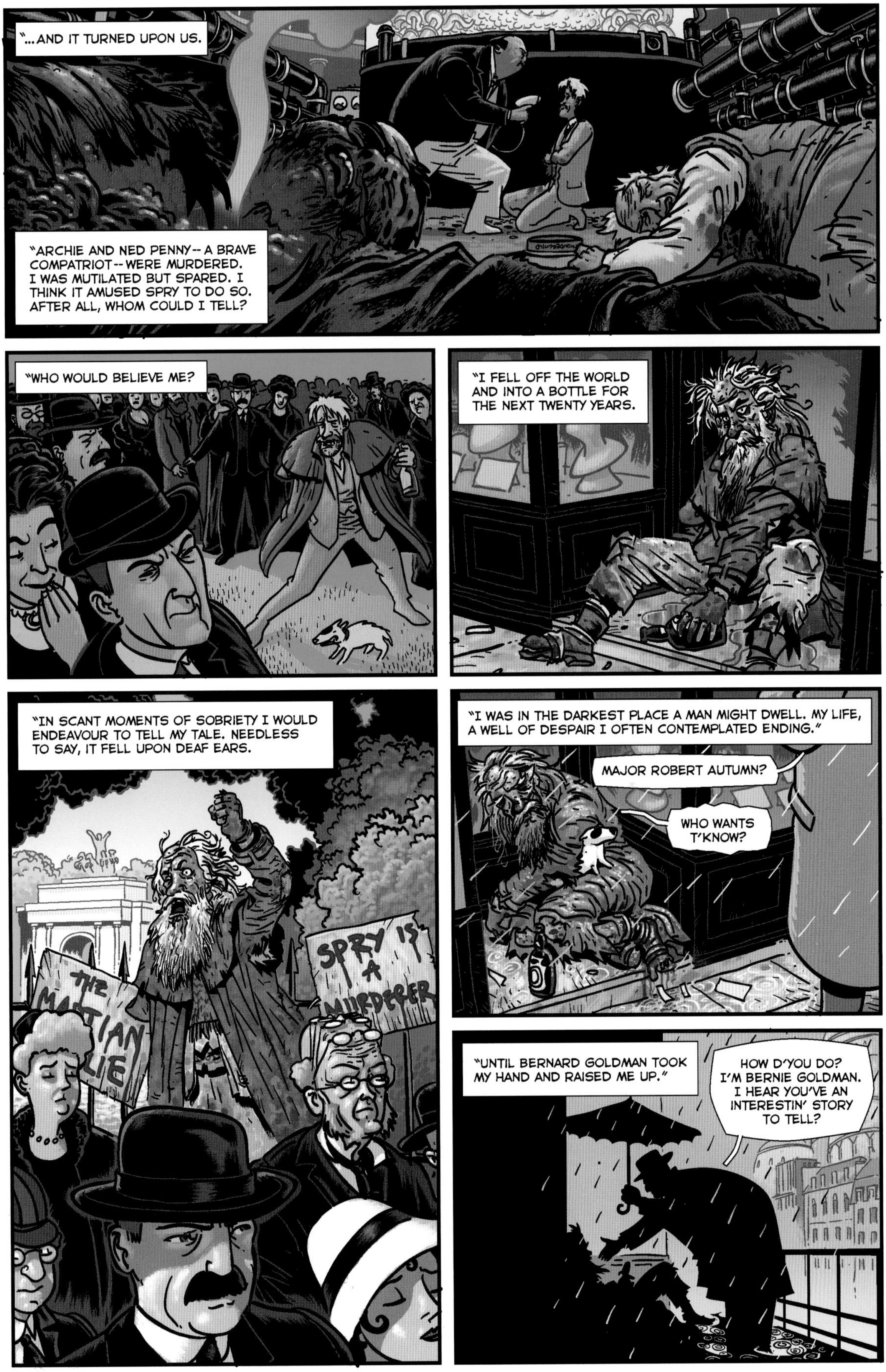
"...AND IT TURNED UPON US.
"ARCHIE AND NED PENNY-- A BRAVE COMPATRIOT--WERE MURDERED. I WAS MUTILATED BUT SPARED. I THINK IT AMUSED SPRY TO DO SO. AFTER ALL, WHOM COULD I TELL?
"WHO WOULD BELIEVE ME?
"I FELL OFF THE WORLD AND INTO A BOTTLE FOR THE NEXT TWENTY YEARS.
"IN SCANT MOMENTS OF SOBRIETY I WOULD ENDEAVOUR TO TELL MY TALE. NEEDLESS TO SAY, IT FELL UPON DEAF EARS.
SPRY IS A MURDERER
"I WAS IN THE DARKEST PLACE A MAN MIGHT DWELL. MY LIFE, A WELL OF DESPAIR I OFTEN CONTEMPLATED ENDING."
MAJOR ROBERT AUTUMN?
WHO WANTS T'KNOW?
"UNTIL BERNARD GOLDMAN TOOK MY HAND AND RAISED ME UP."
HOW D'YOU DO? I'M BERNIE GOLDMAN. I HEAR YOU'VE AN INTERESTIN' STORY TO TELL?

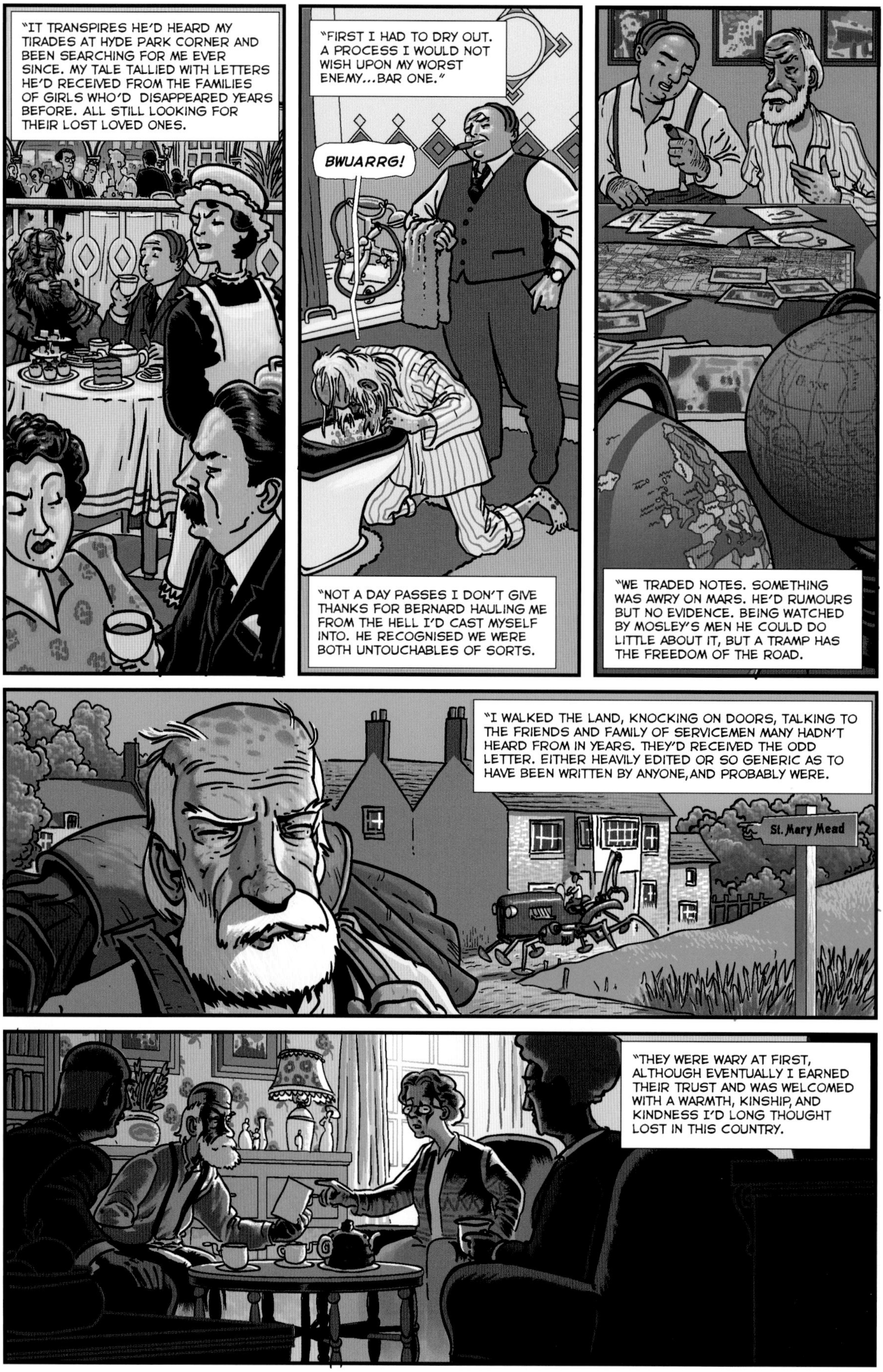
"IT TRANSPIRES HE'D HEARD MY TIRADES AT HYDE PARK CORNER AND BEEN SEARCHING FOR ME EVER SINCE. MY TALE TALLIED WITH LETTERS HE'D RECEIVED FROM THE FAMILIES OF GIRLS WHO'D DISAPPEARED YEARS BEFORE. ALL STILL LOOKING FOR THEIR LOST LOVED ONES.
"FIRST I HAD TO DRY OUT. A PROCESS I WOULD NOT WISH UPON MY WORST ENEMY...BAR ONE."
BWUARRG!
"NOT A DAY PASSES I DON'T GIVE THANKS FOR BERNARD HAULING ME FROM THE HELL I'D CAST MYSELF INTO. HE RECOGNISED WE WERE BOTH UNTOUCHABLES OF SORTS.
"WE TRADED NOTES. SOMETHING WAS AWRY ON MARS. HE'D RUMOURS BUT NO EVIDENCE. BEING WATCHED BY MOSLEY'S MEN HE COULD DO LITTLE ABOUT IT, BUT A TRAMP HAS THE FREEDOM OF THE ROAD.
"I WALKED THE LAND, KNOCKING ON DOORS, TALKING TO THE FRIENDS AND FAMILY OF SERVICEMEN MANY HADN'T HEARD FROM IN YEARS. THEY'D RECEIVED THE ODD LETTER. EITHER HEAVILY EDITED OR SO GENERIC AS TO HAVE BEEN WRITTEN BY ANYONE, AND PROBABLY WERE.
St. Mary Mead
"THEY WERE WARY AT FIRST, ALTHOUGH EVENTUALLY I EARNED THEIR TRUST AND WAS WELCOMED WITH A WARMTH, KINSHIP, AND KINDNESS I'D LONG THOUGHT LOST IN THIS COUNTRY.

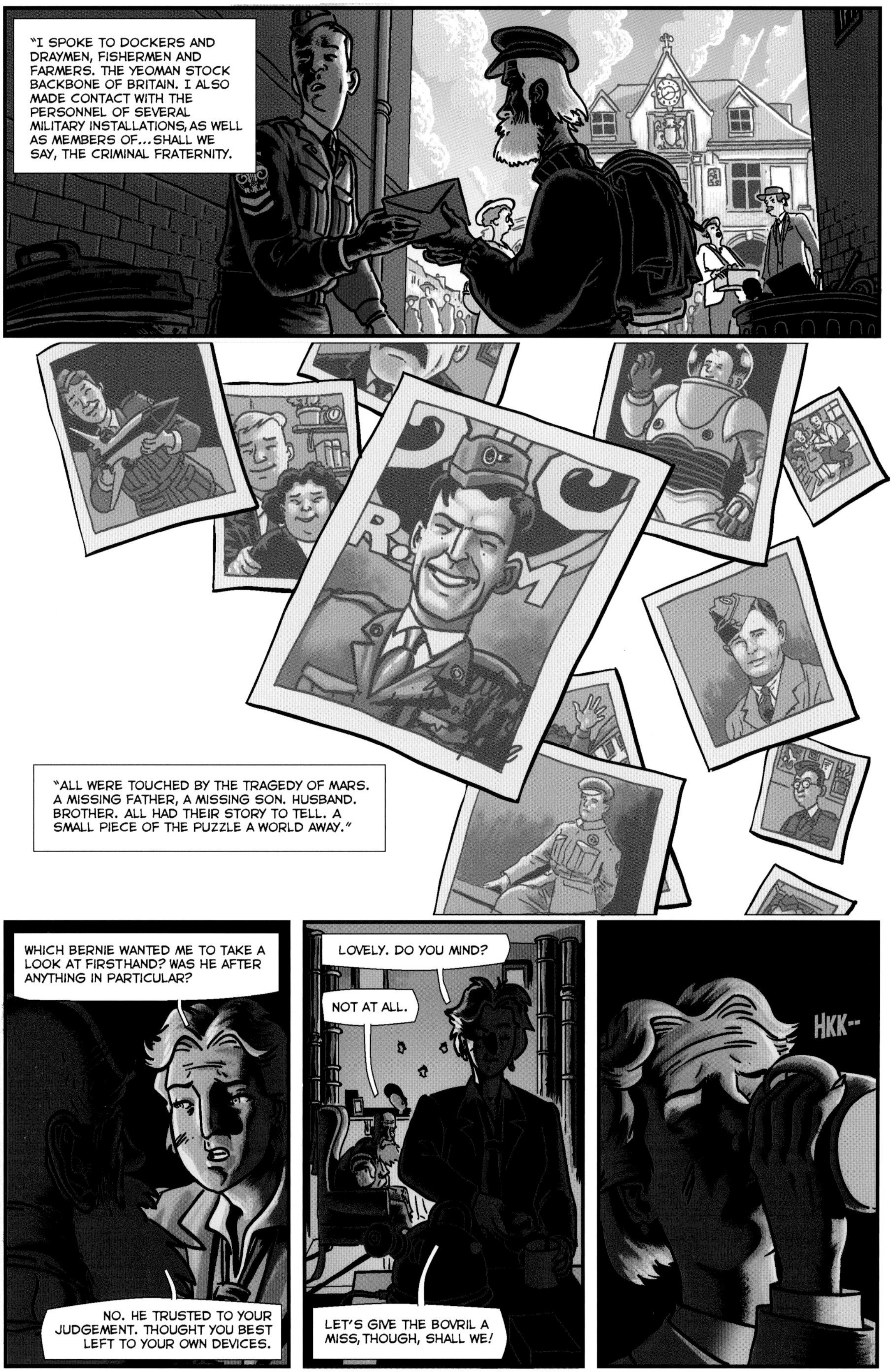
"I SPOKE TO DOCKERS AND DRAYMEN, FISHERMEN AND FARMERS. THE YEOMAN STOCK BACKBONE OF BRITAIN. I ALSO MADE CONTACT WITH THE PERSONNEL OF SEVERAL MILITARY INSTALLATIONS, AS WELL AS MEMBERS OF... SHALL WE SAY, THE CRIMINAL FRATERNITY.
"ALL WERE TOUCHED BY THE TRAGEDY OF MARS. A MISSING FATHER, A MISSING SON. HUSBAND. BROTHER. ALL HAD THEIR STORY TO TELL. A SMALL PIECE OF THE PUZZLE A WORLD AWAY."
WHICH BERNIE WANTED ME TO TAKE A LOOK AT FIRSTHAND? WAS HE AFTER ANYTHING IN PARTICULAR?
NO. HE TRUSTED TO YOUR JUDGEMENT. THOUGHT YOU BEST LEFT TO YOUR OWN DEVICES.
LOVELY. DO YOU MIND?
NOT AT ALL.
LET'S GIVE THE BOVRIL A MISS, THOUGH, SHALL WE!
HKK--

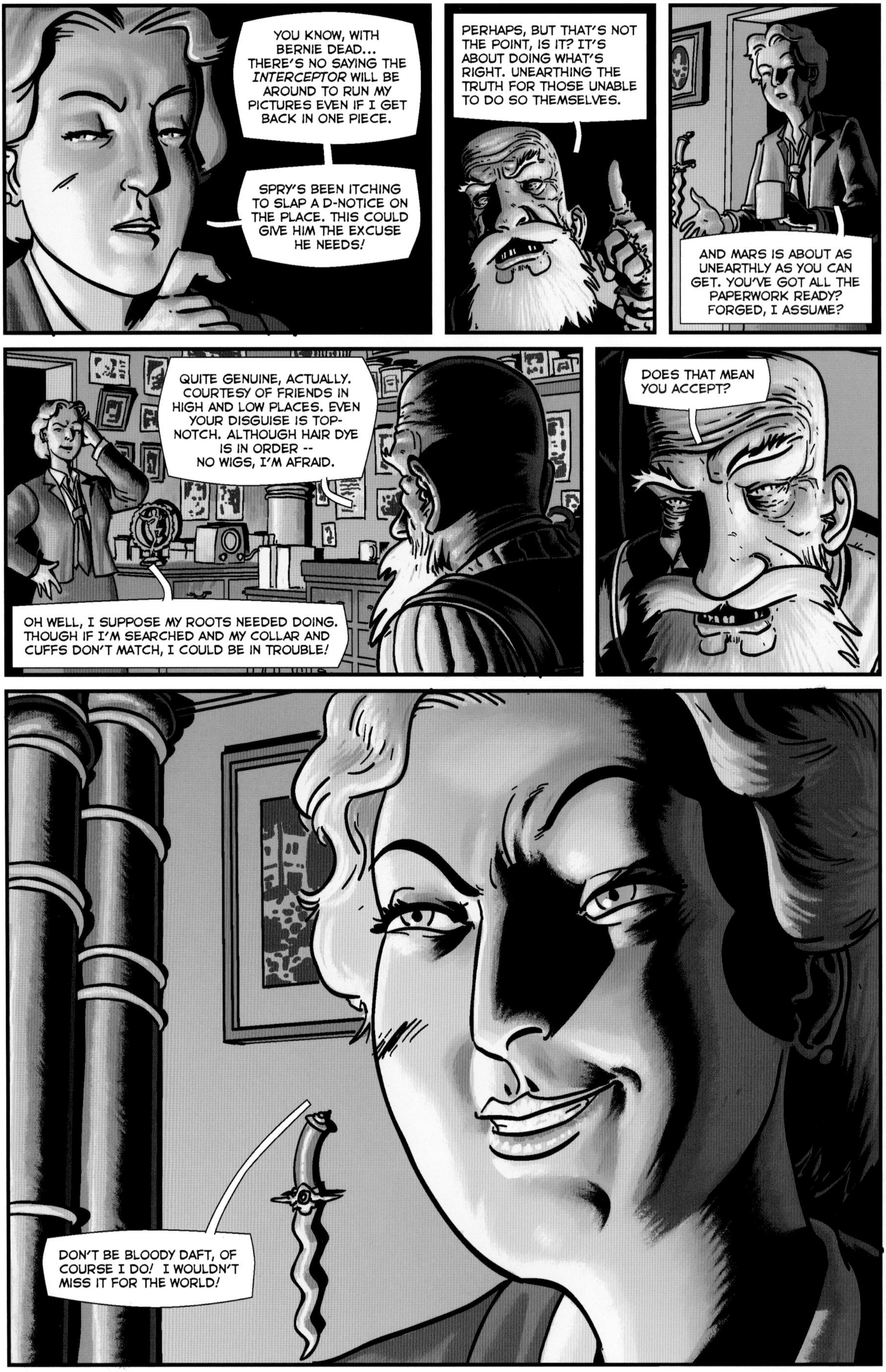
YOU KNOW, WITH BERNIE DEAD... THERE'S NO SAYING THE *INTERCEPTOR* WILL BE AROUND TO RUN MY PICTURES EVEN IF I GET BACK IN ONE PIECE.
SPRY'S BEEN ITCHING TO SLAP A D-NOTICE ON THE PLACE. THIS COULD GIVE HIM THE EXCUSE HE NEEDS!
PERHAPS, BUT THAT'S NOT THE POINT, IS IT? IT'S ABOUT DOING WHAT'S RIGHT. UNEARTHING THE TRUTH FOR THOSE UNABLE TO DO SO THEMSELVES.
AND MARS IS ABOUT AS UNEARTHLY AS YOU CAN GET. YOU'VE GOT ALL THE PAPERWORK READY? FORGED, I ASSUME?
QUITE GENUINE, ACTUALLY. COURTESY OF FRIENDS IN HIGH AND LOW PLACES. EVEN YOUR DISGUISE IS TOP-NOTCH. ALTHOUGH HAIR DYE IS IN ORDER -- NO WIGS, I'M AFRAID.
OH WELL, I SUPPOSE MY ROOTS NEEDED DOING. THOUGH IF I'M SEARCHED AND MY COLLAR AND CUFFS DON'T MATCH, I COULD BE IN TROUBLE!
DOES THAT MEAN YOU ACCEPT?
DON'T BE BLOODY DAFT, OF COURSE I DO! I WOULDN'T MISS IT FOR THE WORLD!

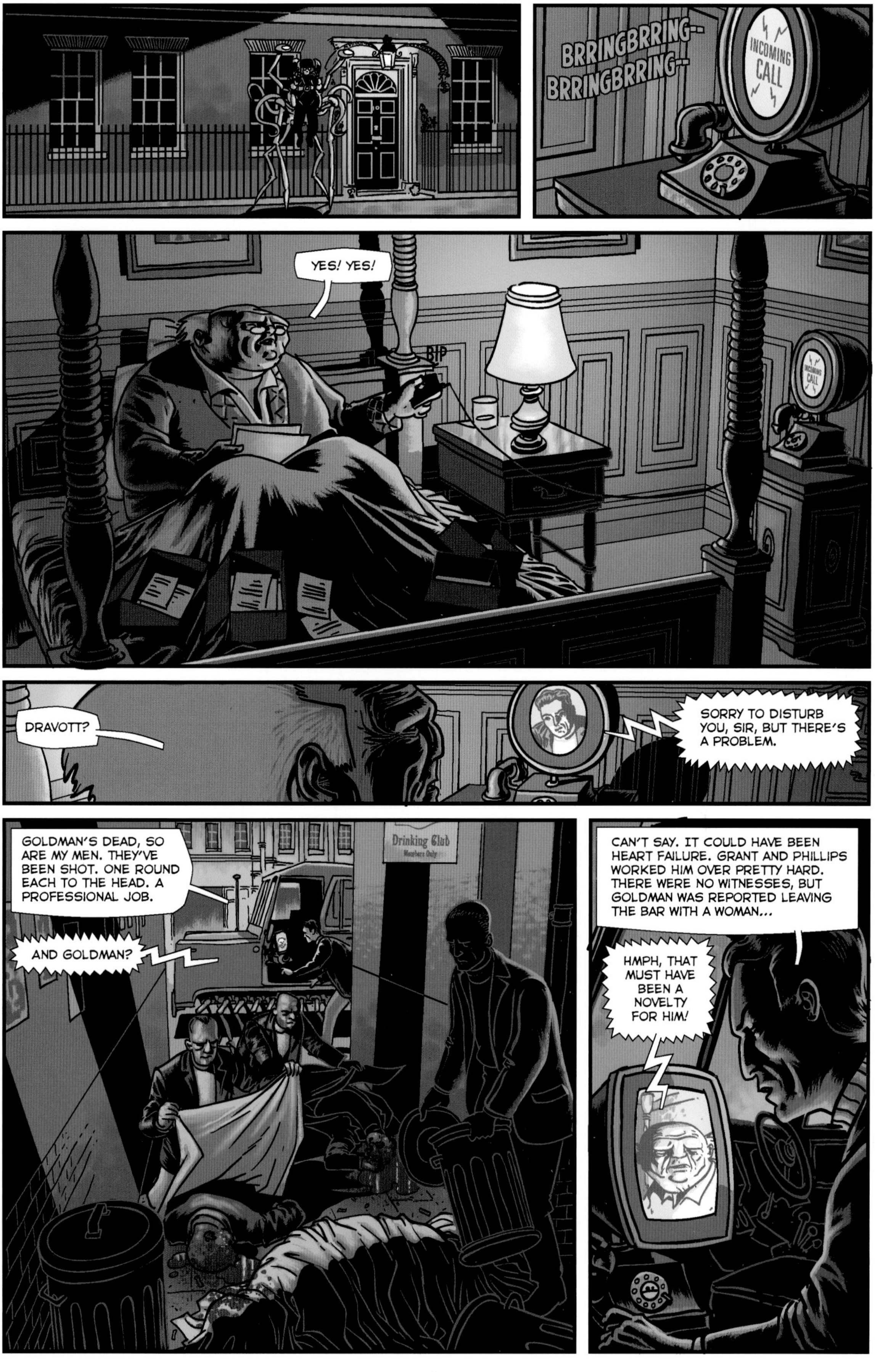
BRRINGBRRING--
BRRINGBRRING--
INCOMING CALL
YES! YES!
BIP
INCOMING CALL
DRAVOTT?
SORRY TO DISTURB YOU, SIR, BUT THERE'S A PROBLEM.
Drinking Club
GOLDMAN'S DEAD, SO ARE MY MEN. THEY'VE BEEN SHOT. ONE ROUND EACH TO THE HEAD. A PROFESSIONAL JOB.
AND GOLDMAN?
CAN'T SAY. IT COULD HAVE BEEN HEART FAILURE. GRANT AND PHILLIPS WORKED HIM OVER PRETTY HARD. THERE WERE NO WITNESSES, BUT GOLDMAN WAS REPORTED LEAVING THE BAR WITH A WOMAN...
HMPH, THAT MUST HAVE BEEN A NOVELTY FOR HIM!

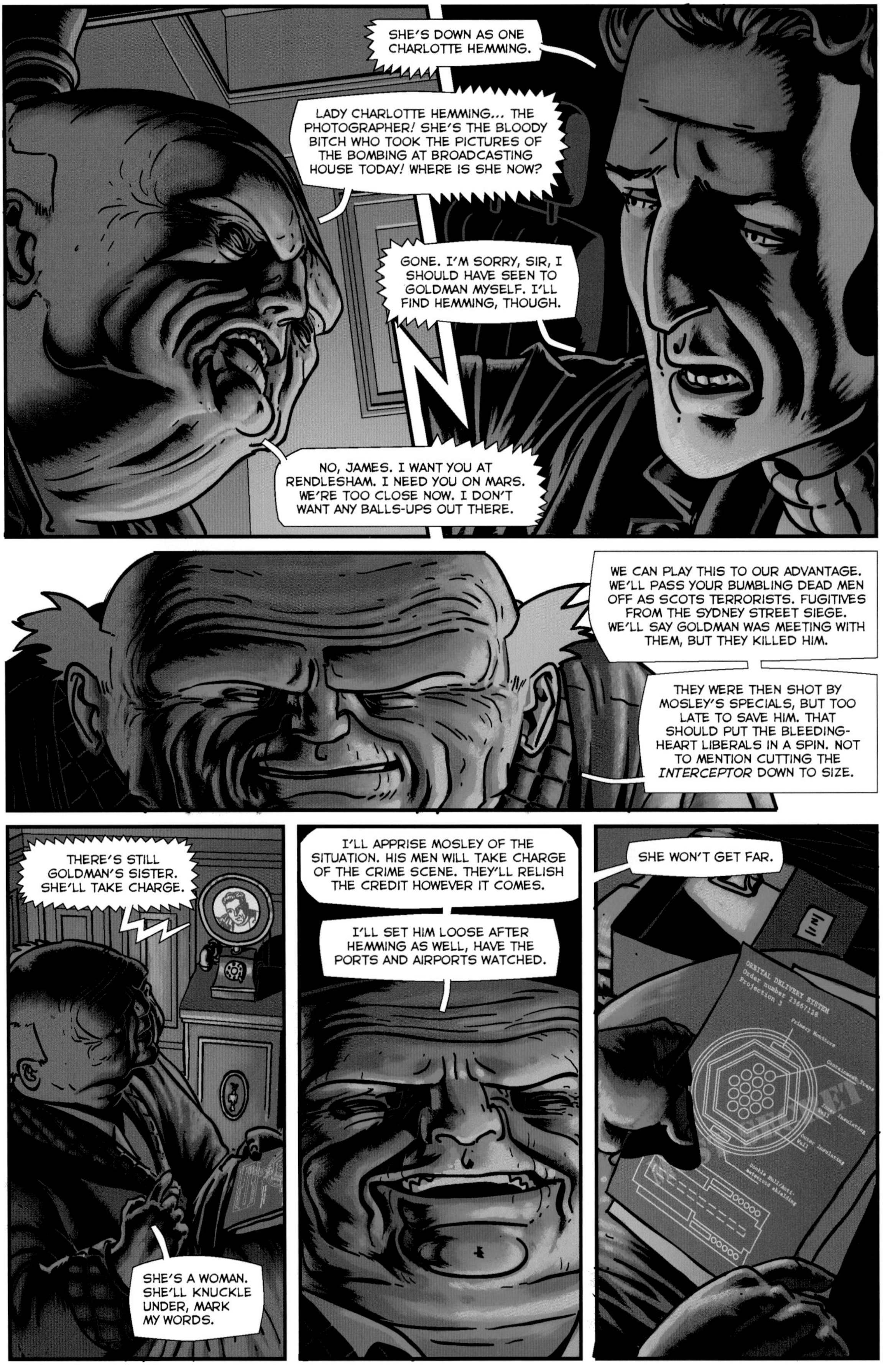
SHE'S DOWN AS ONE CHARLOTTE HEMMING.
LADY CHARLOTTE HEMMING... THE PHOTOGRAPHER! SHE'S THE BLOODY BITCH WHO TOOK THE PICTURES OF THE BOMBING AT BROADCASTING HOUSE TODAY! WHERE IS SHE NOW?
GONE. I'M SORRY, SIR, I SHOULD HAVE SEEN TO GOLDMAN MYSELF. I'LL FIND HEMMING, THOUGH.
NO, JAMES. I WANT YOU AT RENDLESHAM. I NEED YOU ON MARS. WE'RE TOO CLOSE NOW. I DON'T WANT ANY BALLS-UPS OUT THERE.
WE CAN PLAY THIS TO OUR ADVANTAGE. WE'LL PASS YOUR BUMBLING DEAD MEN OFF AS SCOTS TERRORISTS. FUGITIVES FROM THE SYDNEY STREET SIEGE. WE'LL SAY GOLDMAN WAS MEETING WITH THEM, BUT THEY KILLED HIM.
THEY WERE THEN SHOT BY MOSLEY'S SPECIALS, BUT TOO LATE TO SAVE HIM. THAT SHOULD PUT THE BLEEDING-HEART LIBERALS IN A SPIN. NOT TO MENTION CUTTING THE *INTERCEPTOR* DOWN TO SIZE.
THERE'S STILL GOLDMAN'S SISTER. SHE'LL TAKE CHARGE.
SHE'S A WOMAN. SHE'LL KNUCKLE UNDER, MARK MY WORDS.
I'LL APPRISE MOSLEY OF THE SITUATION. HIS MEN WILL TAKE CHARGE OF THE CRIME SCENE. THEY'LL RELISH THE CREDIT HOWEVER IT COMES.
I'LL SET HIM LOOSE AFTER HEMMING AS WELL, HAVE THE PORTS AND AIRPORTS WATCHED.
SHE WON'T GET FAR.
ORBITAL DELIVERY SYSTEM
Order number 23667128
Projection 3
Primary Monitors
Containment Traps
Inner Insulating Wall
Outer Insulating Wall
Double Hull/Anti-meteoroid shielding

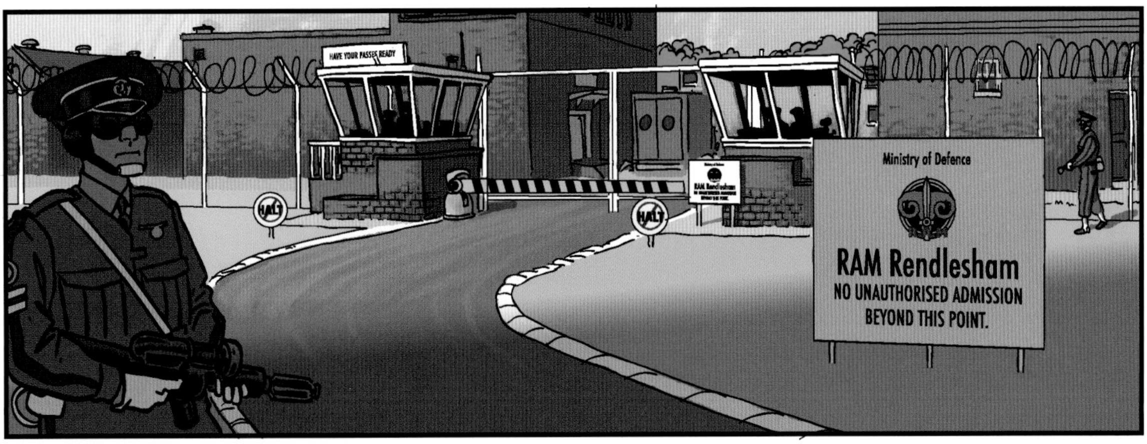
HAVE YOUR PASSES READY
HALT
HALT
Ministry of Defence
RAM Rendlesham
NO UNAUTHORISED ADMISSION
BEYOND THIS POINT.

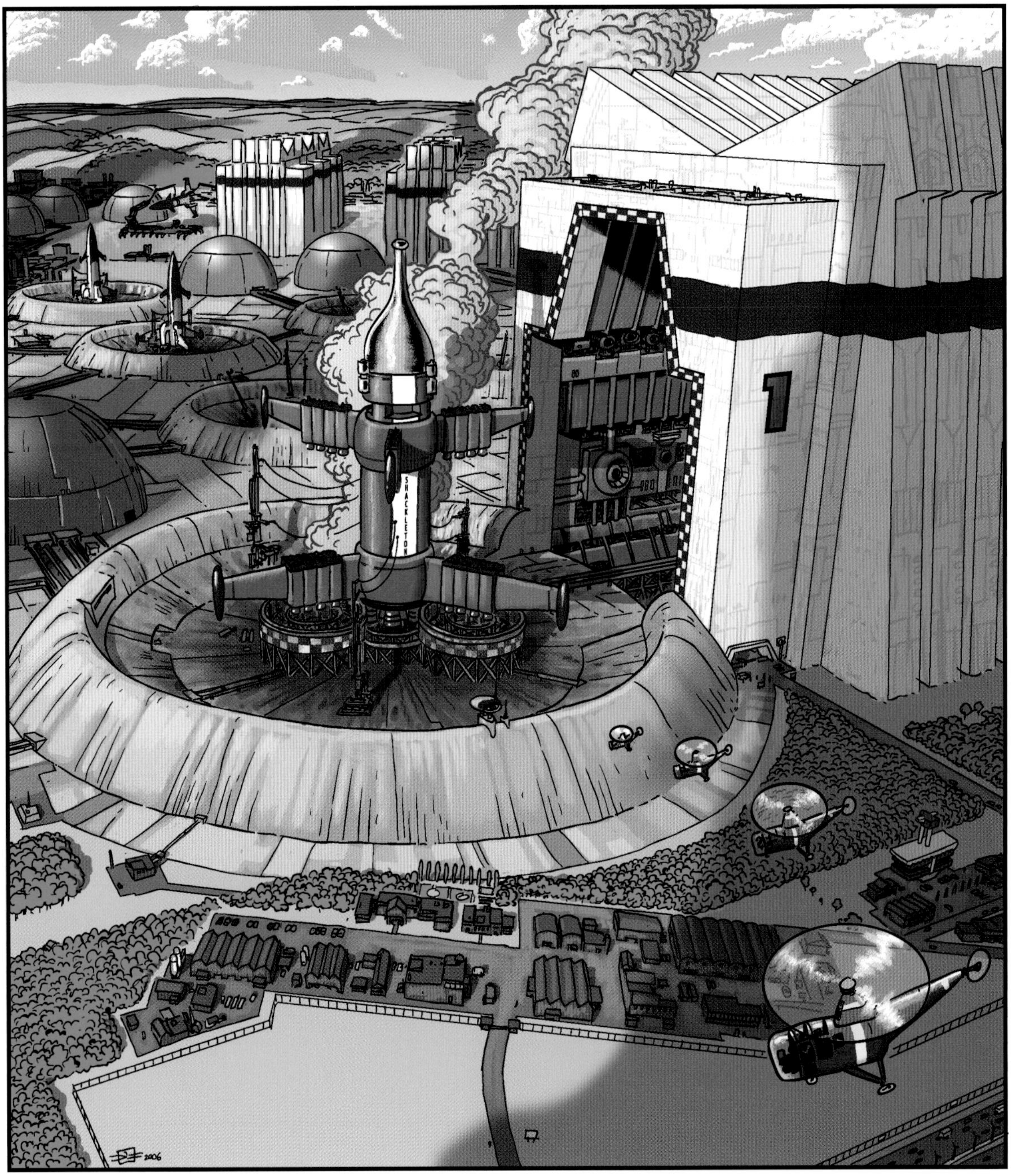
SHACKLETON
1
2006

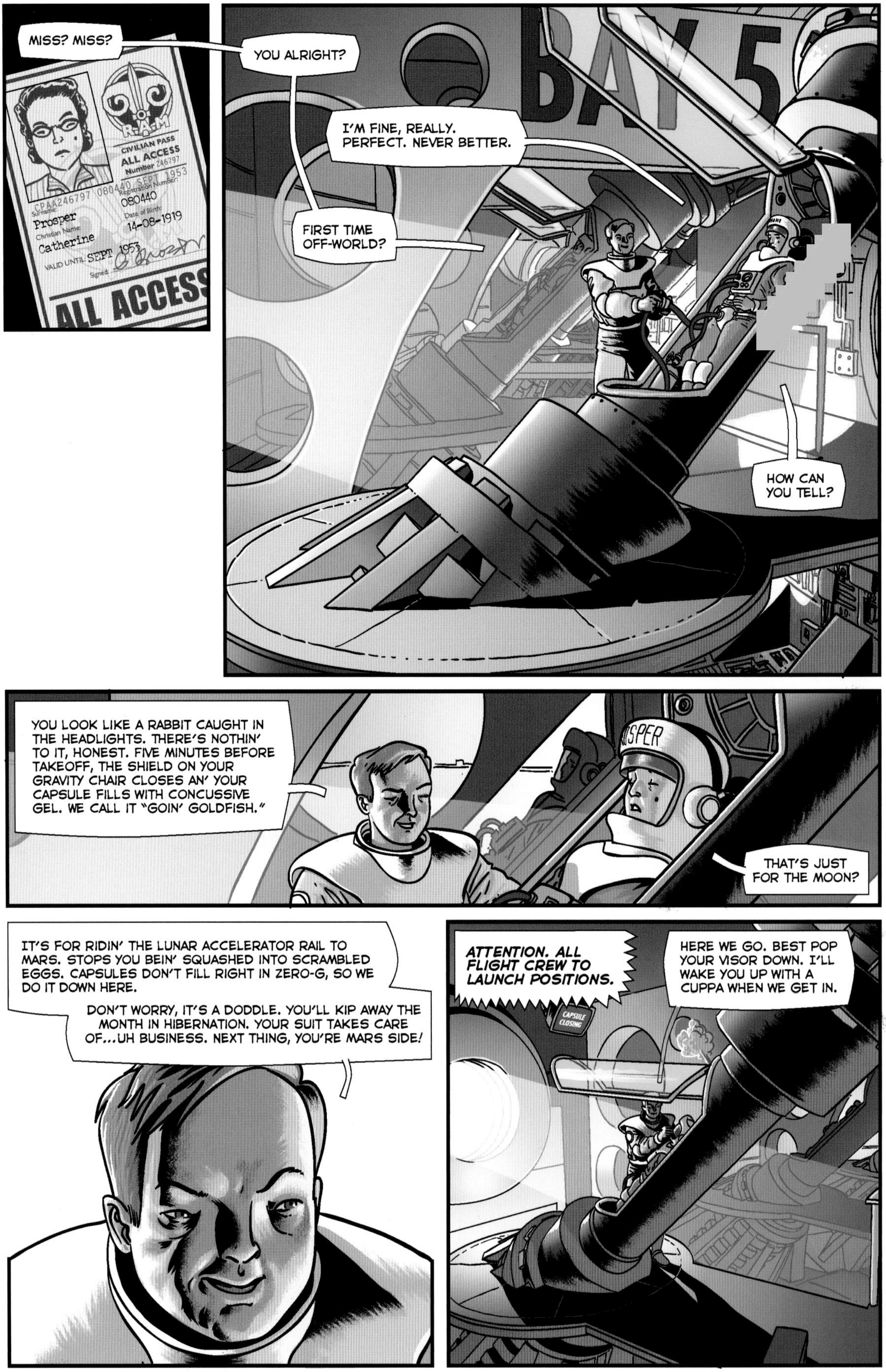
MISS? MISS?
YOU ALRIGHT?
R.A.M
CIVILIAN PASS
ALL ACCESS
Number 246797
CPAA246797 080440 SEPT 1953
Registration Number:
080440
Surname:
Prosper
Christian Name:
Catherine
Date of Birth:
14-08-1919
VALID UNTIL: SEPT 1953
Signed:
ALL ACCESS
BAY 5
I'M FINE, REALLY. PERFECT. NEVER BETTER.
FIRST TIME OFF-WORLD?
HOW CAN YOU TELL?
YOU LOOK LIKE A RABBIT CAUGHT IN THE HEADLIGHTS. THERE'S NOTHIN' TO IT, HONEST. FIVE MINUTES BEFORE TAKEOFF, THE SHIELD ON YOUR GRAVITY CHAIR CLOSES AN' YOUR CAPSULE FILLS WITH CONCUSSIVE GEL. WE CALL IT "GOIN' GOLDFISH."
THAT'S JUST FOR THE MOON?
IT'S FOR RIDIN' THE LUNAR ACCELERATOR RAIL TO MARS. STOPS YOU BEIN' SQUASHED INTO SCRAMBLED EGGS. CAPSULES DON'T FILL RIGHT IN ZERO-G, SO WE DO IT DOWN HERE.
DON'T WORRY, IT'S A DODDLE. YOU'LL KIP AWAY THE MONTH IN HIBERNATION. YOUR SUIT TAKES CARE OF...UH BUSINESS. NEXT THING, YOU'RE MARS SIDE!
ATTENTION. ALL FLIGHT CREW TO LAUNCH POSITIONS.
HERE WE GO. BEST POP YOUR VISOR DOWN. I'LL WAKE YOU UP WITH A CUPPA WHEN WE GET IN.
CAPSULE CLOSING

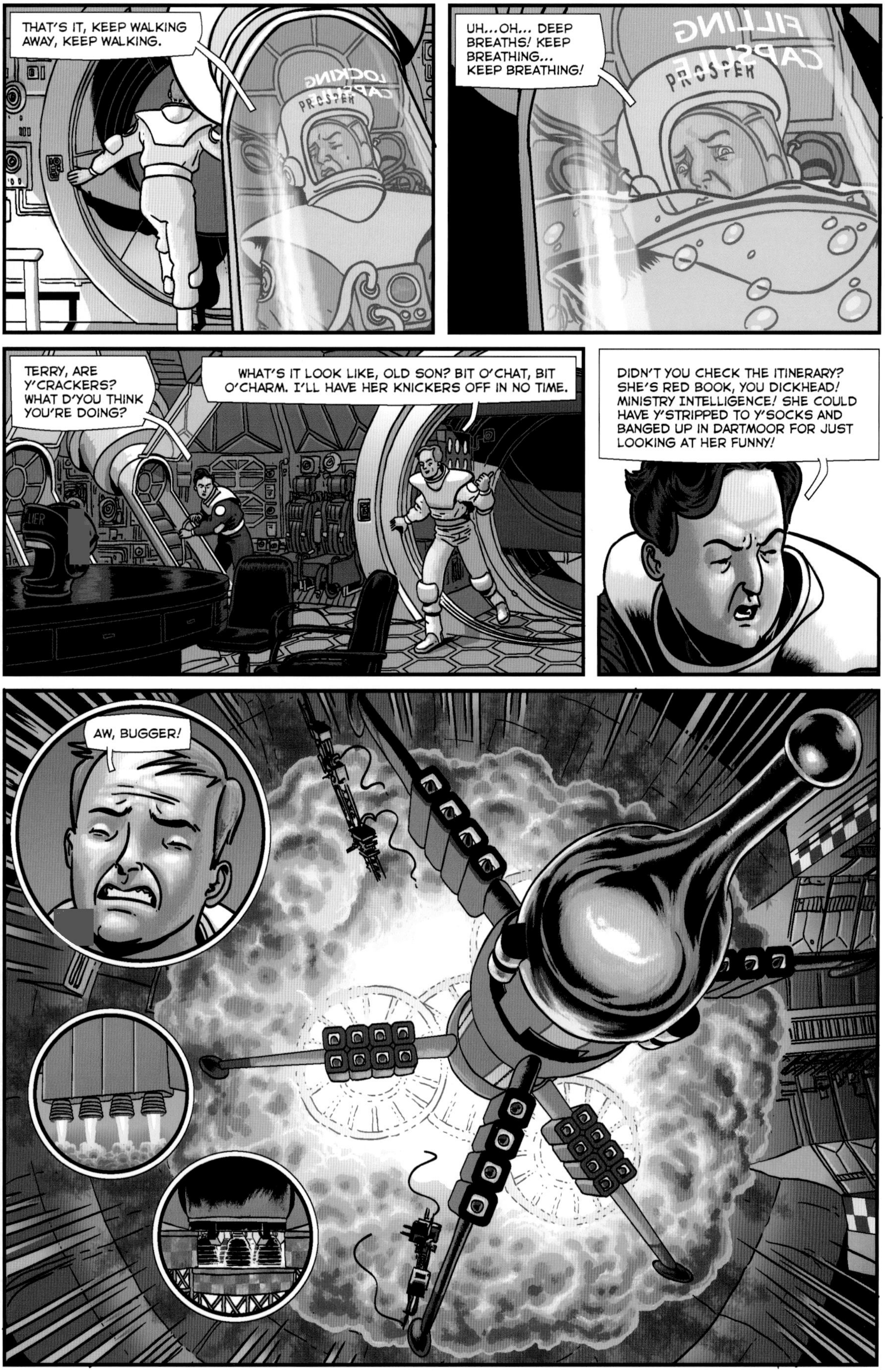
THAT'S IT, KEEP WALKING AWAY, KEEP WALKING.
UH...OH... DEEP BREATHS! KEEP BREATHING... KEEP BREATHING!
TERRY, ARE Y'CRACKERS? WHAT D'YOU THINK YOU'RE DOING?
WHAT'S IT LOOK LIKE, OLD SON? BIT O'CHAT, BIT O'CHARM. I'LL HAVE HER KNICKERS OFF IN NO TIME.
DIDN'T YOU CHECK THE ITINERARY? SHE'S RED BOOK, YOU DICKHEAD! MINISTRY INTELLIGENCE! SHE COULD HAVE Y'STRIPPED TO Y'SOCKS AND BANGED UP IN DARTMOOR FOR JUST LOOKING AT HER FUNNY!
AW, BUGGER!

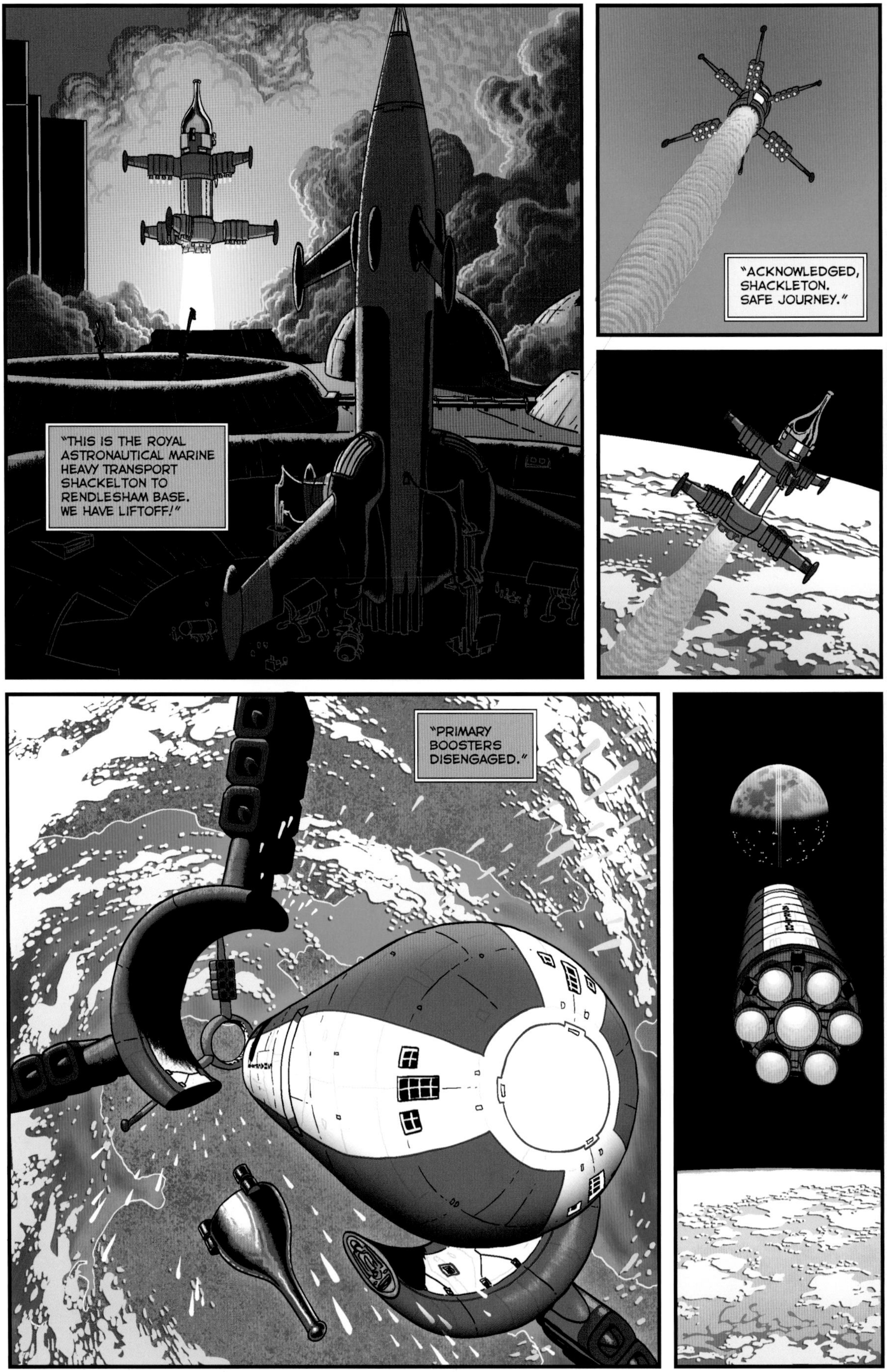
"THIS IS THE ROYAL ASTRONAUTICAL MARINE HEAVY TRANSPORT SHACKLETON TO RENDLESHAM BASE. WE HAVE LIFTOFF!"
"ACKNOWLEDGED, SHACKLETON. SAFE JOURNEY."
"PRIMARY BOOSTERS DISENGAGED."

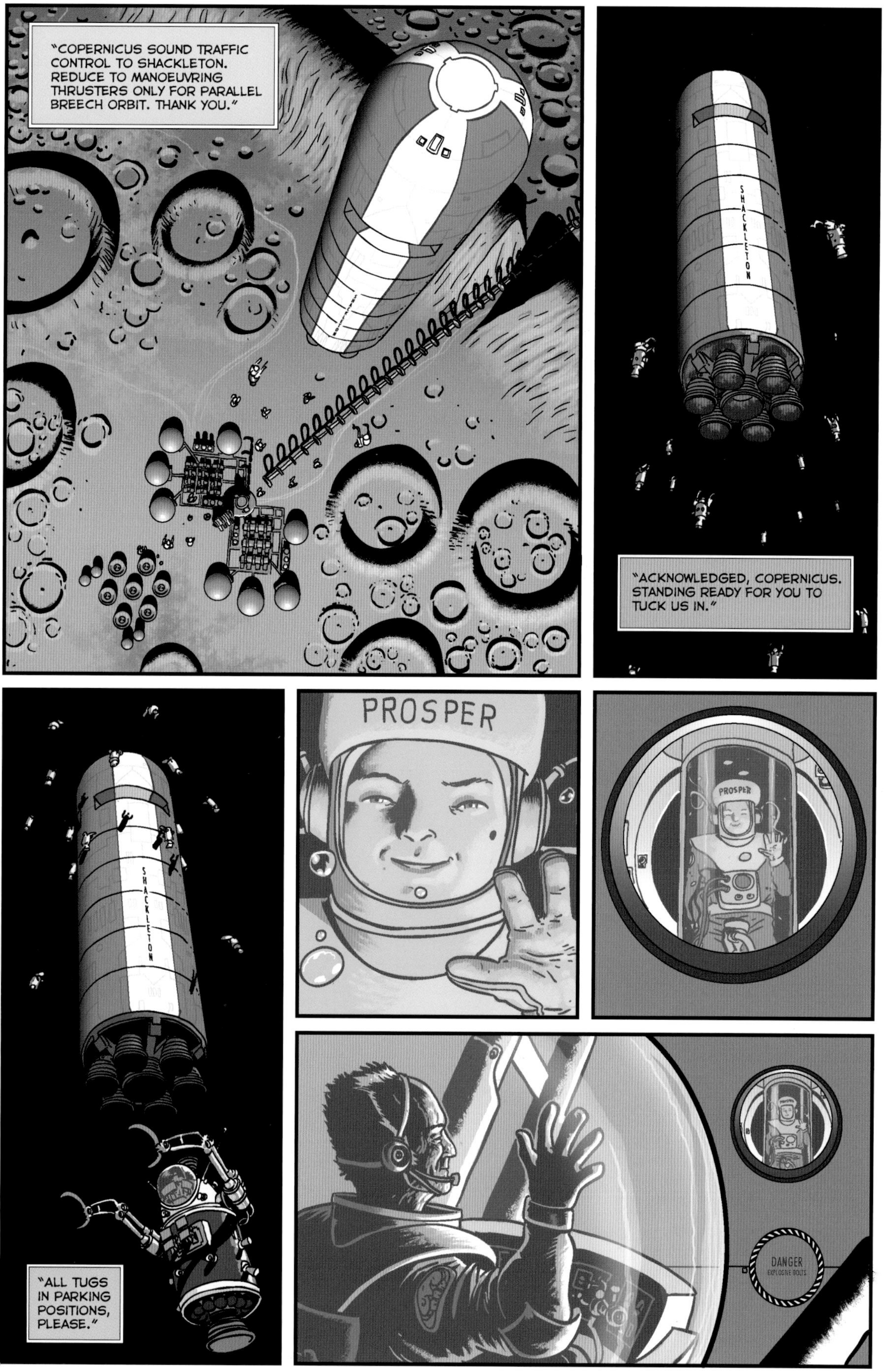
"COPERNICUS SOUND TRAFFIC CONTROL TO SHACKLETON. REDUCE TO MANOEUVRING THRUSTERS ONLY FOR PARALLEL BREECH ORBIT. THANK YOU."
SHACKLETON
"ACKNOWLEDGED, COPERNICUS. STANDING READY FOR YOU TO TUCK US IN."
SHACKLETON
"ALL TUGS IN PARKING POSITIONS, PLEASE."
PROSPER
PROSPER
DANGER
EXPLOSIVE BOLTS

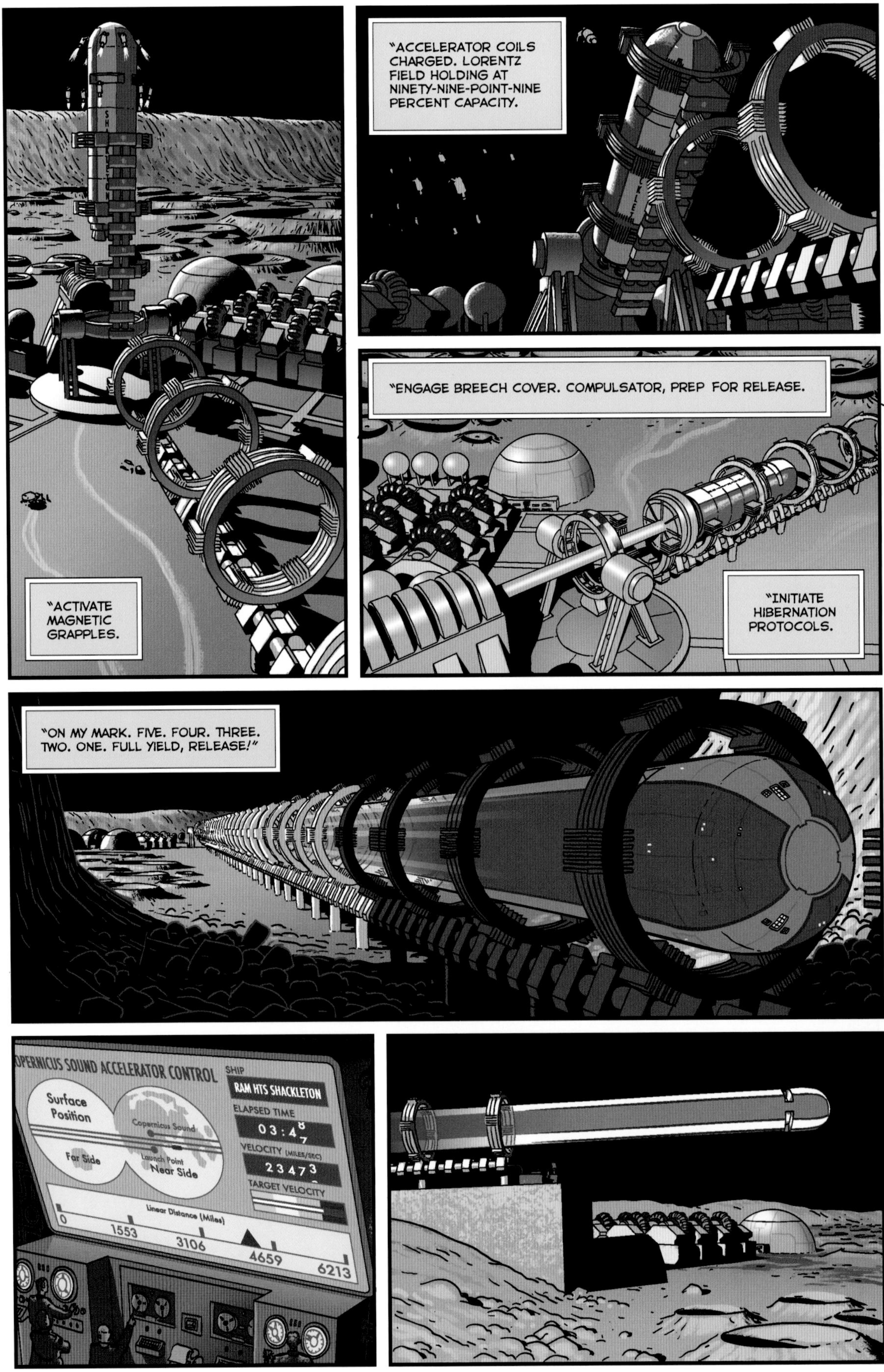
"ACCELERATOR COILS CHARGED. LORENTZ FIELD HOLDING AT NINETY-NINE-POINT-NINE PERCENT CAPACITY.
"ACTIVATE MAGNETIC GRAPPLES.
"ENGAGE BREECH COVER. COMPULSATOR, PREP FOR RELEASE.
"INITIATE HIBERNATION PROTOCOLS.
"ON MY MARK. FIVE. FOUR. THREE. TWO. ONE. FULL YIELD, RELEASE!"
OPERNICUS SOUND ACCELERATOR CONTROL
SHIP
RAM HTS SHACKLETON
ELAPSED TIME
VELOCITY (MILES/SEC)
TARGET VELOCITY
Surface Position
Copernicus Sound
Launch Point
Near Side
Far Side
Linear Distance (Miles)
0
1553
3106
4659
6213

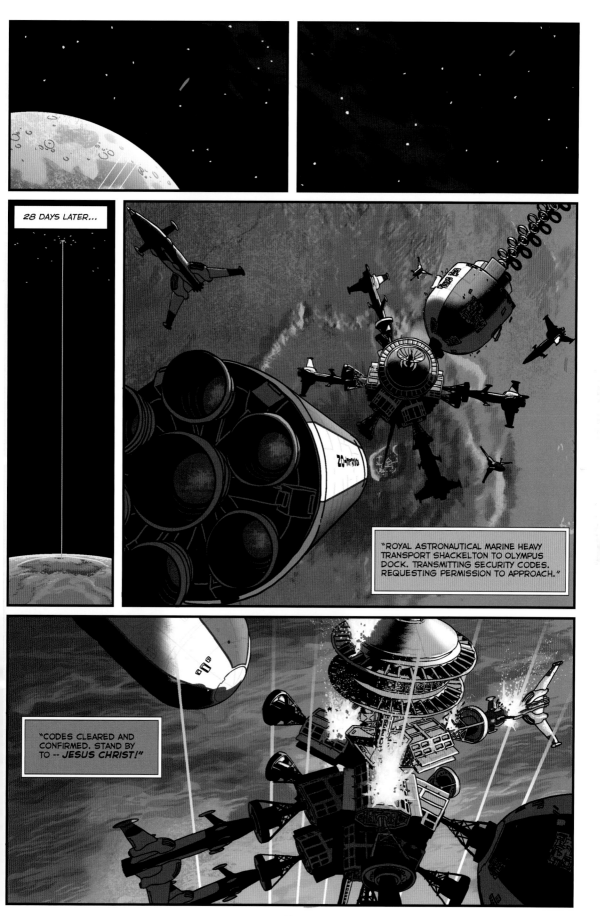

28 DAYS LATER...

"ROYAL ASTRONAUTICAL MARINE HEAVY TRANSPORT SHACKELTON TO OLYMPUS DOCK. TRANSMITTING SECURITY CODES. REQUESTING PERMISSION TO APPROACH."

"CODES CLEARED AND CONFIRMED. STAND BY TO -- *JESUS CHRIST!*"

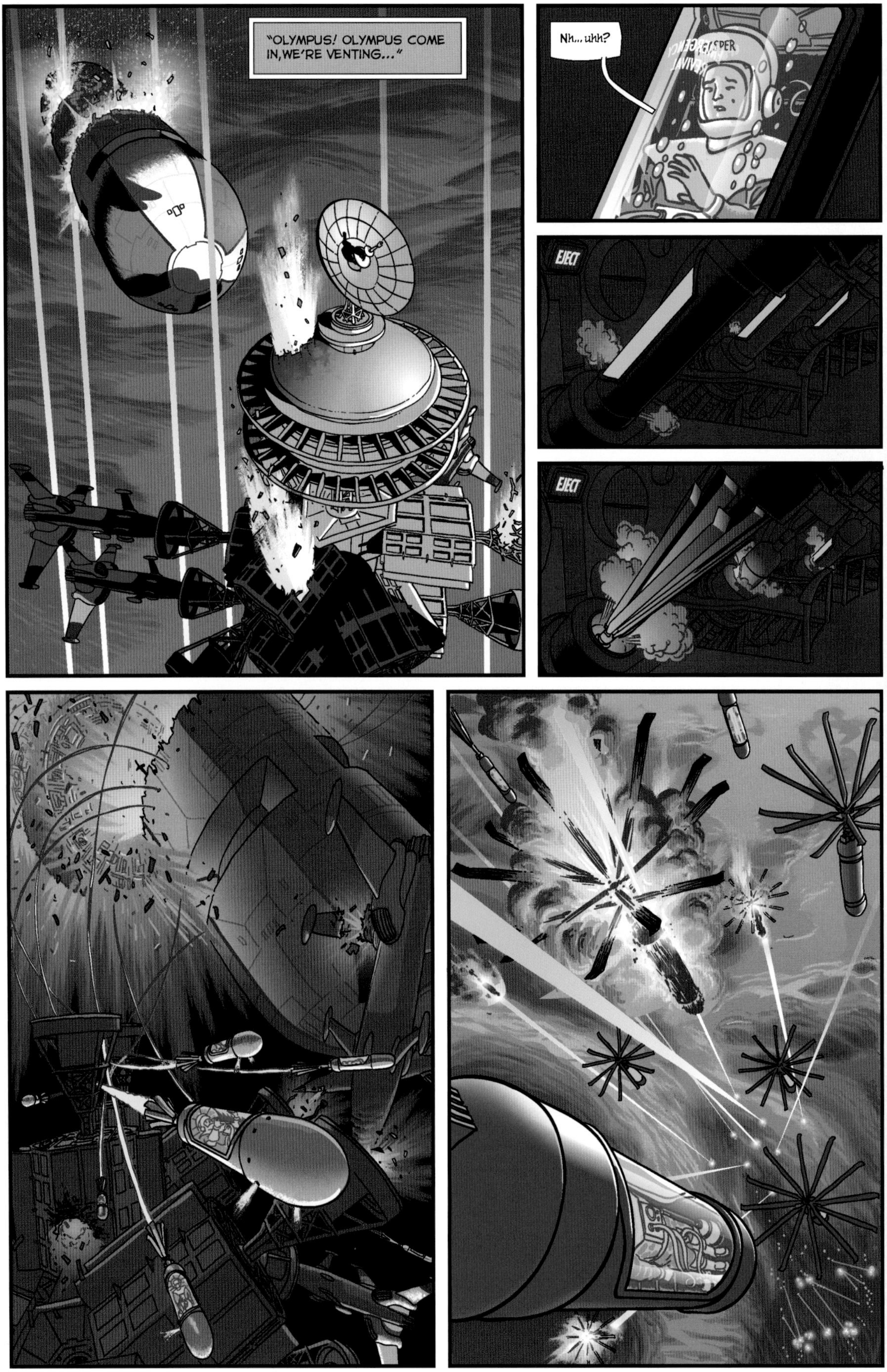
"OLYMPUS! OLYMPUS COME IN, WE'RE VENTING..."
Nh... uhh?
EJECT
EJECT

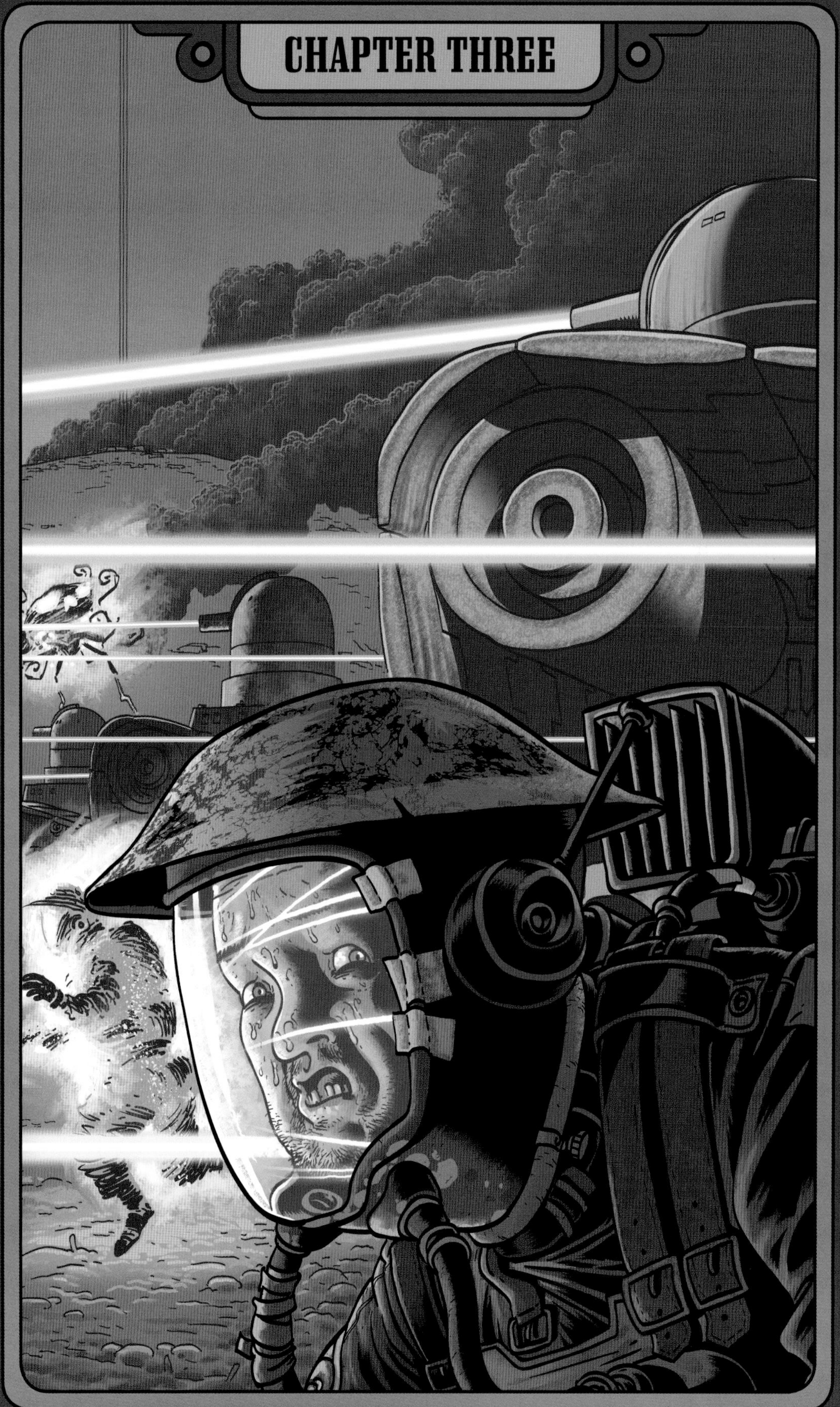
CHAPTER THREE

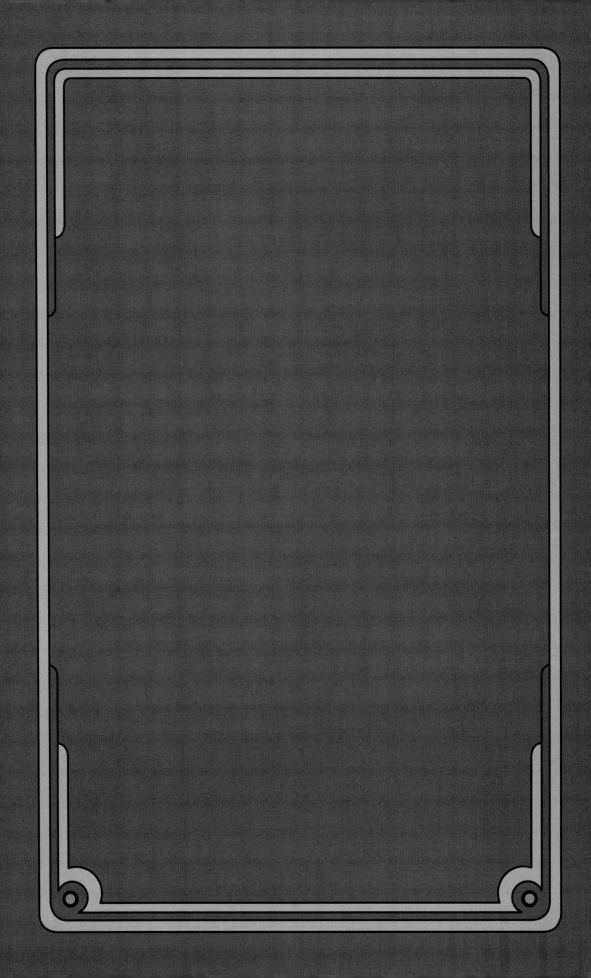

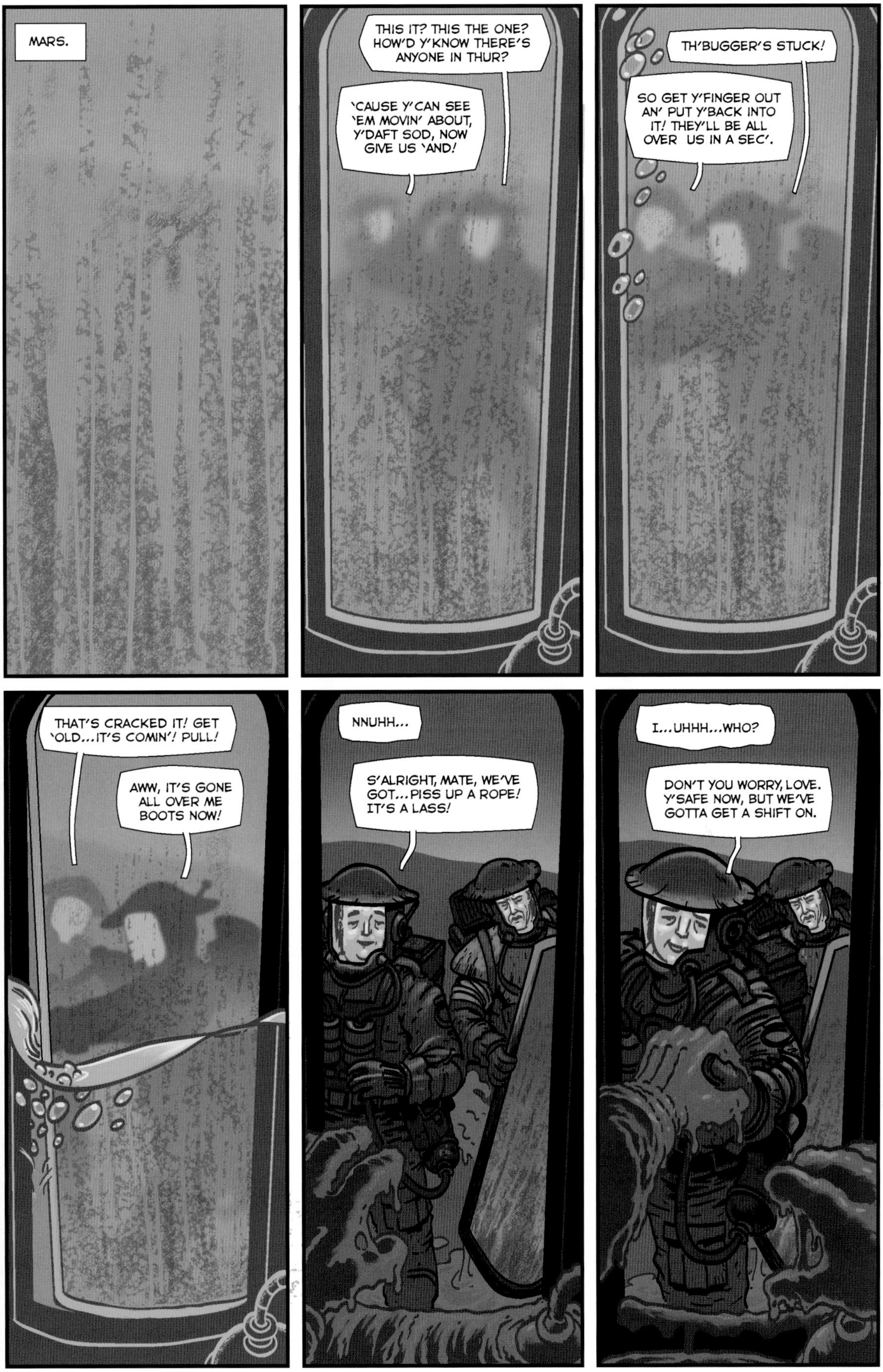
MARS.
THIS IT? THIS THE ONE? HOW'D Y'KNOW THERE'S ANYONE IN THUR?
'CAUSE Y'CAN SEE 'EM MOVIN' ABOUT, Y'DAFT SOD, NOW GIVE US 'AND!
TH'BUGGER'S STUCK!
SO GET Y'FINGER OUT AN' PUT Y'BACK INTO IT! THEY'LL BE ALL OVER US IN A SEC'.
THAT'S CRACKED IT! GET 'OLD...IT'S COMIN'! PULL!
AWW, IT'S GONE ALL OVER ME BOOTS NOW!
NNUHH...
S'ALRIGHT, MATE, WE'VE GOT...PISS UP A ROPE! IT'S A LASS!
I...UHHH...WHO?
DON'T YOU WORRY, LOVE. Y'SAFE NOW, BUT WE'VE GOTTA GET A SHIFT ON.

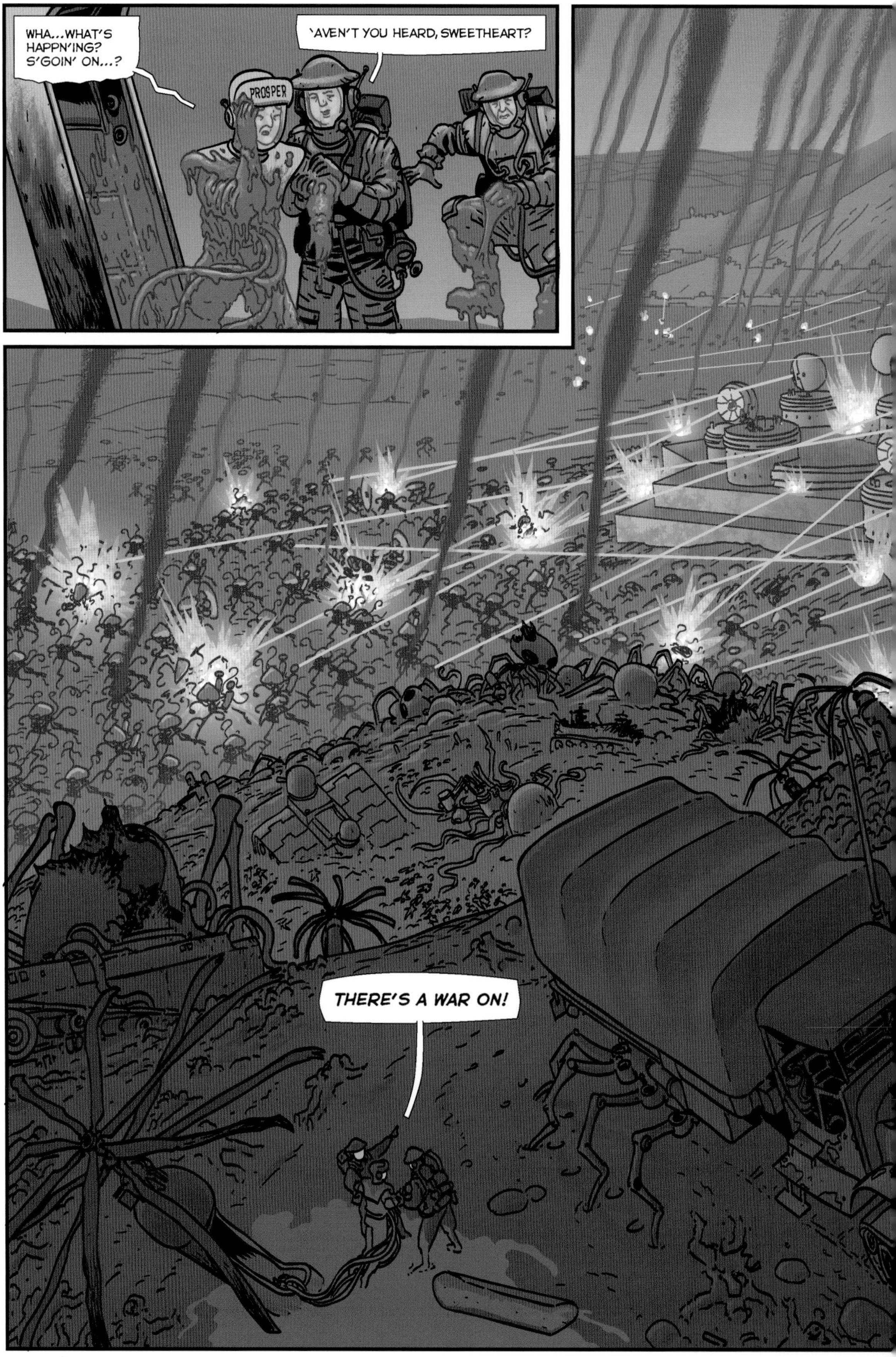
WHA...WHAT'S HAPPN'ING? S'GOIN' ON...?
'AVEN'T YOU HEARD, SWEETHEART?
PROSPER
THERE'S A WAR ON!

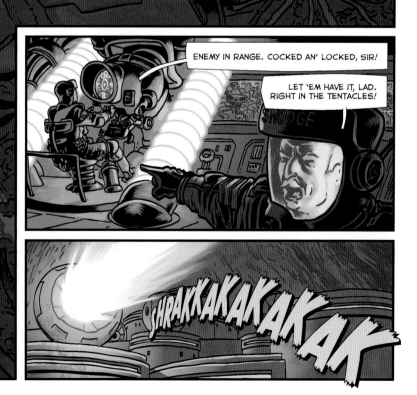

ENEMY IN RANGE. COCKED AN' LOCKED, SIR!

LET 'EM HAVE IT, LAD. RIGHT IN THE TENTACLES!

SHRAKKAKAKAKAK

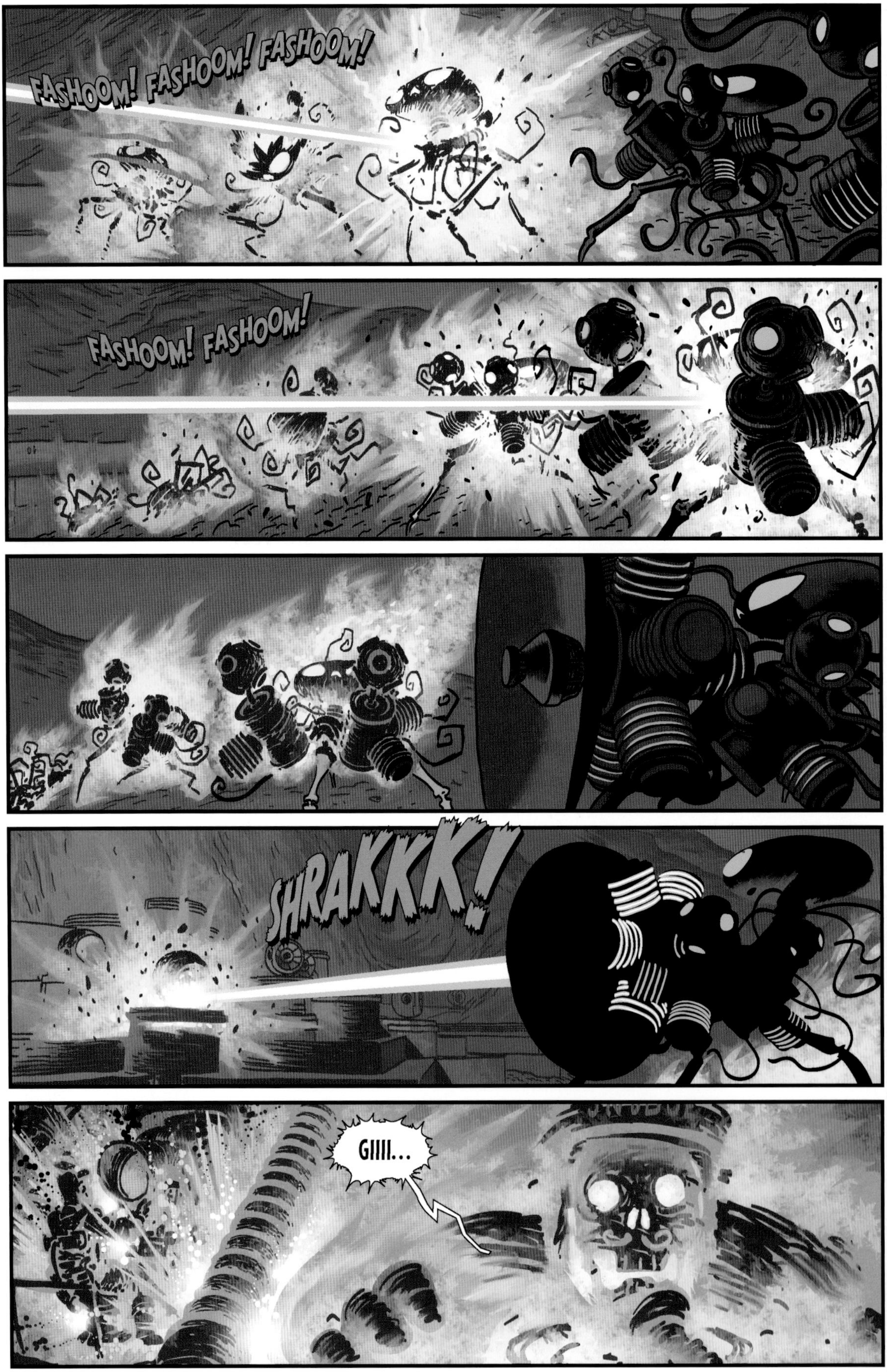
FASHOOM! FASHOOM! FASHOOM!
FASHOOM! FASHOOM!
SHRAKKK!
GIIII...

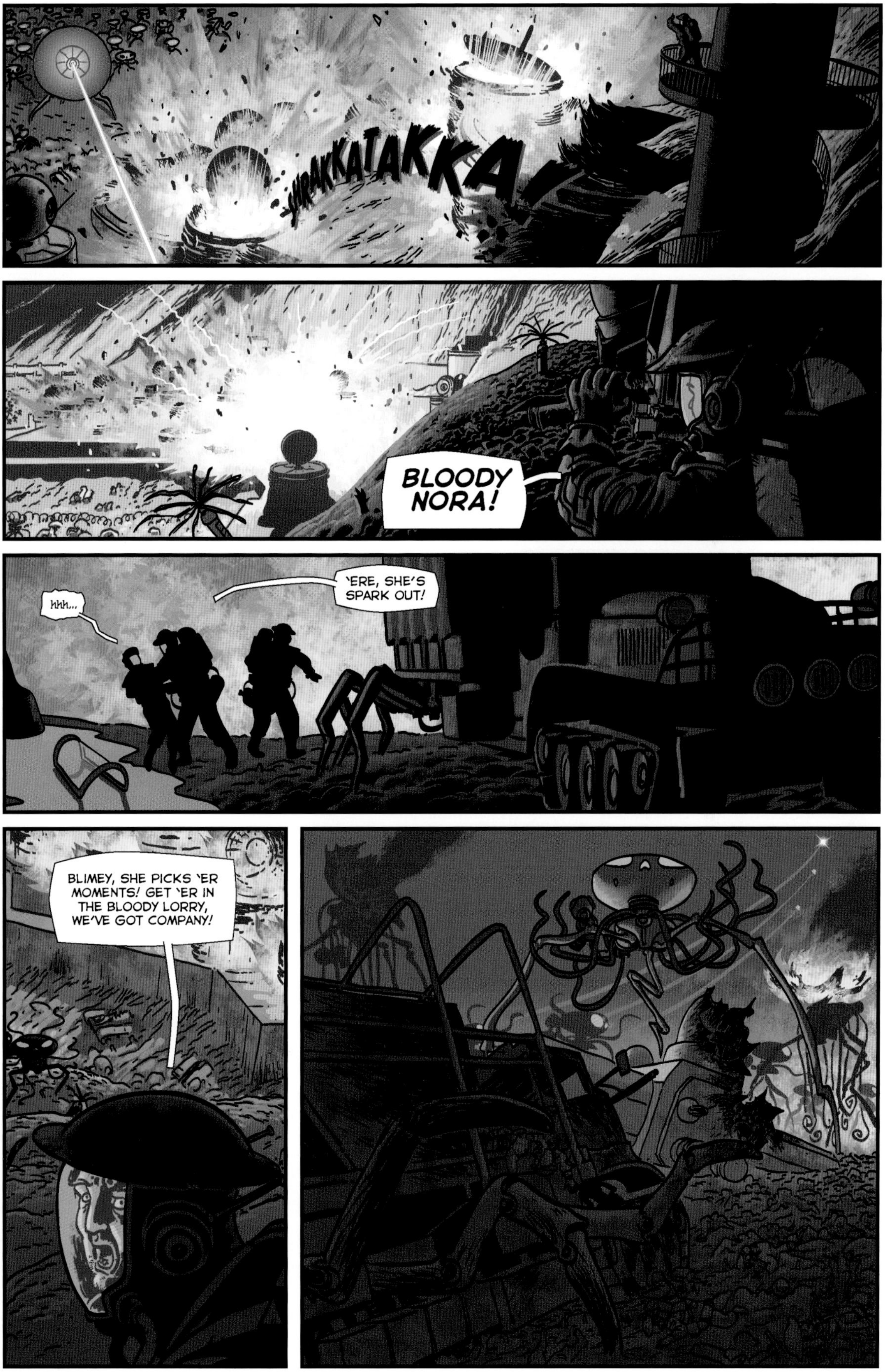
SHRAKKATAKKA
BLOODY NORA!
hhh...
'ERE, SHE'S SPARK OUT!
BLIMEY, SHE PICKS 'ER MOMENTS! GET 'ER IN THE BLOODY LORRY, WE'VE GOT COMPANY!

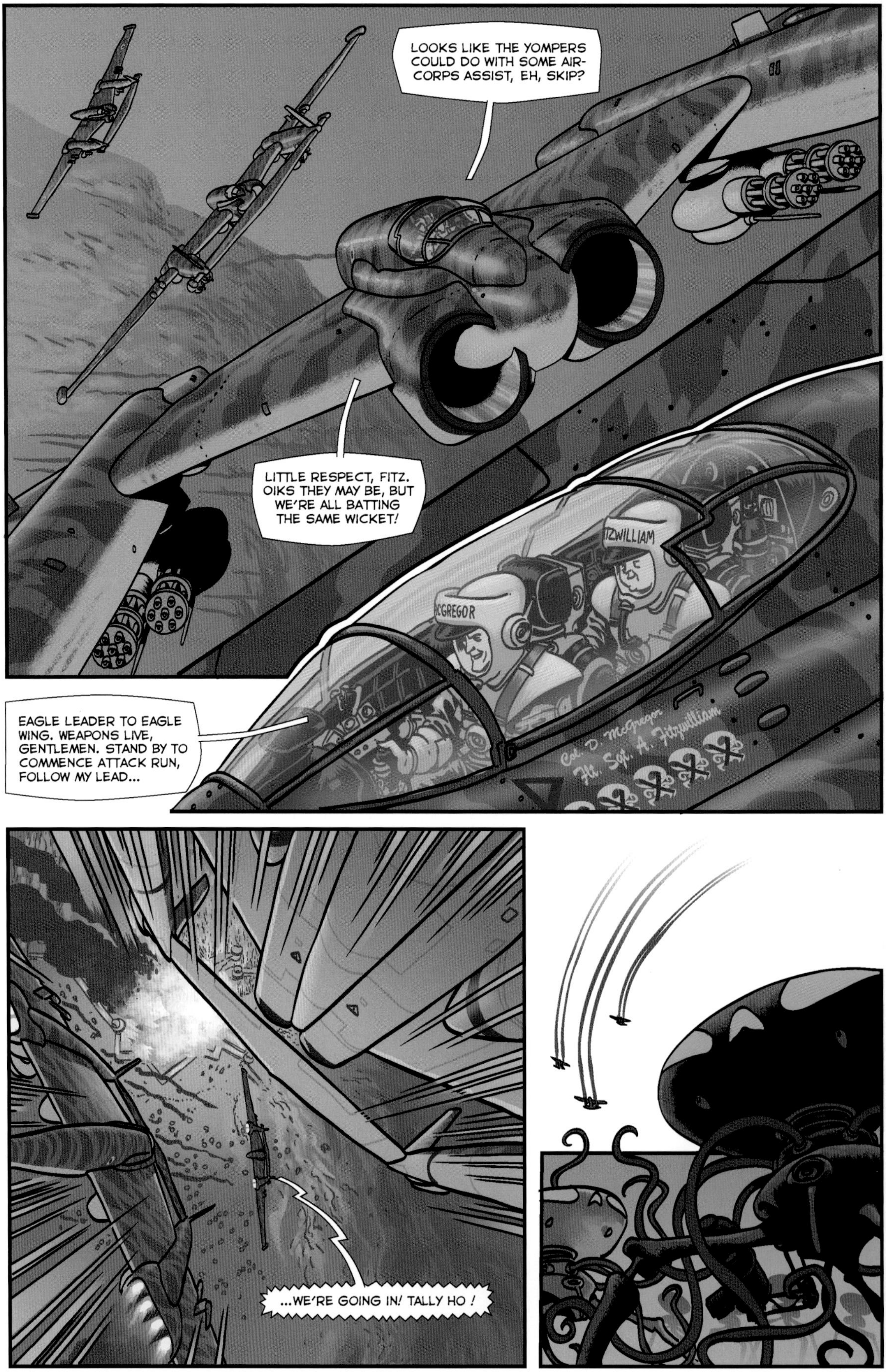
LOOKS LIKE THE YOMPERS COULD DO WITH SOME AIR-CORPS ASSIST, EH, SKIP?
LITTLE RESPECT, FITZ. OIKS THEY MAY BE, BUT WE'RE ALL BATTING THE SAME WICKET!
Col. D. McGregor
Flt. Sgt. A. Fitzwilliam
EAGLE LEADER TO EAGLE WING. WEAPONS LIVE, GENTLEMEN. STAND BY TO COMMENCE ATTACK RUN, FOLLOW MY LEAD...
...WE'RE GOING IN! TALLY HO!

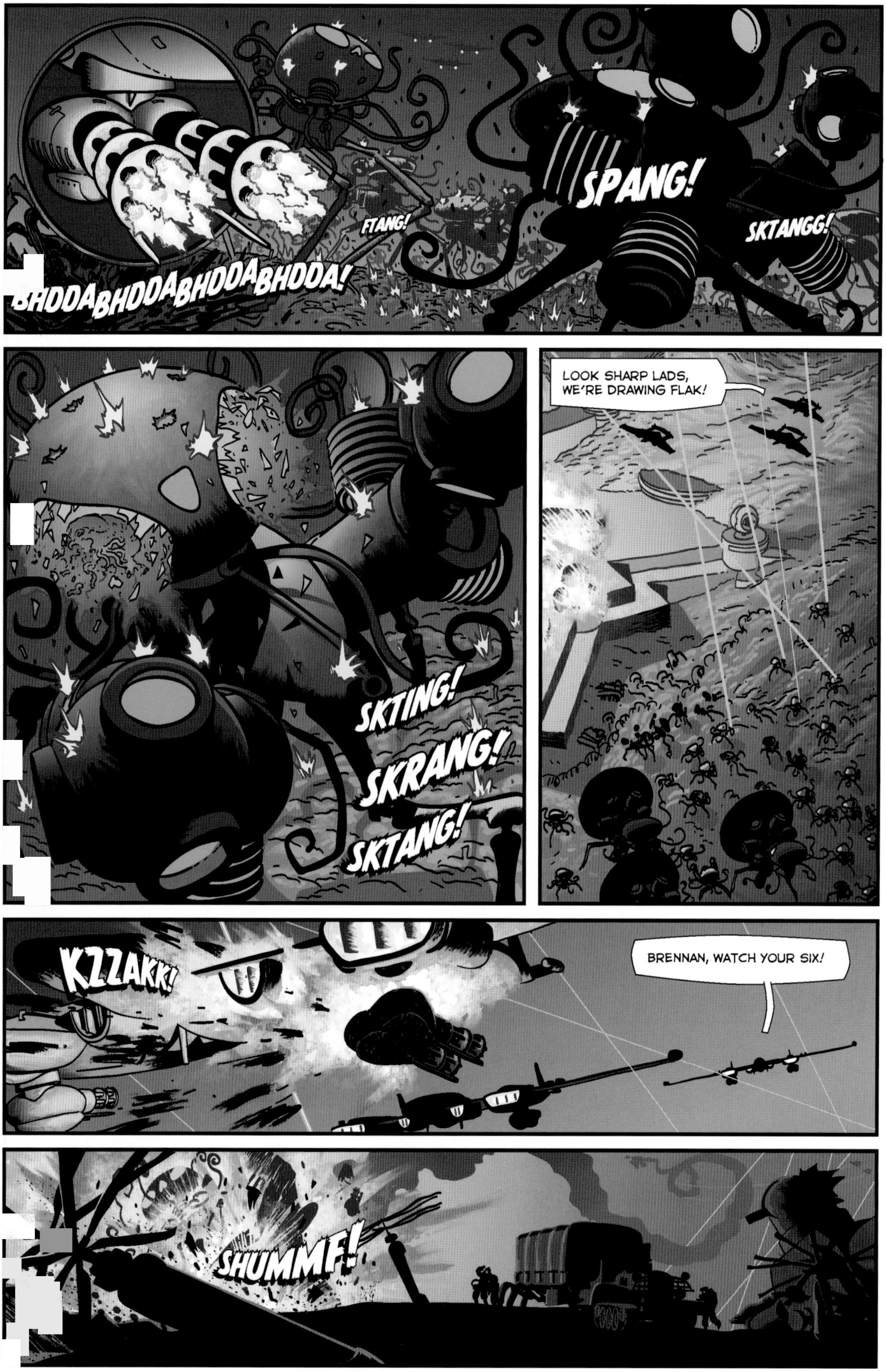
BHDDABHDDABHDDABHDDA!
FTANG!
SPANG!
SKTANGG!
SKTING!
SKRANG!
SKTANG!
LOOK SHARP LADS, WE'RE DRAWING FLAK!
KZZAKK!
BRENNAN, WATCH YOUR SIX!
SHUMMF!

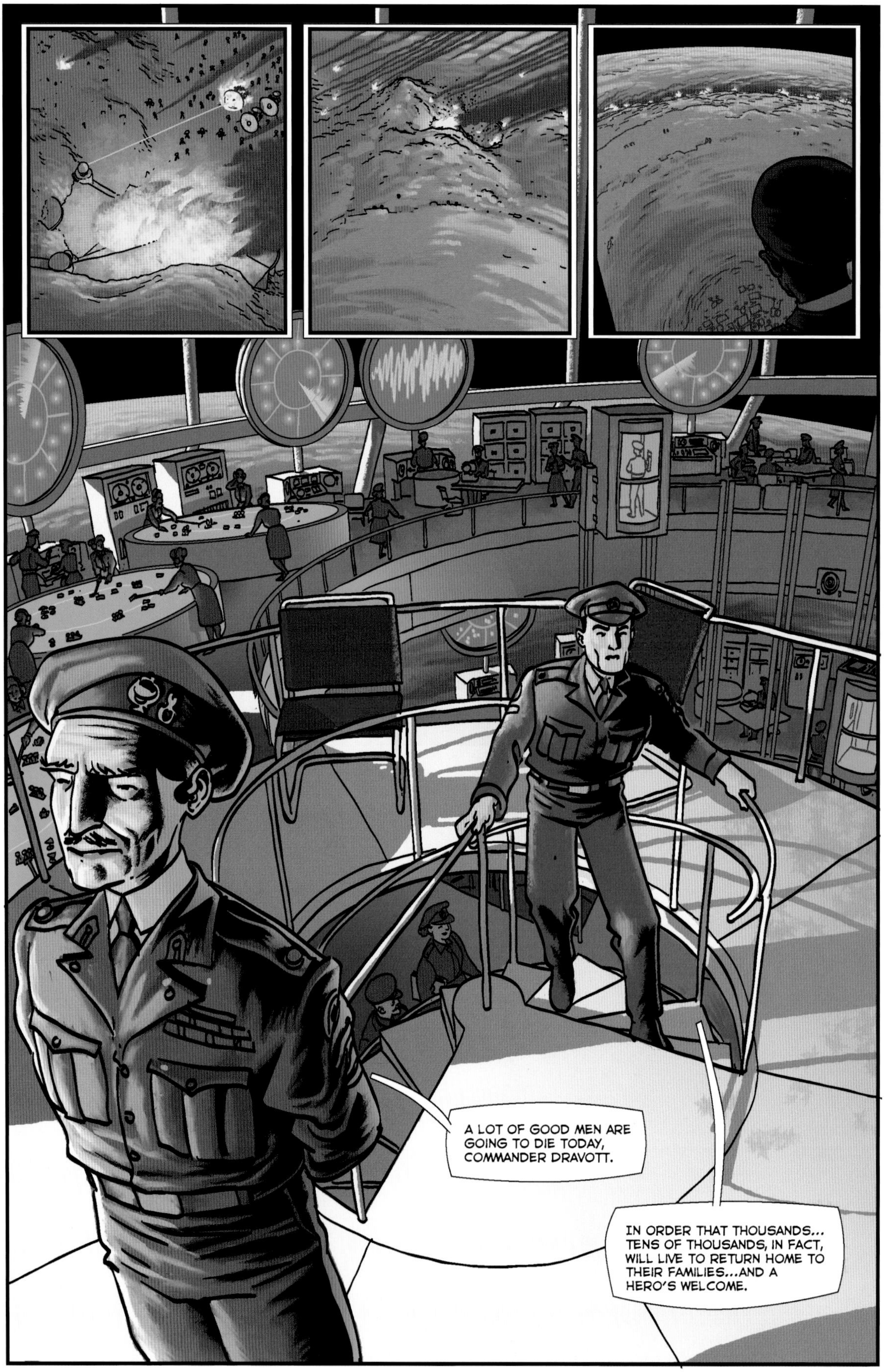
A LOT OF GOOD MEN ARE GOING TO DIE TODAY, COMMANDER DRAVOTT.
IN ORDER THAT THOUSANDS... TENS OF THOUSANDS, IN FACT, WILL LIVE TO RETURN HOME TO THEIR FAMILIES...AND A HERO'S WELCOME.

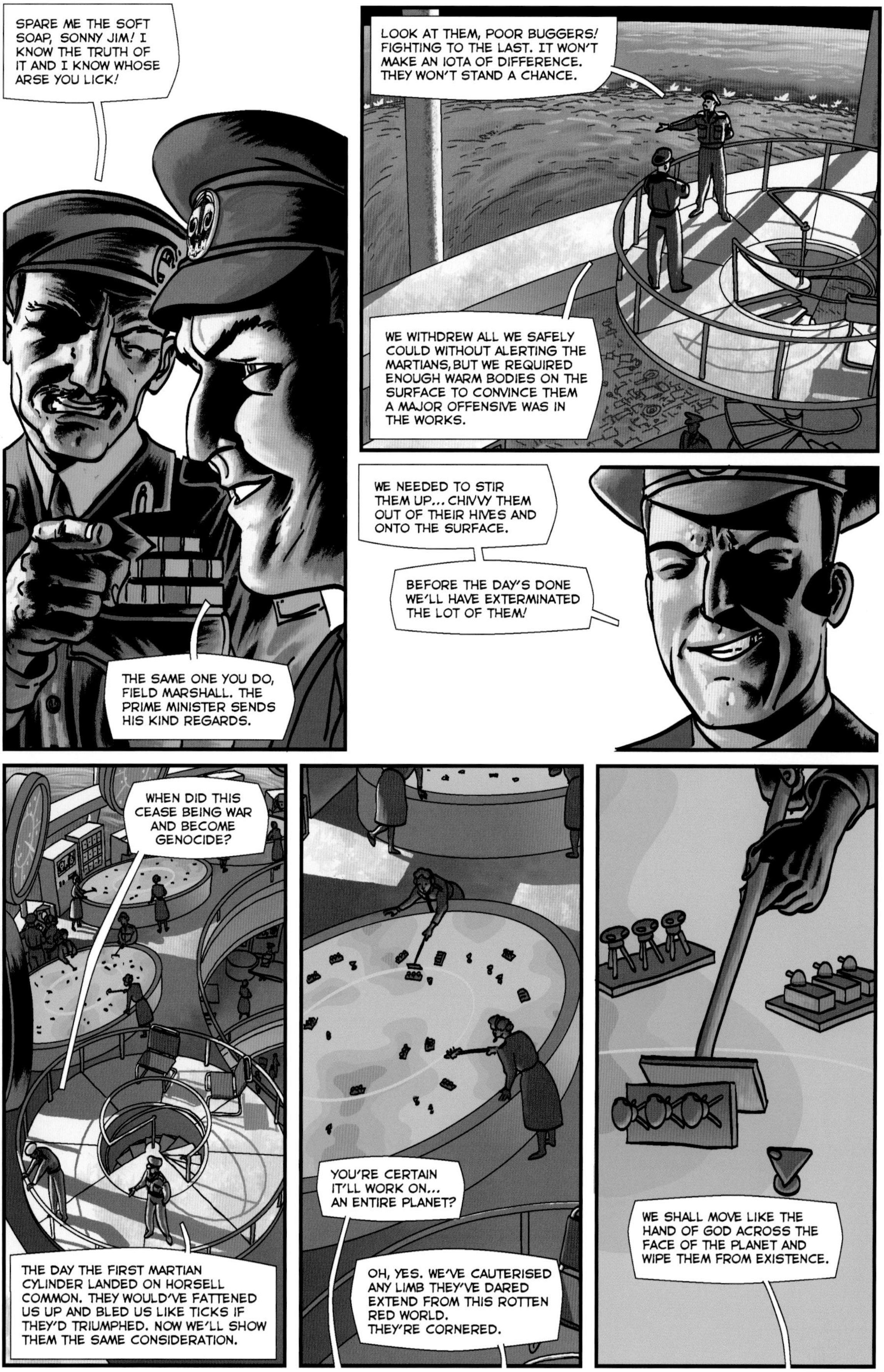
SPARE ME THE SOFT SOAP, SONNY JIM! I KNOW THE TRUTH OF IT AND I KNOW WHOSE ARSE YOU LICK!
THE SAME ONE YOU DO, FIELD MARSHALL. THE PRIME MINISTER SENDS HIS KIND REGARDS.
LOOK AT THEM, POOR BUGGERS! FIGHTING TO THE LAST. IT WON'T MAKE AN IOTA OF DIFFERENCE. THEY WON'T STAND A CHANCE.
WE WITHDREW ALL WE SAFELY COULD WITHOUT ALERTING THE MARTIANS, BUT WE REQUIRED ENOUGH WARM BODIES ON THE SURFACE TO CONVINCE THEM A MAJOR OFFENSIVE WAS IN THE WORKS.
WE NEEDED TO STIR THEM UP... CHIVVY THEM OUT OF THEIR HIVES AND ONTO THE SURFACE.
BEFORE THE DAY'S DONE WE'LL HAVE EXTERMINATED THE LOT OF THEM!
WHEN DID THIS CEASE BEING WAR AND BECOME GENOCIDE?
THE DAY THE FIRST MARTIAN CYLINDER LANDED ON HORSELL COMMON. THEY WOULD'VE FATTENED US UP AND BLED US LIKE TICKS IF THEY'D TRIUMPHED. NOW WE'LL SHOW THEM THE SAME CONSIDERATION.
YOU'RE CERTAIN IT'LL WORK ON... AN ENTIRE PLANET?
OH, YES. WE'VE CAUTERISED ANY LIMB THEY'VE DARED EXTEND FROM THIS ROTTEN RED WORLD. THEY'RE CORNERED.
WE SHALL MOVE LIKE THE HAND OF GOD ACROSS THE FACE OF THE PLANET AND WIPE THEM FROM EXISTENCE.

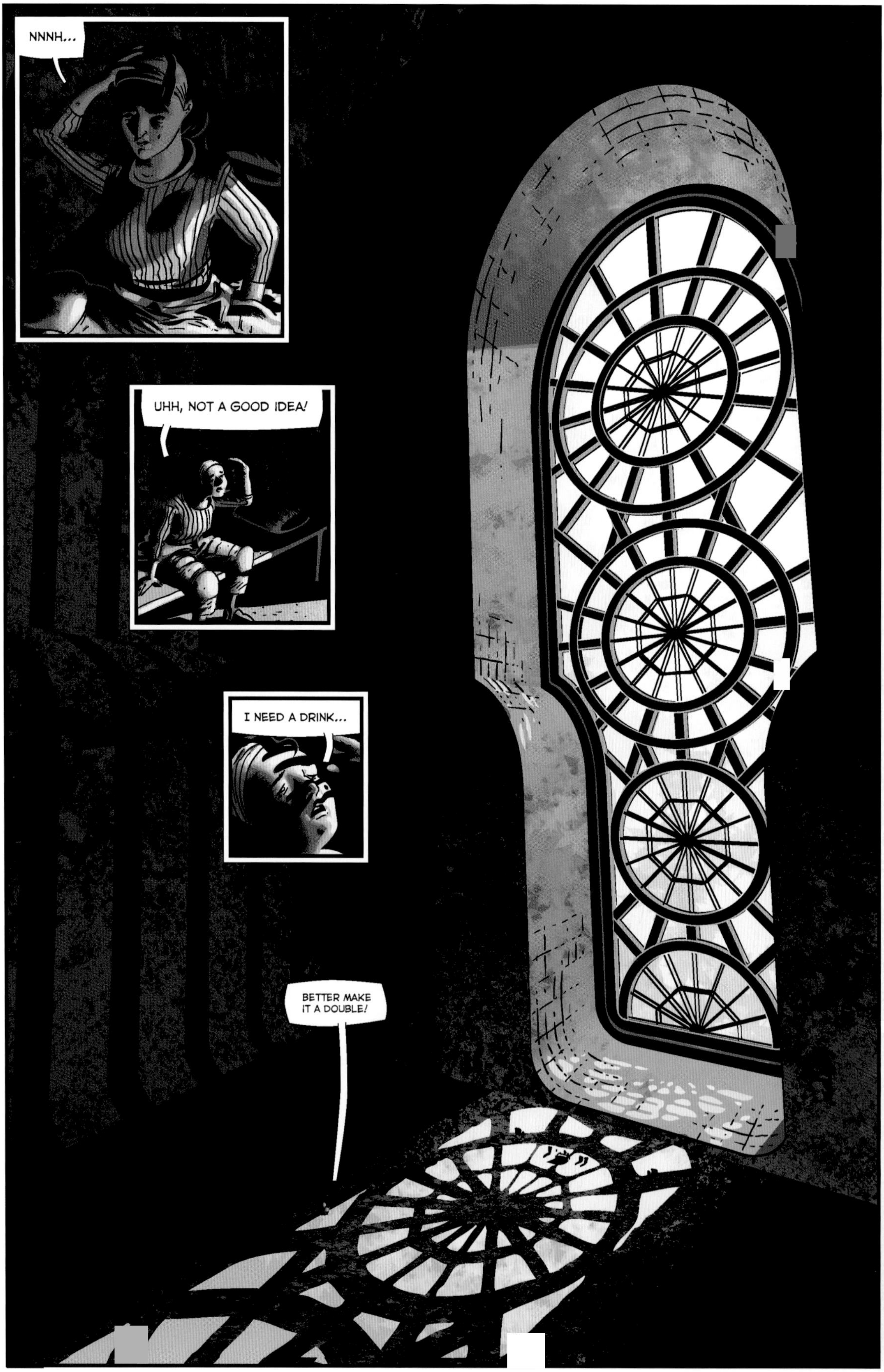
NNNH...
UHH, NOT A GOOD IDEA!
I NEED A DRINK...
BETTER MAKE IT A DOUBLE!

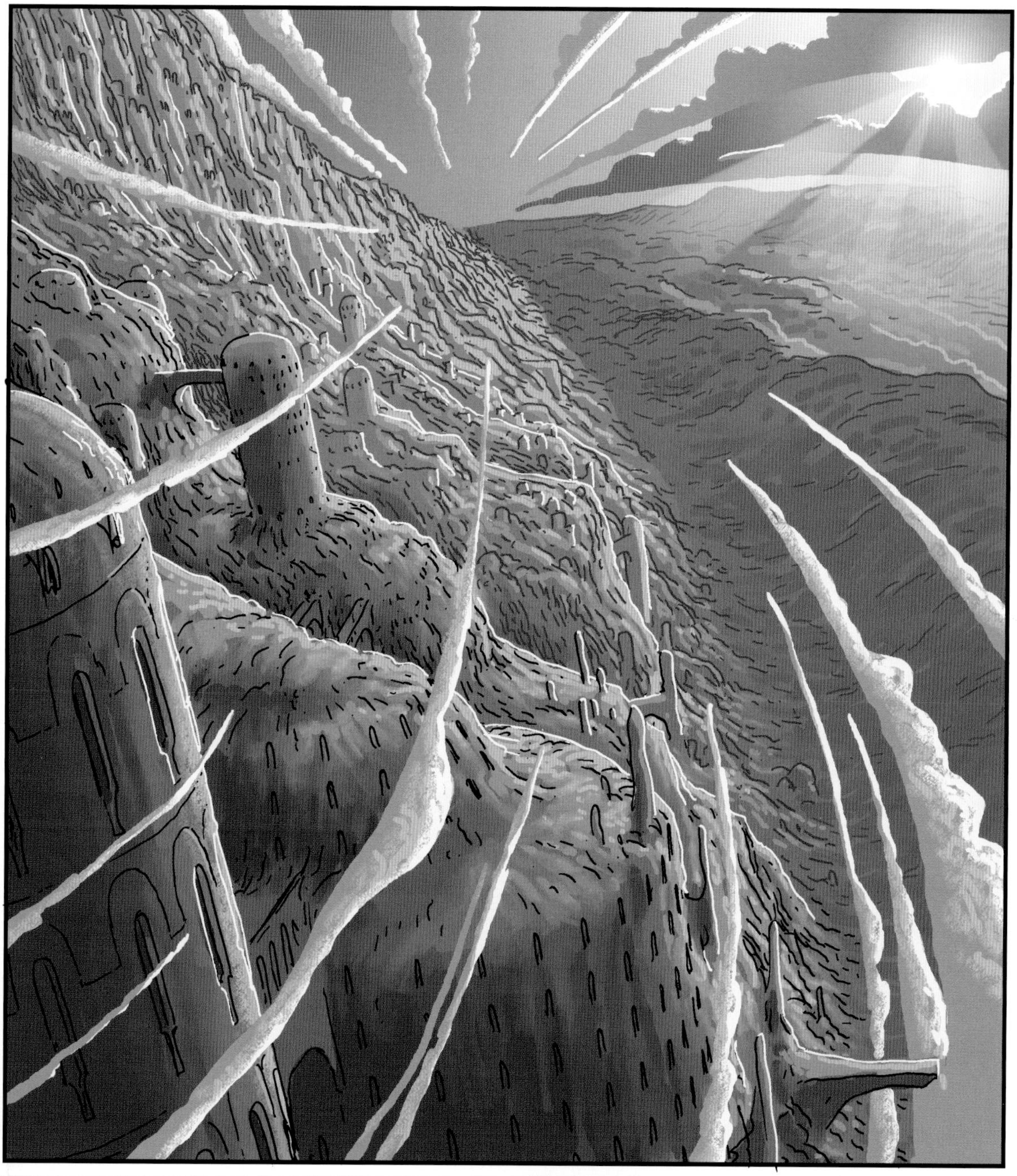

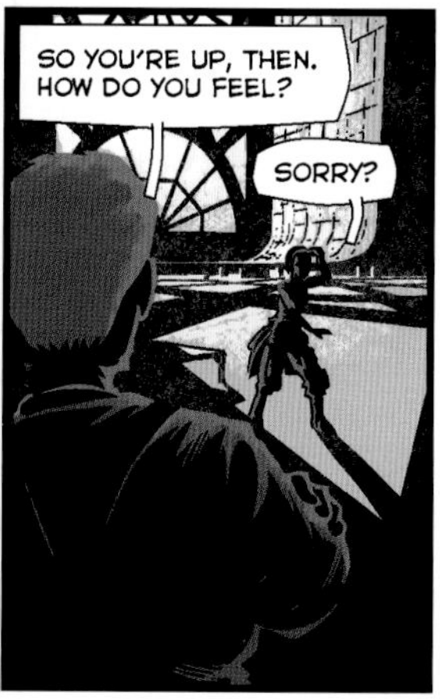
SO YOU'RE UP, THEN. HOW DO YOU FEEL?
SORRY?

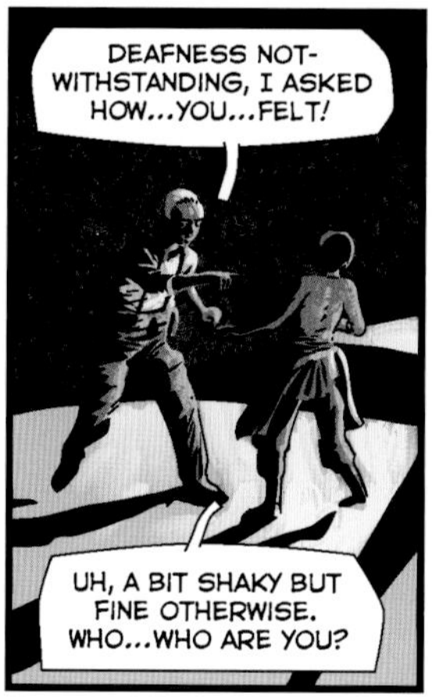
DEAFNESS NOT-WITHSTANDING, I ASKED HOW...YOU...FELT!
UH, A BIT SHAKY BUT FINE OTHERWISE. WHO...WHO ARE YOU?

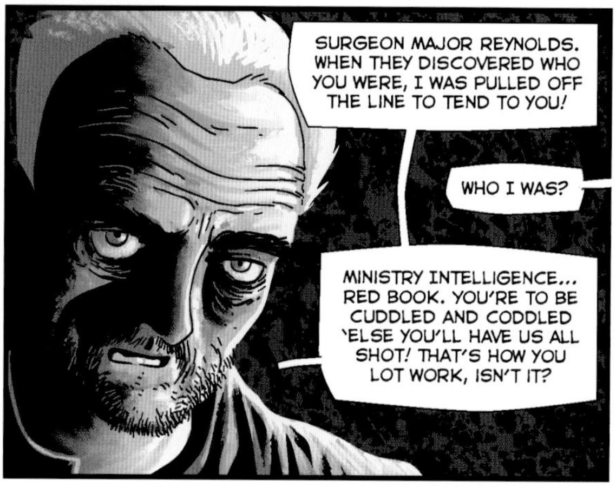
SURGEON MAJOR REYNOLDS. WHEN THEY DISCOVERED WHO YOU WERE, I WAS PULLED OFF THE LINE TO TEND TO YOU!
WHO I WAS?
MINISTRY INTELLIGENCE... RED BOOK. YOU'RE TO BE CUDDLED AND CODDLED 'ELSE YOU'LL HAVE US ALL SHOT! THAT'S HOW YOU LOT WORK, ISN'T IT?

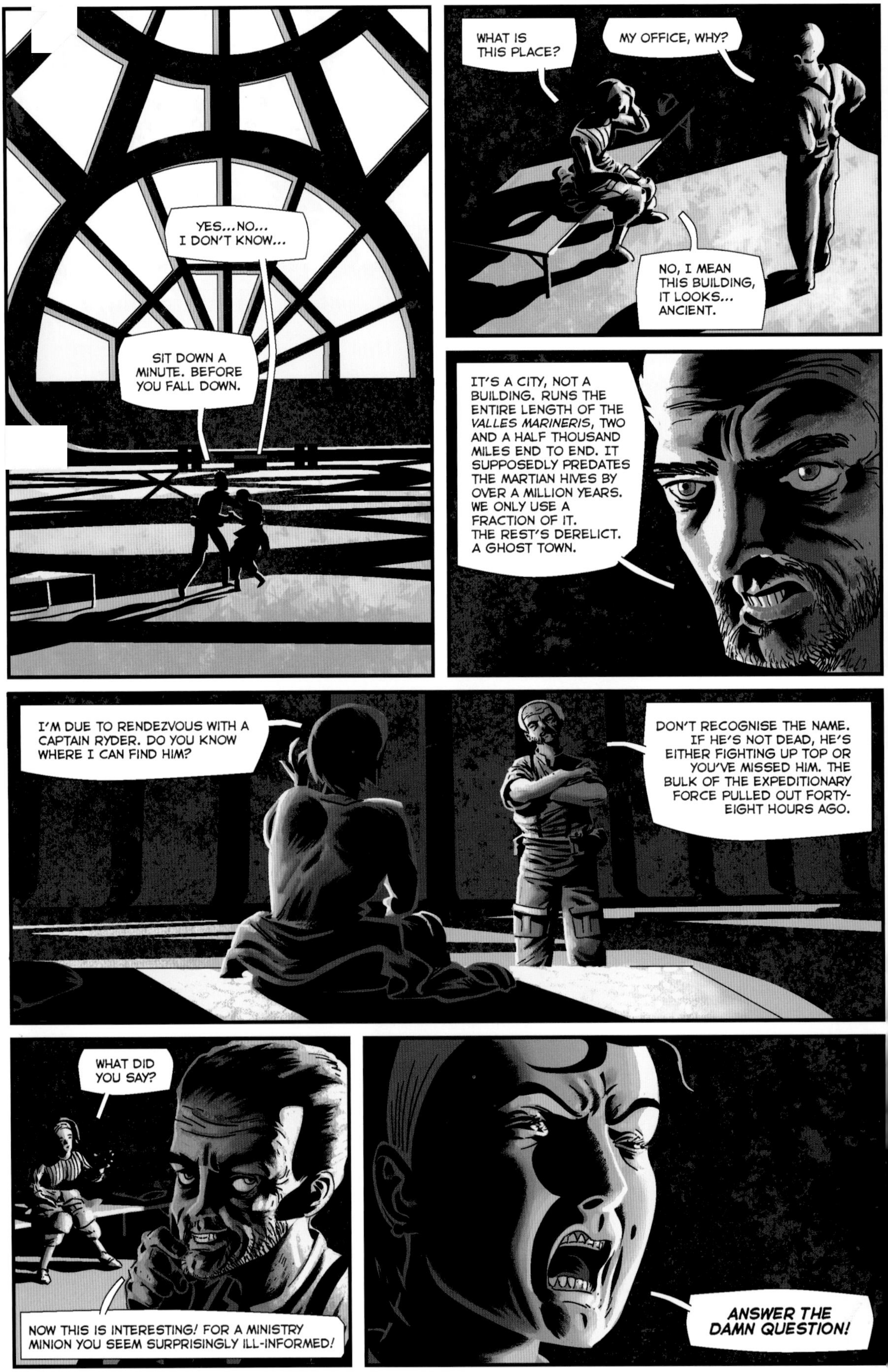
YES...NO...
I DON'T KNOW...
SIT DOWN A MINUTE. BEFORE YOU FALL DOWN.
WHAT IS THIS PLACE?
MY OFFICE, WHY?
NO, I MEAN THIS BUILDING, IT LOOKS... ANCIENT.
IT'S A CITY, NOT A BUILDING. RUNS THE ENTIRE LENGTH OF THE *VALLES MARINERIS*, TWO AND A HALF THOUSAND MILES END TO END. IT SUPPOSEDLY PREDATES THE MARTIAN HIVES BY OVER A MILLION YEARS. WE ONLY USE A FRACTION OF IT. THE REST'S DERELICT. A GHOST TOWN.
I'M DUE TO RENDEZVOUS WITH A CAPTAIN RYDER. DO YOU KNOW WHERE I CAN FIND HIM?
DON'T RECOGNISE THE NAME. IF HE'S NOT DEAD, HE'S EITHER FIGHTING UP TOP OR YOU'VE MISSED HIM. THE BULK OF THE EXPEDITIONARY FORCE PULLED OUT FORTY-EIGHT HOURS AGO.
WHAT DID YOU SAY?
NOW THIS IS INTERESTING! FOR A MINISTRY MINION YOU SEEM SURPRISINGLY ILL-INFORMED!
ANSWER THE DAMN QUESTION!

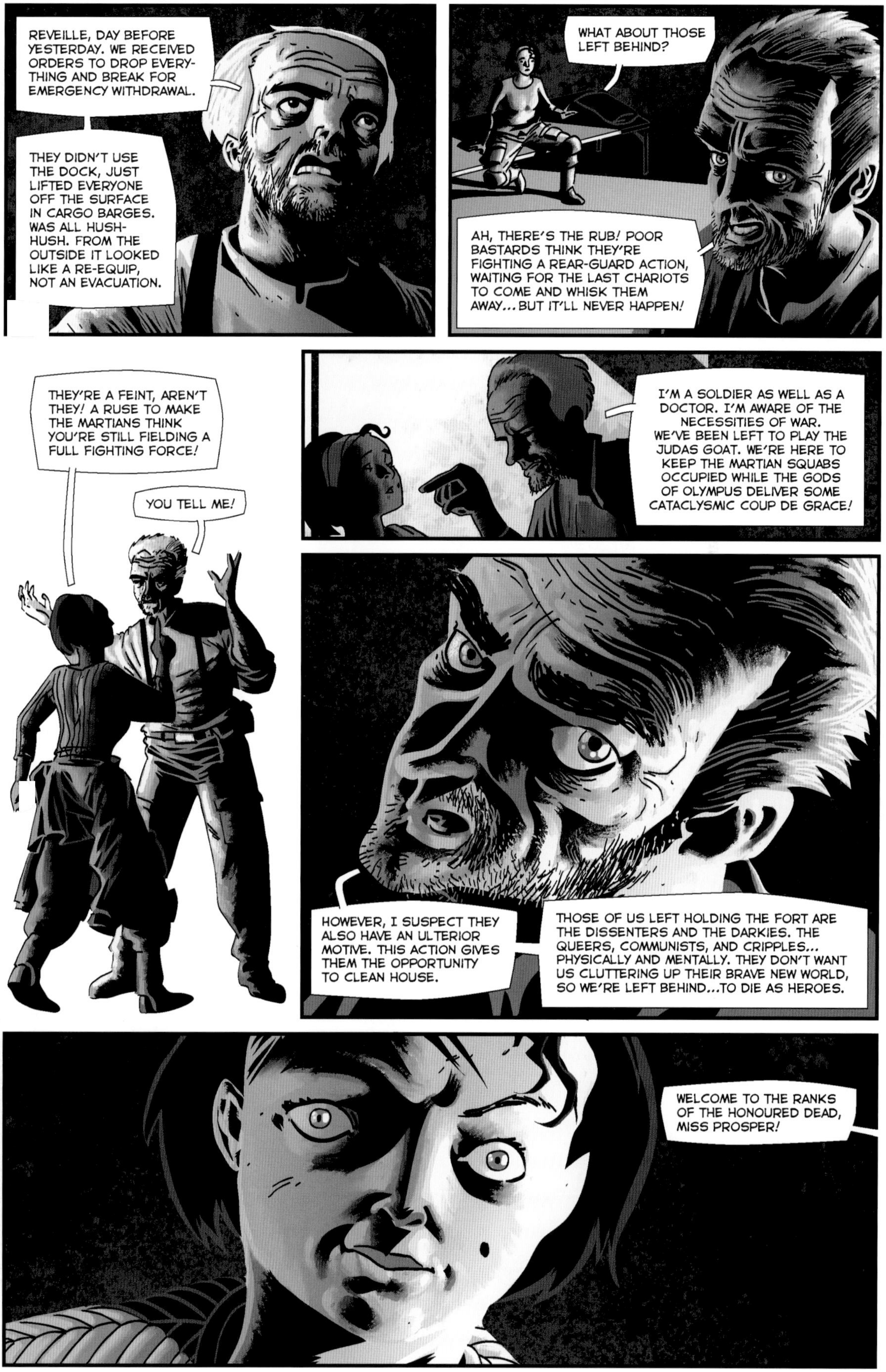
REVEILLE, DAY BEFORE YESTERDAY. WE RECEIVED ORDERS TO DROP EVERYTHING AND BREAK FOR EMERGENCY WITHDRAWAL.
THEY DIDN'T USE THE DOCK, JUST LIFTED EVERYONE OFF THE SURFACE IN CARGO BARGES. WAS ALL HUSH-HUSH. FROM THE OUTSIDE IT LOOKED LIKE A RE-EQUIP, NOT AN EVACUATION.
WHAT ABOUT THOSE LEFT BEHIND?
AH, THERE'S THE RUB! POOR BASTARDS THINK THEY'RE FIGHTING A REAR-GUARD ACTION, WAITING FOR THE LAST CHARIOTS TO COME AND WHISK THEM AWAY... BUT IT'LL NEVER HAPPEN!
THEY'RE A FEINT, AREN'T THEY! A RUSE TO MAKE THE MARTIANS THINK YOU'RE STILL FIELDING A FULL FIGHTING FORCE!
YOU TELL ME!
I'M A SOLDIER AS WELL AS A DOCTOR. I'M AWARE OF THE NECESSITIES OF WAR. WE'VE BEEN LEFT TO PLAY THE JUDAS GOAT. WE'RE HERE TO KEEP THE MARTIAN SQUABS OCCUPIED WHILE THE GODS OF OLYMPUS DELIVER SOME CATACLYSMIC COUP DE GRACE!
HOWEVER, I SUSPECT THEY ALSO HAVE AN ULTERIOR MOTIVE. THIS ACTION GIVES THEM THE OPPORTUNITY TO CLEAN HOUSE.
THOSE OF US LEFT HOLDING THE FORT ARE THE DISSENTERS AND THE DARKIES. THE QUEERS, COMMUNISTS, AND CRIPPLES... PHYSICALLY AND MENTALLY. THEY DON'T WANT US CLUTTERING UP THEIR BRAVE NEW WORLD, SO WE'RE LEFT BEHIND...TO DIE AS HEROES.
WELCOME TO THE RANKS OF THE HONOURED DEAD, MISS PROSPER!

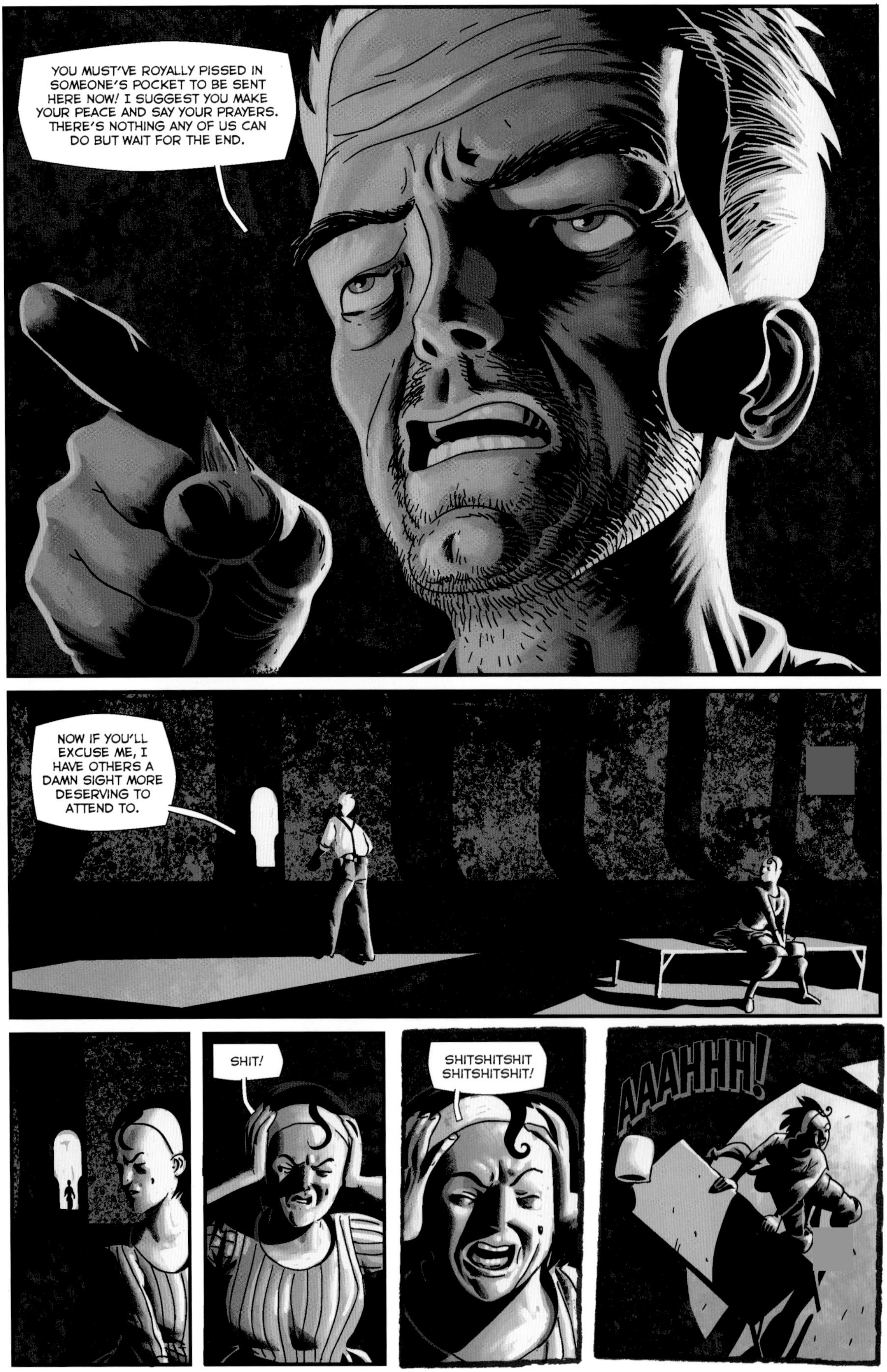
YOU MUST'VE ROYALLY PISSED IN SOMEONE'S POCKET TO BE SENT HERE NOW! I SUGGEST YOU MAKE YOUR PEACE AND SAY YOUR PRAYERS. THERE'S NOTHING ANY OF US CAN DO BUT WAIT FOR THE END.
NOW IF YOU'LL EXCUSE ME, I HAVE OTHERS A DAMN SIGHT MORE DESERVING TO ATTEND TO.
SHIT!
SHITSHITSHIT SHITSHITSHIT!
AAAHHH!

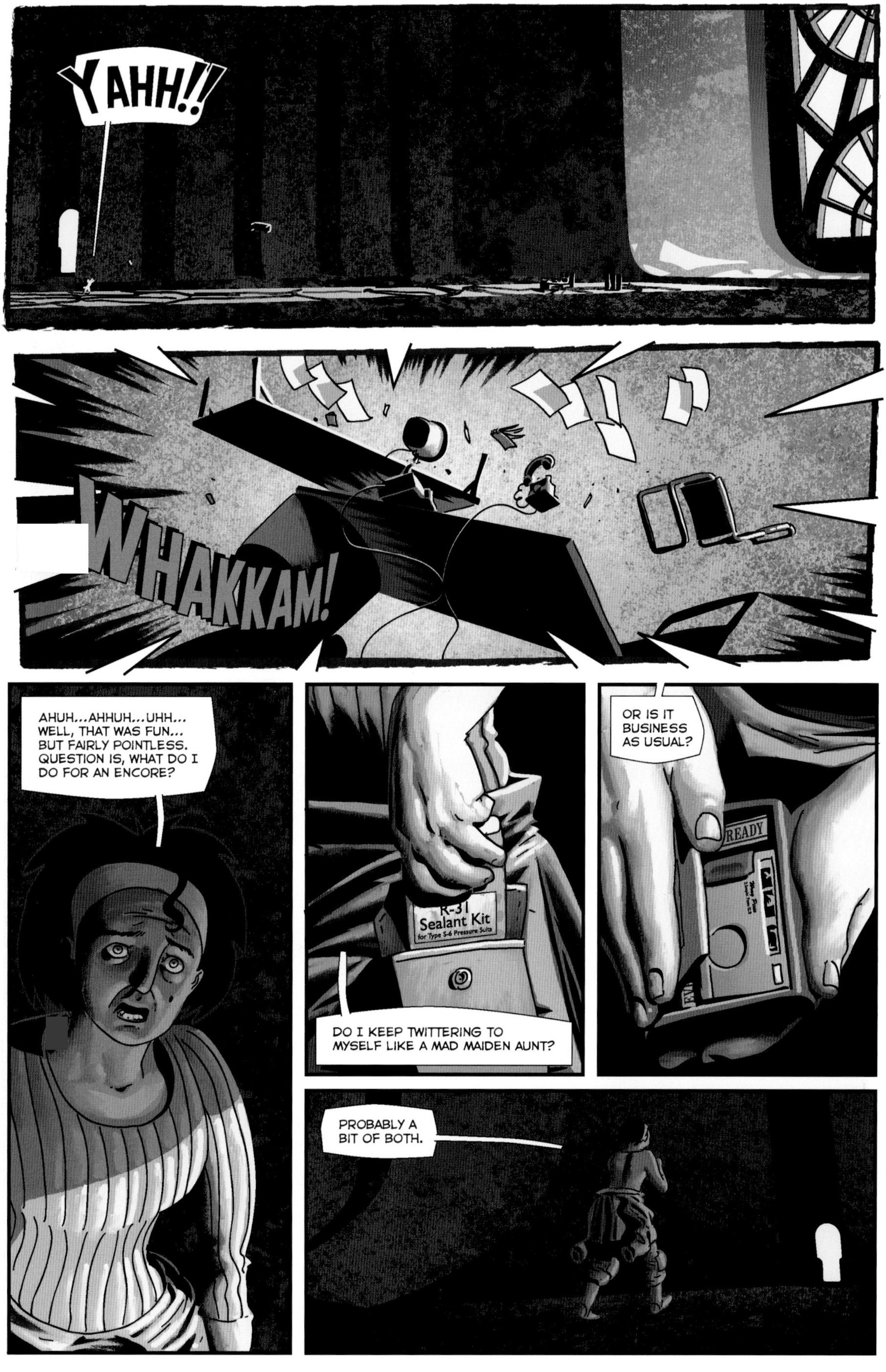
YAHH!!
WHAKKAM!
AHUH...AHHUH...UHH... WELL, THAT WAS FUN... BUT FAIRLY POINTLESS. QUESTION IS, WHAT DO I DO FOR AN ENCORE?
R-31 Sealant Kit for Type S-6 Pressure Suits
DO I KEEP TWITTERING TO MYSELF LIKE A MAD MAIDEN AUNT?
OR IS IT BUSINESS AS USUAL?
READY
PROBABLY A BIT OF BOTH.

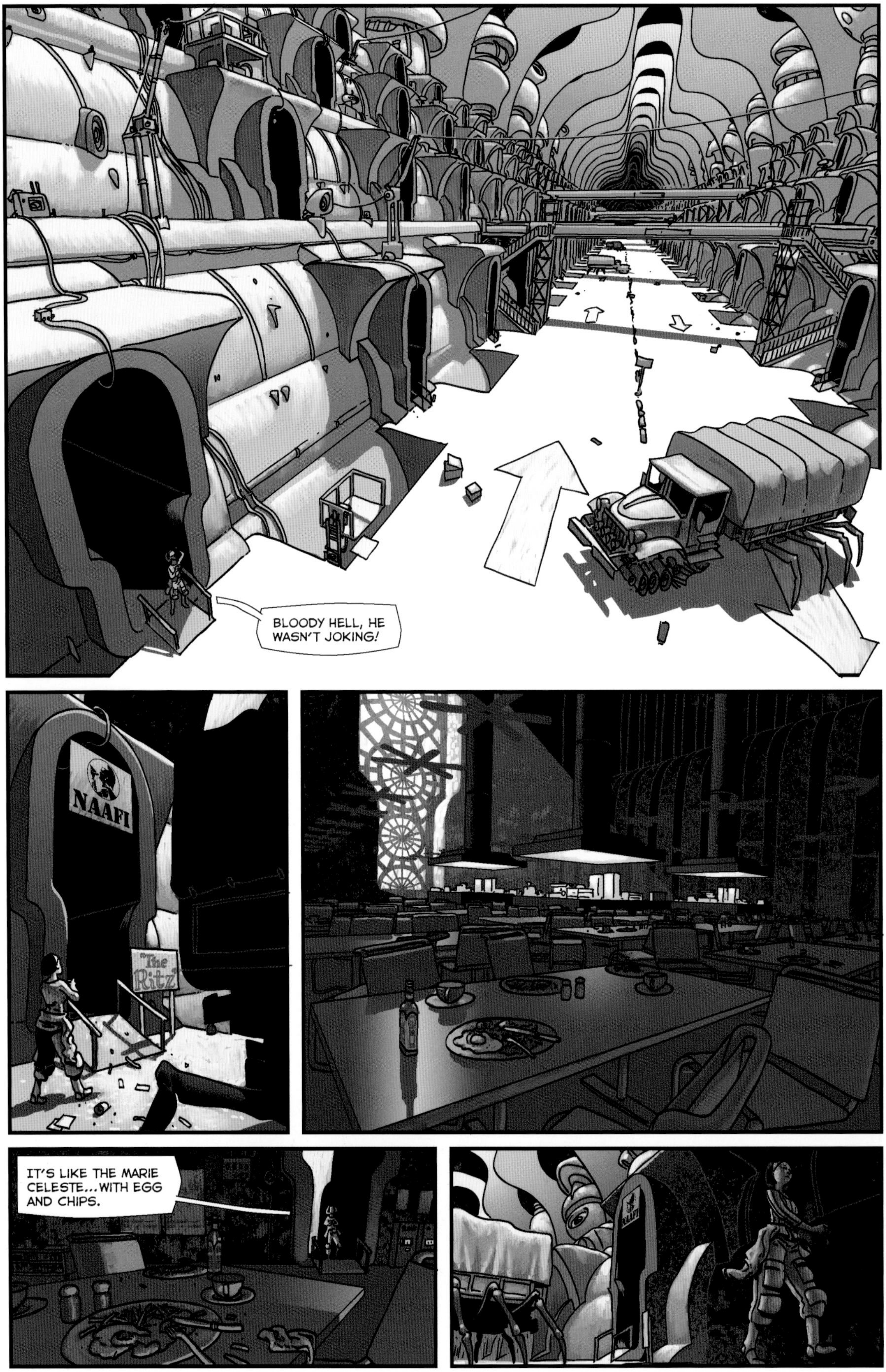
BLOODY HELL, HE WASN'T JOKING!
NAAFI
"The Ritz"
IT'S LIKE THE MARIE CELESTE...WITH EGG AND CHIPS.

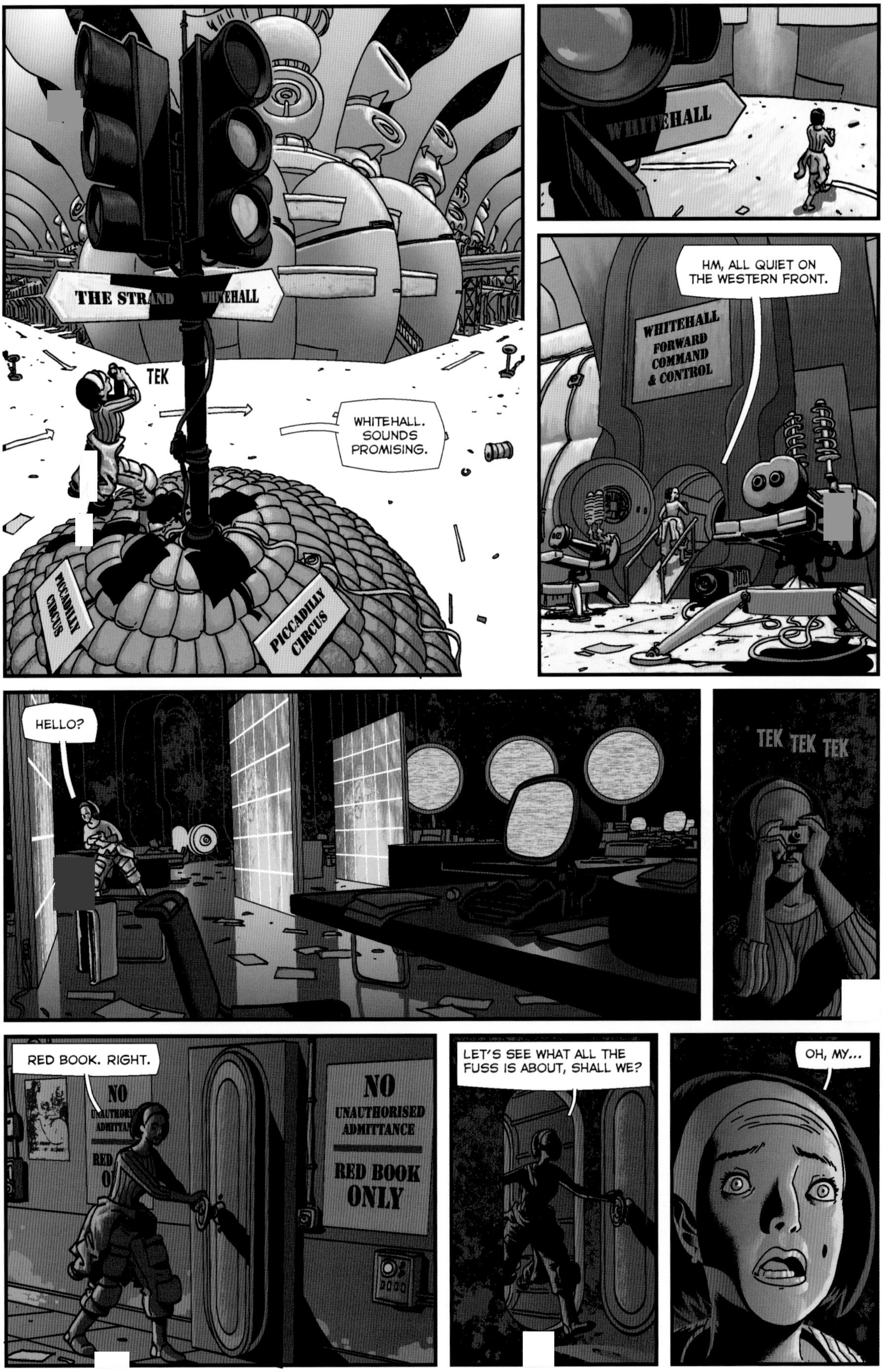
THE STRAND
WHITEHALL
TEK
WHITEHALL. SOUNDS PROMISING.
PICCADILLY CIRCUS
PICCADILLY CIRCUS
WHITEHALL
HM, ALL QUIET ON THE WESTERN FRONT.
WHITEHALL FORWARD COMMAND & CONTROL
HELLO?
TEK TEK TEK
RED BOOK. RIGHT.
NO UNAUTHORISED ADMITTANCE
RED BOOK ONLY
LET'S SEE WHAT ALL THE FUSS IS ABOUT, SHALL WE?
OH, MY...

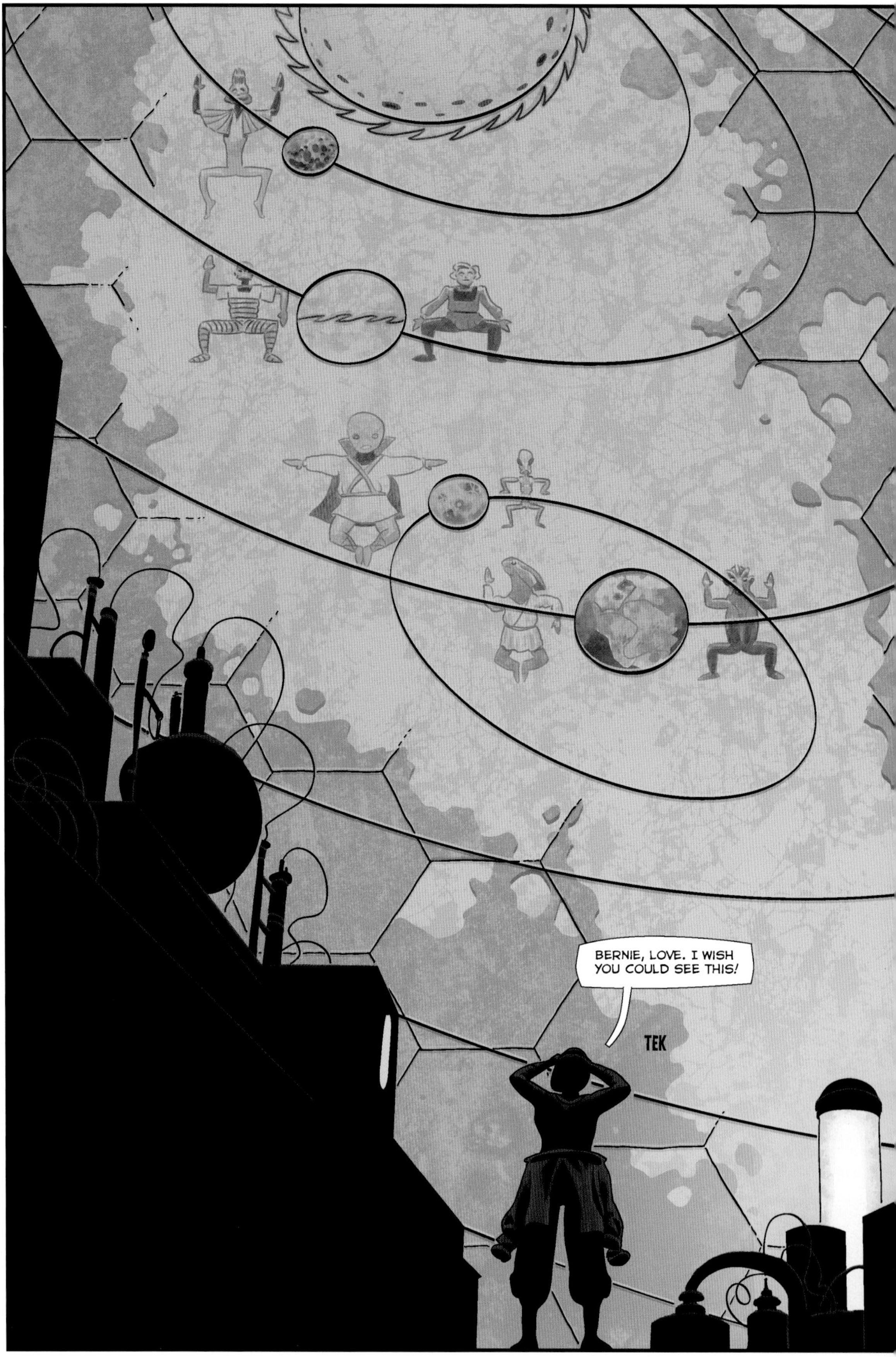
BERNIE, LOVE. I WISH YOU COULD SEE THIS!
TEK

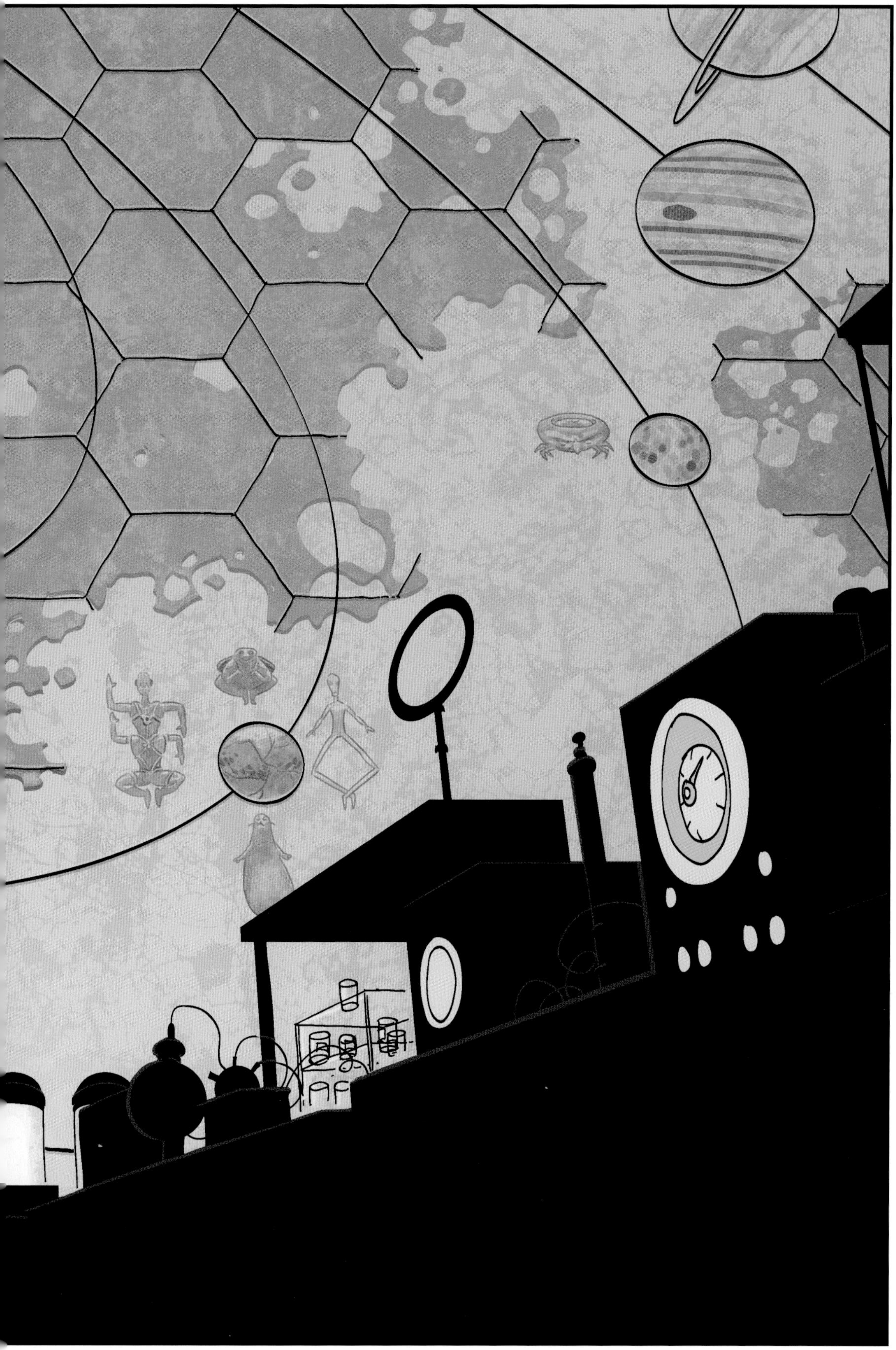

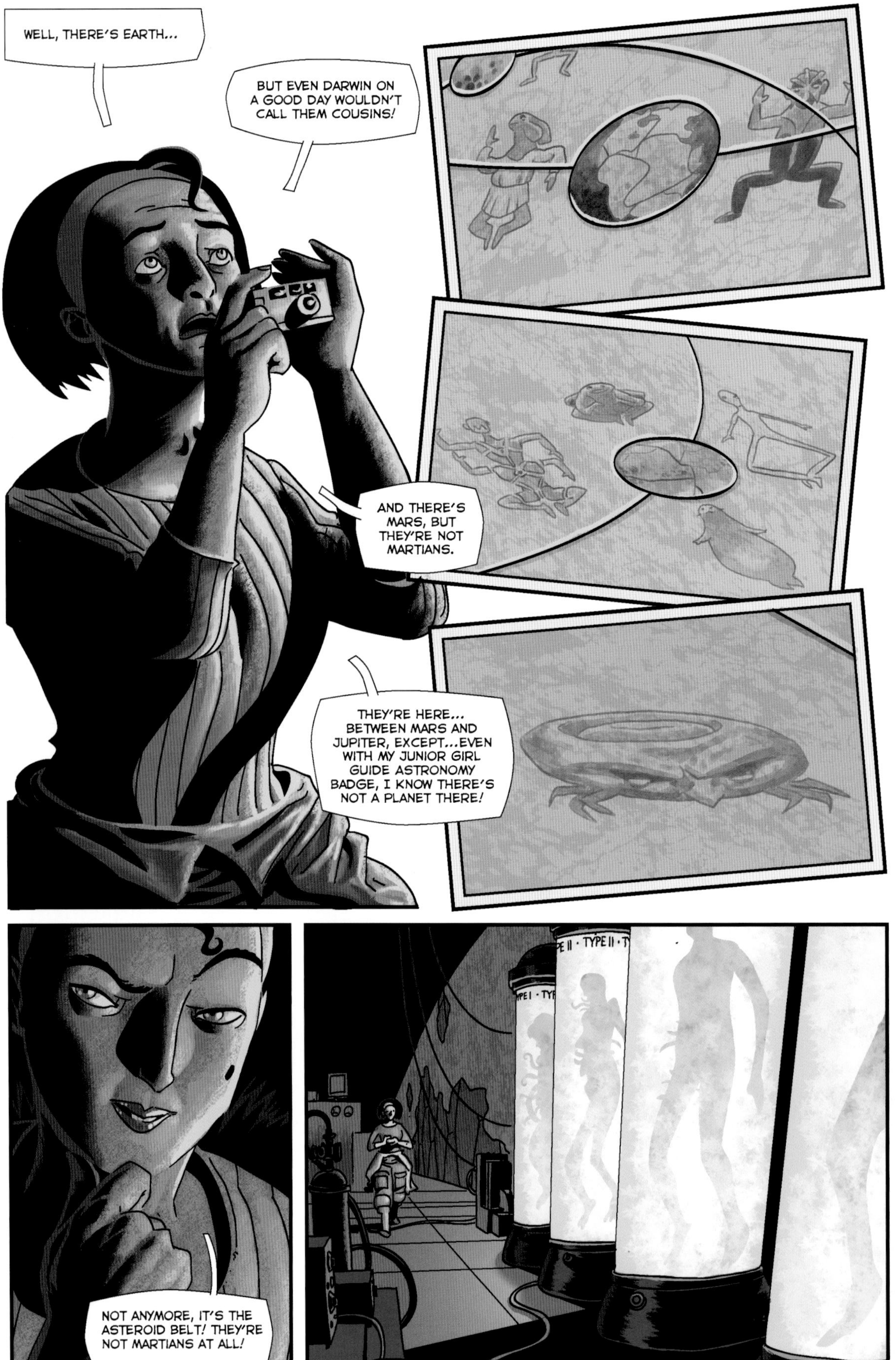
WELL, THERE'S EARTH...
BUT EVEN DARWIN ON A GOOD DAY WOULDN'T CALL THEM COUSINS!
AND THERE'S MARS, BUT THEY'RE NOT MARTIANS.
THEY'RE HERE... BETWEEN MARS AND JUPITER, EXCEPT...EVEN WITH MY JUNIOR GIRL GUIDE ASTRONOMY BADGE, I KNOW THERE'S NOT A PLANET THERE!
NOT ANYMORE, IT'S THE ASTEROID BELT! THEY'RE NOT MARTIANS AT ALL!
TYPE I · TYPE
TYPE II · TYPE II · T

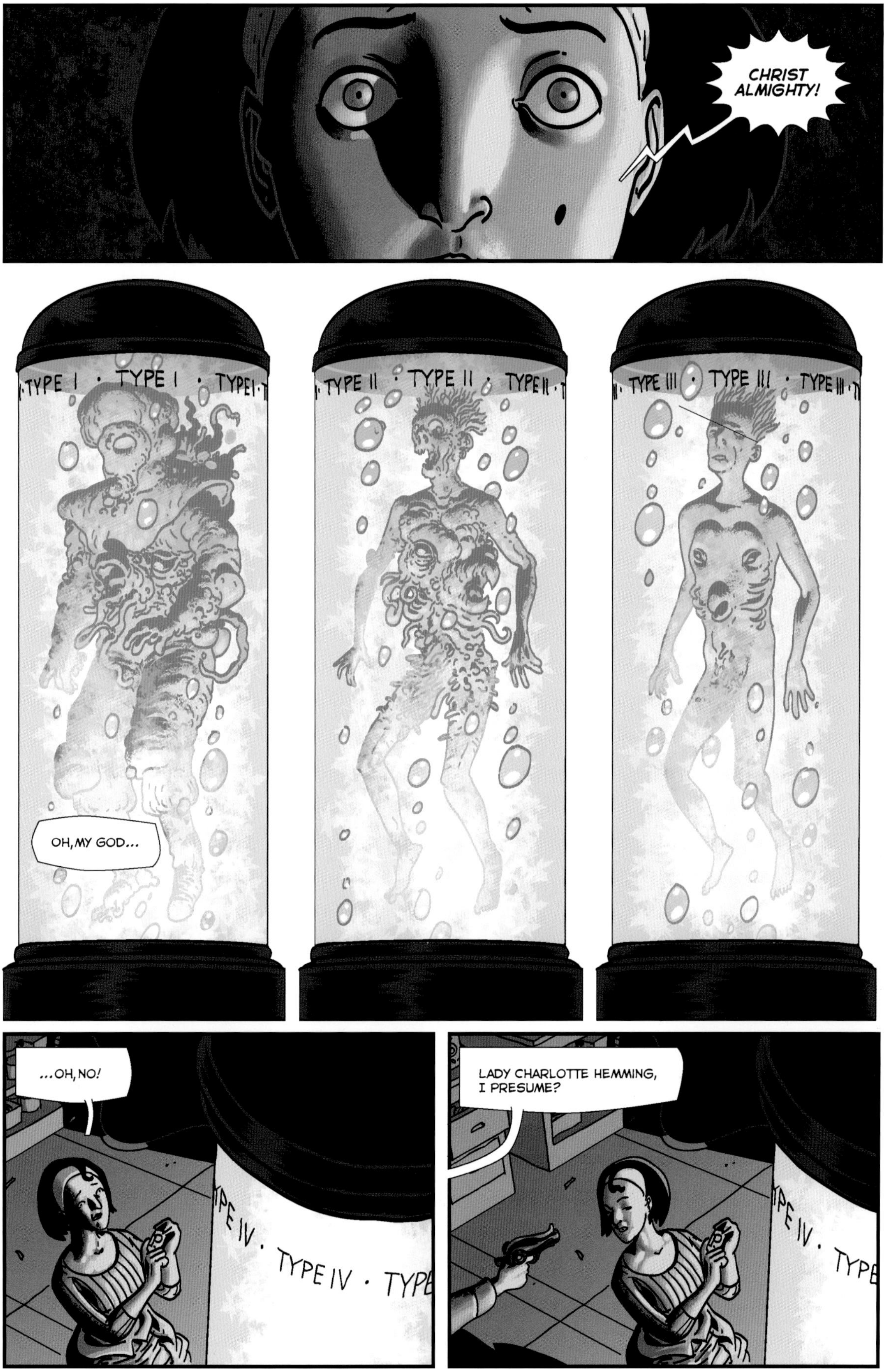
CHRIST ALMIGHTY!
TYPE I · TYPE I · TYPE I
TYPE II · TYPE II · TYPE II
TYPE III · TYPE III · TYPE III
OH, MY GOD...
...OH, NO!
TYPE IV · TYPE IV · TYPE
LADY CHARLOTTE HEMMING, I PRESUME?
TYPE IV · TYPE

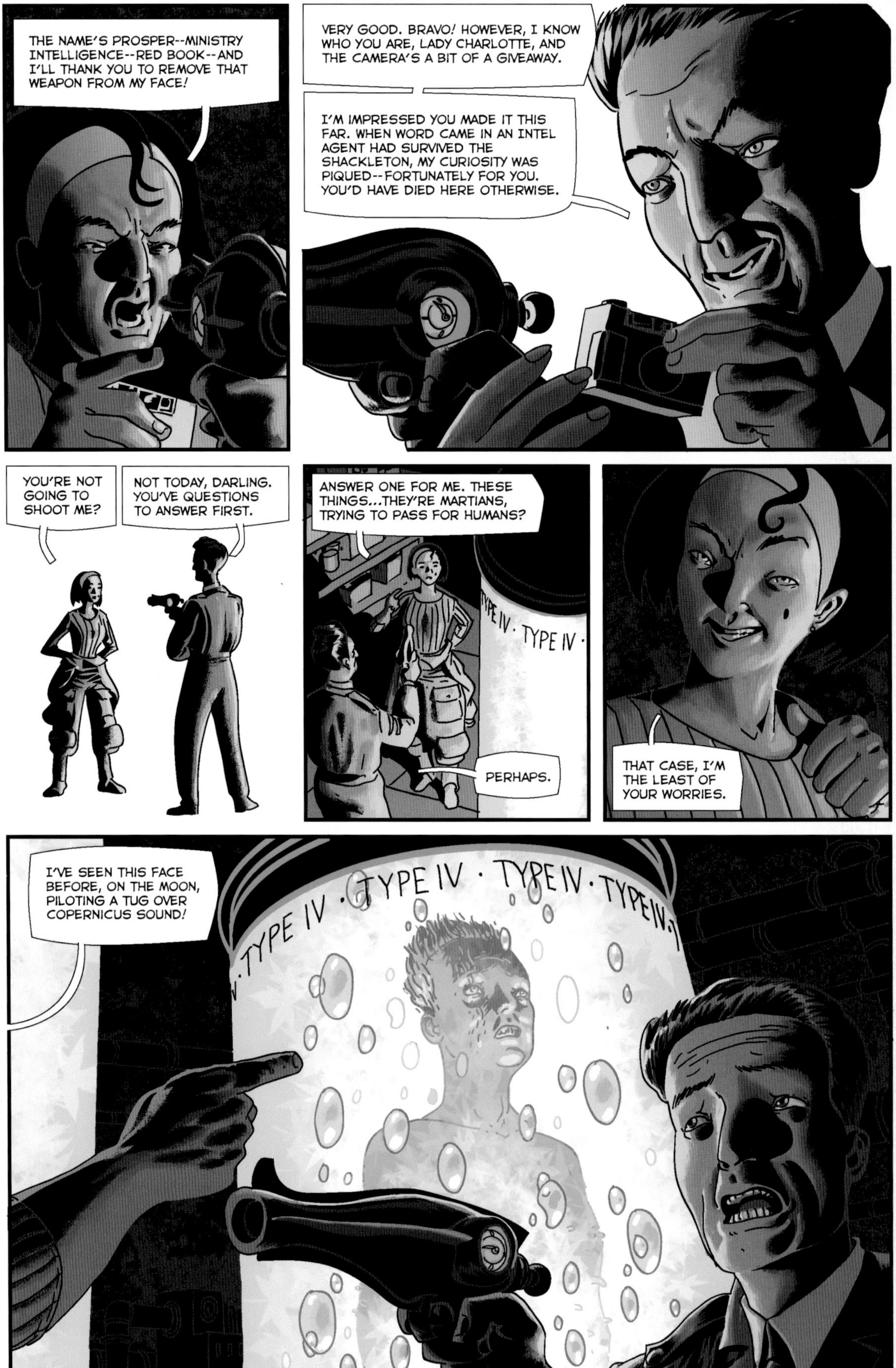
THE NAME'S PROSPER--MINISTRY INTELLIGENCE--RED BOOK--AND I'LL THANK YOU TO REMOVE THAT WEAPON FROM MY FACE!
VERY GOOD. BRAVO! HOWEVER, I KNOW WHO YOU ARE, LADY CHARLOTTE, AND THE CAMERA'S A BIT OF A GIVEAWAY.
I'M IMPRESSED YOU MADE IT THIS FAR. WHEN WORD CAME IN AN INTEL AGENT HAD SURVIVED THE SHACKLETON, MY CURIOSITY WAS PIQUED--FORTUNATELY FOR YOU. YOU'D HAVE DIED HERE OTHERWISE.
YOU'RE NOT GOING TO SHOOT ME?
NOT TODAY, DARLING. YOU'VE QUESTIONS TO ANSWER FIRST.
ANSWER ONE FOR ME. THESE THINGS...THEY'RE MARTIANS, TRYING TO PASS FOR HUMANS?
TYPE IV · TYPE IV ·
PERHAPS.
THAT CASE, I'M THE LEAST OF YOUR WORRIES.
I'VE SEEN THIS FACE BEFORE, ON THE MOON, PILOTING A TUG OVER COPERNICUS SOUND!
TYPE IV · TYPE IV · TYPE IV · TYPE IV ·

CHAPTER FOUR

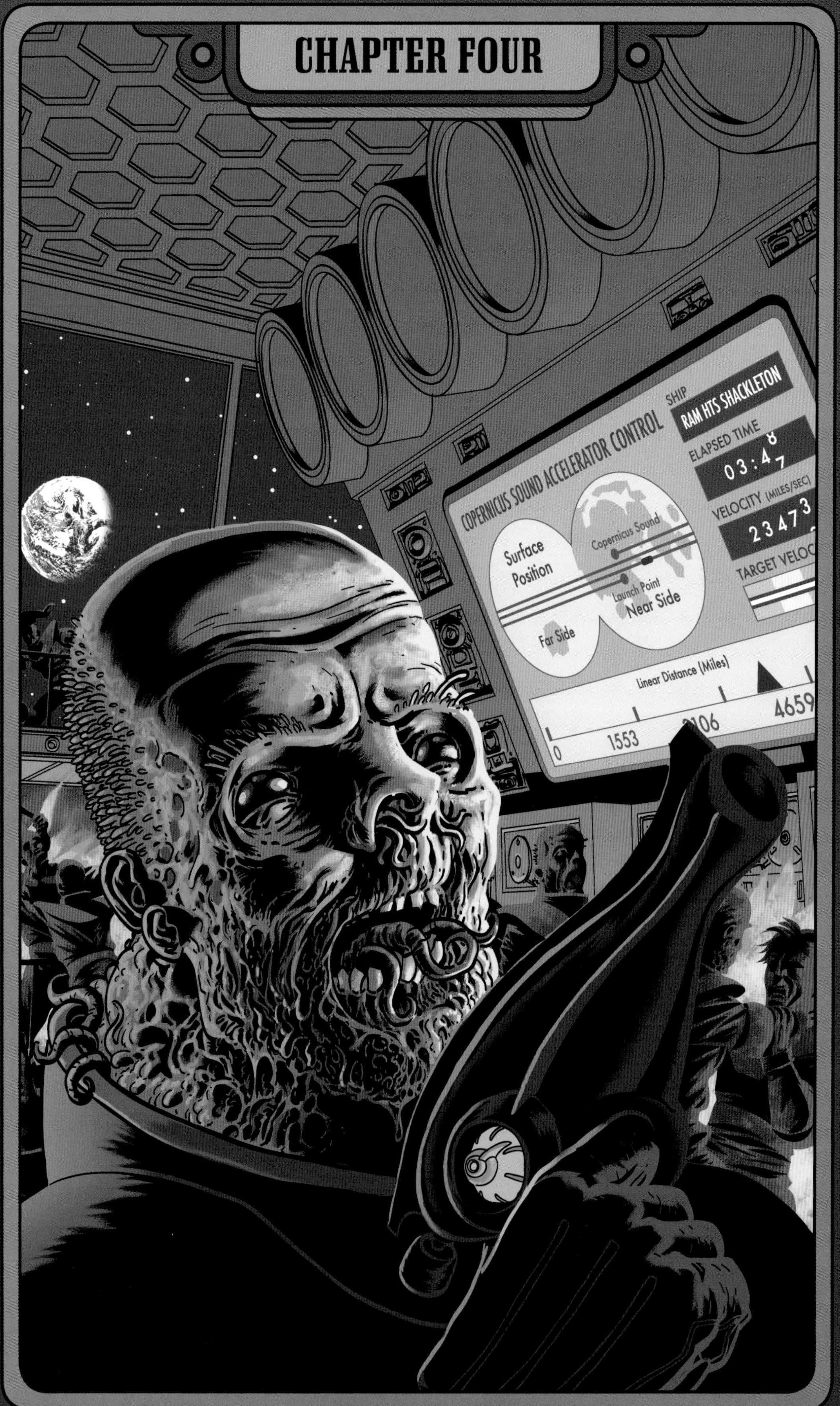

COPERNICUS SOUND ACCELERATOR CONTROL
SHIP
RAM HTS SHACKLETON
ELAPSED TIME
VELOCITY (MILES/SEC)
Surface Position
Copernicus Sound
Launch Point
Near Side
Far Side
Linear Distance (Miles)
0
1553
4659

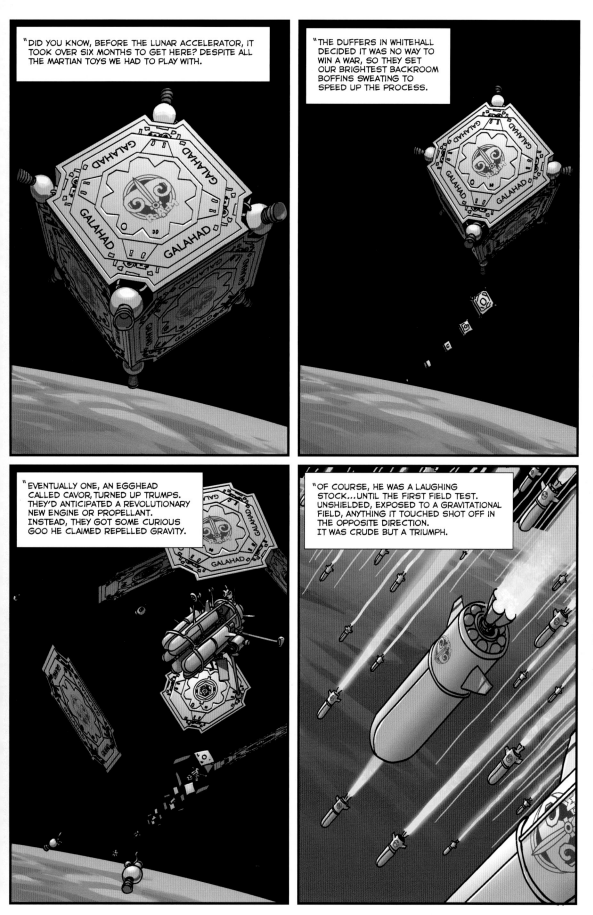

"DID YOU KNOW, BEFORE THE LUNAR ACCELERATOR, IT TOOK OVER SIX MONTHS TO GET HERE? DESPITE ALL THE MARTIAN TOYS WE HAD TO PLAY WITH.

"THE DUFFERS IN WHITEHALL DECIDED IT WAS NO WAY TO WIN A WAR, SO THEY SET OUR BRIGHTEST BACKROOM BOFFINS SWEATING TO SPEED UP THE PROCESS.

"EVENTUALLY ONE, AN EGGHEAD CALLED CAVOR, TURNED UP TRUMPS. THEY'D ANTICIPATED A REVOLUTIONARY NEW ENGINE OR PROPELLANT. INSTEAD, THEY GOT SOME CURIOUS GOO HE CLAIMED REPELLED GRAVITY.

"OF COURSE, HE WAS A LAUGHING STOCK...UNTIL THE FIRST FIELD TEST. UNSHIELDED, EXPOSED TO A GRAVITATIONAL FIELD, ANYTHING IT TOUCHED SHOT OFF IN THE OPPOSITE DIRECTION. IT WAS CRUDE BUT A TRIUMPH.

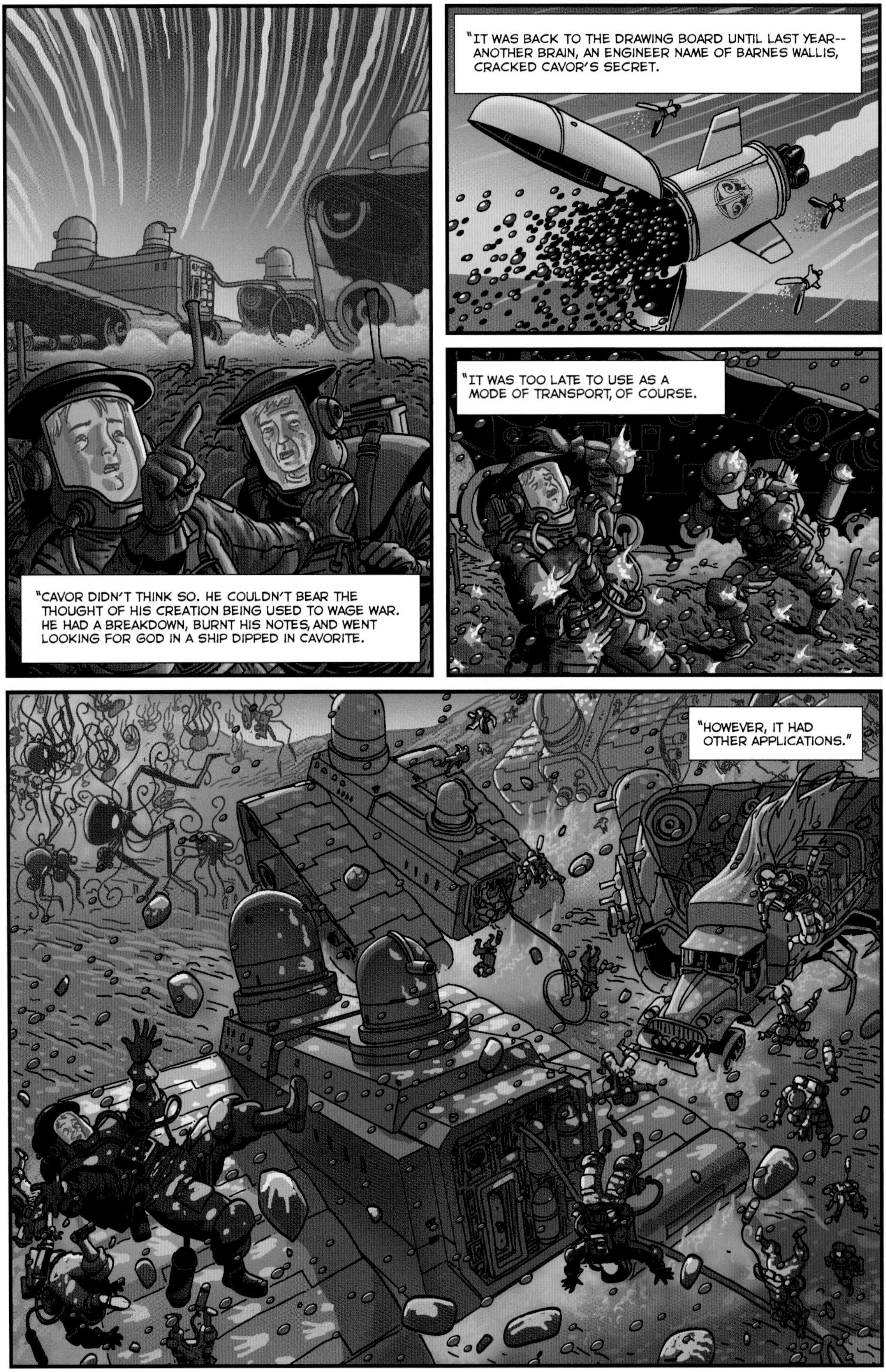
"CAVOR DIDN'T THINK SO. HE COULDN'T BEAR THE THOUGHT OF HIS CREATION BEING USED TO WAGE WAR. HE HAD A BREAKDOWN, BURNT HIS NOTES, AND WENT LOOKING FOR GOD IN A SHIP DIPPED IN CAVORITE.
"IT WAS BACK TO THE DRAWING BOARD UNTIL LAST YEAR-- ANOTHER BRAIN, AN ENGINEER NAME OF BARNES WALLIS, CRACKED CAVOR'S SECRET.
"IT WAS TOO LATE TO USE AS A MODE OF TRANSPORT, OF COURSE.
"HOWEVER, IT HAD OTHER APPLICATIONS."

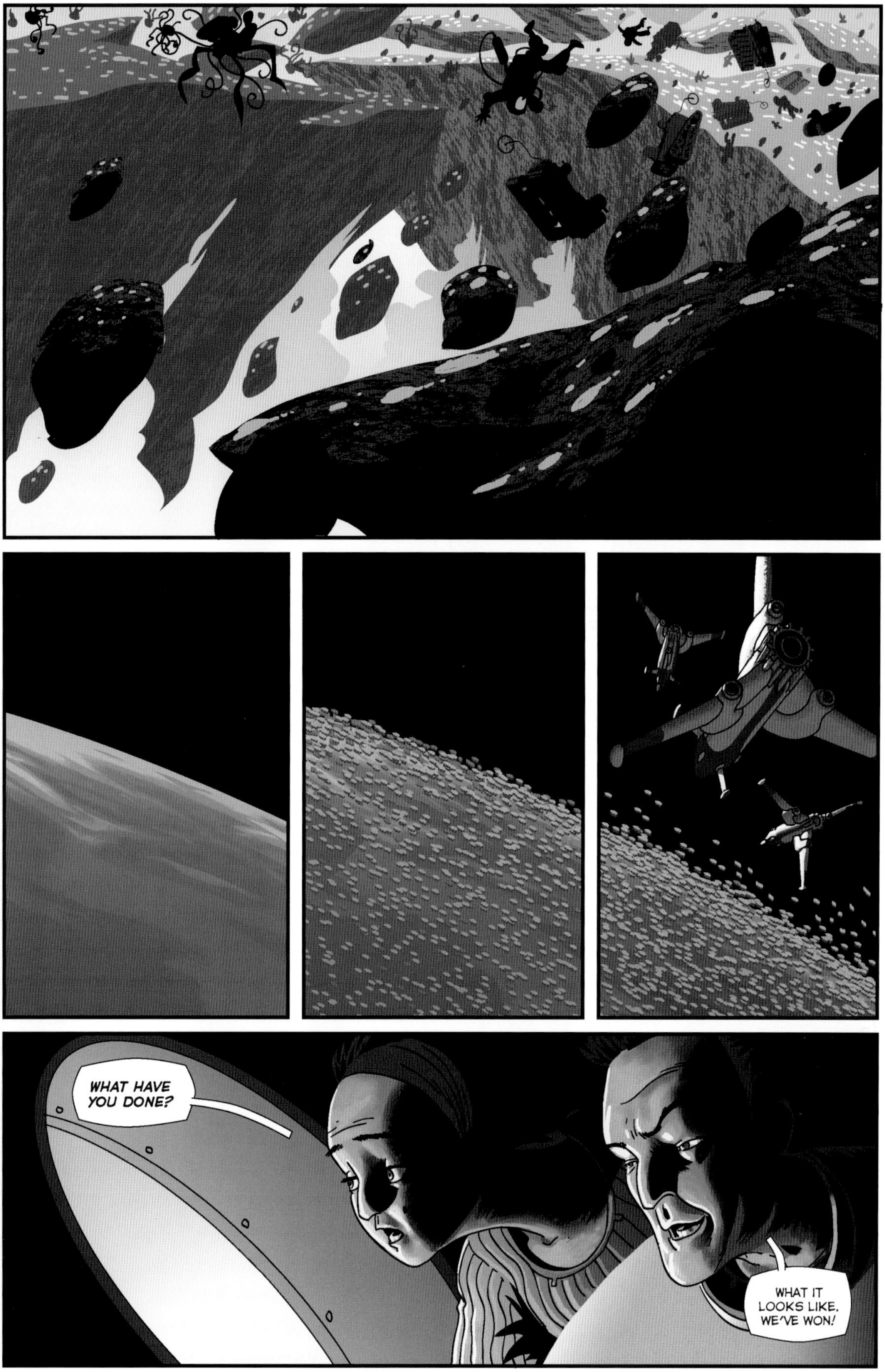
WHAT HAVE YOU DONE?
WHAT IT LOOKS LIKE. WE'VE WON!

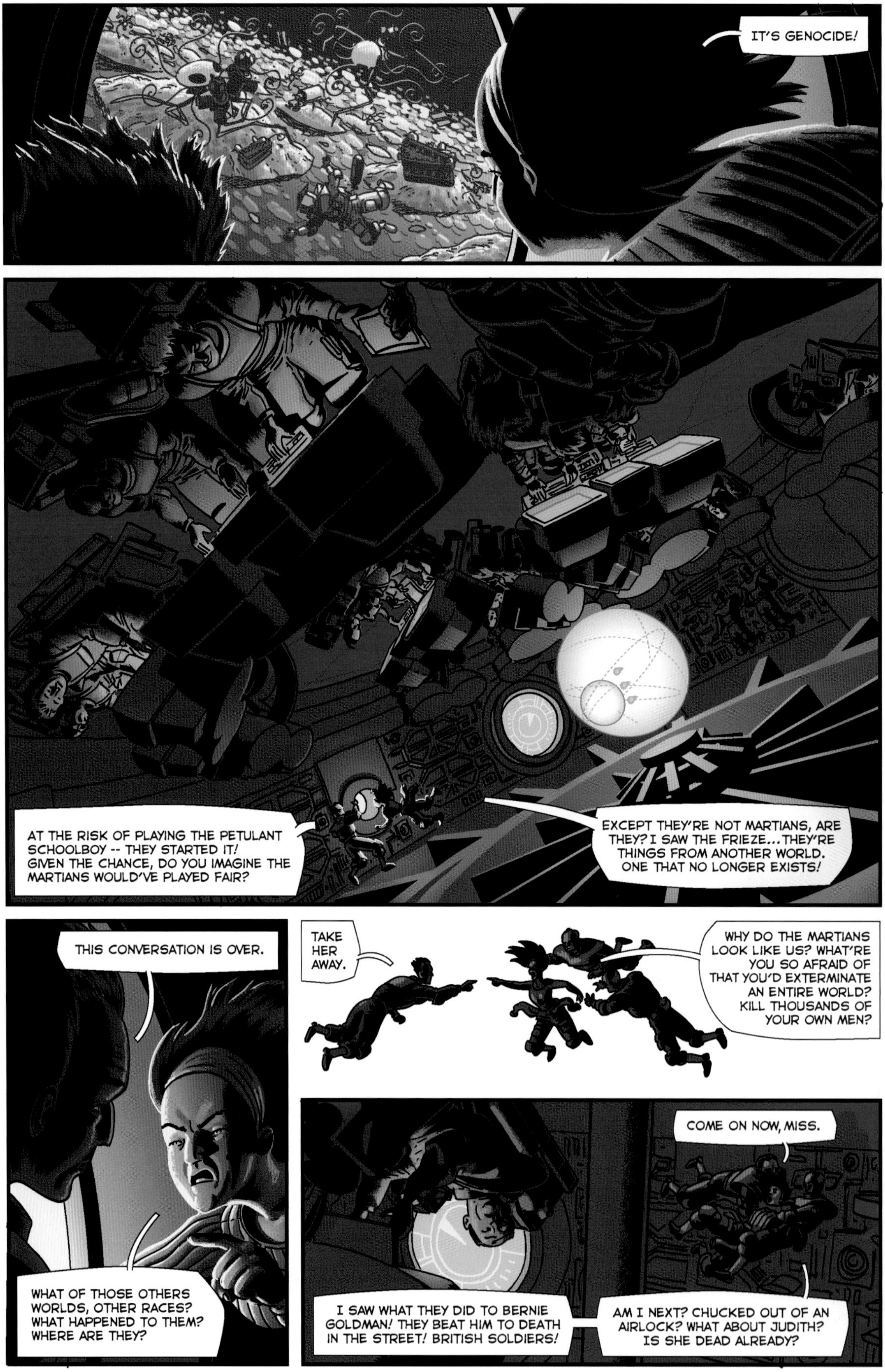
IT'S GENOCIDE!
AT THE RISK OF PLAYING THE PETULANT SCHOOLBOY -- THEY STARTED IT! GIVEN THE CHANCE, DO YOU IMAGINE THE MARTIANS WOULD'VE PLAYED FAIR?
EXCEPT THEY'RE NOT MARTIANS, ARE THEY? I SAW THE FRIEZE... THEY'RE THINGS FROM ANOTHER WORLD. ONE THAT NO LONGER EXISTS!
THIS CONVERSATION IS OVER.
WHAT OF THOSE OTHERS WORLDS, OTHER RACES? WHAT HAPPENED TO THEM? WHERE ARE THEY?
TAKE HER AWAY.
WHY DO THE MARTIANS LOOK LIKE US? WHAT'RE YOU SO AFRAID OF THAT YOU'D EXTERMINATE AN ENTIRE WORLD? KILL THOUSANDS OF YOUR OWN MEN?
COME ON NOW, MISS.
I SAW WHAT THEY DID TO BERNIE GOLDMAN! THEY BEAT HIM TO DEATH IN THE STREET! BRITISH SOLDIERS!
AM I NEXT? CHUCKED OUT OF AN AIRLOCK? WHAT ABOUT JUDITH? IS SHE DEAD ALREADY?

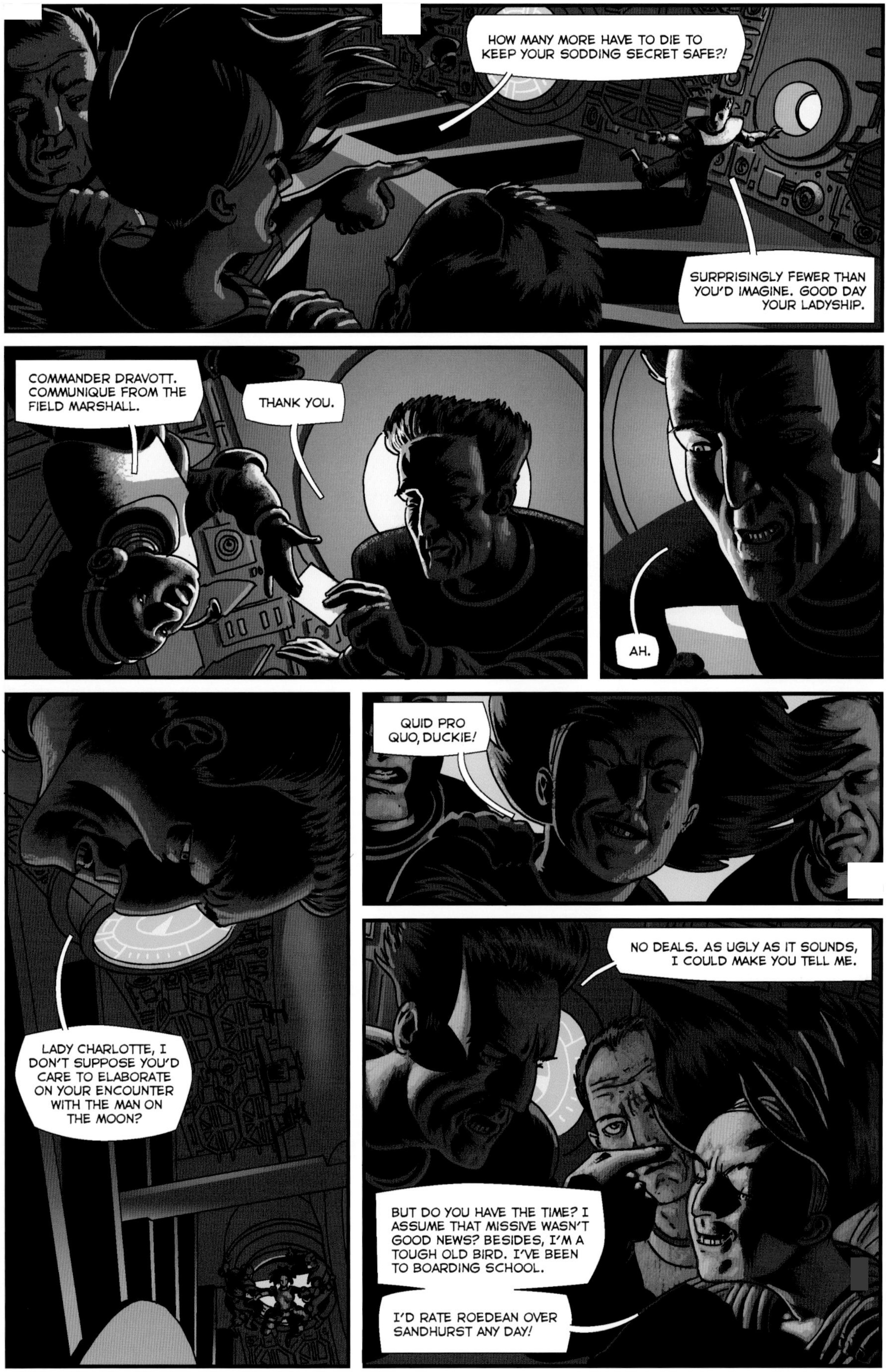
HOW MANY MORE HAVE TO DIE TO KEEP YOUR SODDING SECRET SAFE?!
SURPRISINGLY FEWER THAN YOU'D IMAGINE. GOOD DAY YOUR LADYSHIP.
COMMANDER DRAVOTT. COMMUNIQUE FROM THE FIELD MARSHALL.
THANK YOU.
AH.
LADY CHARLOTTE, I DON'T SUPPOSE YOU'D CARE TO ELABORATE ON YOUR ENCOUNTER WITH THE MAN ON THE MOON?
QUID PRO QUO, DUCKIE!
NO DEALS. AS UGLY AS IT SOUNDS, I COULD MAKE YOU TELL ME.
BUT DO YOU HAVE THE TIME? I ASSUME THAT MISSIVE WASN'T GOOD NEWS? BESIDES, I'M A TOUGH OLD BIRD. I'VE BEEN TO BOARDING SCHOOL.
I'D RATE ROEDEAN OVER SANDHURST ANY DAY!

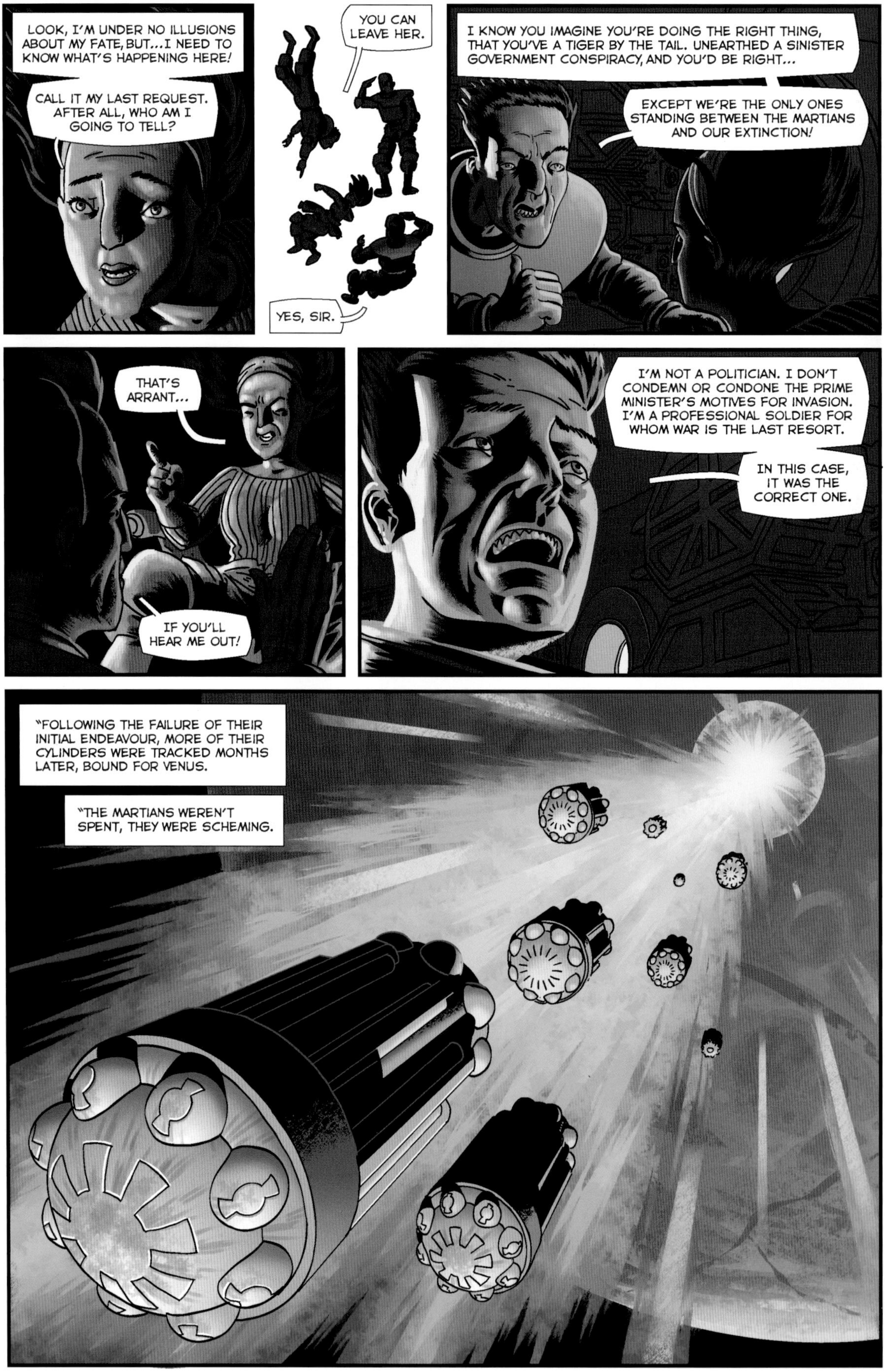
LOOK, I'M UNDER NO ILLUSIONS ABOUT MY FATE, BUT...I NEED TO KNOW WHAT'S HAPPENING HERE!
CALL IT MY LAST REQUEST. AFTER ALL, WHO AM I GOING TO TELL?
YOU CAN LEAVE HER.
YES, SIR.
I KNOW YOU IMAGINE YOU'RE DOING THE RIGHT THING, THAT YOU'VE A TIGER BY THE TAIL. UNEARTHED A SINISTER GOVERNMENT CONSPIRACY, AND YOU'D BE RIGHT...
EXCEPT WE'RE THE ONLY ONES STANDING BETWEEN THE MARTIANS AND OUR EXTINCTION!
THAT'S ARRANT...
IF YOU'LL HEAR ME OUT!
I'M NOT A POLITICIAN. I DON'T CONDEMN OR CONDONE THE PRIME MINISTER'S MOTIVES FOR INVASION. I'M A PROFESSIONAL SOLDIER FOR WHOM WAR IS THE LAST RESORT.
IN THIS CASE, IT WAS THE CORRECT ONE.
"FOLLOWING THE FAILURE OF THEIR INITIAL ENDEAVOUR, MORE OF THEIR CYLINDERS WERE TRACKED MONTHS LATER, BOUND FOR VENUS.
"THE MARTIANS WEREN'T SPENT, THEY WERE SCHEMING.

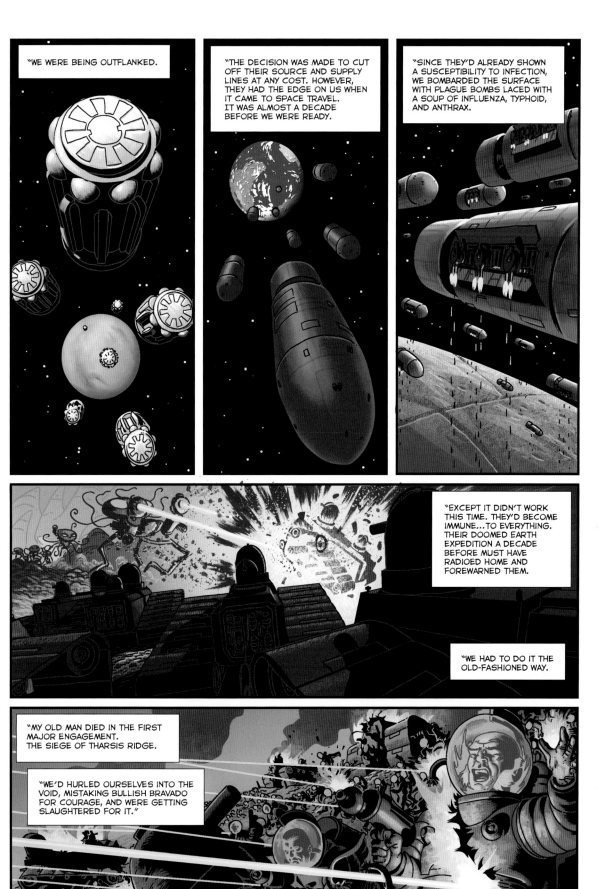

"WE WERE BEING OUTFLANKED.

"THE DECISION WAS MADE TO CUT OFF THEIR SOURCE AND SUPPLY LINES AT ANY COST. HOWEVER, THEY HAD THE EDGE ON US WHEN IT CAME TO SPACE TRAVEL. IT WAS ALMOST A DECADE BEFORE WE WERE READY.

"SINCE THEY'D ALREADY SHOWN A SUSCEPTIBILITY TO INFECTION, WE BOMBARDED THE SURFACE WITH PLAGUE BOMBS LACED WITH A SOUP OF INFLUENZA, TYPHOID, AND ANTHRAX.

"EXCEPT IT DIDN'T WORK THIS TIME. THEY'D BECOME IMMUNE...TO EVERYTHING. THEIR DOOMED EARTH EXPEDITION A DECADE BEFORE MUST HAVE RADIOED HOME AND FOREWARNED THEM.

"WE HAD TO DO IT THE OLD-FASHIONED WAY.

"MY OLD MAN DIED IN THE FIRST MAJOR ENGAGEMENT. THE SIEGE OF THARSIS RIDGE.

"WE'D HURLED OURSELVES INTO THE VOID, MISTAKING BULLISH BRAVADO FOR COURAGE, AND WERE GETTING SLAUGHTERED FOR IT."

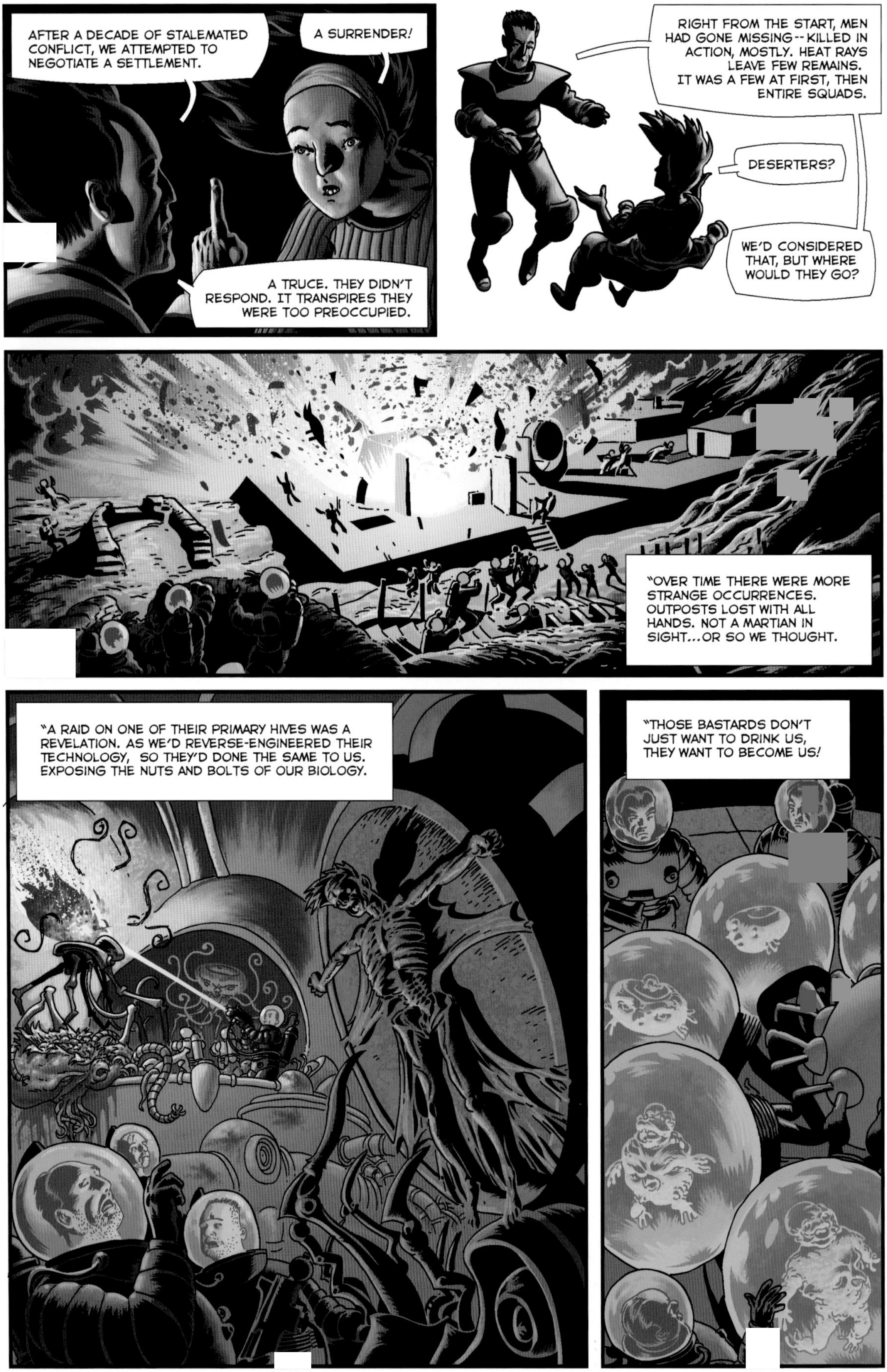
AFTER A DECADE OF STALEMATED CONFLICT, WE ATTEMPTED TO NEGOTIATE A SETTLEMENT.
A SURRENDER!
A TRUCE. THEY DIDN'T RESPOND. IT TRANSPIRES THEY WERE TOO PREOCCUPIED.
RIGHT FROM THE START, MEN HAD GONE MISSING--KILLED IN ACTION, MOSTLY. HEAT RAYS LEAVE FEW REMAINS. IT WAS A FEW AT FIRST, THEN ENTIRE SQUADS.
DESERTERS?
WE'D CONSIDERED THAT, BUT WHERE WOULD THEY GO?
"OVER TIME THERE WERE MORE STRANGE OCCURRENCES. OUTPOSTS LOST WITH ALL HANDS. NOT A MARTIAN IN SIGHT...OR SO WE THOUGHT.
"A RAID ON ONE OF THEIR PRIMARY HIVES WAS A REVELATION. AS WE'D REVERSE-ENGINEERED THEIR TECHNOLOGY, SO THEY'D DONE THE SAME TO US. EXPOSING THE NUTS AND BOLTS OF OUR BIOLOGY.
"THOSE BASTARDS DON'T JUST WANT TO DRINK US, THEY WANT TO BECOME US!

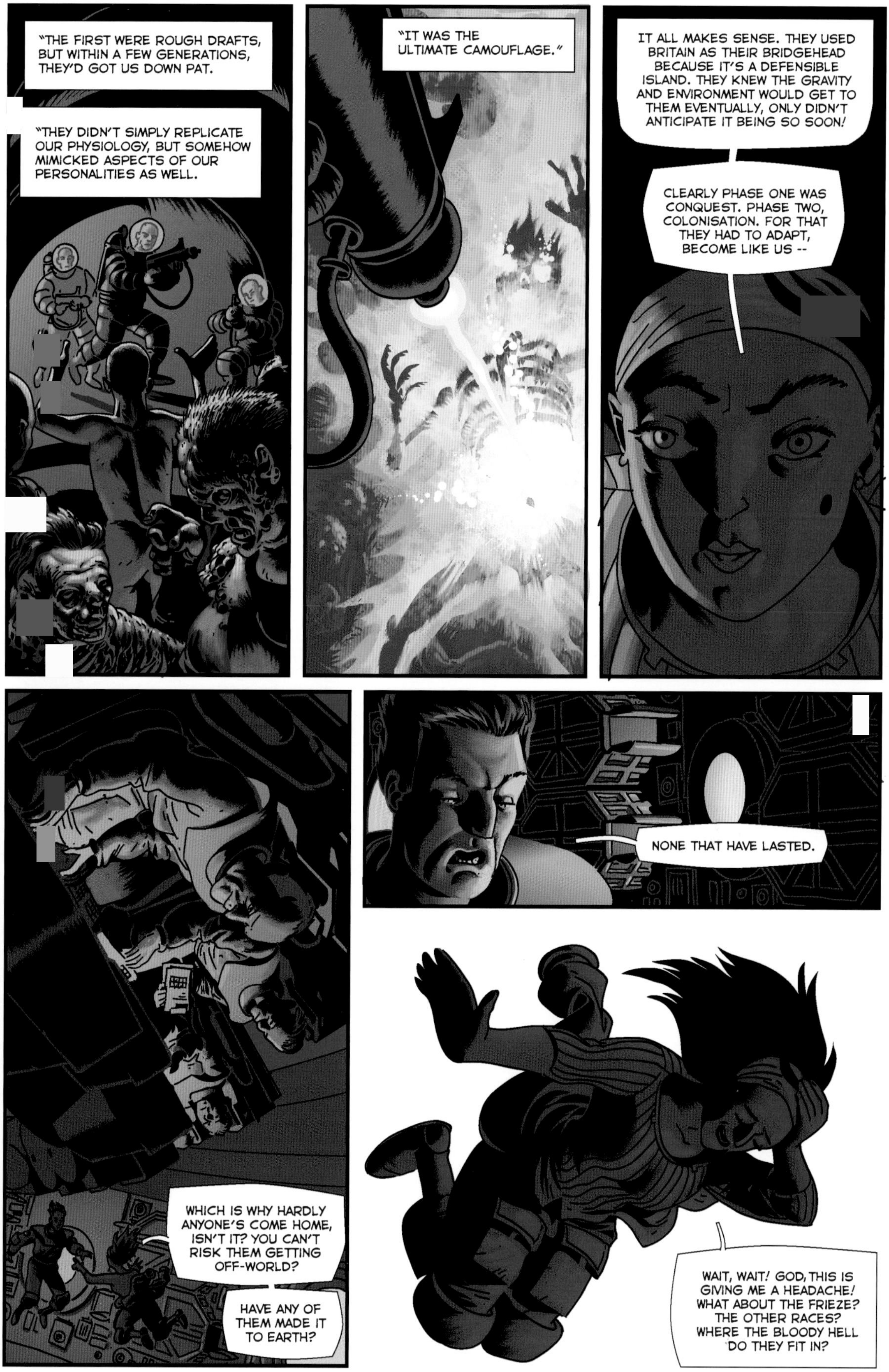
"THE FIRST WERE ROUGH DRAFTS, BUT WITHIN A FEW GENERATIONS, THEY'D GOT US DOWN PAT.
"THEY DIDN'T SIMPLY REPLICATE OUR PHYSIOLOGY, BUT SOMEHOW MIMICKED ASPECTS OF OUR PERSONALITIES AS WELL.
"IT WAS THE ULTIMATE CAMOUFLAGE."
IT ALL MAKES SENSE. THEY USED BRITAIN AS THEIR BRIDGEHEAD BECAUSE IT'S A DEFENSIBLE ISLAND. THEY KNEW THE GRAVITY AND ENVIRONMENT WOULD GET TO THEM EVENTUALLY, ONLY DIDN'T ANTICIPATE IT BEING SO SOON!
CLEARLY PHASE ONE WAS CONQUEST. PHASE TWO, COLONISATION. FOR THAT THEY HAD TO ADAPT, BECOME LIKE US --
WHICH IS WHY HARDLY ANYONE'S COME HOME, ISN'T IT? YOU CAN'T RISK THEM GETTING OFF-WORLD?
HAVE ANY OF THEM MADE IT TO EARTH?
NONE THAT HAVE LASTED.
WAIT, WAIT! GOD, THIS IS GIVING ME A HEADACHE! WHAT ABOUT THE FRIEZE? THE OTHER RACES? WHERE THE BLOODY HELL DO THEY FIT IN?

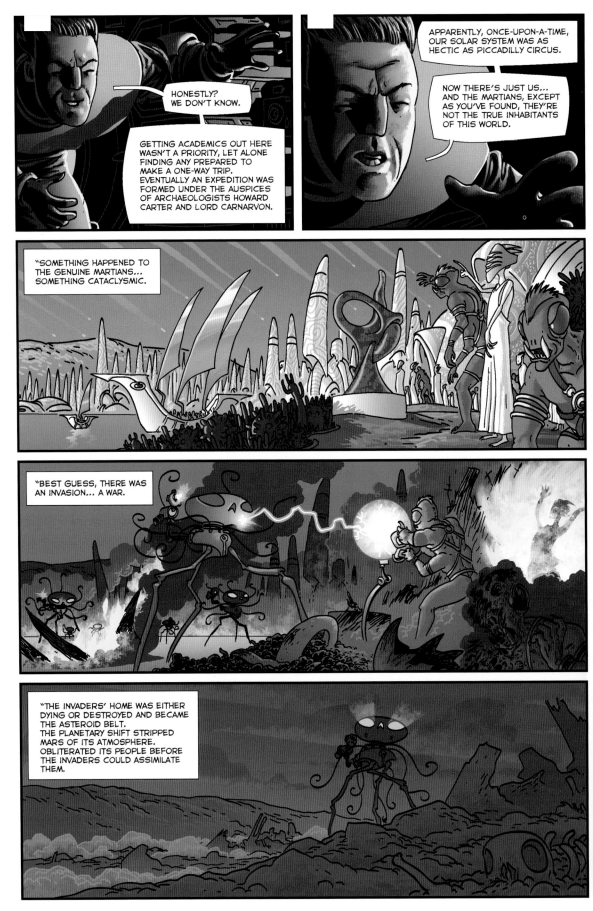

HONESTLY?
WE DON'T KNOW.

APPARENTLY, ONCE-UPON-A-TIME, OUR SOLAR SYSTEM WAS AS HECTIC AS PICCADILLY CIRCUS.

GETTING ACADEMICS OUT HERE WASN'T A PRIORITY, LET ALONE FINDING ANY PREPARED TO MAKE A ONE-WAY TRIP. EVENTUALLY AN EXPEDITION WAS FORMED UNDER THE AUSPICES OF ARCHAEOLOGISTS HOWARD CARTER AND LORD CARNARVON.

NOW THERE'S JUST US... AND THE MARTIANS, EXCEPT AS YOU'VE FOUND, THEY'RE NOT THE TRUE INHABITANTS OF THIS WORLD.

"SOMETHING HAPPENED TO THE GENUINE MARTIANS... SOMETHING CATACLYSMIC.

"BEST GUESS, THERE WAS AN INVASION... A WAR.

"THE INVADERS' HOME WAS EITHER DYING OR DESTROYED AND BECAME THE ASTEROID BELT.
THE PLANETARY SHIFT STRIPPED MARS OF ITS ATMOSPHERE.
OBLITERATED ITS PEOPLE BEFORE THE INVADERS COULD ASSIMILATE THEM.

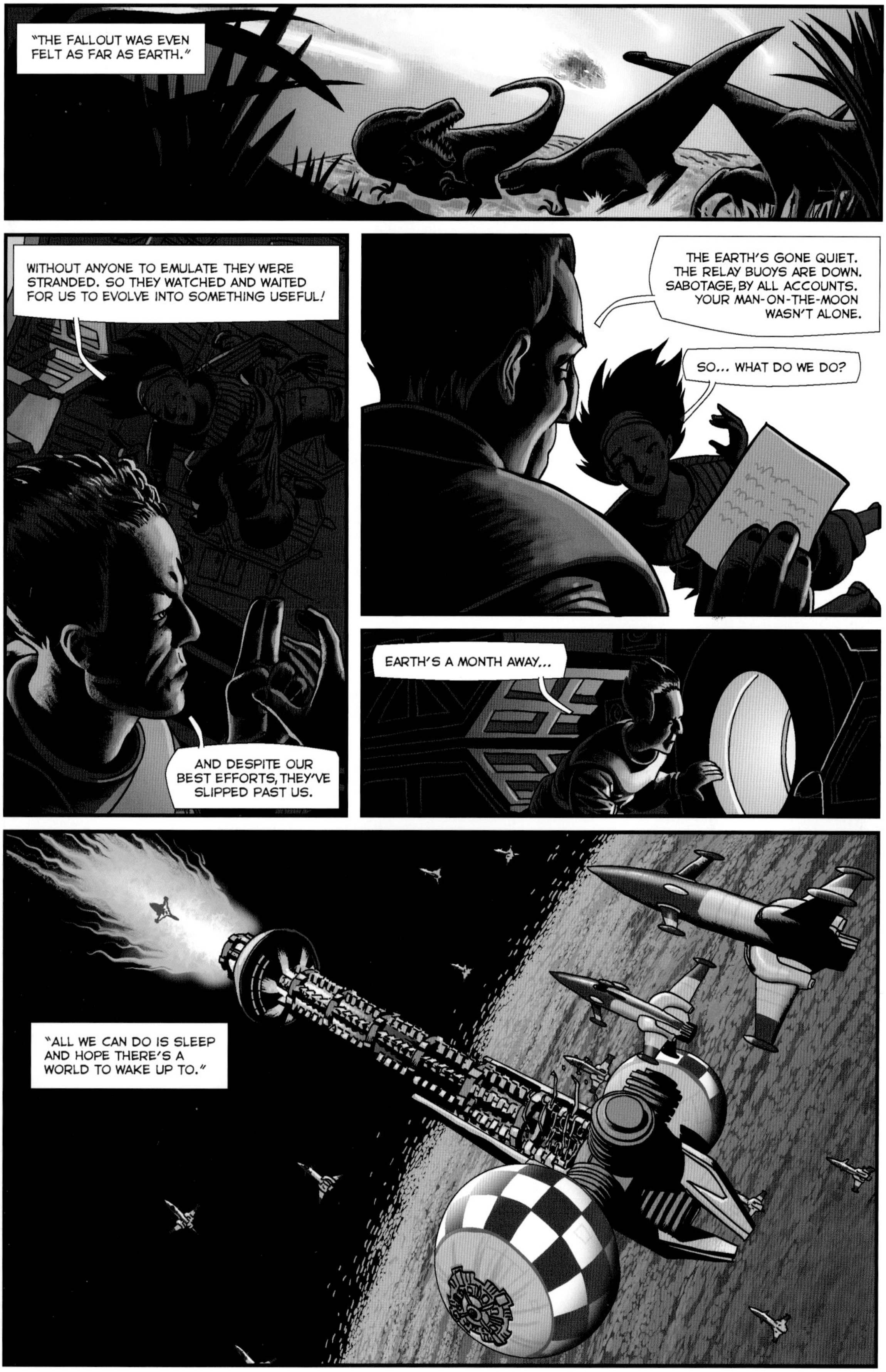
"THE FALLOUT WAS EVEN FELT AS FAR AS EARTH."
WITHOUT ANYONE TO EMULATE THEY WERE STRANDED. SO THEY WATCHED AND WAITED FOR US TO EVOLVE INTO SOMETHING USEFUL!
AND DESPITE OUR BEST EFFORTS, THEY'VE SLIPPED PAST US.
THE EARTH'S GONE QUIET. THE RELAY BUOYS ARE DOWN. SABOTAGE, BY ALL ACCOUNTS. YOUR MAN-ON-THE-MOON WASN'T ALONE.
SO... WHAT DO WE DO?
EARTH'S A MONTH AWAY...
"ALL WE CAN DO IS SLEEP AND HOPE THERE'S A WORLD TO WAKE UP TO."

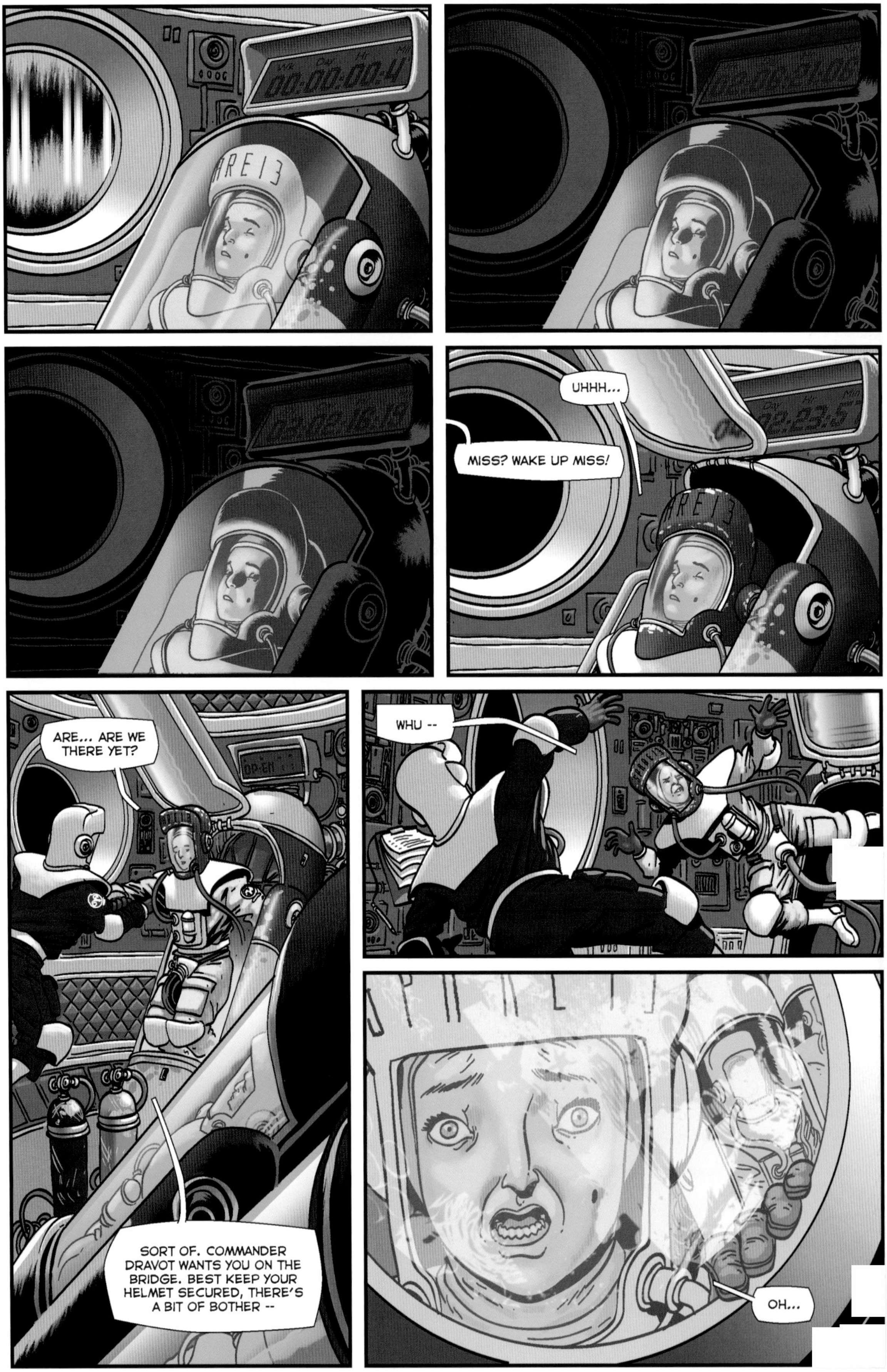

UHHH...
MISS? WAKE UP MISS!
ARE... ARE WE THERE YET?
SORT OF. COMMANDER DRAVOT WANTS YOU ON THE BRIDGE. BEST KEEP YOUR HELMET SECURED, THERE'S A BIT OF BOTHER --
WHU --
OH...

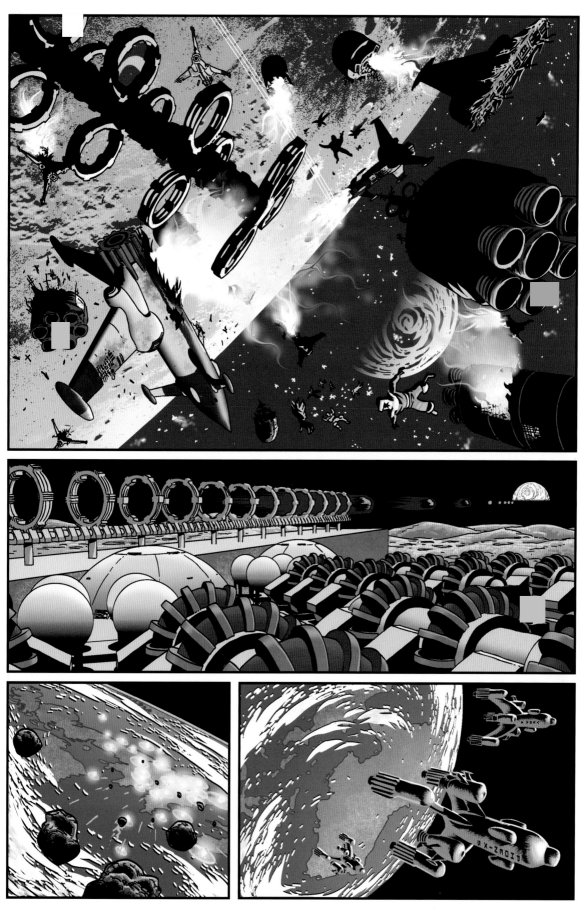

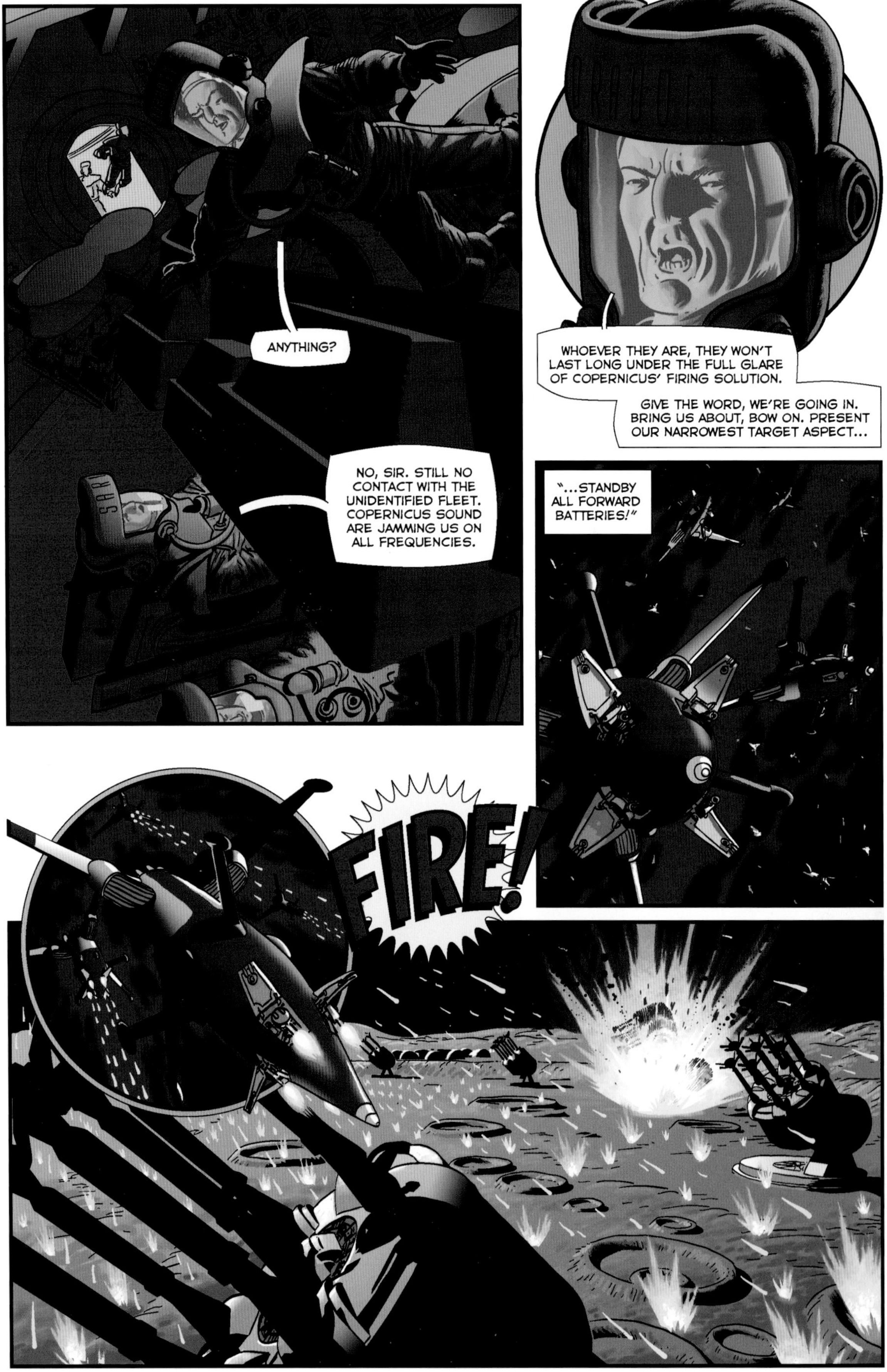
ANYTHING?
NO, SIR. STILL NO CONTACT WITH THE UNIDENTIFIED FLEET. COPERNICUS SOUND ARE JAMMING US ON ALL FREQUENCIES.
WHOEVER THEY ARE, THEY WON'T LAST LONG UNDER THE FULL GLARE OF COPERNICUS' FIRING SOLUTION.
GIVE THE WORD, WE'RE GOING IN. BRING US ABOUT, BOW ON. PRESENT OUR NARROWEST TARGET ASPECT...
"...STANDBY ALL FORWARD BATTERIES!"
FIRE!

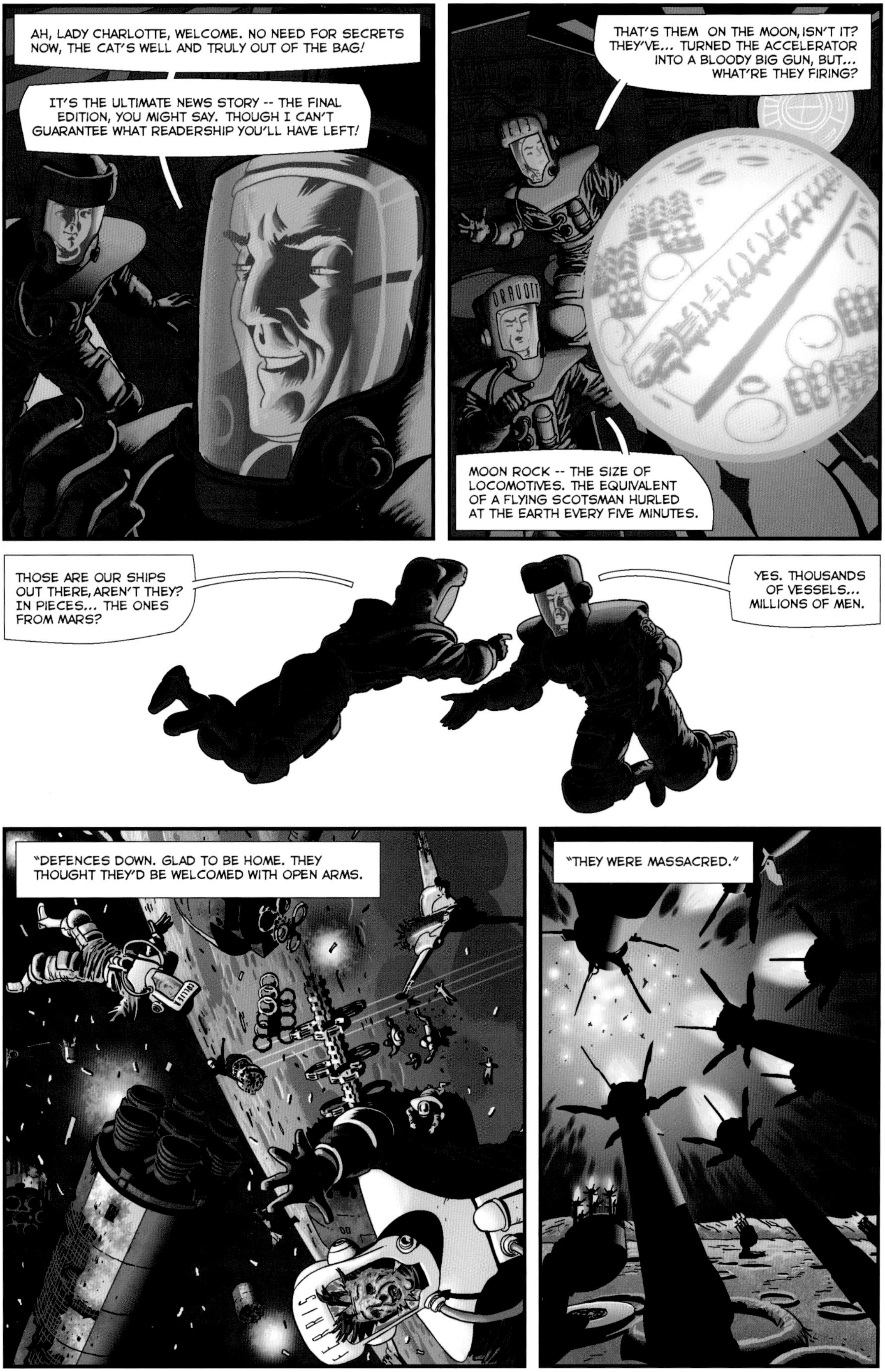

AH, LADY CHARLOTTE, WELCOME. NO NEED FOR SECRETS NOW, THE CAT'S WELL AND TRULY OUT OF THE BAG!
IT'S THE ULTIMATE NEWS STORY -- THE FINAL EDITION, YOU MIGHT SAY. THOUGH I CAN'T GUARANTEE WHAT READERSHIP YOU'LL HAVE LEFT!
THAT'S THEM ON THE MOON, ISN'T IT? THEY'VE... TURNED THE ACCELERATOR INTO A BLOODY BIG GUN, BUT... WHAT'RE THEY FIRING?
MOON ROCK -- THE SIZE OF LOCOMOTIVES. THE EQUIVALENT OF A FLYING SCOTSMAN HURLED AT THE EARTH EVERY FIVE MINUTES.
THOSE ARE OUR SHIPS OUT THERE, AREN'T THEY? IN PIECES... THE ONES FROM MARS?
YES. THOUSANDS OF VESSELS... MILLIONS OF MEN.
"DEFENCES DOWN. GLAD TO BE HOME. THEY THOUGHT THEY'D BE WELCOMED WITH OPEN ARMS.
"THEY WERE MASSACRED."

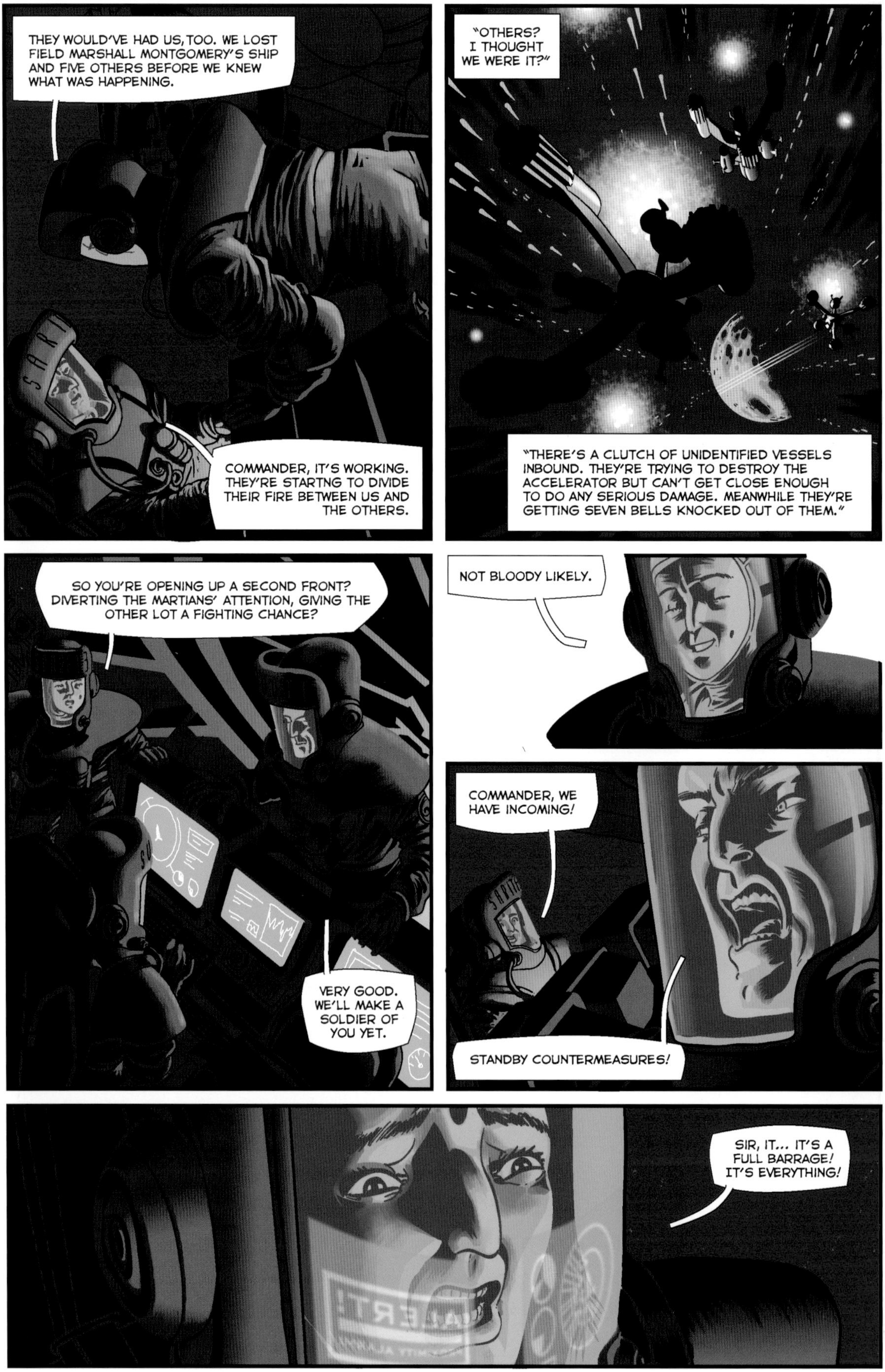
THEY WOULD'VE HAD US, TOO. WE LOST FIELD MARSHALL MONTGOMERY'S SHIP AND FIVE OTHERS BEFORE WE KNEW WHAT WAS HAPPENING.
COMMANDER, IT'S WORKING. THEY'RE STARTNG TO DIVIDE THEIR FIRE BETWEEN US AND THE OTHERS.
"OTHERS? I THOUGHT WE WERE IT?"
"THERE'S A CLUTCH OF UNIDENTIFIED VESSELS INBOUND. THEY'RE TRYING TO DESTROY THE ACCELERATOR BUT CAN'T GET CLOSE ENOUGH TO DO ANY SERIOUS DAMAGE. MEANWHILE THEY'RE GETTING SEVEN BELLS KNOCKED OUT OF THEM."
SO YOU'RE OPENING UP A SECOND FRONT? DIVERTING THE MARTIANS' ATTENTION, GIVING THE OTHER LOT A FIGHTING CHANCE?
VERY GOOD. WE'LL MAKE A SOLDIER OF YOU YET.
NOT BLOODY LIKELY.
COMMANDER, WE HAVE INCOMING!
STANDBY COUNTERMEASURES!
SIR, IT... IT'S A FULL BARRAGE! IT'S EVERYTHING!

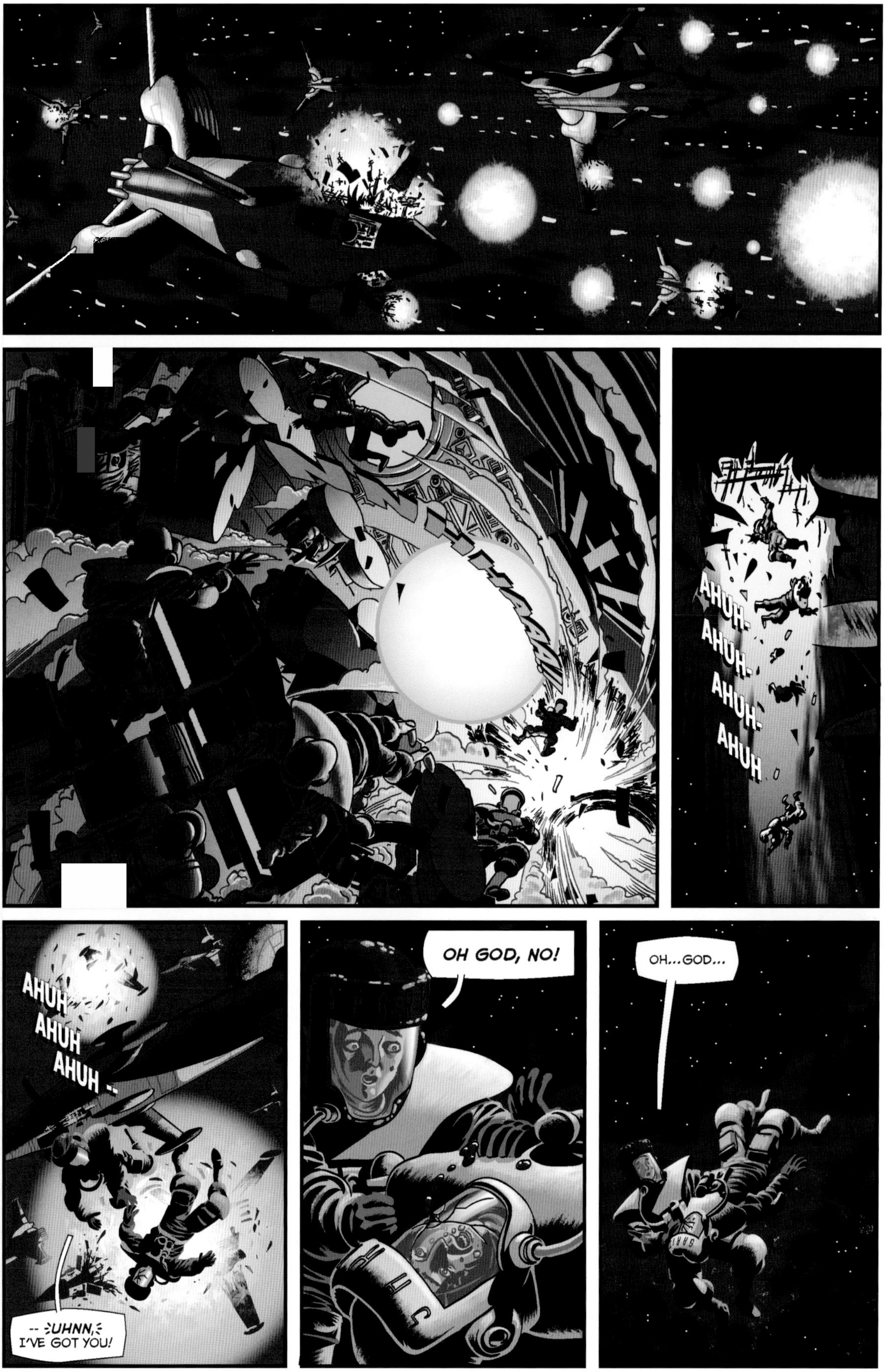
AHUH-
AHUH-
AHUH-
AHUH
AHUH
AHUH
AHUH --
-- UHNN, I'VE GOT YOU!
OH GOD, NO!
OH... GOD...

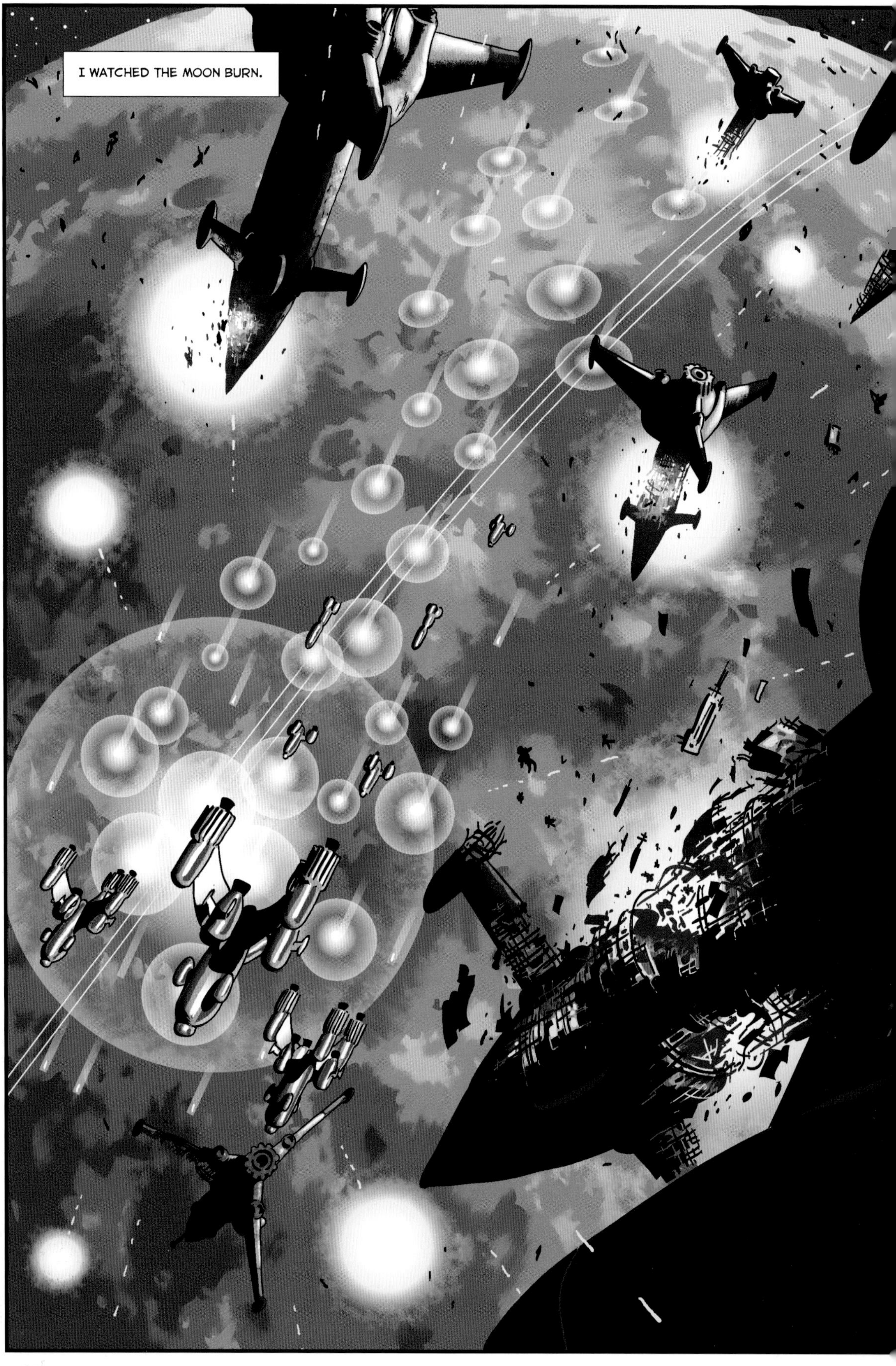
I WATCHED THE MOON BURN.

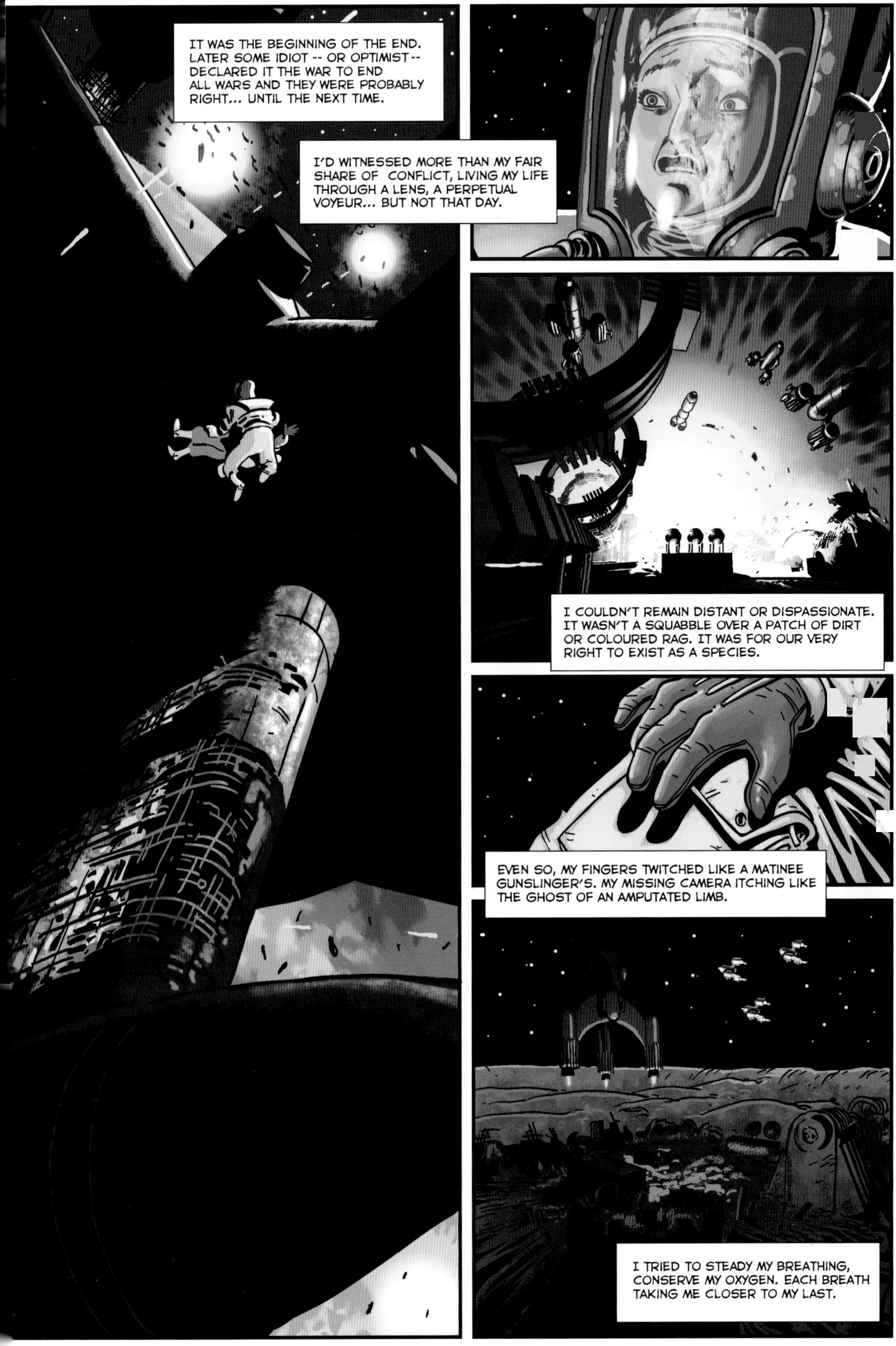

IT WAS THE BEGINNING OF THE END. LATER SOME IDIOT -- OR OPTIMIST -- DECLARED IT THE WAR TO END ALL WARS AND THEY WERE PROBABLY RIGHT... UNTIL THE NEXT TIME.
I'D WITNESSED MORE THAN MY FAIR SHARE OF CONFLICT, LIVING MY LIFE THROUGH A LENS, A PERPETUAL VOYEUR... BUT NOT THAT DAY.
I COULDN'T REMAIN DISTANT OR DISPASSIONATE. IT WASN'T A SQUABBLE OVER A PATCH OF DIRT OR COLOURED RAG. IT WAS FOR OUR VERY RIGHT TO EXIST AS A SPECIES.
EVEN SO, MY FINGERS TWITCHED LIKE A MATINEE GUNSLINGER'S. MY MISSING CAMERA ITCHING LIKE THE GHOST OF AN AMPUTATED LIMB.
I TRIED TO STEADY MY BREATHING, CONSERVE MY OXYGEN. EACH BREATH TAKING ME CLOSER TO MY LAST.

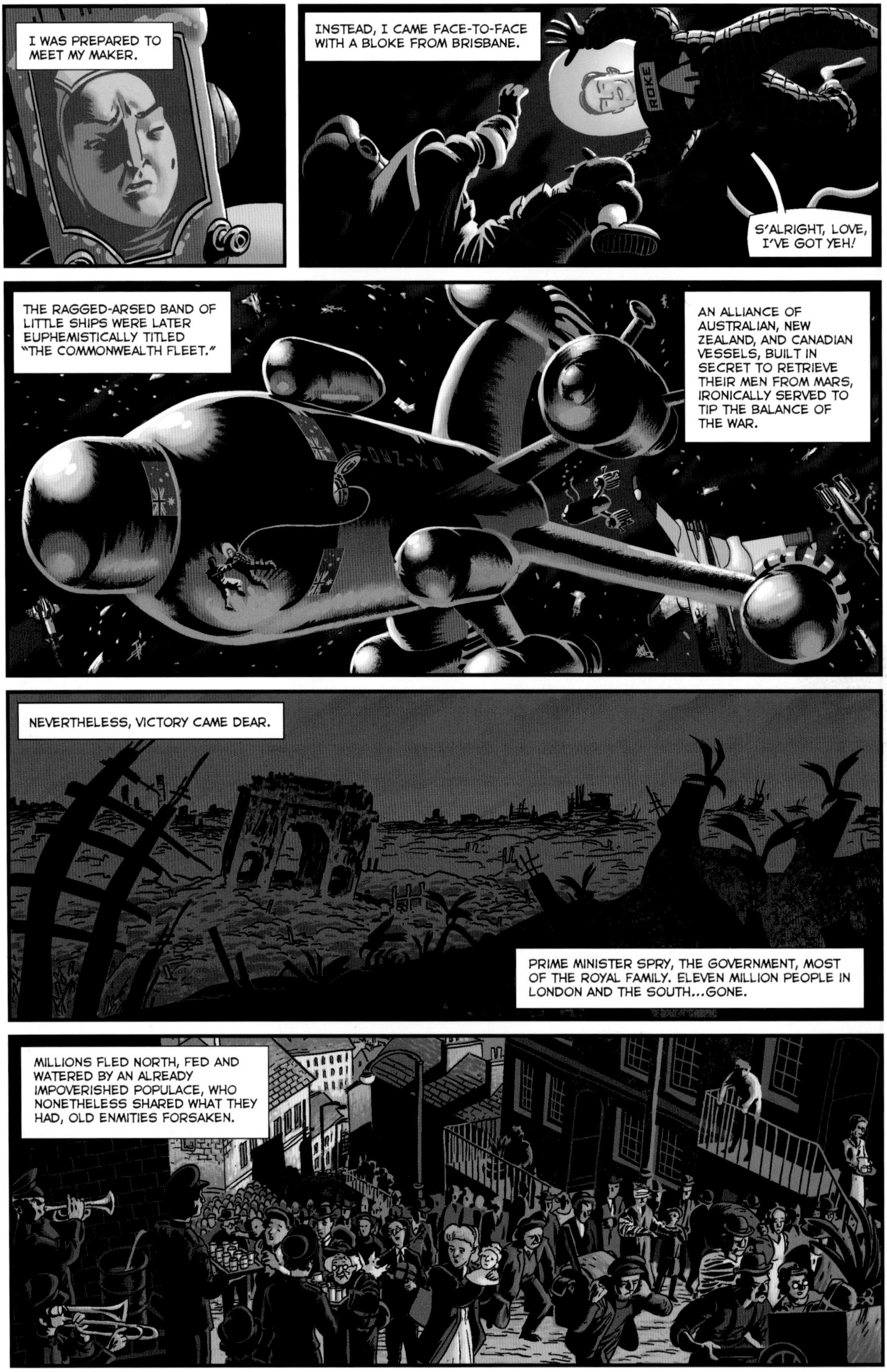
I WAS PREPARED TO MEET MY MAKER.
INSTEAD, I CAME FACE-TO-FACE WITH A BLOKE FROM BRISBANE.
ROKE
S'ALRIGHT, LOVE, I'VE GOT YEH!
THE RAGGED-ARSED BAND OF LITTLE SHIPS WERE LATER EUPHEMISTICALLY TITLED "THE COMMONWEALTH FLEET."
AN ALLIANCE OF AUSTRALIAN, NEW ZEALAND, AND CANADIAN VESSELS, BUILT IN SECRET TO RETRIEVE THEIR MEN FROM MARS, IRONICALLY SERVED TO TIP THE BALANCE OF THE WAR.
NEVERTHELESS, VICTORY CAME DEAR.
PRIME MINISTER SPRY, THE GOVERNMENT, MOST OF THE ROYAL FAMILY. ELEVEN MILLION PEOPLE IN LONDON AND THE SOUTH...GONE.
MILLIONS FLED NORTH, FED AND WATERED BY AN ALREADY IMPOVERISHED POPULACE, WHO NONETHELESS SHARED WHAT THEY HAD, OLD ENMITIES FORSAKEN.

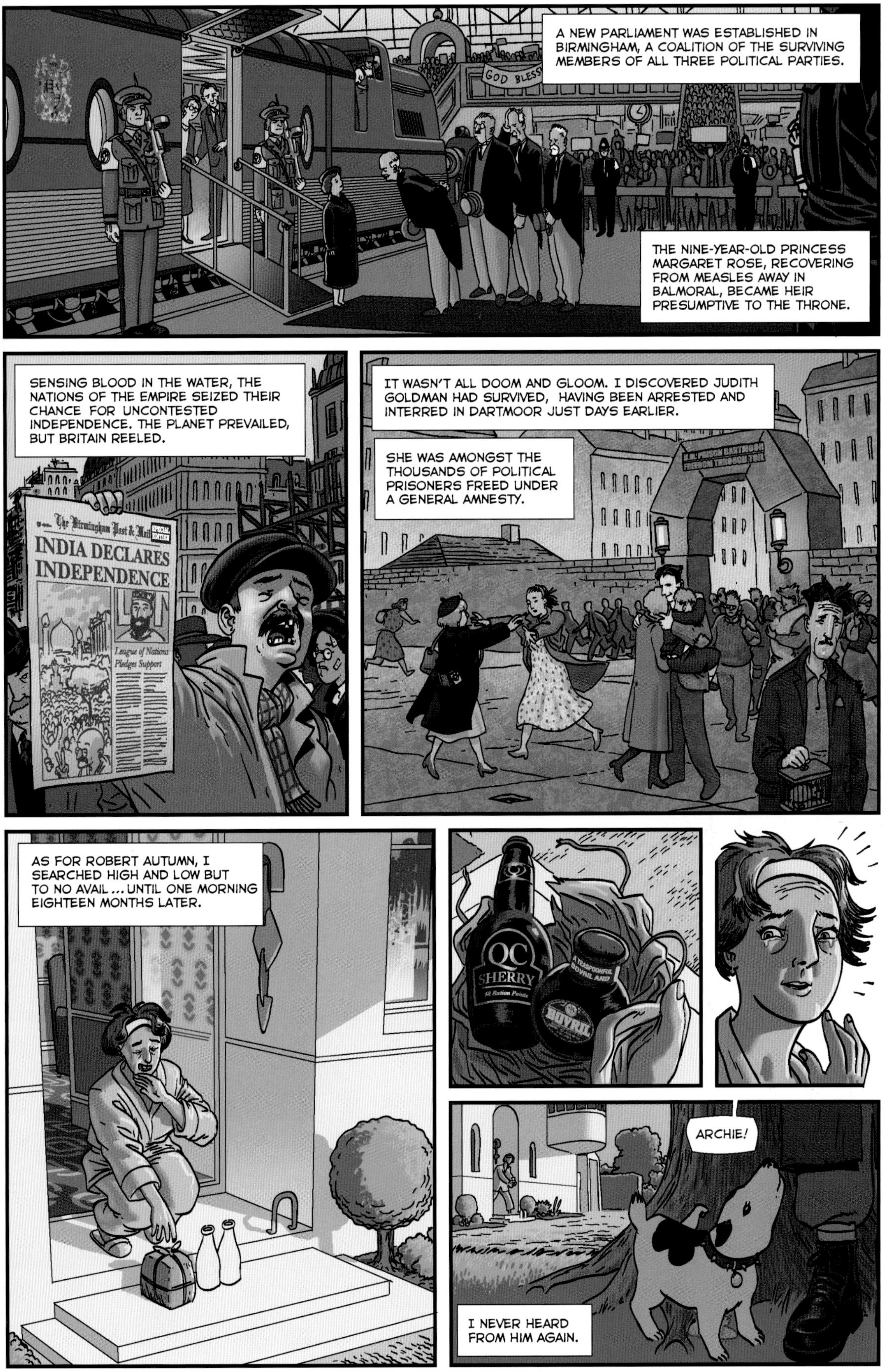
A NEW PARLIAMENT WAS ESTABLISHED IN BIRMINGHAM, A COALITION OF THE SURVIVING MEMBERS OF ALL THREE POLITICAL PARTIES.
GOD BLESS
THE NINE-YEAR-OLD PRINCESS MARGARET ROSE, RECOVERING FROM MEASLES AWAY IN BALMORAL, BECAME HEIR PRESUMPTIVE TO THE THRONE.
SENSING BLOOD IN THE WATER, THE NATIONS OF THE EMPIRE SEIZED THEIR CHANCE FOR UNCONTESTED INDEPENDENCE. THE PLANET PREVAILED, BUT BRITAIN REELED.
The Birmingham Post & Mail
SPECIAL EDITION
INDIA DECLARES INDEPENDENCE
League of Nations Pledges Support
IT WASN'T ALL DOOM AND GLOOM. I DISCOVERED JUDITH GOLDMAN HAD SURVIVED, HAVING BEEN ARRESTED AND INTERRED IN DARTMOOR JUST DAYS EARLIER.
SHE WAS AMONGST THE THOUSANDS OF POLITICAL PRISONERS FREED UNDER A GENERAL AMNESTY.
AS FOR ROBERT AUTUMN, I SEARCHED HIGH AND LOW BUT TO NO AVAIL ... UNTIL ONE MORNING EIGHTEEN MONTHS LATER.
QC
SHERRY
48 Ration Points
A TEASPOONFUL BOVRIL AND
BOVRIL
ARCHIE!
I NEVER HEARD FROM HIM AGAIN.

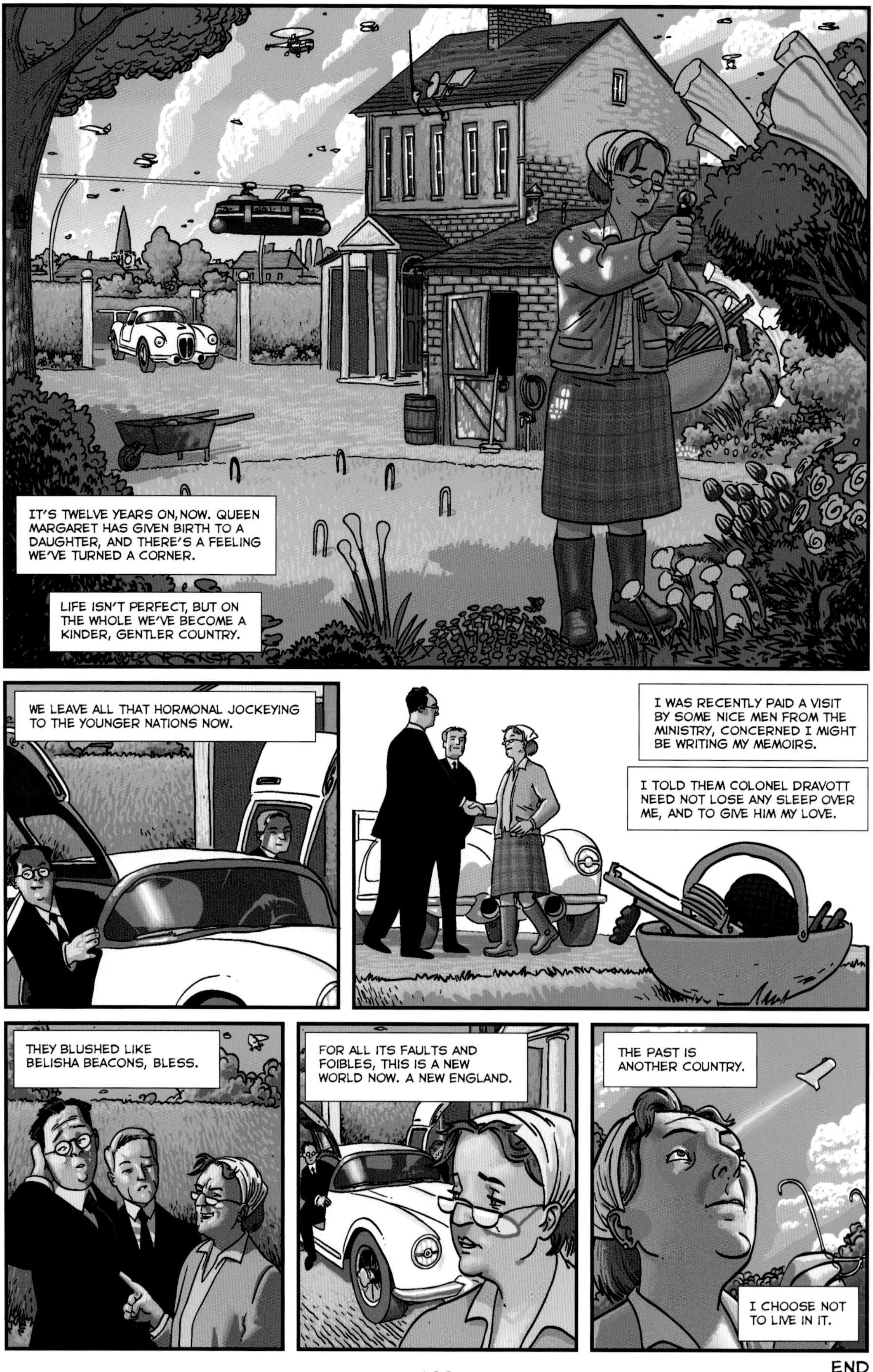
IT'S TWELVE YEARS ON, NOW. QUEEN MARGARET HAS GIVEN BIRTH TO A DAUGHTER, AND THERE'S A FEELING WE'VE TURNED A CORNER.
LIFE ISN'T PERFECT, BUT ON THE WHOLE WE'VE BECOME A KINDER, GENTLER COUNTRY.
WE LEAVE ALL THAT HORMONAL JOCKEYING TO THE YOUNGER NATIONS NOW.
I WAS RECENTLY PAID A VISIT BY SOME NICE MEN FROM THE MINISTRY, CONCERNED I MIGHT BE WRITING MY MEMOIRS.
I TOLD THEM COLONEL DRAVOTT NEED NOT LOSE ANY SLEEP OVER ME, AND TO GIVE HIM MY LOVE.
THEY BLUSHED LIKE BELISHA BEACONS, BLESS.
FOR ALL ITS FAULTS AND FOIBLES, THIS IS A NEW WORLD NOW. A NEW ENGLAND.
THE PAST IS ANOTHER COUNTRY.
I CHOOSE NOT TO LIVE IN IT.
END

SKETCH GALLERY
with commentary by D'Israeli

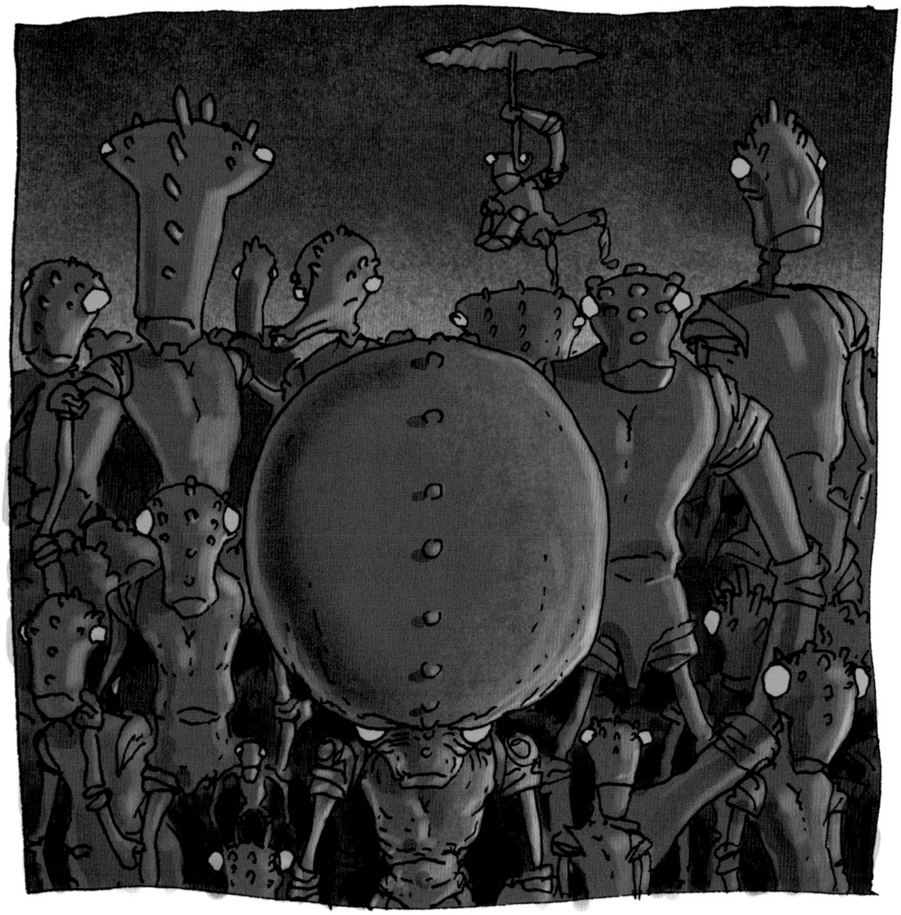

▲ **O**ur first idea for a sequel to *Scarlet Traces* was to feature the Selenites — H. G. Wells' moon-dwellers from his novel *The First Men in the Moon.* The notion of the Selenites entering the Earth-Mars conflict was eventually dropped due to lack of space, but this image was used as part of the project pitch to editor Dave Land.

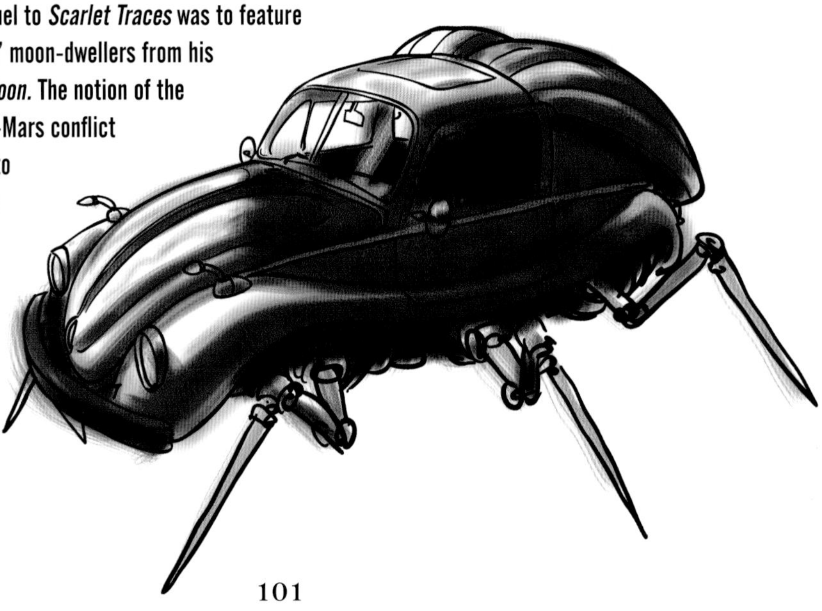

► **A**nother idea that never made it into the finished product — a VW Beetle with wings.

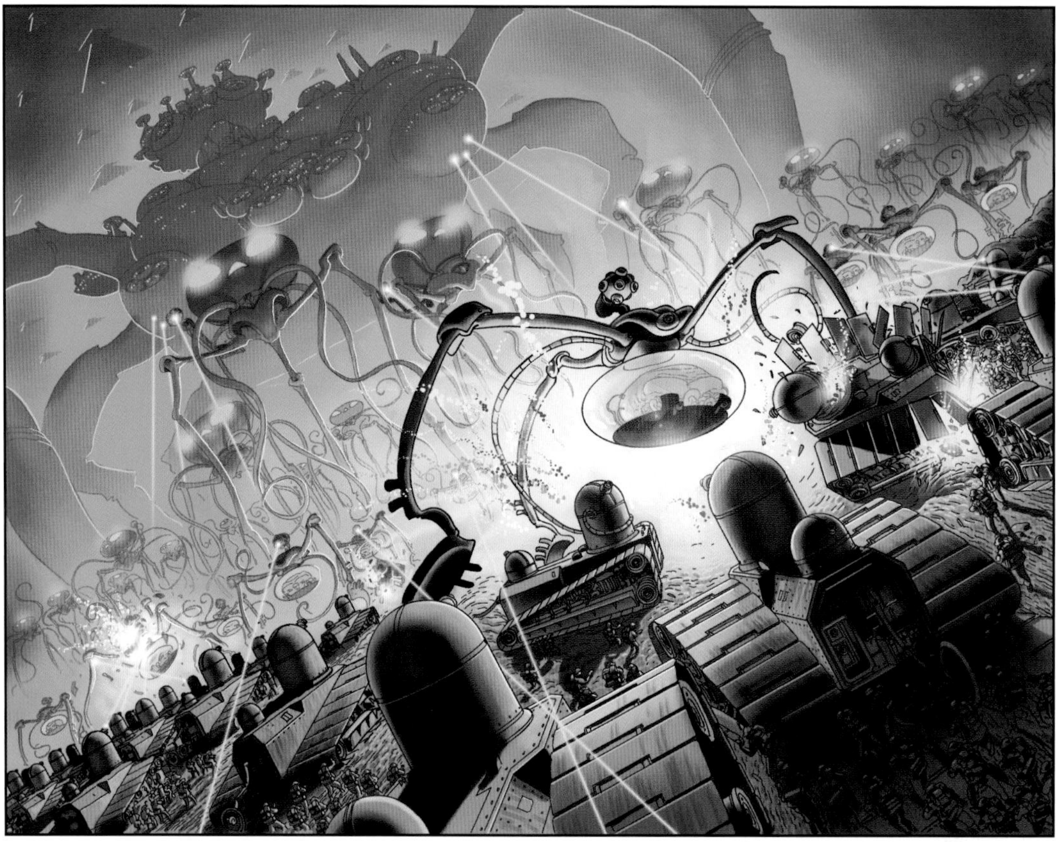

Promotional image for Dark Horse, used to promote the project at Comic-Con, 2004. It was the first finished image of the project. This was before I started using CGI, so all those tanks were drawn by hand.

Charlotte-Anne Hemming was originally conceived as a love interest for Robert Autumn in the original *Scarlet Traces,* but she was edged out of the story when the character of the vagrant, Old Ned, became more prominent. When we were looking for a suitable main character for the sequel, the photojournalists of the 1940s, with their adventurous lifestyles and star status, seemed a suitable starting point. Ian wanted a female lead character, which seemed a bit improbable, until we lit on Lee Miller, who was almost too good to be true — she'd been a fashion model, photojournalist, and writer, as well as the lover of the surrealist artist Man Ray! This first sketch of Charlotte was very closely based on Lee Miller.

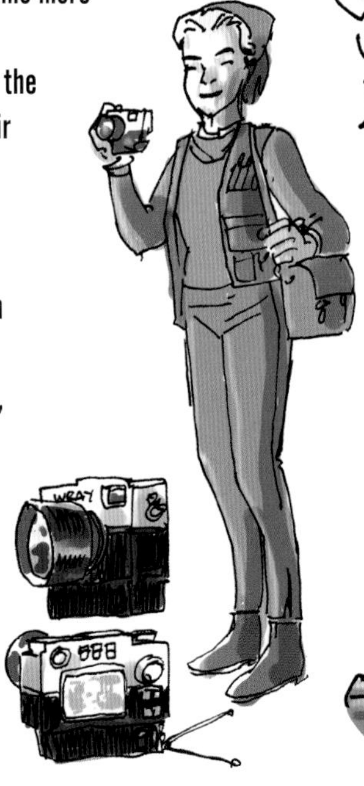

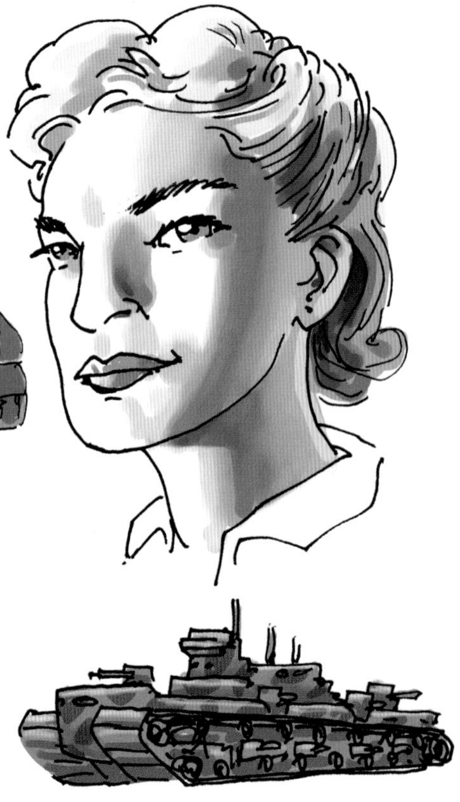

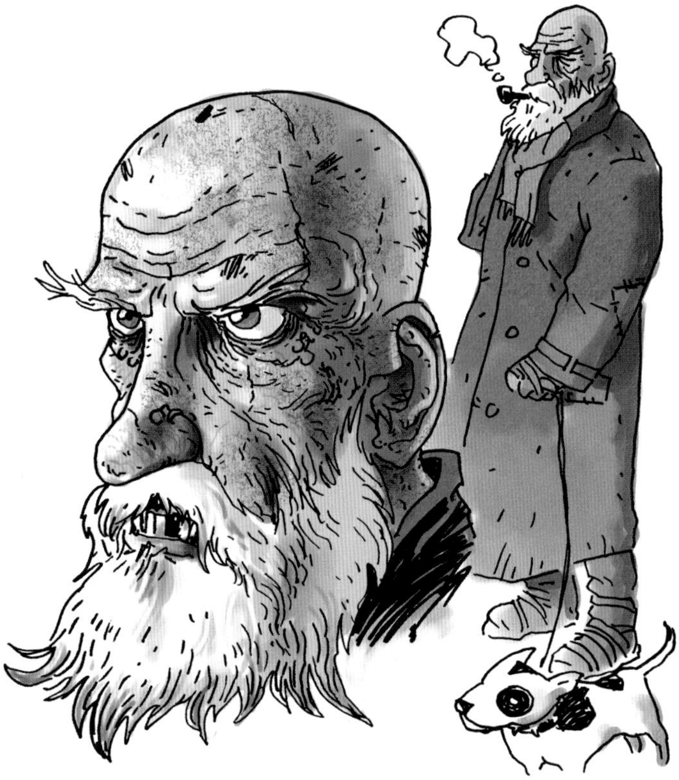

◄ **R**obert Autumn as an old derelict.

▼ **I**nitial design for the British Tommys' vacuum suits; the scuba-style face mask was inspired by the breathing sets described in the Isaac Asimov novel *Space Ranger*. Though this was replaced by a whole-head helmet and the camouflage pattern was dropped, the rest of the design made it into the book.

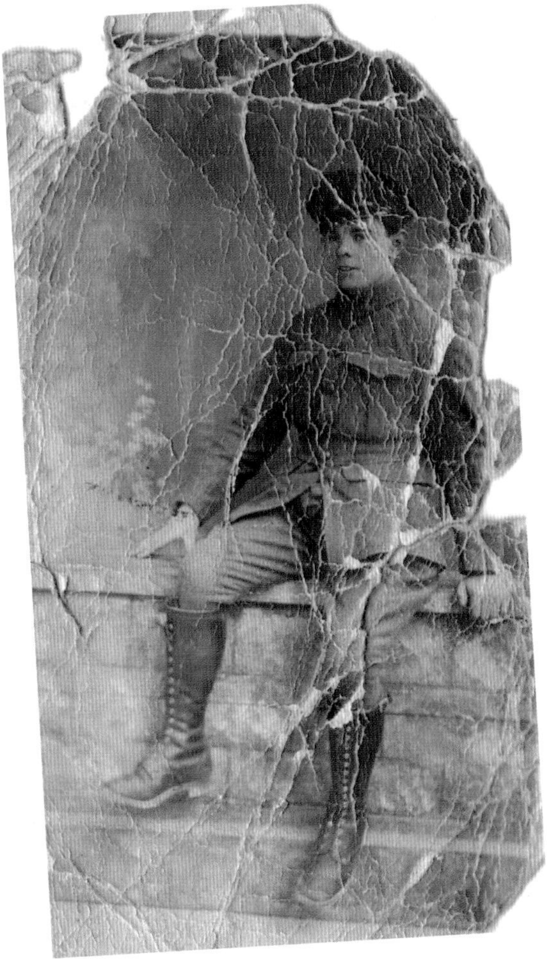

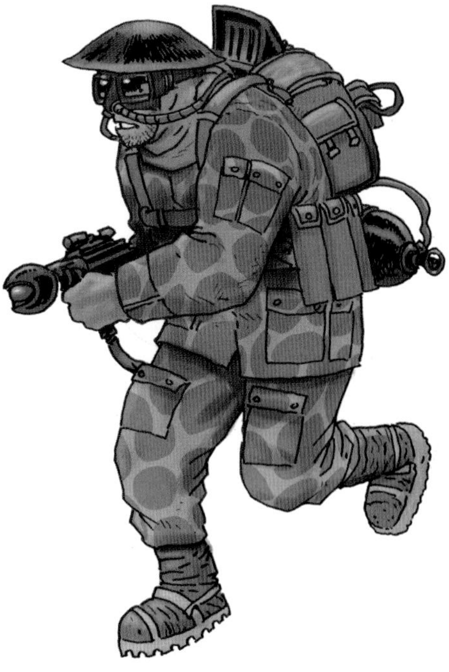

◄ **A** photograph of Ian Edginton's grandfather, dressed to go off and fight the Bolsheviks. Used as the basis for one of the photos in the montage of lost loved ones in Chapter two.

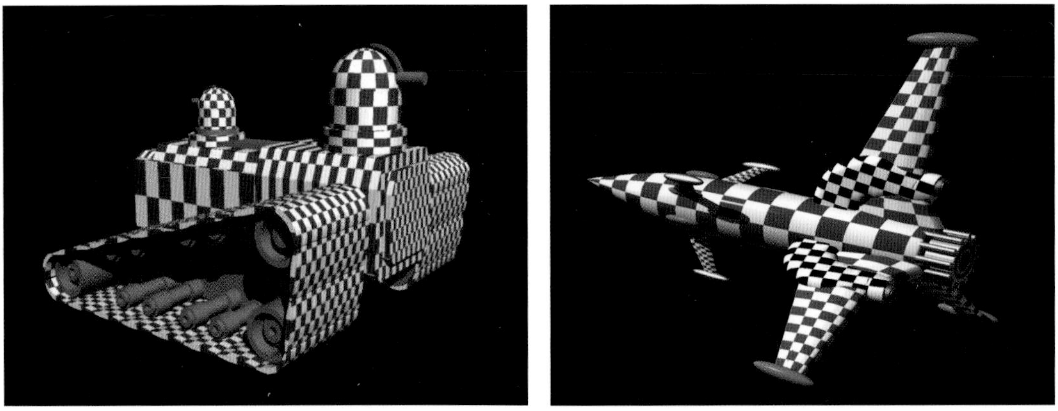

For *The Great Game,* I made extensive use of CGI modeling for reference. These two models of the tank and space cruiser were made to test the model-building and rendering process.

I got the idea after reading about the working methods of Frank Hampson and his studio, who produced the *Dan Dare* comic strip for the *Eagle* comic in the 1950s. Hampson and his assistants made numerous detailed models of vehicles, characters, and props to help with their lavishly detailed renditions of futuristic and alien worlds.

Actual renders of CGI models used as the basis of various panels in *The Great Game*. Because I draw directly on computer using a graphics tablet, it's child's play to import these renders into my pages and to scale, rotate, and even flip them as required to fit the panels.

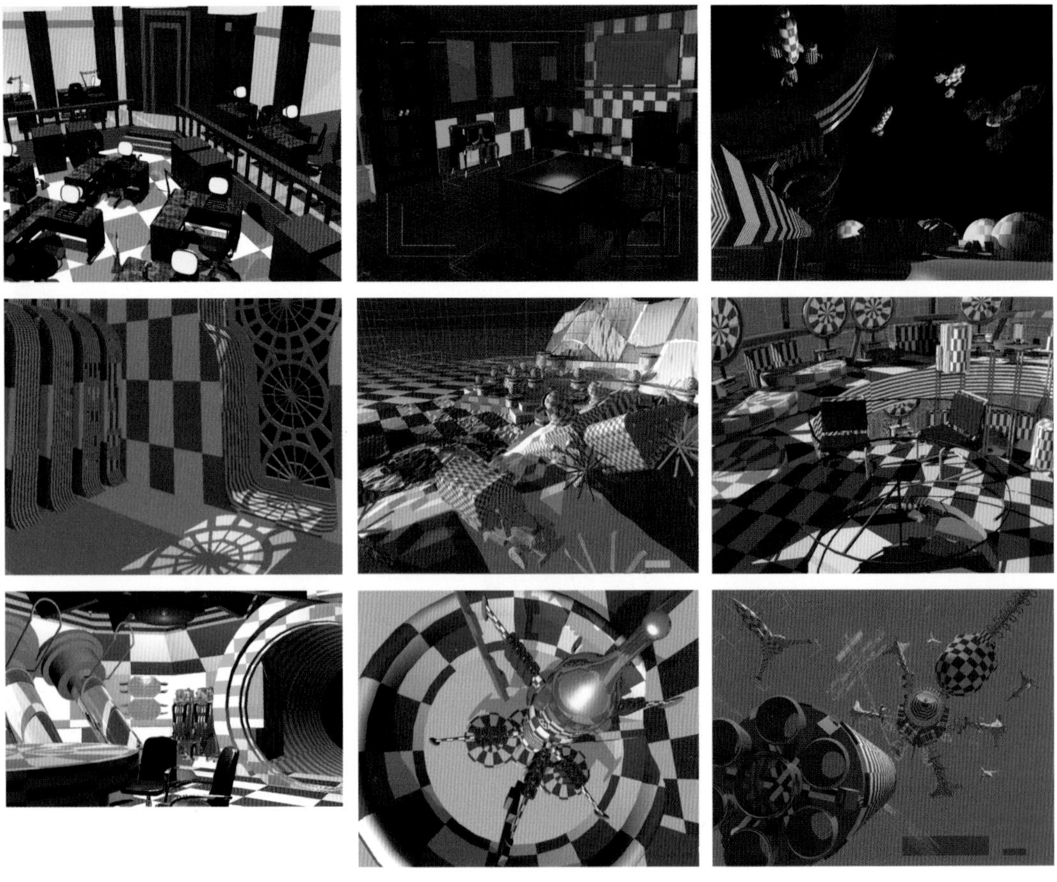